WAKING ANASTASIA

TIMOTHY REYNOLDS

WAKING ANASTASIA

TIMOTHY REYNOLDS

TYCHE BOOKS LTD.

Waking Anastasia
Published by Tyche Books Ltd.
www.TycheBooks.com

First Tyche Books Ltd Edition 2016

Print ISBN: 978-1-928025-55-9
Ebook ISBN: 978-1-928025-56-6

Cover Art by Alexey Tretyakov
Cover Layout by Lucia Starkey
Interior Layout by Ryah Deines
Editorial by M.L.D. Curelas

Author photograph: Cometcatcher Media

This book was funded in part by a grant from the Alberta Media Fund.

As always, for my mother, Ann, and my sisters, Katharine & Nancy, for their continued love & support.

In loving memory of Anastasia Nicholaievna Romanova, The Grand Duchess Shvibzik, who came to me in a dream and told me her story;

Of my grandfather, Major Horton Munro Reynolds, who was there at The House of Special Purpose in Ekaterinburg in the summer of 1918 with the Canadian Expeditionary Forces;

And of Patrick J. Wren & Sally-Ann (Sam) MacGillivray Wren, gone too soon.

PROLOGUE

Kharkiv, Ukraine. May, 1916.

WITH HER EVER-present Kodak Brownie camera in hand, fourteen-year-old Anastasia strolled a short distance away from the Imperial train while the crew replenished the locomotive's tender with water from the adjacent tower. They were less than a day away from Livadiya and the grand summer palace, but she had been cooped up in the train for two days and was restless. Just that morning, she and her sister Tatiana had snapped at each other over the meaning of William Blake's "The Divine Image" from their morning lesson. She took a long, deep breath of the crisp mountain air, yearning for even a hint of the mildly salty Black Sea hundreds of miles to the south.

The Livadiya Palace was one of her all-time favourite places and she, Maria, and Tatiana were looking forward to celebrating all three of their June birthdays with the grandest fancy party ever held in the courtyard. But they weren't there yet, and for the first time in ages the mood on the Imperial train was dark and sullen. Curt words were exchanged and once or twice in the night she thought she'd heard Father's angry voice over the sound of the great steam engine.

Humming to herself, Ana looked around at her family and the off-duty servants, as they stretched out sore muscles or sat on and around the platform, soaking up the cherished sunshine. It had been a cool, damp spring in St. Petersburg and the Ukrainian sunshine felt absolutely marvellous. She snapped a photograph of the tender and the tower, turned the crank to wind the film, then carefully framed and snapped another of the Stationmaster conferring with an Imperial Guard captain. Finally, she turned ever so subtly and faced her sisters, Olga, Tatiana, and Maria.

Olga sat on a box, with her legs straight out and her hat tilted to shade her winter-pale face. Tatiana leaned in the doorway of the royal blue carriage, hatless and sneaking peeks at a guard with whom she had been flirting the entire trip. Beautiful Maria—Mashka—sat on the folded-down step of the compartment she shared with Ana, as tired of being cooped up in the train as Ana herself. It was quite obvious by Mashka's slouched shoulders and downcast gaze that she was already missing Luka back home.

Ana snapped the photo and smiled to herself. Some day she, too, would entertain suitors, and the four Tsarevnas would all marry their true loves and live happily ever after together in one of the royal palaces. She so loved her sisters to pieces. Olga and Tatiana were The Big Pair while Mashka and herself were, appropriately, The Little Pair.

"Mashka, come! Wipe away that frown and let us find Father. He's certain to know how soon we can be bathing in the sea and riding along the beach."

Maria shaded her face from the sun with her hand and looked up at her younger sister. "You, Shvibzik, have far too much energy for your own good. Fine, let's see what news we can squeeze from Father, Little Imp." She stood and with a quick shake of her skirts, chased out the wrinkles as best she could.

"Best to leave Father to his business, Shvibzik." Tatiana stepped down from the carriage and stretched her arms out in the sunlight. "He's meeting with a member of the Ukraine parliament. There has been trouble further west and the guards in the palace have been doubled."

Ana stopped mid-step. She wanted to cheer Mashka up but not at the cost of disturbing Father. "And you know this how, Tatya?"

"The soldiers talk, and I overhear." She nodded toward the carriage. "Come, let's find something cold to drink before Chef gets too busy with dinner."

Ana thought about it for only a moment before she took

Mashka's hand and followed Tatya and Olga to the dining car.

Two Years Later: Ekaterinburg, Russia. The night of July 17-18, 1918.

STUBBORN LIGHT FROM the gibbous moon forced its way through the heavy clouds as though determined to provide illumination for a chance passer-by to witness the "cleansing" taking place. But it was midnight and the only two "citizens" still about stood casually sharing a hand-rolled smoke, awaiting further orders beside the tailgate of an empty, dark-green, canvas-sided truck.

Yellow light spilled out through the propped-open back door of the once-stately Ipatiev House, and scruffy flowering shrubs caught the spill, but neither of the men gave a damn, wanting nothing more than to finish this night's "business" with the Tsar and get back to their bunks. Their commander, Yakov Yurovsky, had ordered them to remain by the truck, and that's exactly what they were doing.

Sharp laughter burst from just inside the building, down in the basement, followed by heavy boot steps quickly ascending wooden stairs. A smirking corporal appeared and crunched across the gravel to the truck's cab, ignoring the lackadaisical attitude of his fellows stationed out in the fresh air. The engine of the truck started with a pair of backfires and a roar that settled down to a rumble. The moment of truth had arrived and when the corporal slammed shut the truck's door, Piotr—the older of the two men on duty—dropped the remains of the cigarette and ground it under his boot. He took his place to the right side of the open tailgate and his nephew, Sergei, followed suit on the left, ready.

The sound of the truck's sputtering engine filled the night, then a gunshot was heard from inside the house. That first shot was followed quickly by two more and a woman's shocked scream, then a fusillade of gun and rifle shots nearly drowned out the horrified screams and cries of two men, eight women, and a young boy. Sergei knew that his fellow Bolsheviks were making quick work of the Tsar, his family, and their servants. Not even the youngest daughter's puppy was to be spared in this decisive action.

The shots came further apart, but the terrified screams went on and on. Sergei thought he recognized the macabre steel-in-flesh sound of bayonets doing their dirty work while gruff, fear-filled voices shouted at the victims to finally die. The two men above smirked, knowing that this night marked the true end of the Tsar's corrupt rule.

Twenty minutes later, two more shots echoed up from the basement and then a shout for Piotr and Sergei to come at once. They rushed down into the killing zone in the bowels of The House of Special Purpose. Smoke filled with the heavy stench of gunpowder, fear, and blood assaulted them, but they listened closely to their commanding officer's orders. Sergei saw the crumpled bodies out of the corner of his eye and hid a smile.

THE TRUCK IDLED away the minutes in the alley above, then all at once the flurry of action from the basement rushed up the stairs and out into the warm night. Wrapped in bloody bed linens, the remains of the Russian Royals and their household were awkwardly and unceremoniously hustled up and into the back of the truck. In the urgency and darkness no one noticed a small, cloth-bound book slip from inside one of the smaller bundles and tumble onto the shrubs beside the doorway. The slim volume teetered there long enough for the wan light to illuminate the bullet-torn, bloodstained cover of William Blake's *Songs of Innocence and of Experience*, before it slipped down between the wall and the shrub. Once it was out of sight, a faint blue glow reached out briefly from the bloodstain, then suddenly was drawn back, absorbed into the book.

Hushed, harsh commands urged the soldiers to finish their grim work. Soon the truck was loaded and the men all seated on the benches beneath its canvas cover. A shadowed officer slammed the tailgate and the vehicle left, the spinning tires spitting gravel while the senior conspirators mounted their own vehicles and followed. Silence quickly re-established itself as the master of the night.

THREE DAYS LATER, outside the dark Ipatiev House, Captain Martin Powell folded his camera, stowed it in its leather case, took a much-needed swig from his canteen, and wiped the back of his tanned hand across his narrow moustache. He was one of forty drab-olive-and-dust-uniformed soldiers, many of whom stood at ease, smoking and batting idle conversation around in the warm sun. Except for a small Russian escort in their midst, the armed men were members of the Canadian Siberian Expeditionary Force, there to reinforce the anti-Bolshevik forces. They'd secured the area and were nearly done investigating, having not found the royal family they'd come to liberate but instead discovering evidence of unknown sinister acts committed in a small, cramped room in the basement. The blood had been hastily washed away, but uncountable bullet holes remained.

The voice of Powell's commander cut through the chatter to his right.

"That's it, lads! We have a train to catch. Load up and move out! Powell, retrieve the team in the basement!"

"Yessir!" Powell snapped off a sharp salute and jogged to the back door of the manor house. The milling soldiers double-timed back to their waiting trucks, still alert for attack, while their Russian escort boarded their own vehicle. Powell leaned inside the dark stairwell and relayed the order. "Basement detail! Move out! Double time!!"

A half-dozen soldiers trotted up the stairs and out into the bright sunlight, carrying battery-operated lanterns and flashlights. To give them room, Powell stepped into the shrubs flanking the doorway. His heel trod on something neither shrub nor soil and he turned to inspect the unexpected.

Casually lost in the soil between the shrub and the wall was a book—small, cloth-bound, simple. Around an estate so utterly stripped of any personal belongings, this one little, torn, and stained item spoke clearly to him of something dark and wrong in this place of revolution. Before he had an opportunity to examine the book closer, a barked command reminded him of duties best not forgotten. He dropped the curious little volume into his satchel with his camera and hurriedly joined his Expeditionary Force fellows on a truck just as the group of vehicles chugged off after their wary Russian hosts.

EVENTUALLY, OVER IMMEASURABLE time, the pain and terror sloughed off and away and an arm's-length-distant warmth surrounded Anastasia. She felt . . . cradled, in a place of safety. But she was restless, too, because somehow it was all wrong and she shouldn't be here, in this place, this formless darkness. In spite of the coziness, fear trickled back in.

There was faint, unfamiliar music and laughter, growing, moving near, and she thought that a special moment, an *important* moment, had at last arrived. Then the music and laughter faded, leaving her with just the arm's-length benevolence. No, that wasn't entirely true, because there was, just beyond the cocoon of warmth, a deeper darkness, a chasm just waiting for her to step away from wherever she was. She steadied herself and waited.

Inside the chasm, the darkness waited, too.

CHAPTER ONE

@TheTaoOfJerr: "It's no good pretending that a relationship has a future if your record collections disagree violently . . ."
~Bruce Hornsby

Present Day

WITH ONLY THREE and a half weeks until Christmas, an unseasonably early deep-freeze slammed Southwestern Ontario and started icing over the Thames River that bisected the dozing town of St. Marys, twenty minutes down-river from Stratford. Jeremy Powell—twenty-four, determined, and stubborn—was bundled tightly against the knife-edged cold in his much-worn, fire-engine-red, Eddie Bauer parka. Refusing to give in to the cold, he snapped another photo of the short icefall forming where the river flowed over the low dam a hundred yards from Queen Street, the town's main thoroughfare. Jerry moved his tripod-mounted Canon to capture another angle, marvelling at how the subtle pastels of the ice-reflected evening light changed the images ever so gently.

He was so bundled against the cold that when his cell phone rang, the theme from *Mission: Impossible* was too muffled for him to be sure he'd heard it at all. He stopped and listened and the second ring seemed clearer. Hurriedly, he yanked his gloves off, stuffed them under his arm, and frantically searched the large pockets of his bulky jacket, trying to find the phone before it went to voice mail. On the final ring, he found it and snapped it open.

"Jerry here."

"Jerr, it's Manny Werinick, out on Vancouver Island." The Aussie accent was thick and the deep voice full of joy.

"Mr. Werinick . . . hi."

"It's 'Manny', mate. Nothing but."

"Manny, then." Jerry smiled. Manny seemed to ooze glee and even standing in the freezing cold a couple thousand kilometres away, Jerry felt the glow. "Did you get the email I sent, with the audio files?"

"I did, Jerr."

"Great! Have you had a chance to listen—"

"With a voice like yours, Jerr, you could woo the joey from a wallaby's pouch. Your résumé kicks ass, too. The job's yours if you want it, mate."

Jerry's breath caught. "Really? Wow. I didn't expect your decision quite so soon. I haven't even told my girlfriend or my family that I applied for it. When do you need my answer by?"

"Monday'll be soon enough, mate. Just think on it over the weekend and get back to me."

"Thanks, Manny. I guess I'll talk to you Monday."

"Looking forward to it, young fella. Have a great weekend, and enjoy the bloody cold one last time, cuz it's never like that here in Victoria."

"One more reason to aim for the West Coast, then."

"One of many, Jerr, one of many. Monday. Gotta run, mate. Cheers."

"Cheers." The call ended, Jerry stared at his phone, now oblivious to the cold, damp air freezing his bare hand. "Sonofabitch. I got it! 'Jerry Powell, Station Manager'. Damn, I like the sound of that!"

TWO HOURS LATER, Jerry sat in the cozy, warm Riverside Diner on the limestone- and heritage-lined main drag of St. Marys, wiping rib sauce off his fingers. It was the kind of retro diner the locals cherished and the tourists expected, with a dozen Formica-topped, steel-trimmed tables and four green-vinyl-wrapped booths. The Riverside was only a third full with the usual post-dinner coffee crowd, mostly due to the cold, but also because the local minor hockey team—the Lincolns—were still beating up the visiting rival London Nationals in the second period. This left Jerry to share the last booth, the one in the shadows at the back, with Haley Simmons, his on-again-off-again, nearly-divorced, live-in girlfriend of the last two years.

The long photo shoot in the cold and a belly full of Riverside ribs had Jerry wanting to be ensconced in the warm comfort of their own apartment, slippers on his feet and Netflix on the big screen. “I don’t know why we couldn’t have had dinner at home, Haley. There are a couple things I wanted to talk to you about.”

“Sorry, Jerry, but there’s something I want to tell you and I really don’t want to do it at the apartment.”

“Oh-kay. That’s a little odd, but what’s up?”

Keeping her eyes downcast, she took a sip from her steaming mug followed by a slow, deep, nervous breath. When she finally looked up and spoke, her voice was soft and the words came quickly. “I won’t be going back to the apartment, Jerry. Steve and I . . .”

Jerry had a good idea where this was headed—where it had been headed for a month or so now—so he shut up and mentally crossed his fingers.

“. . . and for the sake of the girls, I’m moving back and we’re going to give our marriage one more try. You know I love you, but the girls need me.”

“You’re sure this time? Steve’s sure?”

“Yeah. I . . . I need them, too.”

“Haley, I’ve always said that I’d respect your decision if you went back to Steve and the girls, and I do.”

She took his hands in hers and kissed them, grateful. “Thank you, Sweetie. We’ll still be friends. Steve and the girls like you, so maybe you can come over for Sunday dinner every so often.”

Jerry forced a half smile. “Sure.” He was surprised how much actually hearing her say the words hurt.

“You’re not mad?”

“Why would I be mad, Haley? Disappointed, yes. Mad? What would be the point?” He shook his head sadly. “You’ve made your decision. And now I’ve made mine.” He dropped a handful of fives on the table to take care of the bill, then stood up with his heavy coat in hand. “Take care, Haley.”

She reached out to stop him from leaving. “Jerry . . .”

“Have a good life, Haley. No regrets. Call me when you want

to come get your stuff." He turned to leave but only got two steps before her quiet whisper stopped him.

"I love you, Jerry."

"Yeah, me too." He placed a folded ten-dollar bill on the counter in front of their waitress as he passed by. "Thanks, Tanya. G'night."

Both relieved and sad that Haley had finally made up her mind, Jerry stepped firmly out into the night. Once outside, bundled up against the cold, he shook off unexpected tears. Then he steadied himself and headed off up the Queen Street hill, now fervently wishing he'd driven instead of walking the half-mile from the apartment. The throb of a familiar headache was already starting.

He was only a block from home when the mild throb transformed into a full-blown migraine within the space of a heartbeat, causing Jerry to stumble on the freshly plowed sidewalk. His boots scuffed awkward marks in the light dusting of snow as he slammed his eyes shut and jammed his gloved hands against his temples with the hope that just this once he could squeeze out the pain. The movement only seemed to sharpen and define the agony, and he wobbled a few more steps before dropping to his knees into the nearest fluffy snowdrift. The pain of his bruised heart forgotten, he ripped off his woollen toque and slammed two generous handfuls of snow to his temples, crushing them hard to his aching skull.

"Oh God oh God oh God." Unsuccessfully willing away the spikes of torturous current, he groaned and whimpered and tried not to puke.

The vice tightened on his skull, and he was sure his head was going to explode like a grape. Then the worst of the wave passed and he was able to roll over into a sitting position and look around. His vision was blurry as hell but he could see that he was still very much alone beneath the streetlight, in the softly tumbling snowfall. He suspected that everyone else in St. Marys was either inside, barred against the cold, or at the hockey game, screaming encouragement at their team. Not a single car passed by in the five minutes Jerry took to eventually stagger to his feet and start stumbling his way through the final leg of what had just become a marathon journey home. By the time he reached the walk leading up to the scruffy, ninety-year-old former Victorian manor, he felt the beast of a second storm of pain stalking him, close on his heels.

In through the shared entrance, up the Everest of the bending, scream-squeaking, wooden stairs, he fumbled with the key, dropped it once, snatched it up, and gently, deliberately, slipped it into the lock. The entire time, the Riverside ribs threatened to come back up and stain the faded old wallpaper with barbeque sauce. With his weight against the door when he turned the key and the knob, it slammed open, pulling him into the darkness. He managed to stay on his feet just long enough to shoulder the door closed behind him before he succumbed to gravity and crumpled.

Almost blind from the pain, Jerry let instinct guide him. He crawled down the long, semi-dark hallway to the cluttered coffee table in the living room where a distant memory told him that somewhere on the table, amongst the variety of half-read photography magazines and a D. B. Jackson novel, was a huge bottle of some extra-strength painkiller. A quick grope found the bottle, and after a brief struggle to open it, he popped four of the chalky white tablets into his mouth and chewed. With a swallow from a warm, half-empty can of Pepsi on the end table beside him, he washed down the crushed relief, crawled onto the couch, and curled up in a fetal ball, smushing a cushion over his eyes to block out the light he didn't have the energy to turn off. He rocked back and forth, groaning, wanting to puke but not daring to for the further torture it would inflict. Soon tears came, but for the pain, not for Haley or the pseudo life they'd had. It took almost half an hour, but he finally fell asleep, not giving a damn that he was still wearing his snow-wet coat and boots.

JERRY WOKE ONCE during the night, long enough to remove his outdoor clothes, stumble into the bathroom to relieve his bladder of the previous evening's coffee, and then back to the couch. The bedroom was still too far away. By the time the sun came up, he was finally sleeping peacefully and soundly under the old afghan blanket he'd had since he was a kid.

NOON FOUND HIM sitting up, rubbing the sleep out of his eyes, and draining the rest of the Pepsi with a disgusted grimace. He swallowed the warm, syrupy sweetness, and found himself staring at Sushi, his Siamese fighting fish that watched him from the little tank on his desk.

"Ladies and gentlemen, pain has left the building. A couple more skull-crushers like that and I'll have them amputate my damned head, Soosh." He yawned, levered his stiff body up off the long couch, and stretched out the kinks he always got from sleeping there. He was twisting his neck left and right to pop the tendons and get the blood flowing again when there was a rapid, insistent, small-fisted knock at the apartment door.

"Too early for the cleaning lady I should hire, too late for the milkman who no longer delivers," he mumbled as he wandered off to answer the knock. As he shuffled past, Sushi turned and swam behind the ancient Greek ruins dominating his home. The knocker took a break just long enough for Jerry to wander down the hall to answer the pounding before it brought on another headache. He opened the door and found his teenaged neighbour, Isis, with her fist raised to knock again. Lowering her hand to her hip, the bouncy, bubbly, cute, stone-deaf fifteen-year-old looked Jerry up and down with disapproval. She pushed past him and walked down the hall backwards, speaking and flashing sign language at him.

"Jerry, your lights were on all night and you look like shit. You slept in your clothes, too."

"Isis, have you been spying on me again?" Jerry spoke and signed back, fluent from years of volunteering with the hearing impaired. "What did I tell you? Being a friend is good. Being a stalker is bad."

"Sedona had to take a midnight piss, and I was up reading, so I took her. Besides, I'm not stalking you—I watch out for you."

"I know. Thank you, kiddo. Now give me a quick hug and go start the coffee maker, please. I'm going to brush my teeth and change."

Isis glanced around the apartment. "Is she here?"

"No. Haley is gone. Forever. It's over. She's gone back to Steve."

The petite redhead stepped into his arms and gave him a long, strong hug. "I love you, Jerry."

Jerry returned the hug cautiously, like a caring uncle. "I know, Munchkin. Thank you." They broke out of the embrace and Jerry gently shoved Isis toward the kitchen. She spoke over her shoulder.

"Go clean up, Jerry. You smell."

He sighed, shook his head, and shuffled off to the bathroom. "Women."

CHAPTER TWO

@TheTaoOfJerr: "One good thing about music, when it hits you, you feel no pain."

~Bob Marley

ISIS MADE THE coffee and heated up the last two of the dozen apple-banana muffins she'd made and brought over earlier in the week. Jerry brushed, shaved, and got dressed for his job as the junior program director at Stratford's last independent AM radio station. Because his day started at two in the afternoon and Haley's retail work started before ten in the morning, on holidays, weekends, and school PA Days, Isis was a regular visitor in the hours when only Jerry was home and she wouldn't run the risk of running into Haley. She and Jerry had talked about it more than once and while she admitted that she was somewhat jealous of Haley as Jerry's girlfriend, when she put that aside, she really just didn't like the older woman.

It took a little verbal arm-twisting by Isis, but while he wolfed down his muffin, Jerry told her about the headache that was the reason his lights were on all night and why he looked like crap when he answered her knock.

"Was it as bad as the one last week?"

"Worse. I think it was the nitrates in the corned beef sandwich I had for lunch."

"Then stop eating that shit if it makes you sick. Peanut butter makes me sick and I'm smart enough to stay away from it."

"You're allergic—there's a big difference. I don't go into anaphylactic shock, I just get a headache."

"I don't care. Use your head for something besides having migraines."

BY THE TIME Jerry got to work he was feeling human again, the headache a faded memory. With his nearly empty Tim Hortons extra-large, double-double decaf coffee on his desk in front of him, he was just wrapping up a phone conversation when the station's owner, Derek, popped his head into the office. From the speaker mounted above the door, Steven Page's "Leave Her Alone" played.

Jerry acknowledged Derek with a quick nod. "Four o'clock will be great, Lisa. Tell Doc Wallis I appreciate him staying late on a Friday." He hung up and gave Derek all of his attention.

"The latest numbers are in, Jerry. They look great. Drop by my office after you're done your show." He ducked back out before Jerry had a chance to answer him, the door swinging shut behind him.

Jerry's reply went no further than the "Gordon Lightfoot Live in Stratford" poster on the back of the closed door. "Um, sure, Derek." He refilled his cup from the coffee maker on top of the file cabinet and returned to the desk to check his emails. He sipped the fresh brew and reached for the computer mouse. The first message was from Manny Werinick and the subject was "Manny's Plea".

Jerry opened the email, saw that it was actually a video message, and clicked on the attachment. Manny's greying, balding, long face suddenly filled the computer screen.

"G'day, Jerry. Like you, I've been thinking about that offer I made yesterday. It's not enough, mate. I like your work and I want my new station manager here in Victoria by Christmas so how 'bout I bump the salary up 5k, and we've got a beauty of a flat two blocks from the Inner Harbour that's yours to rent for a whole lot less than it's worth . . ." Manny laughed, " . . . cuz we own the bloody building! I can still wait for Monday, if I have to, but I just wanted to sweeten the pot. Hate to lose the Golden Voice of Stratford because I didn't throw everything I have at you.

You still have my cell number, just on the off chance you make your decision before Monday. Don't be afraid to use it. Have a good weekend, Jerr. Talk atcha on Monday."

The message came to an end and Manny's face froze on the screen. Jerry smiled and shook his head in disbelief. "That man was born a salesman. He probably sold advertising space on his diapers." He checked the computer screen again. "Let's see . . . two spam, today's '*horror*scope', three new Twitter followers, one Chicken Soup for the Soul and . . . oh, great. Two from Mom. 'Time for a Haircut' and 'Eating Properly'. E-nagging at its best. They'll wait. They'll *all* wait." Coffee in hand, he got up and left the office, turning his back on the maternal missives.

After two minutes the computer went on stand-by, about the same time the song coming out of the speaker ended and Jerry's too-smooth-for-his-age voice came on the air.

"It's that time again, Stratford—it's Powell in the PM. Two hours of all-request, all-oldies, to get you through that post-lunch dead zone on a wintery Friday."

AT FIVE MINUTES after four, Jerry found himself standing in his chiropractor's treatment room. With one hand on Jerry's shoulder to steady him, Dr. Wallis adjusted Jerry's vertebrae with the spine gun. With every click of the gun, Jerry winced.

"When is the new desk chair being delivered, Jerry?"

"Next week. Monday, I hope."

"And you're doing the exercises we went over last time?"

"Daily."

"Good. How about the caffeine?"

"I've cut back to 90% decaf, no tea, and only one Pepsi a day."

"That should help your health in other ways but I wonder if maybe reducing your intake so much so fast isn't bringing on a few headaches, too. Did your blood work come back?"

"It did. Your brother says that I'm mildly hypoglycemic but nothing to worry about, yet."

"Good. How are you sleeping on the harder mattress?"

"Last night I didn't get as far as the bedroom, but when I do it gives me the best sleep I've had in years."

"Good, good. How about stress? Life is treating you well?"

"Well, Haley's gone back to Steve, and I have to decide if I want to move to a station manager's job in British Columbia."

"Station Manager? That's great! And Haley's gone back to Steve and the girls? That should relieve quite a bit of the stress. I know my cousin and she definitely has her stressful moments, except in her case they're usually days or weeks instead of moments."

Jerry chuckled between adjustments. "True enough."

"Now, this job offer—are you considering it?"

"More and more by the minute. Know any good back-crackers in Victoria?"

"Please lie down face-down on the bench, with your arms at your sides." Jerry followed the directions and Wallis continued his examination and adjustment. "Not off-hand, but I'll do some checking with the Association. No other stresses? Work? Home? Family?"

"Work is good, I'll have the apartment to myself after Haley moves her stuff out and as for family, I'll be seeing my mother tomorrow."

"Bingo!"

"What?"

"Your mother. When you mentioned her, the muscles in your back tightened right up."

"Yeah, well, she has that effect on people."

"She shouldn't be the cause of headaches the magnitude of yours, but when added to the physiological factors we've discussed, it could be that last straw. You know, Jerry, I'll miss you as a patient, but, without knowing any of the specifics, I think that job in Victoria is a great opportunity."

"Thanks, Doc. I really needed to hear that from someone other than the little voice in my head."

JUST BEFORE NOON the next morning, Jerry pulled up in front of his Great Aunt Mavis' home in King City, north of Toronto. Seeing the driveway occupied by a minivan with the engine running, he parked his Jeep Grand Cherokee next to the curb. The day was blanketed in a soft grey cloud cover but there wasn't the amount of snow they had in St. Marys, two hours west. The air had a little less bite, but Jerry still grabbed the duct-tape-patched blue down-filled coat from the back seat.

He transferred his wallet, keys, and iPhone over to the coat's zippered pocket then walked over and knocked on the window of the van, startling the driver out of a daze or a reverie. Knowing his slightly older cousin, Geoff, it was probably a daze. Geoff jumped in his seat and turned to look at Jerry. Recognizing him, he powered the window down. Geoff's older brother, Ty, leaned over the centre console.

"Hey, Cuz."

"Mr. Radio, Jer-Man."

"Hey, guys. You know, you could have gone in—Aunt Mavis doesn't bite."

"No, but the place smells weird and she's always yapping on with stories about 'the old days' like the Depression or the Sixties or other shit. Who cares? What's past is past."

"Yeah, if it doesn't help me make the rent or cover child support, it doesn't matter, Jerr."

"It never hurts to know where you come from, guys."

"I came from the grocery store. Before that I was at Walmart, buying spark plugs." The brothers laughed at the joke.

"Exactly," Ty added. "And before that, the Liquor Barn."

"Whatever you say, guys. Let's just get loaded up and get the stuff to storage. If she wants to talk about the past, nod, smile, and go on with whatever you're doing. She's been lonely since Uncle Tyrone died, so at least pretend to care. This is a tough move for her."

"Why? She's not doing any of the damned lifting."

Jerry gave up, shaking his head in frustration. He climbed the three steps to the front door. "Are you guys sure we're related?" The brothers closed up the van and followed him.

The door opened before he could ring the bell, and Great Aunt Mavis stood there, flashing a mischievous smile. "You and Ty are definitely cousins but we're not sure about Geoff. I think he was a foundling, left by a family of living heart donors."

Jerry and Ty laughed, but Geoff grunted. "Yeah, yeah. Whatever. How are you today, Aunt Mavis?" The three men each give her a hug as they entered the old house.

"Fair to middling, boys. You don't realize how much bric-a-brac a person can collect until it comes time to pack it up and move it. Both of your mothers got it all into boxes, so I really appreciate your help with the heavy part. There are sandwiches and coffee in the kitchen, and if you walk only on the runners, you can keep your boots on." She pointed to where she'd carefully laid down old carpet remnants nap-down to protect the hardwood floors.

Jerry undid his jacket in the warmth of the house and kissed her lovingly on the top of her head. "Thanks, Auntie M."

Geoff and Ty wordlessly followed the path of carpet pieces into the living room where they grabbed small boxes and started the process. Jerry bent his knees to grab a larger box but Mavis stopped him.

"Jerry, why don't you join me in the sewing room for a minute." She picked up a shoebox and shuffled down the short hall to her sewing room. The pink macramé slippers probably from a church craft sale slid almost soundlessly along the oak floor beside the carpet path. Jerry stayed to the improvised walkway and followed along.

The tiny sewing room was stripped bare except for an empty sewing table, a rocking chair, and a rickety old card-table chair folded and leaning against the wall. Jerry looked at it and sympathized, thinking that was pretty much how he'd been feeling the last little while—well used and ready for a garage sale. On the rocker, a second-hand romance paperback sat tent-style, saving Mavis' place. Mavis carefully moved the book to the table and lowered herself into the rocker. She pointed at the folded chair.

"Grab yourself that chair, young man—your cousins may miss you, but with the snail's pace they work at, it won't take you long to catch up."

Jerry opened the chair of questionable solidity and sat his slender frame down, slowly, cautiously. Mavis didn't seem to notice his hesitation, and when he was seated she leaned over and gently placed the tied-up Hush Puppies shoebox in his hands.

"This is for you. It's a few things my father, your great-grandfather, wanted you to have, plus a couple more from Tyrone and me. When Grandad found out how sick he was in his last year, he started gathering family relics for you. I'd forgotten all about it until I found it at the back of the linen closet. There's an old book, his first camera, the pocket watch my mother gave him one birthday, and some photos, amongst other things."

"But I was just a little kid when he died."

"Even so, he believed—and I do, too—that you're the only member of this clan of misfits that's ever given a damn about our history. You did a school project that year about the family tree, and spent one entire Saturday asking him questions about the family that no one had ever thought to ask before. You were only six, but you impressed the hell out of him."

"Auntie M, I don't know what to say—thank you." He started to remove the string to check out the box's contents, but Mavis put her tiny hand on his to stop him.

"Wait until you get home, dear. You'll have more time to relax and go through it. A few of the things may be quite valuable, so don't leave the box lying around where it can grow legs."

Jerry smiled and gave her a tender kiss on her pale, feather-soft cheek. "Thank you, Aunt Mavis. I'd better get back out there before Tweedle Dumb and Tweedle Dumber start playing football with your treasures."

She winked at him. "Smart boy."

THERE WAS WARMTH to the darkness that had been absent for so long. It was a welcoming, gentle warmth, radiating from a source nearby. There was a distant familiarity to it, but also strangeness she couldn't identify. She thought it might be someone she knew, but a cold corner of the emptiness slithered in and crushed that hope.

HALF AN HOUR later Jerry had the Jeep nearly full of Mavis' boxes. He had the back open and was gently sliding in a large, blue plastic tub of bubble-wrapped dishes when he heard a car pull up behind him. He turned to see his mother's dark blue Honda Accord across the end of the driveway. He smiled and raised a hand in greeting. A few seconds later, tiny Jane Powell locked her car, zipped up her long winter coat, and made her way to her only son. Jerry once described her to a new girlfriend as being all of ten feet of attitude in a five-foot-nothing, hundred-pound package. He'd spent twenty-four years trying to find her elusive approval and had the headaches to prove it.

"Hey, Mom. How was the drive up?" Jerry took a step toward her and gave her a hug.

She returned the embrace half-heartedly. "The city plow blocked the driveway with snow and that lazy kid I pay to shovel it couldn't be there until two. I don't know why I pay him."

"Maybe because you can't do it yourself."

"What's that got to do with anything, Jeremy? You know, if you still lived in Toronto I wouldn't have to pay some scruffy, skateboarding hoodlum with a ring in his nose to do it."

Jerry tried to let his mother's cynicism and disdain slough off him like a shed snake skin. The routine was an old one for both of them, though only Jerry seemed to be tired of it.

"Yes, Mom. Whatever you say." He returned to the back of the Jeep and tried snugging the bin into place, to make more room for the next one. When he turned around, his mother was standing right, tight there, in his space and his face, looking up at him.

"Jeremy Powell, what are you doing wearing that old jacket? People will think we're poor."

Jerry winced slightly and felt a headache coming on. "Or they could think that I'm doing lifting and toting and don't want to rip a good coat. Mom, are you here to help carry?" He pulled down the rear door of the SUV but stopped short of latching it shut so he could get the next load in without fumbling with the release.

"Don't be smart with me, mister. That's what you boys are here for."

Jerry sighed and started back to the house where his cousins were inside, getting another load. His mother followed.

"Did you ask your cousins how their sister's health is?"

Jerry stopped and turned back to face her. "No, Mom."

"Then how am I supposed to find out how she's doing?"

"Maybe you could call and ask her."

"It's long distance. It costs money."

"Everything costs money, Mom. You can't go through life without spending some of it."

"I don't like your attitude, Jeremy. When you finish here we'll talk about it."

Jerry took a deep breath to fight the encroaching pain and straightened his back to relieve the pressure of slouching and carrying the heavy boxes. "Mom, by the time we finish loading here and then unloading at the storage depot, I won't have time for one of your lectures. I'd like to be back in St. Marys before the storm moves in and clogs the roads."

"I expected you to be staying in town tonight, and I'd have your sister over for dinner. We'd even have that boyfriend of hers over, too."

"You mean Jean-Marc?"

"He doesn't speak English, he's Roman Catholic, and he has a tattoo, for God's sake."

"He speaks six languages, including fluent English with only a faint accent, Mom. And so what if he's Roman Catholic? I'm considering Christian Science as my own faith of choice."

"Don't even joke about that!"

"It's my life to do as I choose, and if I decide to worship, say, Hostess Twinkies and chesty redheads named Bambi, it's my choice. I guess you don't want to see my rearing cobra tattoo, then." He made like he was going to undo his pants.

"Why are you always so difficult? You have a smart ass answer for everything!"

"And you have . . . never mind. I've got work to do." He went back up the steps, kicking the road dirt off his boots when he reached the mat at the front door. He went back into the house, passing his cousins who each had a small box under one arm and one of Mavis' crust-free cucumber sandwiches in the other hand.

Jane followed Jerry inside. "Hello, boys. How's the move coming along?"

"Having a real ball, Aunt Jane."

"Nice to hear, Geoffrey." Jerry wondered whether she was oblivious to his cousin's sarcasm or just chose not to acknowledge it because it wasn't from her own son. Jerry fished a small plastic bottle of painkillers from his coat pocket, popped two of them, and then headed for the kitchen to get a mouthful of water to wash them down. Mavis stepped out of the sewing room to meet her niece, and patted Jerry's arm in understanding as she passed him.

"Jane? What brings you back here? Did you forget something, dear?"

"No, Aunt Mavis, I just wanted to make sure this was being done properly."

Jerry came back into the hallway from the dining room, ending up behind his mother, but she was surveying the house, really seeing neither Mavis nor Jerry. She sighed, either at the emptiness or the fact that there were still boxes to be moved. Mavis winked at Jerry, unseen by Jane.

"Well, dear, it took two training videos and a written test in both official languages, but after the boys figured out how to use two hands to carry a box, things moved along just fine."

Jane turned back to Mavis and released another world-shattering sigh. "I'm glad to see you're in good spirits. Now I know where Jeremy gets his attitude."

"Yes, dear. Whatever you say, dear." Mavis shuffled back to the novel on her rocker, and Jerry started back outside with another box, chuckling as he went. His mirth was short-lived.

"Jeremy, if you carry two boxes at a time, you'll get finished faster and then you can come shovel the driveway."

Jerry didn't slow, but just tossed his exhausted reply over his shoulder. "I thought you invited me for *dinner*, Mom."

"Of course, but while you're there, I have a list . . ."

As he walked toward the Jeep, he heard Aunt Mavis interrupt his mother. "You always have a list for him when he visits, dear. Do you ever have him over without getting him to do jobs around your house?" Jerry smiled again. He definitely got his sense of humour from Aunt Mavis and his father's side of the family.

CHAPTER THREE

@TheTaoOfJerr: "Without deviation from the norm, progress is not possible."

~Frank Zappa

THREE HOURS LATER the sun had just set and Jerry was finally on the road back home to St. Marys, having used the excuse of the two-hour winter drive to turn down his mother's insistent dinner invitation, and the no-doubt long list of tasks that always awaited his attention at her townhouse. She'd not been happy, but Jerry was worn out and beyond worrying about either his mother's driveway or her mood. If nothing else had come of the day, he'd made his decision about the West Coast. He opened a cold can of Pepsi and took a long, thirsty sip.

"Ahhh . . . pure ambrosia." With one hand on the steering wheel he slipped a white ear bud into his right ear and pulled his iPhone out of his pocket. Grabbing quick peeks at the road between button pushes, Jerry dialled Manny in Victoria. Manny answered on the third ring.

"JERRY! Talk to me, mate!"

"Manny, I have to give two weeks' notice here and will need another week to ship my stuff and drive out, but I can be there by Christmas."

"Bloody marvellous, Jerr! I knew you'd come 'round sooner or later. Glad it was sooner. Will your girlfriend be joining you?"

"She's now the ex-girlfriend."

"Damn. Sorry to hear it. But don't you worry none, Jerr—lots of beauties here on the island and some of them are even under fifty."

"To be honest, Manny, I'm looking forward to losing myself in the new job for a while. Some days I think my luck with women has been bad since birth."

"You got it, Jerr. You want me to take care of the apartment for you?"

"That'd be great, Manny. I'm going to have enough stuff to worry about at this end that if I know there's a warm, dry roof over my head waiting for me out there, it'll take a lot of pressure off."

"You name it, mate, we'll have it done for you. Just put my phone number on anything you ship out and we'll take care of it when it arrives. I can't tell you how much we're really looking forward to your joining us, Jerr."

"Likewise. It's just the kick-in-the-ass my life needs."

"Perfect! Call me Monday in the A.M., and we'll get the paperwork scanned and emailed to you for signing. In the meantime, have a great weekend, cuz I know I will."

"I'll do my best. Thanks, Manny."

TIME ONCE AGAIN drifted along aimlessly, but she'd long ago grown accustomed to it, so she relaxed. Wherever she was, it now had at least a veneer of safety to it, and that was just fine with her.

A WEEK LATER, Jerry's apartment looked like Mavis' had the week before, with everything in boxes, and boxes everywhere. The key difference was that many of Jerry's boxes were labelled "For Salvation Army", and the music playing was Harry Chapin's "Old College Avenue", rather than Glenn Miller. He picked up an empty liquor store box to fill with books but stopped when he saw the still unopened shoebox on the floor behind it.

"That's where you've been hiding. No time better than the present to open a present." Jerry took the shoebox over to the box-covered couch and coffee table. He fit into a narrow spot left on the couch and placed the Hush Puppies box on top of a sealed-and-ready-to-go bin on the rustic barn-board coffee table. With a gentle pull of one end of the string it was undone and fell away. Carefully, reverently, Jerry opened the box, finding the $20 bill first.

"Good old Aunt M. I'm twenty-four and she still slips me money whenever she can." Next was an envelope with his name on it, but he caught sight of a photo beneath it and put the envelope to one side. He wiped his hands on his jeans, then, as an afterthought looked down at them. They were filthy from moving and packing. "Damn. Not good." He left the box on top of the bigger box, went into the bathroom, and washed and dried his hands thoroughly.

When he was sure his hands were as clean as he could get them, he returned to the task and carefully lifted up the old black-and-white photo of the stately, walled home. Beneath it was an old, almost ancient camera. Though intrigued by the camera, Jerry took a close look at the photo. "Very nice. The old family homestead, maybe?" He placed it to one side, carefully removed the camera and put it next to the photograph. Beneath the camera was a copy of William Blake's *Songs of Innocence and Experience*. Its dark cloth cover was stained and torn, but the phone rang before he could take a closer look, to see how extensive the damage was. He put it back in the shoebox and went in search of his cell phone. He found it on the fourth ring, hidden beneath a dropped t-shirt.

"Talk to me." Jerry returned to packing while talking on the phone. "Oh. Hi, Mom."

"What? No, Mom, I told you not to expect me in Toronto this weekend—I have plans." Distracted, he stuck the envelope, the photo, and the camera back in the shoebox, placed the shoebox into a larger box, and then padded in and around it with clean clothes from a pile on a worn chair.

"Well, if you must know, my drug dealer is due any minute now with the fifty keys of heroine I ordered. My pregnant, teenage, prostitute girlfriend and I are going to spend the afternoon cutting the stuff with laundry soap and putting it all in little baggies so we can give them away free to the Sunday School kids tomorrow morning. Rabbi Schmuck and Mahatma Sherpa are going to help." He shoved a box out of his way and sat heavily on the couch.

"No? What's not to believe? You're right. I was lying . . . she's not pregnant, the Rabbi is, and it's not my baby. Fine, Mom. I'm still packing. I told you that I have to be in Victoria by Christmas to start the new job." Seeing a recently opened bottle of vitamin water, he grabbed it and took a gulp.

"Mom, I could tell you the absolute truth, and if it didn't fit with your view of how your world should be, you'd disbelieve it. Look, I love you, this chat is fun, and I'm glad you called, but I really can't talk right now. How about I call you tomorrow after breakfast? A quick call before I leave." He rolled his eyes and took another drink. "Of course I'm not brushing you off. Yes, I'll call. Tomorrow morning. Bye, Mom."

He hung up. "Holy shit, that woman drives me nuts. I need a run before I explode." He checked his watch. "Forty minutes until dinner downstairs. Thirty minutes of pulse-pounding stress-relief and then ten minutes to clean up. Easy peasy." Changing quickly into his Gortex winter running gear, he was down the stairs and out the door in record time. He turned right and headed south, setting the countdown timer on his watch for fifteen minutes. With every pounding step along the snowy sidewalks and gulping breath of cold air, Jerry felt his frustration with his mother fade. He let his mind slip into run-mode, counting steps in tens, then counting breaths in fives. The houses slipped past, unnoticed. The only thought that inserted its way into his running mind was an image of the cover of the book from his great-grandfather. Why would he keep a stained and damaged book?

His pace was steady until his watch beeped at him, then he picked up the pace and began to make his way back home. He pushed himself hard, breathing in through his nose and out through his mouth. His pulse pounded in his ears and it felt great, not even a hint of a headache. By the time he ran up the stairs and let himself into the apartment, he was soaked with sweat and felt great. He even had five extra minutes to get cleaned up for dinner. With so many boxes already packed and taped shut, the shoebox's antique contents stood out. He didn't dare put it away until he'd had a shower, but he couldn't resist taking another look at the book of poetry sitting innocently in the bottom of the box. He leaned over and squinted for a better look, but a big glob of sweat dropped off his brow and landed on the stained cloth.

"Shit!" He bolted to the bathroom, peeled a foot of toilet paper off the roll, and then charged back into the living room where he gently dipped a corner of the absorbent paper into the drop as it rolled slowly across the brown stain. The drop was quickly sucked up and the book seemed no worse for wear. "What a dumb ass."

He left everything else right where it was, and charged into the bathroom, slamming the door behind him.

SHE FELT, OR rather *saw*, a spark in the interminable darkness, and it seemed to push away some of the cold, growly emptiness. That was new, she thought. There was a warmth to the spark, but it was fleeting. She watched for another spark, but it was apparently a solo effort. Nonetheless, the dark didn't seem so empty now, and the weight of her world seemed a bit less oppressive.

FIVE MINUTES LATER Jerry rushed out of the steamy bathroom, wearing a dark green bath towel around his lower half, drying his shaggy hair with a smaller hand towel. Singing along with another Harry Chapin song now filling the apartment, he walked into the living room, refreshed and happy.

He stopped in his tracks, letting Harry go on about being a taxi driver on a rainy night, without Jerry's disharmony. Sitting on the couch, watching him and grinning much too widely, was Isis.

Jerry dropped the smaller towel in shock and grabbed the larger one as if it might fall off. While holding the shifting towel with one hand, he tried to sign and talk, too.

"Damn, girl! What are you doing here?" He moved toward the bedroom, trying to keep stacks of boxes between himself and Isis.

"Mom sent me to get you. Dad made a fresh batch of Irish Cream and thought we could try it before dinner."

"I'll be ready in a couple minutes, so go tell them I'll be right there."

"Oh no. I'm not leaving. If this is as close as I get to seeing you naked, I'm not missing a second of it."

"Isis! You're only fifteen! And you have a boyfriend!" He stopped behind a stack of boxes as high as his chest and signed with both hands over the top box. "I could get arrested for just standing here talking to you like this."

Isis stayed on the couch but leaned left then right, trying to see around the boxes blocking her view. "Don't be silly. I'll never tell."

"That's not the point."

"No, the point is that Chad is sweet, but he's too immature. He doesn't understand me like you do."

"You've been out on a total of three dates with him. Give him a chance, Isis. Love takes time. It doesn't happen in a couple weeks." The towel slipped but he caught it before it revealed anything. "Damn! Go or stay, but I'm going into my bedroom, *alone*, so I can get dressed for dinner, with your whole family. If your dad walked in right now he'd kill me. No questions asked, just a bullet between the eyes. He's a cop—he could get away with it."

"You're no fun."

"Right. Remember that. Me old man, you jailbait. No fun. No fun at all." He backed into the bedroom, both hands holding the towel securely in place and then closed the door with a resounding thump.

JERRY EVENTUALLY RE-EMERGED from the bedroom, dressed in jeans and a faded red Fanshawe College sweatshirt fit for a casual dinner with friends.

"There. Shall we—" Isis sat on the couch, crying softly and clutching his bulky, olive-green, cable-knit sweater. "Hey, I'm sorry, Kiddo." He moved a couple boxes off the couch and sat down beside her, keeping a polite distance between them.

"It's not your fault I'm going to miss you, Jerry."

"But, Isis . . ." He had no idea what to say and she interrupted him before he could come up with anything.

"Can I ask a big favour?"

"Of course."

"This sweater. Can . . . can I have it? I'll buy you a new one, but I want this one."

"Um . . ." The sweater had been a Christmas gift from his mother, four or five years before.

"It's my favourite. I just want something to remember you by."

"You betcha. It's yours, for a trade." He'd started to think that leaving his friends in St. Marys wasn't going to be as painless as he'd first thought.

"What trade?"

"Something of yours, something I will remember you by. And

nothing kinky." The last thing he needed was to get caught driving across the continent with the cute frilly nightie of a fifteen-year-old girl in his suitcase. His hopes of taking the shortcut through the States would be dashed.

"Oh, yes! Can I pick it? I want it to be something special!"

"Sure. Your choice, but with your mom's full approval. Now, we have to go—your folks will wonder what's keeping us."

"Don't worry." She wiped way the last of her tears and grinned. "I told them I was going to give you a blow-job before we join them for the Irish Cream."

He leaped off the couch and nearly fell over a box on the floor. "WHAT?!!"

"Psych! Mom said you'll be late like always and I was to stay and hurry you up." With the sweater held close she got up from the couch and started down the hall to leave the apartment, laughing as she went.

Jerry relaxed and followed her. "Then let's go get some Irish Cream." Her back was turned so she didn't hear him, but at the door she stopped and faced him, then threw her arms around him. He hugged her back, lightly, and broke the embrace first. Isis stepped back, pulling the cherished sweater to her chest.

"Thank you, Jerry."

DINNER WITH ISIS' family went well, and her parents were grateful when they saw the sweater and understood it had been a gift of sorts to their daughter. They knew all about Isis' crush on their upstairs neighbour, but they also knew that Jerry had never treated Isis with anything but respect and kindness. He'd been their neighbour since Isis was twelve and they trusted him completely.

When he got back to his apartment, the hot meal and Irish cream teamed up to give him a sense that everything was right in the world, and he was making the best decision he could. He gently packed up the shoebox again, slipped it into a nearly full liquor box, and padded around it with one of the sweaters Isis left him with. He was so tired that he didn't even bother to turn off the lamp on Sushi's bowl, letting the glow show him the way to bed.

LIKE THE FIRST rays of morning sun cresting a hill and breaching her window, she felt warmth and light and an invitation to simply move up and out of the dark. She shed that absolute absence of light like a blanket, and emerged into a dream world. The dream around her was dim and without form at first, but eventually it began to take the shape of a small flat with nice high ceilings. It was not *her* bedroom, of that she was quite certain. Nor was it any room she knew in either the Palace or that last bleak house she remembered before . . . before . . . before she remembered nothing. She was not dreaming of a familiar place, but there was no darkness. There were also no soldiers, no guns, and no screams. She knew it was obviously a dream, but it was a much more pleasant dream than the ones she had been haunted by for so very long. This was a dream she could linger in.

Never before had she experienced a dream of such rich, clear detail. It appeared to be a flat, but full of boxes. Why would she dream of such a strange place? And where was Alexei? Or Olga or Tatiana? *Where was Mashka?!* She spun around, thinking they could be behind her, out of sight, but she was alone. She worried but then she felt an irresistible draw, a tug of sorts, pulling her away from the dream. The dream faded back into the darkness she had become so accustomed to.

THE NEXT MORNING, Isis' parents were as sad as their daughter when Jerry finally placed his camera bag in the packed-full Jeep and backed out of his parking spot for the last time. They waved, he waved, Isis cried, and even Jerry shed a tear or two.

HE CROSSED THE Canada-USA border at Sarnia rather than Windsor to the south, in order to bypass Detroit, a city he liked to visit but hated to drive through in any weather, let alone winter ice and snow. For the most part, road crews kept the interstates as clear of snow as could be done and every few miles he came upon sand-and-salt crews spreading their traction-assisting mix.

Stopping only for gas and one hot meal, Jerry made it through Michigan, the top of Indiana, through the always-congested Chicago, and up the I-90 to Rockford, where he let his GPS lead him to the closest Super 8. He got a room for himself and Sushi, and after a quick chat with the desk clerk for directions just before he closed up for the night, Jerry was off to the local Little Caesars for his favourite comfort food—a medium veggie pizza and a bottle of Coke.

Back at the Super 8 he dropped some food flakes in Sushi's bowl and watched the local news while munching pizza, propped up on a stack of pillows on one of the two double beds. He had three texts from Isis so he quickly rattled off an "I'm okay, Sushi is a lousy co-pilot, miss you, too" reply. He couldn't spend the entire trip hearing the beep of waiting texts from a sweet but infatuated teen, so he muted the ringer and placed the phone on top of his wallet on the bedside table.

He couldn't believe that he'd finally left Ontario and the road was under his feet. Like Jack Kerouac and Neal Cassady in the late 1940s, Jerry felt the electrifying thrill of being on the road, leaving behind the known and facing into the unknown. Thankful he wasn't hitchhiking like his two heroes had, Jerry tossed the empty pizza box onto the other bed and fell asleep sometime after midnight.

SHE FELT STRONGER than she had in ages and sensed that she was finally moving in a direction she was destined to go. An energy reached for her that was in defiance of the darkness and she listened to it, heeded its call. Pushing away the solitude, though, she found only more darkness . . . then within that darkness there appeared light, so she pushed further out into it and found herself in a brightly lit yard full of the oddest looking automobiles, with smooth lines and curved glass, nothing like the boxy conveyances her family rode in.

There appeared to be snow on the ground and on some of the vehicles, but she couldn't feel the cold. It was all the oddest of dreams, but unlike most of her dreams since she tumbled into the darkness, this was peaceful. Odd, but peaceful. She gained some strength in knowing that there was now light and life, even in her dreams. When the darkness tugged at her once again, she returned to it, no longer as afraid as she had been.

DAY TWO FOUND Jerry following I-90 up through Wisconsin, into Minnesota and on to South Dakota. Except for stops to sample real Wisconsin cheese, pick up a souvenir ceramic mouse-and-cheese salt-and-pepper set, dip his toe into the mighty Mississippi River near Lacrosse, and a half-hour detour south on I-35 over the Minnesota-Iowa state line—just so he could say he'd been to Captain James T. Kirk's home state—he made good time to Chamberlain, South Dakota. The Best Western he found was a block away from the Missouri River. He didn't know a lot of American history, but knew enough to be awed for the second time that day. He must have stood on the Chamberlain Bridge for half-an-hour watching what Google said was once North America's longest river, as it flowed beneath his feet. He soaked up the rhythm and found a peace he hadn't felt in a really long time. Eventually he wandered back to the motel for much-needed sleep.

In addition to his camera gear and computer bag, he grabbed one box from the back of the Jeep, to keep safe in the motel room with him and Sushi. The further he travelled from home, away from his family, the more Jerry thought about the odd little treasures left to him by his great-grandfather, and the more he felt the need to protect them. They were pieces of his own history, far more than silly knick-knacks, and definitely worthy of care.

He fed Sushi, drank a glass of cold South Dakota tap water, and climbed between the crisp, starched motel sheets. Sleep caught up with him almost as soon as he clicked off the mock-brass bedside lamp.

SOMETHING WAS CHANGED. She sensed warmth that had been missing. She stretched and moved out of the darkness, and found herself in a simple room. She couldn't see clearly, but it seemed to have basic, blocky furniture devoid of any adornments, including a desk on which a small fish bowl sat. She watched the beautiful red and purple beauty swim back and forth as if it could see her. Eventually it settled down and relaxed just above the gravel on the bottom of the simple bowl. She found it peaceful to just watch the fins and gills move. Did it sleep? She had no idea. Drifting around the hazy room, she wandered through the bed and inadvertently passed through its occupant. She got a sense of a young man and backed away quickly, embarrassed to have invaded his privacy even in the dream. Her dark cocoon soon beckoned to her so she willingly returned to its familiarity.

EXCITEMENT WOKE HIM earlier the next morning than he'd planned, and an odd dream he'd had about a pretty girl watching over him in silence stuck with him as he fixed himself a cup of decaf, had a quick shower, packed everything up, and loaded it all into the Jeep. Eventually thoughts of seeing Rushmore pushed the dream girl into the background.

Despite a light dusting of snow, man and fish were off before sunrise in an attempt to make it across the state to the Black Hills to see Mount Rushmore by lunch. He knew Sushi didn't give a damn about where they had lunch, but Jerry felt that if they could get there by mid-day, he could take some time to see one of the great man-made wonders of the modern world. For him, Rushmore was to be the highlight of the whole road trip. As he'd told Isis when they'd gone over his itinerary the night before he left, there were two reasons he was driving through the U.S.—to avoid much of the Canadian prairie winter weather, and to see Mount Rushmore. They'd spent an hour on her laptop looking up the mountain-carved monument on Wikipedia, and before they were done, Isis was so excited that she wanted to go with him just so she could see the faces of the four presidents carved into the side of a mountain.

"That is too cool, Jerry! Take lots of pictures and email them to me. Promise?"

"I promise, Kiddo."

WITHIN THE INKY blackness enveloping and winding through her, she could sense motion again, as if the darkness was on the move. She lacked the energy to stretch beyond her prison again, and she wanted to cry out, for anyone, friend of foe, but she still couldn't find her voice. Exhausted, she was isolated, suspended . . . lost.

CHAPTER FOUR

@TheTaoOfJerr: "Music gives a soul to the universe, wings to the mind, flight to the imagination and life to everything."

~Plato

JERRY DIDN'T ARRIVE in Custer, South Dakota until after lunch, but that was only because he'd spent an hour wandering around Wall Drugs—"America's Biggest Roadside Attraction". He bought a carved, lifelike, two-inch tall rattlesnake for Isis, and got the requisite free bumper sticker from the bin at the exit from one of the shops, but in his excitement to reach Rushmore, he was disappointed in the massive Wild West tourist trap in the simply-named town of Wall. Under different circumstances, he thought he probably could have appreciated the shops, galleries, and museums more, but the Jeep's tires spit gravel and snow as he fled the parking lot and made his way back to I-90 and west to the turnoff south to the town of Custer and Mount Rushmore.

HE COULD HAVE spent years researching the mountain-tall memorial and still not been prepared for the thrill of seeing it in person, towering above him, beyond the Avenue of the Flags, the Grand View Terrace, and the amphitheatre. Someone back east had once told him that they were disappointed with how small the memorial was, but standing there, looking up at its immensity, Jerry had to wonder what the hell they were expecting if they considered this small. He was blown away.

Knowing that he couldn't leave Sushi in the Jeep for too long without heat, he snapped pictures from every angle imaginable, walked the short Presidential Trail, ducked into the Lincoln Borglum Museum, and scooted through the gift shop in record time. He hated to leave the magnificence of Gutzon Borglum's masterpiece of engineering, but the mountain temperatures were dropping quickly, the forecast was for wet snow out of nearby Wyoming, and Sushi, patient and sturdy though he was, deserved to spend the night in a warm hotel room.

He promised himself that someday soon he'd return to fully appreciate the human and natural history of the Black Hills, then Jerry reluctantly drove back north to I-90 and west into Wyoming. A roast beef sandwich and an orange Gatorade grabbed in Rapid City kept his stomach from growling too much, but just south of Sheridan, Wyoming, at almost 4000 feet above sea level, a headache hit like a bullet to the brain.

With one hand pressed against his temple to feebly try and suppress the chainsaw in his head, and one eye barely open, Jerry swerved off the highway and into a closed truck weigh scale. As soon as the Jeep skidded to a stop, he slammed it into PARK, staggered out into the snow, and collapsed, vomiting up the orange mess that had once been the sandwich and the sports drink. Gentle flakes of loving snow drifted calmly down to blanket him in a thin layer of cooling, crisp white, but it took plunging his head face-first into a snow drift to push the pain back.

The sword of agony was eventually supplanted by the spear of cold, so Jerry hauled himself to his feet and stumbled to the still-running Jeep. A quick look at his watch said that he'd only been there for ten minutes, but he felt like it had been years. He rinsed his mouth out with warm water from the bottle in the console, popped in some gum, and pulled back out onto the quiet interstate. Twenty minutes later he and Sushi were in a beige room in a beige motel somewhere just off the interstate. Sushi gobbled up the food flakes Jerry dropped in his bowl while Jerry nibbled a Subway tuna wrap and sipped Coke in a feeble attempt to resurrect his blood sugar. He fell asleep with Garth Brooks' "The Beaches of Cheyenne" whispering out of the tinny clock radio, courtesy of Sheridan's own KYTI 93.7, and slept until nine the next morning.

SHE SENSED A great deal of pain nearby and so stayed in her darkness. Although she was curious about the young man she had bumped into in that stark dream room, the great pain frightened her and hinted that something may have happened to herself recently that involved more pain than she could ever imagine. She curled around herself and pushed all thoughts of agony away.

THE HEADACHE STAYED close to the surface this time, so the next day and a half were a bit of a blur for Jerry as he continued west until he could drive no more. He reached Missoula, Montana and found a clean bed and a hot bath, having driven like an automaton, not fully appreciating the stunning snow-dressed scenery as he'd passed through it. His reflexes kept him safe on the road and his body told him when to eat, so it was just miles of asphalt, gas stations, and roadside eateries, which continued the next mentally hazy day all the way to Seattle and up to Port Angeles. He missed the last ferry of the day across to Vancouver Island by a couple hours, so he once again fed Sushi, fed himself, and hit the sack in a convenient motel.

THE PAIN SHE sensed subsided eventually, and beneath the sense of movement within the darkness, there was now an ancient, ceaseless rhythm, a deep pulse like the sea she had once dipped her toes in. She had toes? Maybe not now, but she was certain that she once had, and they had felt the rhythm of waves and the pull of a tide. Serenity enveloped her, and she drifted into something more like a sleep than the usual limbo.

A DENNY'S BREAKFAST of raspberry pancakes and scrambled eggs all smothered in maple syrup fuelled him up for the day, but it took a conversation with ferry-ticket-seller Rachelle—a cute, pierced, and tattooed platinum blonde—to finally drag him away from the world of the living dead and into the light.

"So, dude, we were house-boating up off the Sunshine Coast when Shade, like, was hanging a chummed line off the stern and smoking a home-rolled, when the rod was near yanked from his hand. He stuffed the rolly between his lips and started the fight of his life. He was no rookie, though, dude. He let the line out and let whatever it was run. It didn't go far, though. Once it thought the threat was gone, it chilled. Shade passed the smoke and started a slow reel in. He'd reel for a minute, feel the resistance build, and let it out. Then he'd reel a bit more, and then let it out. All the time, man, he was pulling it in, closer and closer, tiring it out, wearing it down. Judging by the bend on that deep-sea rod, we figured he had a salmon-and-a-half on the line.

"He danced with this baby for an hour before he finally got it up to the port side where we rushed with the net. We nearly crapped ourselves when we saw it. Man, it was a beauty."

"What was it? A Coho? Sockeye?"

"*Shark*, dude."

"Shark? No way!"

"Way. It was just a little thing, a meter, meter-and-a-half, but it was big enough to snap the line when we tried to get a net under it."

"Cool."

"Beyond cool. But that's life on the Strait, dude."

The morning was slow, and Rachelle was hopped up on Red Bull and happy to chat chat chat about the Port, and her many visits north to The Island to party with her cousin Rod in Nanaimo. By the time the *M.V. Coho* ferry pulled out of port with Jerry on the outside deck, he'd rediscovered his smile.

Exhausted, but relaxed, Jerry sat by himself on the deck, in the wan, early morning sun. The light snowfall stopped and the clouds parted, just for his departure, it seemed to him. He closed his eyes and breathed deeply, taking in the sea air, purging the road grime and exhaust fumes of the last five days. Seagulls screeched and wheeled in the sky above the ferry, begging for handouts from the few passengers brave enough to face the near-freezing, moist, winter air of the strait, but Jerry paid no attention to either them nor to the less-than-perfect weather. The thick, tangy, sea breeze intoxicated him, drawing out his exhaustion and scattering it far and wide. With his camera tucked inside his heavy red jacket, and a steaming, hot decaf in his gloved hand, he was at peace. *I could get used to being near the ocean*, he thought. He took a couple snap shots with his iPhone and emailed them to Isis before sitting back, closing his eyes, and surrendering to the moment completely.

SHORTLY AFTER NINE, Jerry called Manny from the ship.

"Tell me you're here, Jerry! Tell me my new star station manager is in town!"

"About half-an-hour out, or so one of the regular passengers just told me."

"The ferry from Tsawassan?"

"From where? I'm coming over from Port Angeles. I drove through the States the whole way."

"Right-oh, mate. You're on the *Coho*, then. Good ship and true and all that. Your flat is all ready for you. You want the address and I'll meet you there, or do you want to come to the station and pick up the keys?"

"Do you mind meeting me at the apartment? I have it programmed into Maggie-Sue, my GPS. It's been a long trip and I'd like to clean up before meeting the team at the station. Or are they expecting me today?"

"Tomorrow's soon enough, young fella. That's one helluva long drive to do alone, so you take the night. Your stuff has been arriving all week, and the boxes are all sitting in the middle of the flat waiting for you to turn it into a home. I left the furniture like you saw in the photos I emailed over, and we found a couple beauty chairs on the weekend that I've tossed in, but don't feel obligated to take 'em. I've got two other rental properties I can use 'em in."

"Sounds great, Manny. I really do appreciate everything you've done."

"You're one of the family now, Jerry, and family takes care of each other. Besides, I'm going to get my time and money's worth out of you—there's a lot of work to be done to get us through this downturn. But all that can wait another day or two, mate. Give me a call when you're about to dock and I'll make my way over to the flat."

"Will do. I'll let you get back to work."

"Yeah, must do—year end and all. Finally see you in an hour or so, Jerr."

"Yeah, I guess you will, Manny. I'm looking forward to it."

Jerry disconnected, dropped the phone back into his pocket, and relaxed. He was tempted to put the headphones on and listen to some soul-fixing jazz, but the hum of the ship's engine, the cry of the gulls, and the rhythm of the sea were all the music he needed, so far from where he'd started only days before.

MANNY MET JERRY at the apartment, just as promised, and Jerry was knocked speechless by Manny's sheer tallness. Jerry estimated his new employer to be over six-and-a-half-feet tall and most of it was smile. Right up to the moment Manny grabbed Jerry's hand in his massive paw and pumped it like an old friend, Jerry was sure the giant Aussie was going to sweep him up in a hug. After the long drive so far from his roots back east, Jerry probably would have been okay with a hug.

"Welcome to the City of Gardens, Jerry. Not many flowers to see now, but give it a few months and it'll be a bloody riot of colour. But never mind that. I'm so excited, I'm rambling like a schoolgirl. Let's get you upstairs and settled in, mate."

"After you, Boss."

Together the two of them climbed the gently worn, dark-stained oak stairs to the third floor—Jerry holding Sushi's travel bowl in one hand and his laptop bag in the other, while Manny carried one of Jerry's bags in a long-fingered hand, and the apartment keys in the other. He led the way up the stairs and stopped at a spacious landing with only two apartments leading off from it.

Unlocking the knob and the deadbolt, Manny reached in, flicked a light switch with his key hand, and stepped back to let Jerry go in first. Half expecting Manny to simply lead the rest of the way into the apartment, Jerry hesitated, afraid there would be a surprise party waiting for him. He had the impression that when Manny said the station staff were as close as a family, he meant that the little things were taken care of, such as welcoming the new team member with a party, like a long-lost relative returned home. He was relieved to find no one waiting, but the relief was quickly replaced by amazement at the beauty of his new digs.

Twelve-foot-high ceilings, dark-stained oak trim, polished hardwood floors with expensive-looking, imported, oriental carpets, and sparkling stained-glass-crowned windows greeted him. The place begged him to kick off his shoes, drop his worries by the door, and just sink back into the leather couch forever, protected from stress, strain, and everything else he'd left behind. Then he saw the Christmas tree, lit with simple white LEDs and decorated with silver and red glass balls. At six-feet, it wasn't much taller than him, and it was tucked in a corner, but it was definitely the heart of the amazing space.

"Wow."

"Right you are, Jerr. This little haven was my own bachelor pad before I met Carmella, and we even spent the first year of our marriage up here, cloistered from the world but close to the slow, steady pulse of Victoria. Conceived our son here, though not on that couch—don't worry. We loved this little place so much I bought the whole building when it came on the market a few years back."

His eyes moist with emotion and the release of the stress that had been building for so long, Jerry turned back to Manny. Without a word he reached his hand out to clasp the big man's own in thanks, but Manny had other ideas though and finally took Jerry into a quick hug. "Like I said, welcome to the family."

"I . . ."

"No worries. I understand. Carmella stocked the fridge and freezer with a few basics, stuck the numbers of a half-dozen local fast food joints on the fridge, and even made up the bed with some of our spare linens, just so you don't have to do anything but settle in. Basic HD cable is included, so the flat-screen you shipped out is all hooked up." He took a few seconds to collect his thoughts. "We know you've made a big move here, Jerr, and we wanna do everything we can to make Victoria your new home. Hell, if my daughter wasn't already married to a great fella . . . "

Jerry laughed. "Thanks, Manny. I appreciate the thought. I now understand the depth of the sentiments behind the rave reviews when I checked your references. I've got a bottle of Crown Royal in one of my bags if you'd care to join me in a toast to this new life—before I pass out on that couch from exhaustion."

"Let's get everything out of your truck and up here, first, then we can toast and you can pass out, knowing you've got nothing to do but relax until tomorrow. And just so you know, tomorrow is just a quickie, Jerr. You'll swing by the station for the welcome and see your office, but no work for you, yet." Manny handed Jerry the keys and led the way out of the apartment and down to the street.

"Take a day or so to settle into this place. My old Gran used to say that an unsettled home was no haven, and everyone needs a haven. Cable is set, but if you want a land-line the number to call is on the fridge, too. And if you haven't called yer insurance company with the new info, you'll wanna do that, too. The only thing I'm a stickler for is tenant's insurance, for everyone concerned. If you need an agent for that, just ask."

Jerry unlocked the Jeep with the remote, and the two men each grabbed an armful of whatever was within reach. "You've thought of everything, Manny. Wow." They headed back up the stairs.

"I can't take all the credit, lad. Carmella is the organizational queen. It's all been her doing. I'd forget my own birthday if she wasn't on top of things. She even programs my Blackberry for me. Hell, I get reminders for events I don't even know I'm going to. I'd have hired *her* to manage the station for me, but she knows little to nothing about market shares and music. She thinks Billboard is where she uses a stick-pin to leave Honey-Do lists for me when she goes out. Besides, if I paid her to organize, she'd have to find a new hobby, and I think she loves doing it just for the fun of it."

"She sounds like quite a lady."

"The best, Jerr. The best."

The two men placed their loads inside the apartment and went back out for more of Jerry's transplanted possessions. The conversation shifted to the various features and services in the neighbourhood, and by the time the Jeep was empty and secured in Jerry's reserved spot, he felt like he knew more about downtown Victoria after half an hour with Manny than he did about St. Marys or Stratford after three years in that area.

He carried his last load into the well-appointed kitchen, knowing that somewhere in the bag were the bottle of rye and a set of bubbled-wrapped crystal rocks glasses he hadn't wanted to leave in the hands of the shippers. He found it all and poured out a couple shots while Manny pulled a bag of ice out of the freezer. Jerry chuckled. "She really did think of everything, didn't she?"

"This one was my idea. There's a six-pack of cold beer in the fridge, too. I hope you like Keith's."

"A pale ale is perfect."

Two ice cubes went into each family heirloom tumbler, and

Jerry handed one to Manny. He raised his own glass. "I'll keep it simple and not too eloquent. To new beginnings, and to new friends who feel like old friends destined to become best friends."

"Well said, young fella." Manny raised his rye in response. "To new beginnings, and new friends who feel like old friends destined to become best friends."

They clinked glasses, sipped the still-warm Crown Royal, and looked around the box-cluttered apartment in silence. Jerry sighed, then put his glass on the counter and wandered over to look behind a mountain of boxes, something having caught his eye.

"A fireplace? I've got a *fireplace*?"

"Every good home does, Jerr." Manny placed his own glass in the sink. "Firewood's in the hall closet for now. West Coast cedar. But you can find that on your own because I do have to get back to the station before the end of the work day."

"Yeah, sorry, Manny. I'll let you get out of here. Thanks for—"

"Any time, Jerr. See you at noon tomorrow. Call me if you need directions to the station." He let himself out, closing the apartment door as he went.

Jerry returned to the kitchen, splashed another shot of whiskey into his glass, and then went looking for the firewood. Manny had comforted him for uprooting himself to come to Victoria, but Jerry saw it in a totally different light. He was strengthened by the idea of being able to "plant" himself somewhere healthy for a change. This was a perfect chance to purge and distance himself from the various unhealthy relationships back east in Ontario. He had a chance to start again, and a rye-on-the-rocks by a cedar-burning fire was the perfect start.

"Let the cleansing of my soul begin."

It had been a long time since he'd had to set and start a fire, but when the few steps came back to him, Jerry was sure he'd found in them the ritual he needed for his new home. Manny had left newspaper on the hearth, kindling in a copper scuttle, and plenty of already-split logs in the huge closet to get him started, so Jerry began by opening the flue, gingerly leaning in and looking up the chimney, to confirm that it was clear. It was. No squirrel's nest, and no last-year's Santa, sooty and frozen in rigor, his underestimated girth caught in an overestimated chimney.

He pulled a copy of the *Victoria Times Colonist* from the top of the pile and slid out the classified section. As a kid he'd always saved the front section for last, figuring that while the fire was sputtering and grasping, he might as well catch up on the news. These days he had the Internet for that, but there was something solid and reassuring about sitting cross-legged by the fireplace with the front page—or the comics—waiting for the sparks to jump from the crumpled balls of paper to the soft, feathered kindling set up like the poles of a tepee over the paper. When he was growing up, he'd sat on an old camel saddle his father had brought home from a business trip to Egypt in the '90s. His mother still had that saddle, next to her own hearth, so instead Jerry pulled up the oxblood-red leather ottoman and sat. New hearth, new tradition.

The kindling caught but the paper burned too fast. Jerry quickly crumpled and twisted three more "sticks", tighter than the first ones, and carefully slid them into the centre of the tepee. The flames found them and grew, this time slowly enough to grab hold of the kindling and consume them gently with a flickering embrace. The kindling crackled and popped as the fire heated the dry sap within, then the flames expanded enough to caress the thicker logs leaning on the tepee, and the whole, contained structure became involved. Fuel was consumed, heat was generated, and his new home was warmed immeasurably.

THERE WAS AN odd change to the tone of the black abyss. The near constant vibration faded away and there was a new radiant warmth like she hadn't felt since another lifetime. It offered a gentle reassurance she now clung to as the blackness tried to crowd back in. Thoughts of the young man interrupted her reverie, though, and she was heartened to think she might dream of him again soon.

CHAPTER FIVE

@TheTaoOfJerr: "Music in the soul can be heard by the universe."

~Lao Tzu

JERRY EVENTUALLY MOVED from the ottoman to the couch where he tumbled into a nearly dreamless sleep for two hours. He didn't exactly dream, but there were hints of the young woman in black drifting at the edge of his mind. When he finally awoke, her fleeting images wafted away like mist in the sun. The fire was too low to generate much heat but still had plenty of energy to ignite the fresh log Jerry put on before wandering off to splash cold water on his face and relieve himself.

Back at the couch, he checked his phone for messages then logged onto his browser to check his email account. There were two messages from Isis, his own copy of his pre-written and weekly-scheduled photography blog, and a reply from his insurance broker, Mostafah. On this one thing, he'd already been ahead of Manny. He'd emailed Mostafah as soon as he knew the new address and the move-in date.

Not yet awake enough to deal with Isis, and not needing to read his own blog, Jerry opened Mostafah's message confirming the change of address and recommending that he get an appraisal done on the little box of antiquities Mavis had bestowed upon him. An attachment listed three antique shops Mostafah's Victoria counterparts recommended. The note pointed out that one of them was only a few blocks away from Jerry's new home address.

IN SPITE OF the gradual shift from driving through the various time zones between St. Marys and Victoria, Jerry's body was still on Eastern Time, so he was up at five, scrambling a half-dozen eggs, chopping vegetables, and grating a small brick of cheese for a monster-sized omelette. He would have loved ham in it or bacon on the side, but since the headaches had started, the menu held no meat with nitrates for this sick puppy. He missed ham and bacon a bit, but what he really missed from the nitrate-rich, no-go-list was corned beef. There were days he nearly cried out for a Shopsy's of Toronto corned beef stacked on rye with Dijon mustard and Swiss cheese. With luck, maybe he could find a place in Victoria that did for seafood what Shopsy's did for deli dining. He just might be able to get used to the idea of fresh scallops, salmon, and a dill cream sauce instead of corned beef on rye. Maybe.

He slipped the finished culinary masterpiece onto a plate, sprinkled the last of the cheddar and dill on top, then ground fresh pepper generously over the whole works. He used as little salt as possible, but loved his fresh-ground Telecherry pepper. He would have liked to relax and chill out, but he also hated sitting still when there was so much to do. He looked up Ipatiev Antiques online and found that they were three blocks away and opened at nine. He didn't have to be at the station until noon—though he would arrive early as always—so including a walk to the antique store, he had plenty of time to unpack and get the place looking more like a home and less like a storage locker.

He ate at the kitchen counter, high atop an oak stool, re-establishing his oldest tradition of reading while eating. It used to drive Haley crazy, so he'd stopped, at least when she was home. Today he was deep into the last chapter of D. B. Jackson's historical fantasy, *Thieftaker: Dead Man's Reach*—Jackson's best to date, and Jerry had been hooked on the series since discovering that his own family was from pre-revolutionary Boston, where the *Thieftaker* series was set. He ate and read in silence, kept company by Sushi, whose flexed and fanned fins indicated that he was happy to be back in his own tank and on a solid countertop rather than in a sloshing, unadorned bowl in a box bouncing in the back seat and not feeling like eating much at all. Jerry grinned at his sturdy companion, dropped a pinch of food into the bowl, and went back to savouring both the book and the omelette.

HAVING USED GOOGLE Street View to find the antique store, he knew exactly what to look for when he rounded the corner and looked up at a small shop with fine gold and black lettering on the windows indicating he'd found Ipatiev Antiques & Fine Furniture. The storefront was only fifteen feet or so wide, with the inset door bracketed by the two bay windows. Whereas some of the shops sharing the street were showing a little bit of wear and tear, the front of Ipatiev Antiques was in impeccable condition. There wasn't a chip in the paint or a spot of rust on the iron fittings. The brass door knob and plate were gleaming and the windows all looked like they'd been hand-polished to invisibility. Jerry was impressed.

The display in the left window featured a variety of small European pieces on a solidly carved dining table. The antiques in the other window were all of an Asian origin, from Indian brass to Chinese jade. Jerry had no idea how old or valuable any of it was, but he was definitely impressed by the spotless selection spread out before him. Oh, to have a job that could allow him to purchase such luxuries, he thought. Someday, he supposed.

He checked his watch to confirm that it was after nine, then entered the shop with the old Kodak camera and the book of Blake's poems wrapped in left-over bubble wrap in a cloth grocery bag. A pair of delicate brass bells announced his arrival as the door bumped their spring hanger and set them to ringing. Inside, the shop was as dust-free as the window displays, yet the area was full of pieces of all sizes, from French armoires to Fabergé-type jewelled eggs in a strong, stunningly lit display case. A gentle voice with the soft rasp of a lifetime smoker and a decidedly Russian accent addressed him.

"Good morning, sir. Welcome to Ipatiev Antiques. How can I be of service? I am Ivan Petrov."

Jerry turned to find a diminutive man about seventy-five years old, dressed like an old-school banker in tailored, navy blue, wool trousers and vest, with a jeweller's loupe hanging from a chain around his neck. "Doing a little Christmas shopping, sir?"

"Sorry, but no. You've got some gorgeous stuff, but right now I'm hoping you can do a rough appraisal on a couple of things I've inherited. I just moved here and my insurance agent wants to know their value as soon as possible, so he can include them in the coverage. You were recommended by one of his Victoria associates."

"Of course, sir. I am honoured by the recommendation. If you have the items with you, I would be pleased to take a look." He moved behind the display case, reached behind it, and came up with a rubber-backed, dark green velvet matt. He flicked a switch on the back of the display case and the lights inside it were replaced by a crisp halogen lamp from above.

Jerry could see that Petrov was obviously a professional who took what he did very seriously. Placing the bag on the glass next to the matt, Jerry gingerly retrieved his great-grandfather's camera and book. Petrov put on a pair of fine cotton gloves and waited patiently while Jerry unwrapped the treasures and placed them on the velvet. As the old man examined the camera, Jerry retrieved the pocket watch from inside his jacket and gently placed it on the velvet next to the book.

"Very nice. The camera is a Number 3A Folding Brownie, made by the Eastman Kodak Company starting in April 1909. It has seen better days, but it is still in very good condition." He picked up the watch, opened it, and examined it closely with the loupe. "I would have to open it up to be sure, but I'm nearly certain that this is a 1922 Longines. White gold, not silver, as many people assume. Seventeen jewels. Swiss-made. Very nice." He pulled a pen and a small coil-bound notebook from his shirt pocket and made some notes.

Jerry was pleased. "It all belonged to my great-grandfather."

Petrov barely heard Jerry as he examined the book. "A nice edition but a shame the cover is stained and torn—that will affect its value, obviously." He opened it and read the inscription. "'To Ana, love Mama. Christmas 1915.' Lovely. Very sweet. This Ana was a family member?"

Jerry chuckled. "Of mine? Oh, no. My great-grandfather picked it up in Russia in the summer of 1918. He was in some place called Ekaterinburg. I've been meaning to do some research on the Internet but just haven't had the time, what with the move and all."

If at all possible, Petrov held the book with an even lighter touch than before, visibly shaken. With trembling hands, he placed the Blake volume down on the velvet. "Ekaterinburg in 1918? He was a soldier?"

"A captain in an Expeditionary Force of some kind. There's a photo inside the back cover that might help."

Petrov picked up the book once again. He opened the back cover and the scalloped-edged black-and-white photo of the Ipatiev House slid out and dropped onto the glass cabinet top. "Very interesting." He looked again at the cover, using the loupe once more to get detail his old eyes alone couldn't. "But with no way to corroborate the origin of this curious little volume, in addition to the damage, I'm afraid it has little value other than as a personal family treasure. Is that stain wine, perhaps?"

Jerry shrugged. "I have no idea. I suppose it could be." He'd originally thought it was blood, but now he wasn't so sure. "Mr. Petrov, do you have an estimate I can give my insurance agent until a formal appraisal can be done? Please?"

Petrov wrote two numbers on the back of his business card and handed it to Jerry. "These are estimates of the values of the watch and the camera. The book, maybe $50, because of its age. I can prepare something formal for your insurance company; if you give me an address, I can drop it off."

Jerry read the note and put it into his wallet. "Thank you. Or you can email it. Whatever is easiest for you. I'll give you my email, my cell number, and my address. I live around the corner on Broad Street. Not too far away." He took another of Petrov's business cards from the jade cardholder on the counter top and wrote the information on the back.

Petrov took it, read it, and tucked it carefully in his vest pocket. "Very good. I should have something later today or early tomorrow." He smiled warmly, and Jerry's doubts evaporated. "That'd be great, sir." He left the shop, his heirlooms held close.

ANA WAS QUITE certain that she no longer needed to breathe, but nonetheless she'd been holding her breath. She sensed a movement and the warmth of a nearby kind soul, but then there was a malignance, a jumbled, confused sense of others in the darkness, or at least other darknesses near at hand. She willed herself to be as small and unnoticeable as she could. Whatever she was sensing, it was not friendly to her.

PETROV WAS ON the phone before the echo of the door bells had died. Working from memory, he fumbled over the last two numbers, remembered them, and finished dialling. It only took two rings before it was answered.

"Mr. Petrov. Merry Christmas."

Petrov sat his old bones down on his stool. "How did you know it was me?"

"Call Display. You really need to catch up with the rest of us, old man. Now, what's so important that you're calling my personal cell phone during Christmas break?"

"Yes, I am sorry about that Doctor Professor. I have only just held in my hands the most extraordinary piece of Romanov memorabilia. What would you say to a book belonging to Anastasia herself, which may have actually been in her possession when she died?"

"I'd say 'bullshit'. It's too hard to prove."

"Prove conclusively? Of course it is too hard. But the owner claims it was picked up at the House of Special Purpose days after the killings. It has what appears to be a bullet hole, blood stains, and an inscription to Ana from her mother in script which looks too similar to your own collection of Alexandra's letters to ignore."

"Good God! I must see it. I'll be in Victoria for three days for the New Year's Gala at The Empress Hotel. I'll come to the shop to see it on New Year's Day."

"I'm afraid I do not have the piece in my possession, Doctor Professor. It was part of a small insurance appraisal I was doing. But I do have the young man's name and address. Perhaps you can make him an offer. I told him it was nearly worthless, so maybe the boy will take a few hundred dollars for it. He is young and will most likely just spend it on drugs and alcohol anyway."

"He has no idea what it's worth? You're sure?"

"Most positive. He will take it home, shove it on a shelf, and forget about it."

"Perfect! Find out as much as you can about him. I like to know my opponents' weaknesses before I face them."

"Would you like me to make a low-ball offer for the book? Perhaps I can have it for you by the time you arrive."

"No. I don't want him thinking that it might be worth something and then try to sell it on eBay or Kijiji." Petrov heard the academic take a deep breath on the other end of the line. "Mr. Petrov, you're quite certain about this piece?"

"As certain as I can be without doing DNA tests on the blood and chemical analysis on what looks like gunpowder residue. I would stake my reputation on it."

"Reputations can be reinvented and rebuilt. Would you stake your *life* on it?"

"I am an old man. A book belonging to Anastasia is probably worth more than my life and would be a poor exchange."

"Maybe so, but I will not be made a fool of like Ramirez and his fake Romanov Fabergé egg." He hung up abruptly, and the old man sighed at the poor manners.

CHAPTER SIX

@TheTaoOfJerr: "Most people die with their music still locked up inside them."

~Benjamin Disraeli

BY THE TIME Jerry walked to the radio station at noon, he was pushing back another dull thumper of a headache, so the tour, the handshakes, and the welcome-aboards were all a bit of a blur. He remembered some pretty faces, some lopsided smiles, and some very eclectic personalities, but it was all he could do to remember where he was. He smiled and nodded and eventually Manny caught on that something was wrong.

"You don't look so good, Jerr. A bit pale, even."

"I get headaches. I'm fighting this one and winning, but it's exhausting."

"Then get out of here. Go relax, and enjoy the sea air. I find it's a cure-all like no other."

"You're the boss, Boss."

With the GPS on his iPhone to guide him should he get lost, Jerry just let his feet lead him out of the station and take him wherever they wanted. He eventually found himself strolling along Victoria's Inner Harbour with only a trace of the headache remaining. Seeing all of the Christmas decorations on shop fronts and vessels in port, Jerry decided he'd better make it up to his new staff. He called Manny.

"Jerr! Miss us already? Ready to start work?"

Jerry chuckled. "Yes and almost. There's one thing I'd like to do first and that's have everyone over to the loft for a Christmas gathering."

"Great idea. When?"

"Well, tomorrow is Christmas Eve. Would that be too short of notice? I just want sort of a drop-in gathering so people can do what they want with their families earlier and then swing by for a bite to eat or a cocktail, and chat for a bit."

"I like it. Want help?"

"That's why I was calling. How would Carmella feel about being my right-hand-lady on this? She knows the people and the city. I don't want her doing the work, just being the voice in my ear that says 'yay' or 'nay'."

"She'd love it! She loves nothing better than planning and executing a party, Jerr, especially on short notice. She just left the office so I'll text her and have her give you a call."

"Thanks, Manny. I'll send out an email telling everyone when and where as soon as we hang up."

"Then go, do."

Jerry sent out the email to his list of station staff and ten minutes later Carmella called.

"Jerry, dear, I hear we're planning a party."

"Just a casual gathering, Carmella. You don't mind giving me a hand?"

"Don't tell Manny this, but I'm tired of shopping for presents and this is the perfect little break I need. Besides, I think it's a great idea. We had a staff party last week but it was a sit-down dinner and we were missing our handsome new station manager with the voice made for radio. We need a relaxed, mingly-thing to start the Christmas week off."

"Just a simple thing. You know the staff and you know where to find supplies, so I'm in desperate need of a wing-man, or wing-woman as the case may be."

"Then I'm your girl."

In five minutes Jerry sketched out what he needed and in another five the two of them had the simple gathering all planned out.

"Jerry, you go home and finish unpacking and settling in. Get a good night's sleep, and I'll be at your door bright and early at nine so we can hit the markets early."

"Nine it is, Carmella. Thanks."

THE FRESH SEA air eventually shoved the headache away and Jerry let his iPhone guide him back to the loft. He tossed together a simple salad, then spent the rest of the afternoon and most of the evening unpacking, replying to emails and texts, tweeting a few words of wit and wisdom, and checking the spelling of his pre-written blog post before letting it go live. He scribbled down a couple ideas for future posts, and then went to bed early.

Between the effects of the sea air and finding renewed hope in this far off place, Jerry slipped into a deep sleep so quickly that at first he didn't realize he was dreaming when the hazy, see-through girl appeared and sat on the foot of his bed. She didn't say anything, but while her smile was welcoming, her eyes seemed confused and maybe a little lost. He smiled, waved, and fell deeper into sleep, where the dreams rarely followed.

THE DARKNESS PARTED and she stepped through the gap into her dream. The blurry flat was still and dark but for the light on the small fish tank. The little fish wiggled at her as she drifted around trying to focus on things and not succeeding. It was a small space, but quite well furnished if her eyes were to be trusted. Once again, it was an unusually calm place for a dream. Until recently her dreams involved screams, shouts, gunfire, and blood, but in this dream she could not, in fact, hear anything at all. Was she deaf here? Or was this a dream world of no sound?

She drifted around, exploring the room, and came across a young man in bed behind a lovely ornate dressing screen. She stopped for a closer look, but couldn't see his face clearly enough to know whether it was the same man from other dreams. The fact that the fish was in this dream as well suggested that this was the same man. The darkness beckoned once again so she let her world draw her back in.

JERRY LOOKED AROUND the loft at the first party he'd hosted in a couple years. The gathering was perfect, and if Carmella were twenty years younger and single, Jerry would have fallen head-over-heels in love with her. She was funny, smart, and made Jerry feel like he'd lived in Victoria his whole life and she, Manny, and he had always been life-long friends. Manny was a lucky SOB, Jerry thought as he watched Carmella blush when one of his new staff complimented her on the pastries she'd whipped up in Jerry's kitchen that afternoon. He looked around the loft at the smiles and camaraderie and realized that it was about time he surrounded himself with some positive, healthy relationships.

Jerry had sort of expected staff to drop in for a half-hour or so and then drift off to do what they'd first planned for the holy night, but most of them were there by seven and—Jerry checked his watch—at eleven o'clock there were still eighteen people there, all laughing and joking like a functional family who actually enjoyed each other's company.

Dean Martin's 1966 *Christmas Album* played softly in the background, some of Jerry's new staff chatted next to the Christmas tree, some hung out near the desk where his laptop sat folded next to a lava lamp, Sushi's hexagonal tank, and a few of Jerry's photos and sketches of St. Marys. On the mantle sat a framed photo of Isis on which she'd written "To Jerry. Always and Forever, Love Isis" and two of the younger women on the team were laughing kindly and examining the photo and the attached lock of hair taped to the frame. Jerry looked up from the couch and saw them, and for the first time in a long time didn't feel the need to defend his life to anyone. These people were just curious about their new boss.

Turning back to the conversation, Jerry smiled. He and Manny chatted with three eager staff members about his own age. Jerry was coming to see that the West Coast staffers who believed they were so much more liberal in appearance and thought than people back east were in fact really not so different from the crew he worked with in Stratford, the Pork Congress of Canada. Mika was a tall, attractively bookish, mahogany-brunette with some far eastern, spiritually inspired tattoos, and a peaceful calm about her. Rolf was only twenty-one, and with his short stature and long, shaggy blond hair, was the closest thing Jerry had ever seen in the real world to Cousin Itt of the Addams Family. Andy, like Rolf, was just out of college and seemed to be the most conservative of the bunch with a dull, moneyed, prep school look and attitude.

And then there was Lee-Anne. Jerry had quickly decided that she was far too much like the small-town women back in

Stratford. She was a curvy, dark-blonde a couple years older than himself, and, as became quickly apparent to Jerry, she was the married company flirt. She wasn't participating very much in the conversation, but she leaned over the back of the couch near Jerry, hanging on his every word while she made sure he could see her cleavage out of the corner of his eye. Not staring was taking all the self-control he could muster, because he had to admit to himself that she had *really* nice cleavage. He'd had a couple drinks and was feeling quite relaxed, so he had to concentrate on the conversation at hand. At the moment, though, Mika had his complete attention, even without flashing her breasts.

"You saw a pod of killer whales?" Jerry was astounded. "While you were just walking down the beach?"

"Yeah. We were collecting shells." She carefully placed the Blake book down on the coffee table.

Rolf nodded and took a sip of his beer. "I see them all the time, man. Orcas, greys . . ."

"Grey whales?! Where can—?" A headache bumped into him, interrupting him. He put a hand to his temple, massaging.

Rolf leaned in. "Jerry?"

"Just a bit of a headache." It drilled a hole in his skull. His two-drink limit was down to zero for the rest of the holidays, he decided. He closed his eyes for a second. He felt Lee-Anne's hands on his shoulders, rubbing slowly, sensuously, and opened his eyes abruptly. She leaned closer and her breasts caressed the back of his head. His eyes went wide with shock.

"Here, Jerry. This'll get rid of your headache, hon."

"Uh . . ." He was stumped. He had to stop her, but maybe this was what happened at parties on the West Coast. He tried to pull away, even though the rub actually seemed to be helping his headache. Not only was she married, but Jerry was pretty sure her husband, Tom, was still somewhere in the loft.

Manny saw Jerry's discomfort and came to his rescue, quietly. "Down, Lee-Anne. Good girl. Sit. It's late and you're massaging under the influence again."

Lee-Anne ignored her boss's boss and kept rubbing, forcing Jerry to lean forward to escape her reach. But, even tipsy, she was faster than he was and pulled him right back again. The rest of the group was starting to notice and, as Jerry feared, they were curious how he'd respond. Lee-Anne's husband decided for him.

"Lee-Anne!"

Mika chuckled. "Lee-Anne, I think your *husband* is calling."

"Let him take a number—I only have one set of hands." She held her hands up to show them and Jerry lurched up and out of reach.

He stood up too quickly and the headrush made him wobble a bit, with the headache slamming back in. One hand returned to his temple, feebly trying to squeeze the pain out. The headrush passed in a flash and he was able to ignore the headache for a moment.

"Yes, you do, Lee-Anne, and I think Tom is holding a coat up for them." Jerry gestured towards a slouched, push-over of a man standing by the front door with a long, supple, red leather coat in his outstretched hands. Tom stepped over with Lee-Anne's coat and shot Jerry a hard look as if Jerry had been the one to start the flirtatious interchange.

He kept his voice low and Jerry could hear that he was pissed off, but Jerry could also tell that this was probably not the first time Tom had had to stop Lee-Anne from rubbing the wrong shoulders. "Time to go, Honey. The sitter has to be home by 11:30."

Manny stepped up and gently steered Lee-Anne towards Tom. "That's a good cue for the rest of us, too. Jerr . . . great party, lad. Sleep that headache away, and we'll see you when we get back from the mainland in a couple days."

Jerry smiled through the headache, forcing it back by sheer will. "Thanks for coming out, everyone. Those of you who have time off, enjoy it. Those of you holding down the fort, I'll see you tomorrow."

The guests all wished each other Merry Christmas, Happy Chanukah, Happy Kwanza, and even Happy Festivus-for-the-rest-of-us, and thanked Jerry for the party, amidst hugs, cheek kisses, and gathering up of coats and sweaters.

TEN MINUTES LATER, Jerry was alone, having scooted Manny and Carmella out the door when they offered to help him clean up. "You've already done enough. Please, go home, have a Christmas Eve nightcap and get some sleep." Their hugs and warm farewells made Jerry feel like he had family for holidays for the first time in too many years. He smiled to no one in particular, and then, as he passed the picture of Isis, he kissed two fingertips and placed them on the forehead of her image. “You’d like these people, Munchkin. I’m in good hands.”

CHAPTER SEVEN

@TheTaoOfJerr: "Love is friendship set to music."
~Jackson Pollock

JERRY LOOKED AROUND at the cluttered loft and realized that Carmella must have been picking up all along because there were only the glasses and coffee cups each of his guests had been using when the party broke up. Dean Martin continued on in the background, a bit louder to Jerry's ears now that the place was empty of conversation. As he went around picking up the dirty glasses and coffee cups, he sang along with Dino's smooth version of "White Christmas".

The headache had receded briefly, but when Jerry picked up a long-stemmed wine glass on the coffee table next to the book of Blake's poetry, the pain slammed back in like a boxer's fist. He spasmed and fell to his knees, the wine glass stem snapping in his hand and slicing open his palm when he reached for the support of the table.

"Son of a . . . ! Shit!" The rolling wave of pain receded enough so that he could see again, but was still intense enough to keep him down on his knees. He slowly and deliberately placed the wine glass remnants on the table as the pain of the cut intruded on the misery of the headache. When he opened his hand to let go of the glass, blood flowed freely, dripping onto the tabletop. Sighting a stack of paper cocktail napkins, he grabbed at them, needing to staunch the bleeding, but unable to keep a few drops from landing on the book of poetry. He jammed the entire stack of poinsettia-decorated napkins into his damaged palm and dragged himself to his feet, aiming for the kitchen and the stainless steel countertop.

IN SPITE OF the pain, Jerry moved fast and didn't notice that the blood, which dropped onto the book, was absorbed quickly into the dark, century-old stain already there. As he stood over the sink, peeling back the crimson-soaked paper napkin, he missed the blue glow that pulsed from the combined stain. In the bright light over the sink, he was too busy washing what had turned out to be a shallow cut and resisting the urge to slam his bloody hands to his forehead to compress the pain of the raging headache to notice when the blue glow enveloped the book, flowed up and out from the stain, and expanded in the air above the coffee table.

SOMETHING *WAS* VERY different. What had previously been a weak, almost casual force inviting her out of the darkness and into her dreams, was now a powerful, insistent, *welcoming* pull she simply could not resist. It was such a wonderful feeling she didn't *want* to resist. She flowed and ebbed and finally remembered her own shape after so long without anything but pure thought and emotion. This was like no dream she had experienced before. Life flowed into her and a deep memory of her self caught at her heart. She thought of a photo of herself, one she took facing the big mirror in her bedroom at the Winter Palace, but it was an old photo, when she was just a child. She then remembered one of her and her sisters, much more recent, all standing tall and smiling. She felt herself slip into that shape, so familiar.

ONCE HE WAS sure there was no glass in his palm and it was thoroughly washed, Jerry grabbed a fresh, clean dishcloth from the drawer with his free hand and jammed it onto the cut. Gripping it with as tight a fist as he could manage, he went in search of painkillers and the first aid kit in the bathroom. He rummaged around in the medicine cabinet, oblivious to anything but the pain and the blood. He found the ibuprofen, fought with the child-proof cap, got it open, dumped a handful of capsules into his shaking palm, tossed four of them back and dropped the rest back into the bottle. He stuck his face under the tap and gulped hard to get enough water to wash the pills down. While he was hunched over the sink, he splashed cold water on his face with his good hand. After a moment or two he stood up, dried his hand on the towel and, from the first aid kit on the counter next to the sink, took out a tube of antibiotic cream and squeezed a small amount into the cut. He slapped a large adhesive bandage over it all and returned to the living room where he could sit in comfort and let the painkillers do their job.

Although he was a firm believer that everything is possible and nothing is certain, Jerry nearly tripped over his own feet when he came face-to-face with a transparent, teenaged girl with golden hair cut in a scruffy bob, dressed in a simple, bullet-hole-riddled and blood-stained, black linen dress taking shape in the middle of his IKEA coffee table. Blood-loss was making him hallucinate a ghost! "Holy crap–! Wha–?! Who?!"

SHE WASN'T ALONE! There was the man, again, from her dream. He stumbled back to the kitchen island, as shocked to see her as she was to see him. He flinched and she was hurt. She was harmless. She was Ana, and she would never hurt a flea! Just ask her younger brother. "Where am I? Who are you?"

FREAKED OUT, BUT pretty sure a hazy, glowing girl couldn't hurt him, Jerry stepped toward the coffee table where he could get a better look at his "houseguest". "Who the hell are you?" Could she be the girl he'd been dreaming about?

The ghost tilted her head as if to hear better, but shook it, frustrated. She pointed at her ears and shook her head again. Jerry guessed that she couldn't hear him any more than he could hear her. With the headache still thumping but slipping slowly into the background, he took another step closer. The ghost moved back, eyes wide and hands raised just a bit defensively. Recognizing fear when he saw it, Jerry stopped advancing and held up his hands in an "I'm-unarmed-and-come-in-peace" gesture. As he addressed the girl again, he accompanied his spoken words with sign language.

"Hello. My name is Jerry."

ANA COULD SEE his lips move, but she still heard no sounds

whatsoever. She shook her head. “I do not understand.” The man held out his hands to show that he was no threat and stepped toward the table, pointing at a pen next to a book. Ana shifted warily to the side but didn’t feel the need to flee. He carefully picked up the pen in a bandaged hand, held up a greeting card of some sort with the other hand, and began writing on the back of the card. After a moment he held it up for her to see. She took a tentative, floating step so she could see what he’d written.

“My name is Jerry. Who are you?”

She smiled.

THE GHOST GIRL pointed at Jerry, mouthing words. Understanding, Jerry grinned and nodded. “Yes, I am Jerry.” While Jerry signed, the ghost watched closely. “Yes! My name is Jerry. J-E-R-R-Y.”

The ghost copied the signs to spell his name and Jerry laughed. “Yes! Jerry!”

The girl continued, signing slowly, a look of concentration on her face as she tried to remember what Jerry had just shown her. “My name is . . .” Not having the signs for the necessary letters, she silently mouthed her name. Jerry didn’t understand her. He could sign with the best of them but he never needed to develop his lip-reading until now. The ghost held out her hand for the pen but when Jerry handed it to her it fell through her fingers and onto the table, landing on the book of poetry. The girl looked at the pen, frustrated, but then she pointed at it excitedly. Jerry picked it up and offered it to her again but she waved it off and pressed her finger down and into the book.

Understanding finally dawned on Jerry so he picked up the book and offered it to her. With a half-smile she shook her head “no” and mimed for him to open it. Jerry opened the cover and showed her the note inside the cover. Written on the title page in faded blue fountain pen was “To Ana, Love Mama. Christmas 1915.” The girl pointed at the inscription and then at herself.

Jerry got the message clearly, if not loudly. “That’s you?” he signed and spoke. “You’re Ana? Anastasia?” He signed slowly. “Your name is A-N-A?”

ANA NODDED VIGOROUSLY. Hand signs! She put her palm over her heart like she had seen him do and made the finger shapes for her name. "I am Ana."

"Hello, Ana." His words were simple so she could both read his lips and follow his hand signs.

"Hello, Jerry."

THE HEADACHE SWEPT in again and grabbed Jerry's attention. His eyes went wide and he stumbled to the closest seat, dropping the book back onto the coffee table. Ana followed him, a look of concern evident on her transparent face.

Jerry pressed on his temples with both hands. "Headache. Bad one."

Ana glanced around the apartment, saw the kitchen sink, pointed at it, and mimed that Jerry should drink lots of water and then sleep.

"You're pretty smart for a ghost. Sleep. I need a week's worth of sleep." He forced a smile, levered himself slowly up out the chair and stumbled to the kitchen area. When he got to the sink, he grabbed a clean tumbler with his good hand and held it up for his guest to see that he understood what she'd suggested.

ANA SMILED BACK, pleased that Jerry was able to understand her, but suddenly the darkness was there again, beckoning her, pulling her away from this new world of light and colour and Jerry. No! It couldn't be over! Dream or no dream, she wanted to stay. She reached out for him, as if he could grab her hands and pull her into his world, but that world was fading fast. The darkness swirled up and out of the book but she finally realized that it wasn't dragging her back in; it was simply embracing her while her strength waned. Suddenly she was so very tired and the dark seemed like a perfectly reasonable place to rest and get strong enough to return to the world of this Jerry person.

She looked up as she left the dream, and waved to Jerry to say "goodnight". Jerry waved back, but she thought he looked more than a little bit confused. Then her world went black, and she was once again alone, but now it didn't bother her in the least. She knew now that there was somewhere other than the darkness, and in that dream place there lived a very sweet, somewhat handsome, man named Jerry.

JERRY RUBBED HIS eyes, shook his head, and took another swig of water. He wanted to pick up the little book but didn't dare touch it. She was gone, but he wasn't even sure she'd actually ever even been there. Had his headaches gotten so bad that he was hallucinating? Had one of his new West Coast friends slipped something into his drink? Were the mushrooms on the crackers magic ones? He had no idea, and if he were honest with himself, he didn't have the energy to think about it much longer. He needed sleep more than he needed answers right now. To that end, he tugged off his party clothes, dragged on his grandpa-style flannel pajamas, and crawled into his antique, solid pine, spindle bed in the loft's screened-off sleeping area. He fell asleep quickly, feeling much older than his years.

SOME HOURS LATER, Ana reached in the darkness for the seam of light that led to the dream world where Jerry lived. Much about it was familiar, yet there were differences she couldn't, yet, put her finger on. Unsure of what to expect, she pushed just her face through. She kept her eyes closed at first, fearing what might be truly beyond in the light, but then realized that she was being silly. She was quite certain that she was dead and so what could possibly be the worst that could happen to her? There were no tales she'd ever heard of people dying twice, except maybe vampyres. Even Our Lord Jesus Christ died just the once.

Ana snuck one eye open. She appeared to be alone, so she opened the other, and "pulled" herself fully into the flat. She turned a circle, admiring the beauty of the space. She was certainly used to much grander, but near the end of their exile, this would have been truly luxurious. The warm woods and plush furniture were so sumptuous compared to the sparse, drafty conditions of the rooms they had been confined to for their last days. She admired the beautiful, dark, hardwood floors and the Persian rug—and then she saw that she was floating eight inches above the floor. *Well, that's silly!* She frowned, scrunched her face up to focus her considerable will, and "told" her feet to go lower. She dropped too quickly and ended up four inches into the floor. Disappointed, she put her hands on her hips, concentrated harder and, a moment later, Anastasia "stood" on the flat's floor, quite pleased with herself. *I wonder if . . .* She concentrated a bit harder and soon she could actually feel the solidity of the floor through the leather soles of her lace-up boots.

Not seeing her host, but knowing that he had intended to retire for the night, she wandered around the flat until she saw the corner of Jerry's bed not hidden by the screen. She hesitantly poked her head through the privacy screen, saw by the rhythm of his breathing that he slept soundly, then withdrew, and turned back to the wonderful flat around her.

She floated up in the air, moving around the loft, then caught herself. *This will not do at all!* She shook her head, closed her eyes, and imagined herself on the floor, walking across the room and not floating all willy-nilly through the air. When her feet touched down once again, she smiled, quite pleased with herself. *Much better! Where to now?* That's when she saw a foot-tall, electrically-lit jar on Jerry's desk containing a slowly undulating green liquid. A soundless giggle escaped her lips as she skipped over to examine the strangeness.

Carefully slipping her diaphanous hand through the glass of the jar, Ana slid her fingertips into the heart of the illuminated green fluid. She focused and imagined just her fingertips being a bit more solid and then suddenly there was less light visible through them. She concentrated a bit harder and the slowly rising ooze deflected around the new obstacles, like green magma around rocks. A silent giggle shook her ghostly form, and she willed her fingertips to be transparent, once again. She pulled her hand back, slowly, not wanting to break the odd little lamp.

Another movement on the desk caught her eye. *I'm not alone!* She turned to examine the one-gallon fish tank and once again saw the beautiful, long-finned, red and purple fish, swimming alone, nibbling at something on the blue gravel that covered the bottom of the little enclosure. A quick glance in Jerry's direction assured her that he still slept, and a silly, impish grin spread across her face as she closed her eyes and pushed her face through the glass, into the water beyond. When she opened her eyes, the little fish peered out at her from behind his miniature Greek ruins.

She stared back at the little creature, then with a quick flick of his tail, he was out from behind the ruins with his fins flared, ready for a fight. She tried to blow bubbles at him but with no air to blow or solid body to do the blowing, she ended up just making a face at him. Nonplussed at the odd threat, the majestic little fighter swam in her nose and out through her left cheek, quite effectively calling her bluff. She blew him a kiss and left him to his meal.

As she withdrew her face from the tank, a faint reflection of twinkling white lights caught her eye. She spun to find a Christmas tree standing tall in the corner of the flat. The beauty and care in its decoration were quickly apparent. As she walked over to it, she felt more and more solid with each step. And then she could hear her own footsteps. By the time she bent over to peer at her own distorted reflection in a giant red glass ball, Ana was as solid as the world around her.

A gentle poke with her finger sent the ball swinging slowly on its metal hook and she smiled, delighted. She moved from one ornament to another, admiring the delicate glass balls and bells, what appeared to be slender crystal icicles, and tin ornaments similar in style and workmanship to those on her own simple trees over the years. These miniature train engines, soldiers, and sewing machines looked to be antiques, though, not new, like her own.

"Curiouser and curiouser." Ana's voice, unheard for so long, was magnified in the darkness of the loft. She spun a pirouette of joy, muffled a giggle with her hand, tossed a wiggle and a wave at the privacy screen, and stopped suddenly. How she had missed it up to now she had no idea, but in one corner was an enormous, black mirror on a stand at waist level. Thinking it extremely odd and highly impractical, she moved around directly in front of it to see what kind of reflection she got in the silly thing.

No! Her dress was riddled with holes and covered in blood! It was all true! In the darkness she thought she was having nightmares, but here was proof that they were memories. She had been *murdered*. She collapsed into a ball on the floor, her arms wrapped tight around herself, and for the first time since the killing ground of the basement of the cursed Ipatiev House, Anastasia Romanova wept tears of both heartache and fury.

There were no gunshots or bayonet stabs or screams of her family and servants to deafen her here. There wasn't even Jimmy, her beloved spaniel, his whimpers of confusion and fear cut short by a bullet as the hot, choking gunpowder smoke filled the tiny basement room. True loss finally came home to the young Grand Duchess, and her tears flowed in a torrent, only to fade to nothing as they ran off her face.

Ana let the emotion rip through her and she faded, nearly slipping back into the book, but she held on. Although she drew no air, she took a deep breath and straightened. *I am already dead, am I not? Which means that it cannot get any worse. And, if I must be somewhere other than with my family, this place is good.* She squinted and dared to look again at her horrific reflection in the strange black mirror. She concentrated on the damage to her dress and imagined the holes being stitched up and the blood blown away by the wind. At first nothing happened, but after a moment she could see a slight change. She concentrated harder, and the holes slowly closed up and the blood stains faded.

With that simple, monumental task achieved, Ana half-smiled, and returned to exploring the flat, though with a bit less bounce in her ghostly step.

JERRY'S MIND FELT like it was wrapped in a huge woolen blanket. Everything was dull and fuzzy as the effects of the painkillers faded and soft morning light begged to be noticed. Between the wine, the scotch, and the meds, his memory of the previous evening was spotty at best. Then a soft female voice in his semi-dream gave him something to focus on. It was a sweet voice, with a British accent and a hint of something else, something Eastern European, maybe. He couldn't remember any of the station's staff having such a unique blend of voice so he tried to drift back toward deep slumber to find out who the dream girl was.

"How are we feeling this morning, good sir?"

Jerry's eyes snapped open. He clumsily blinked off the sleep and found a young woman perched politely on the foot of his bed. He struggled to sit upright, the sheets and blanket confounding him for a moment.

"What the hell?"

She smiled politely, almost regally. "And a pleasant good morning to *you*, fine sir."

He blinked, shook his head free of a headache that wasn't there, and then the memory found him. She was the ghost. "But last night, you couldn't . . . you were . . . but . . ."

"Now I can. Quite *stránno*, strange. Anastasia Romanova, at your service." She made a little curtsy.

Anastasia Romanova? There was a Russian *princess* in his

apartment? Jerry reached for his dark green, terry robe draped over the chair beside the bed. The young *Royal* turned her head away out of politeness. Although he was wearing pajamas, Jerry still threw on the robe after tossing the covers aside and standing up.

"Are you a—"

"A ghost? That is the only conclusion I can reach, unless you have another suggestion we can entertain. I have put a lot of thought into it, and the possibilities are quite limited. Any suggestions, sir?"

Holy shit, what was happening? Had he finally snapped? "No, nothing, Your Majesty." He led the way out to the living room area. Still shaken, he looked over his shoulder to see if she was following, which she was.

She smiled. "Officially, it is, or *was*, 'Your Imperial Highness', but among my dear friends I was Anastasia, Ana, or even, to those who dared, *Shvibzik*—'Little Imp'."

Jerry wandered into the kitchen, sleep still clouding his eyes, and started the coffee maker with Colombian roast. This was no time for decaf. "'Little Imp'?"

"A nickname."

Jerry leaned back against the counter, waiting for the much-needed coffee. "Your English is excellent, for a Russian Princess."

Ana leaned forward, her elbows on the kitchen island. "My Great-Grandmother was Victoria, Queen of England. My mother insisted that we be fluent in both languages, in addition to French. Until our last few months, when our captors forbade it, Mother preferred to speak English with us in our own quarters. As for my title, I am, or *was*, in fact, a Grand Duchess, not a Princess. I have always thought of princesses more as characters from fairytales."

"Sorry. My Russian history is a bit weak, to say the least." The single-serve coffee filled the cup behind him.

"Please do not worry yourself over it, Jerry. I neither asked for the title, nor did I ever really enjoy using it except in play. Call me Ana, please. And you may not know Russia's history, but I do not know Russia's *predstavit'*—present—so we both have much to teach each other."

Jerry glanced at the wall clock. Eleven o'clock. "Sorry, but I have to be at work soon, Ana, so I'm afraid the lessons will have to wait. Make yourself at home. It's been almost a hundred years since your . . . since you were . . . it's a new millennium but ghosts still aren't all that common. Matter of fact, you're my first."

"It is my first time, too. What year is it, Jerry?" The sadness in her voice broke through Jerry's confusion.

"The year? Now? 2016."

"Twenty-sixteen? Two thousand and sixteen?" Her sadness became deep loss. Her entire demeanour deflated. Her shoulders sagged, her head hung down, and her clasped hands trembled.

"I'm sorry, Ana. What I'm trying to say is that you might not want to let anyone else see you. Hell, I don't even know if anyone else *can* see you."

"I understand. I will remain here, Jerry. I have a great deal to think on. To the world it has been nearly a century since my family was murdered in cold blood, but for me it feels much more recent."

"I hadn't thought of that. How much do you remember?" He sipped his coffee, welcoming the heat as it pushed a little against the damp of Victoria's winter. "I'm sorry. Would you like a cup?" He nodded at his own steaming cup.

"No, thank you. I am not certain if I can." She frowned, thinking about his question. "I remember quite a lot, but as a wise man once said, 'I do not know how much I cannot remember.'" She leaned close, her voice lowering. "I am *boyashchiysya*—afraid—Jerry. I do not think I should be here. Why am I? *Where* am I?"

"Where? That's easy. Believe it or not, this is Victoria, British Columbia, Canada—the city named after your great-grandmother. As for 'why', I have no idea, but we'll figure it all out. In the meantime, relax. You're safe here—I live alone, except for the fish, Sushi."

"Sushi?" She said the name slowly, smiling. "Such a gentle, beautiful name."

Moving to the couch, Jerry picked up the remote control and turned on the television. "Maybe, but it means a Japanese rice dish often topped with raw fish." The date, time, and channel appeared briefly on the flatscreen as it started up.

Ana clapped her hands, excitedly. "So this is not a dark mirror after all!"

"It's a television. Sometimes the stuff on here is violent and depressing, but there are a few chuckles—laughs—to be had, too. Think of it as radio, with pictures."

"Or motion pictures with sound," Ana added.

"Exactly! This is the remote control." He held it up for her to see. "These two buttons change the channels—there are over two hundred. The buttons are all labelled. Enjoy."

"I will." She sat on the other end of the couch. "My sincere thanks, Jerry. Now, should you not be preparing to go to your workplace?"

"Definitely." He put the remote on the table in front of Ana and got up.

"Jerry?

"Yeah? *Yes?*"

"*S Roždestvom Khristovym!* Merry Christmas."

Jerry was caught off guard, having forgotten what day it was. "Oh. Merry Christmas, Ana. How did you know?"

"A little trick I learned from Grigori: 'See everything. Miss nothing.' When you turned on the telly-vision, the date appeared."

"Smart girl. Grigori?"

"Grigori Rasputin—a monk who was trying to heal my brother. He, too, was murdered. Have you heard of Grigori?"

He chuckled. "Definitely. He's almost as famous as you are. They even have a song about him."

"A song about *Grigori*?"

"I'll see if I can track down a copy of it for you."

Ana smiled and Jerry saw the imp in her. "Yes, please. Now, go—you have responsibilities, and I need to rest again. I never thought a ghost could get tired, but I find that it is taking a great deal of strength just to speak and hear. Now that I know that there is more than the dark and shadows of the book, I am less afraid to return to it for short times."

"No problem. You rest and I'll work. Merry Christmas, Anastasia—Shvibzik."

The young Grand Duchess giggled, and returned to the book, but not before she winked at her host.

When she was gone, Jerry rubbed his eyes with both palms and then blinked to clear his head. "What the hell is going on here?"

CHAPTER EIGHT

@TheTaoOfJerr: "Life is like a beautiful melody, only the lyrics are messed up."

~Hans Christian Andersen

HIS FIRST SHORT day of actually tackling some of his new Station Manager duties went smoothly, in Jerry's humble opinion. Being Christmas Day there was only a skeleton crew working—the current on-air personality, the producer, the security guard, and one or two others who dropped in briefly to wish the on-duty staff a Merry Christmas. Jerry was able to relax and take his time to discover some of the subtle differences between British Columbia advertising regulations and the ones he was accustomed to back in Ontario, as well as getting a better handle on his new staff, their duties, and their skills.

His email in-box held pass-codes and H/R file locations from Manny, so Jerry took some time to appreciate both the depth and the talent of his new radio family. He was impressed. As he'd seen at his party, Manny had hired some really off-the-wall characters, but now that Jerry could peruse their resumes and accomplishments, he saw that Manny knew exactly what he had in each one of them. Yes, Jerry was *definitely* impressed. Unfortunately, it probably took him twice as long as it should have to get through the files because he kept getting distracted by thoughts of the strange, ghostly girl back in the loft. He wasted nearly an hour researching Anastasia and her life and family on the web, and emailing the results to his personal email account for later perusal.

There was no shortage of theories, both political and social, of what had happened to Ana and her family, but at least now he was pretty sure he could put to rest all of the stories of her survival and later life. If he was going to believe in a ghost, he might as well believe that she was Anastasia Romanova. Once the first big stretch was made, a second one seemed so easy. "Of course I could get home and discover that it was all a delusion brought on by last night's alcohol and pain meds, which would really suck."

A soft beep came from the clock on the wall and Jerry looked up to see that it was already six o'clock. The time had floated by, its passing unnoticed. He blinked, rubbed his eyes, shot back the last of the lukewarm herbal tea at the bottom of his new CKVB mug, winced at the bitterness, then stretched his neck left and right and in slow circles in both directions to get the kinks out. He logged off his computer, and while it was shutting down, he changed his voicemail message.

He was tired, but happy, and it took very little effort to put energy into his voice. "Feliz Navidad, you've reached Jerry Powell at CKVB, I'll be back at the station at noon on the 26th. Please leave a message at whatever sound you hear after my voice, and I'll get back to you when I return to the office. Ciao for now." He pressed the buttons to save and set the message. "Good enough."

He grabbed his duffel coat off the hook behind the door and turned off the lights, but before he could close the office door, the Account Manager, Lee-Anne, seemed to appear out of nowhere, dressed in a long, tight, red, curve-announcing cashmere sweater, and black yoga tights, her own jacket draped over her shoulder. She moved in close, in what Jerry now thought of as "full-flirt mode".

"Jerry, how's your headache, hon? I never did finish the neck rub I started last night. What do you say? In your office?"

"Lee-Anne, *hon*, my headache is long gone, but thanks for the offer." Politely squeezing past her, Jerry shut his door and started down the hall, shouldering his way into his coat as he went. "Besides, I wouldn't dream of letting one of my headaches keep you from getting home to Tom and the kids, especially on Christmas."

Lee-Anne followed at his side, making it a tight fit in the hall. She brushed her long, impossibly silky hair back over her shoulder. "Oh, they're at my Mom's. I'm meeting them there for dinner, but I still have some time." They reached the front reception desk and the uniformed security guard sitting at his evening post.

"Well, I appreciate you bringing in that Sales Summary, Lee-Anne, but it could have waited a few days." He smiled at the guard. "Good night, Samhail. Thank you for watching over us. Have a good night, and I'll see your relief around noon tomorrow."

"Goodnight, Mr. Powell. Merry Christmas, sir."

"Merry Christmas, Samhail." He was still having trouble remembering it was Christmas, especially without the obligatory dinner with his family. As stressful as it could be, he'd never missed Christmas with his family before.

Lee-Anne wasn't finished. "Trust me, Jerry—some things can't wait." They left the building and stepped into the parking lot and a chill wind. She struggled with her coat and although Jerry knew the struggling was an act, he stepped behind her and helped by lifting up the jacket. Lee-Anne tried to lean back into his arms but Jerry was ready and side-stepped her move.

"You're right, Lee-Anne, and there are two terrific little kids who can't wait for their Mommy, so why don't I walk you to your car so they don't have to wait another minute?"

"You're so sweet, Jerry. I must compliment Manny on his choice of a Station Manager."

"Why, thank you, Mrs. Johansen. And I think he has good taste in Sales Reps." In spite of her need to flirt with the new station manager, Jerry knew from her file that Lee-Anne was very good at what she did. He was sure she used her sex appeal to aid her in her work, but she also had a wall of local and national sales awards to prove she wasn't all tits-and-giggles.

"And this Sales Rep tastes good, too." Having reached her little red Lexus, she leaned over to kiss Jerry, but he smoothly and deftly slipped out of her reach.

"Merry Christmas, Lee-Anne. Drive safely."

Visibly disappointed, Lee-Anne pressed the remote and

unlocked the car with a beep. "Merry Christmas, Jerr-bear."

She drove off, throwing him a very flirty finger-wave as she went. Jerry laughed, and started off for home, his stride strong and invigorated by the brisk sea air.

"Women—can't live with 'em, pass the pretzels. Now I suppose I should get home and see how my house ghost is doing." He hummed to himself, then started to sing, "All I want for Christmas is a normal life, a normal life."

TEN MINUTES LATER he unlocked the door of the loft and stepped inside. The television was off but one warm light banished the shadows. There was no sign of Ana, though. He walked over to the Blake book on the coffee table, speaking as though she could hear him from her world to his.

"Ana, I'm home."

Ana answered him, in an almost perfect Ricky Ricardo Cuban accent. "Jerry, you got some s'plainin' to do!"

Jerry looked up at the source of the voice and nearly wet himself—solid-appearing Ana was casually floating around near the high ceiling above his head.

"Crap!"

Ana drifted down to the floor. "Good evening, Jerry. I've learned a few things today."

"I can see that." He dropped his keys back into his coat pocket and hung it up on the coat tree behind the door. "Was the first thing how to scare the living to death?"

"No. That I knew already. Something else. Observe!" She concentrated, and although Jerry couldn't see any marked difference in her appearance, when she reached for his old university sweatshirt her hand didn't pass through it but rather gripped it, just as his would have. She picked up the sweatshirt and slipped it over her head. Jerry couldn't believe it when it stayed put and she spun around, modelling it for him.

"Wow. You have been busy."

"At first I could only keep it on for a few moments before one arm or the other fell through, but now I can do it for an hour or more."

"I'm impressed. How did you—" His cell phone rang in his coat pocket, cutting him off. He retrieved his phone quickly, afraid that Ana would try to answer it; but she only followed him to the couch, politely curious.

"Hello? . . . Mom. Hi. Merry Christmas . . . Well, I haven't returned your call because I just walked through the door and haven't had a chance to listen to my messages. I usually wait until I've got my coat off and maybe closed the front door before I retrieve them . . . Yes, I had to work . . . No, I haven't opened my presents, yet."

Ana made a face at Jerry, trying to distract him. When it didn't work, she grabbed her ears and pulled them until her arms were straight out to the sides and her ears were stretched almost two-feet-long. Jerry laughed, losing the battle.

"Sorry, Mom. I have a guest who's clowning around. Are you going to be up for a while so I can call you back? . . . Oh-kay. How about I open my presents this evening, and give you a call tomorrow morning? . . . Who's my guest? Her name is Ana. She's my, uh, 'neighbour' . . . Well, we thought we'd have coffee and get acquainted . . . WHAT?! Goodnight, Mom. I'll call you at noon, your time." He disconnected the call and put the phone down on the coffee table.

"What did she say to upset you so?"

"Nothing I can repeat to a seventeen-year-old Grand Duchess."

Ana's concern changed to joy in a flash. "Oh! That is the other thing I learned! And it is quite simple. Observe!" She made a grand flourish with her hands. "*Abrakadabra*!"

Jerry watched, half-expecting her to try on his shoes or start the coffee maker, but, right before his eyes, Anastasia Romanova aged a couple years. Gone was her short, slightly plump, teenage figure as she morphed into a slightly taller, almost slender, graceful young woman.

"Son of a—"

"Do *not* say it, Jerry." Her smile was heart-stopping.

"Wow. Who are you now?" He got up and walked around her, inspecting the new look.

"*Me*. I simply decided to be me at twenty-two. I was seventeen when I died, but since I was born in 1901, I am, in theory, a centurion. I modelled myself after my sister, Olga. I thought you might be more comfortable with a twenty-two-year-old me."

"Definitely. I don't feel like we should be chaperoned simply because of the theoretical age difference. Though, who would chaperone a ghost is beyond me."

"I am glad you like it because it does not take any effort on my part, unlike wearing this sweater." The sweatshirt dropped through her to the floor. She picked it up and draped it over the back of the chair.

Jerry made his way to the kitchen area, glancing at the television as he went past it. "Ana, didn't I leave the TV on?"

"I closed it—except for *I Love Lucy*, it was all so annoying. If they took only the good things from all 287 channels, could they fill even two channels?"

"Probably not." He laughed. Even a century-old ghost knew that what was on TV was crap. He opened the fridge, looking at her over his shoulder. "Do you eat?"

"I do not think so. I am not hungry in the least."

"Well, I am, so please don't think me rude if I fix myself some dinner."

"Not at all. While you eat I can tell you what else I have learned today. I learned that I cannot travel too far from the book. I made it to the landing outside your door and could go no further. At that distance, I also found it difficult to concentrate."

"That's weird." He placed a plastic-boxed grocery-store salad on the counter and poured himself a full glass from the two-litre bottle of caffeine-free Coke on the bottom shelf.

"Jerry, why am I here?"

"I've been wondering about that, too, and one school of thought about ghosts is that they're souls who've left something important unfinished. Was there something you didn't finish?"

"Do you mean, something other than my life?"

He leaned back against the sink, his favourite kitchen stance. "Good point. But if that was it, your sisters and your brother would be here, too. Is there something more specific? A message you needed to give? A promise to keep?"

"*Nyet*. No. Nothing big."

"What about the curse put on your family by Rasputin?"

"What curse?"

"I was reading something on the internet at work about a curse he made a couple years before he was murdered."

Ana huffed. "That is silly. Grigori was not cursing us, he was making a prediction that if he died at the hands of any Russian nobility, then my family was in danger, too. It was a warning to watch close to home, and he was absolutely correct." She tipped her head slightly to one side. "Time has not treated Grigori's memory very well, has it, Jerry?"

"I'm afraid not."

"That is so unfortunate. He was a good man. He was *strannyy*—strange—but quite wise and very kind, at least with Mother and us children."

Jerry pulled two frozen chicken cordon-bleu packets from the freezer, opened them, placed them on a plate and stuck them in the toaster oven, setting the timer before dumping his salad on a plate. Ana hopped up to sit on the counter to watch.

"I have an idea for after dinner, Jerry."

"Sure. Shoot."

CHAPTER NINE

@TheTaoOfJerr: "Music is the mediator between the spiritual and the sensual life."

~Ludwig van Beethoven

BY TEN O'CLOCK, the night chill had gripped Victoria's Inner Harbour and few people were out near the provincial parliament buildings. It rarely snowed in coastal Victoria, but on this evening, the feathery-light white fluff drifted down onto the streets, adding to the seasonal mood set by the Christmas lights everywhere. A short walk from the loft, the outline of the beautiful, light-grey, copper-domed, century-old government building was lit with white lights, rendering the large structure almost fairy-like in the distance.

Jerry sat facing the parliament buildings, alone on the marble base of the statue of Queen Victoria. Although he wasn't completely hidden from view, shrubs shielded him from the nearby street. He took a small, plastic grocery bag-wrapped package out of his jacket pocket, gently removed the Blake book, and placed it on the bag beside him on the snow damp bench. He glanced to his right and then his left to make sure no one was watching, and when he looked back, Ana was sitting beside him, nearly bursting with pure joy. Her simple dress and lace-up boots from 1918 lent a touch of nostalgic elegance in the soft light of the

Inner Harbour. Ecstatic, she leapt to her feet. Jerry rewrapped the book and put it back in his jacket.

"Oh, Jerry! I am *outside*!"

"Shhh! Let's not push our luck. So far, so good."

Ignoring his concern, Ana spun and twirled and laughed, looking every bit as solid as Jerry in the cloud-softened moonlight. "This is glorious! Look at the snow! And the lights—look at the Christmas lights! Every tree, every post, *everywhere*! It's all so beautiful!"

Knowing there was no way he could contain her enthusiasm, Jerry stepped up beside her and shared the view.

"It is, isn't it?"

"This is the best Christmas present anyone has ever given me. Thank you!"

She darted in and quickly kissed him on the cheek.

"Hey! I felt that." He raised his hand and felt his cheek where the kiss was planted.

"Good! So did I. Jerry, let us go for a walk."

"I'm not so sure, Ana. We're out of the way here but if we walk along the streets—I don't know if anyone else can see you and I might look like I'm talking to myself."

"Do not get your knickers in a knot, Jerry. Let us just walk now and worry later."

"This is important to you, isn't it?"

"Oh, yes! *Da*!"

"Then let's walk." He led the way to the street-side sidewalk and Ana caught up and took his hand in hers. Surprised, Jerry looked down at their linked fingers but didn't let go. They walked on, and Jerry smiled to himself.

"Your hand is warm."

"What were you expecting?"

"Well, you *are* dead. I guess I was expecting you to be cold to the touch."

"Not right now. I am so happy I feel warm all over."

A dapper gentleman in his seventies strolled towards them, tipping his houndstooth hat in greeting. "Merry Christmas, folks."

"Merry Christmas," Jerry returned.

Ana gripped his hand tightly and whispered, excitement lighting up her voice, "He said 'folks'!"

"I noticed that." He squeezed her hand back.

"*Plural.* He saw me!"

"Yeah, it sure sounded like it."

They walked on, Jerry warmed by the idea that he might not be the only person who could see his ectoplasmic date. Eventually they came upon two women in their forties, holding hands and chatting quietly under the streetlamp. Ana gave a small wave with her free hand and greeted them cheerfully. "Merry Christmas, ladies. Lovely night, is it not?"

The couple smiled at Ana's enthusiasm, and the taller woman answered. "Merry Christmas. It's a perfect night."

"Yes, it is. Merry Christmas," Jerry added. He and Ana strolled on past and the couple went back to each other. Ana was so excited she floated up a few inches above the damp sidewalk.

Jerry tugged her hand and whispered sharply, "Hey! Get down." She snickered and came back down to where her feet once again tread the sidewalk.

"Oh, Jerry! They *heard* me. They *saw* me." She kissed him on the cheek.

He smiled, caught off guard. "Yeah, they sure did, didn't they. Wow."

Fingers laced warmly together, and the chill air ignored, Jerry and Ana explored Victoria's Inner Harbour, greeting others on the promenade as they drifted past, everyone simply soaking up the peace of the late evening and the lights of the season.

TWO HOURS LATER Ana danced around the loft alone, humming quietly, happily to herself. She danced along the floor, passing through the furniture, and then up the walls and onto the ceiling, waltzing and twirling with an imaginary partner. She spun in mid-air and then began to fade as her strength finally waned and she was gently pulled back into the book. A second before she vanished, though, she blew a kiss in Jerry's direction, and he stirred in his sleep as if he felt it.

THE NEXT MORNING Jerry was up bright and early, having slept more soundly than he had for months. After a quick breakfast of microwave-poached eggs and toast, he steeled himself and returned his mother's call. While he verbally jousted with his mother, he watched Ana, who was partially hidden by the oriental dressing screen that blocked off the loft's sleeping area. A pair of his jeans and a freshly unwrapped pale yellow dress shirt hung over the screen. He'd told her to pick anything she liked and Ana had gone directly to the jeans and shirt as if she knew how much they meant to him. It was like Isis all over again. *Oh, well,* he thought, *they're only clothes*. Ana tossed her dress over the screen and pulled the shirt and jeans over to her side. The dress faded away, in a spooky, back-to-wherever-the-dead-go kind of way. Jerry shivered, then answered his mother's query.

"That's right, Mom, I have to work today, a holiday . . . Well, being the new guy, I get to cover the station over the holidays. Also, I'm trying to learn the ropes and I can't do that at home on the couch . . . Yes, the shirt looks great. Thank you. I'll be wearing it today at the office."

Ana pirouetted out from behind the screen, dressed in Jerry's new shirt and old jeans. She danced around him, making faces and coquettishly flashing wrists and ankles at him.

"Great—I'll talk to you next week, then. Have a good time at the flower show, Mom . . . Yes, Mom, I'll be seeing Ana again . . . I know you're glad I've met someone. She's quite a—*what*? Meet her? When? Do I have any say in this? This is my home, Mom, so it only follows that you wait for an invitation to come visit . . . Well, that particular week in February I'm in Seattle for a trade show. Let me check my schedule and see what—no, don't buy your ticket, yet. That would be stupid . . . Mom, I'm not calling *you* stupid, I'm just saying don't buy your ticket until I know if I'm even going to be in the city . . . Mom—*Mother*! Would you please—" His mother interrupted him again so he gave up trying to explain to her. "Good bye, Mom." He hung up without waiting for her reply.

Ana settled beside him on the couch. Jerry sipped his decaf, trying to calm himself.

"She sounds like a *Zhenshchina s siloy*—a strong woman—Jerry."

"That's one of the more polite ways to put it."

"Does she live alone?" Ana tucked one leg up under herself and turned to face him.

"My father chose death over life with her nagging."

"He took his own life?!" She was shocked.

"No, it was a heart attack."

"Then he did *not* choose, did he?"

"No, but I wouldn't have been surprised if he did."

"Do you miss him?"

"Of course." He really did. Every day.

"Was he a stupid man?"

"Stubborn yes; stupid . . . far from it."

"Then do you not think that if he had a choice, he would have chosen life with his family rather than death without?"

"Well, I was really only joking."

"Jerry, death is no joke—trust me on this." A tear tracked down her cheek and she wiped it away. "I have been given a chance to taste life again, but my family . . . where are they? What has happened to Alexei? Is my little brother happy where he is? Is he anywhere? What about Mashka? And Tatya and Olga? Are they all ghosts somewhere else?"

"I . . . don't know."

"Neither do I, but I do not think that they are."

"How do you know?"

"How do I speak? How do I float? Why am I connected to a book of old poetry my mother gave me one Christmas? Jerry, your mother cares about you. If she did not care, she would not even waste breath, let alone time and money to telephone you."

"But she's—"

"*Da*. I know. She infuriates you, makes you angry."

"She drives me crazy, and lately it's been a really short trip."

"Nurture patience."

"Okay." He smiled. "Who am I to argue with royalty?"

"Exactly! A commoner does not argue with a Royal—even a dead one. And for that reason, I wish to ask one further favour."

"Couldn't you just command me?"

"I would not dream of it."

Jerry surrendered. "Then ask away."

"Can we go for another walk?"

"Of course. It's supposed to be a nice evening, again."

"This afternoon. While it is light out."

"I'm sorry, Ana, but I have to work. Besides, are you really ready for the glare of sunlight?"

"I . . . I think so. If not today, tomorrow then?"

"I have tomorrow off, so sure, I guess so. Maybe we should go for a drive, just to start with."

"Yes! A drive! You have an automobile?"

"Sure. It's parked out on the street." He pointed at the window while he walked over to his desk and turned on his laptop. "I prefer to walk, but I have wheels. Tomorrow we'll get out and explore. Deal?"

"Deal! I have not been in an automobile in so very long."

"Then tomorrow it is. Now, I'd better get back to my proposal for Manny."

He sat at the desk and suddenly Ana popped her head through the laptop's screen so that it came right out of his document.

"All work and no play—"

"Pays the bills, young lady."

Ana stuck her tongue out and withdrew from the computer.

JERRY STOOD QUIETLY in the doorway of the tech booth, proudly watching his staff at work. On the other side of the glass the on-air personality was interviewing a now-vacationing Santa. Santa was definitely just Rolf in a Santa hat and a false beard hanging around his neck, but in radio anything is possible.

"So, Santa, what are you going to do with your spare time now that the gifts have all been delivered?"

"Mrs. Claus gave me a home gym for Christmas so I'm going to exercise, I suppose."

"Exercise? Is Santa going on a diet, too?"

"I don't have a choice, young fella. The reindeer all unionized this year and say I have to lose weight, for safety reasons. They claim they're getting old and can't carry the weight like they used to."

"Does that mean you have to cut back on gifts, too?"

"Not a chance, lad. My gift sack is multi-dimensional so it actually doesn't have any weight to it in this dimension. The science behind it is all a bit complicated so I leave the technical stuff to my head elf, Bobo."

Jerry laughed at the natural chemistry in the banter, then a new migraine spiked his skull. He winced, ground his fists into his temples and tried not to throw up in the hallway. Eventually he felt steadier and returned slowly to his office, one hand on the wall for balance.

ANA STOOD AT the window, the sun streaming in, bathing her in its warmth. She held one hand up to the light, examining herself for solidity, and was pleased with the results. Jerry's forgotten iPhone vibrated on the coffee table and she turned to look at it but made no move to answer it.

JERRY'S HEADACHE SLAMMED into him without mercy. He made it back to his office eventually but now leaned hard on his desk, trying to catch his breath. He risked taking his hand off the desk and fumbled through a drawer where he stashed his pills. Before he could open the bottle, though, the agony crushed him and he collapsed to the floor, knocking over his in-basket with a crash on his way down.

STARTLED BY THE sound, Jerry's assistant, Mika, called out from her office across the hall. "Jerry? Boss? You okay?" She wandered over to see what was up and when she stepped around the corner, she saw Jerry on the floor. "Someone call 9-1-1! Jerry's collapsed!"

CHAPTER TEN

@TheTaoOfJerr: "If I should ever die . . . let this be my epitaph: The only proof he needed of the existence of God was music."
~Kurt Vonnegut

MIKA, RED-EYED and emotionally frazzled, sat next to Jerry's hospital bed, keeping vigil while Jerry slept. She tried to read a magazine from the nurse's station but couldn't concentrate. She was reading the same paragraph about ski vacations in Utah for the fifth time when Manny slipped into the room. "Hey, Boss."

"How is he, girl?" He put a comforting hand on her shoulder and she reached up and squeezed it.

"Sedated. They took x-rays and have scheduled an MRI for next week, I guess. I'm not family, so they're only giving me hints of what's going on. Damned frustrating."

"An MRI for a headache?" He picked up the chair next to the empty bed across the room and placed it next to Mika's, careful not to let the feet scrape the floor.

"The doctor says the symptoms look familiar."

"How long does he expect to keep Jerr here?"

"Overnight, at least. He'll know more in a couple hours."

"Damnation."

"Yeah."

ANA DRIFTED UP out of her book and glanced around the flat. The lights were off, so she thought that maybe Jerry had come home and gone to bed, although she really wish he'd said hello before he went to sleep. She shook off the remnants of the darkness that seemed to cling to her less and less when she exited the book's other realm, and stood solidly on the floor. Jerry's college sweatshirt lay folded on the table, so she slipped it on over her dress. She then tiptoed over to peek behind the privacy screen, but was stopped abruptly at the end of her ethereal leash, a yard short of the screen.

This is rather silly, only being able to travel a few yards. She stalked back to the coffee table and the tiny book with the weight of a world. *Why do you do this to me? Why can I not simply—?* And then it dawned on her. Very carefully, as if expecting to be shocked or burned, Ana reached over and picked up the book.

"*O, moy dorogoy Gospod'*!" *Oh, my Dear Lord!* She hugged the book tight to her chest and giggled. *Mashka would mock me so, for being silly and not thinking of this sooner*. To test the new development, Ana walked back to Jerry's privacy screen. Unlike her first attempt, this time nothing stopped her. She did a little skip of joy and peeked behind the screen. The bed was empty.

She turned back to the main room. "Jerry?" Now that she knew he wasn't asleep, she could risk calling out. She could see that the door to the toilet was open and the small area beyond was dark, but she knew that meant nothing conclusive. Afraid of what she might find, she walked through the kitchen to assure herself that Jerry wasn't lying out of sight on the floor behind the counter. Relieved that he wasn't there, she tapped lightly on the bathroom door. No answer came. "Jerry? I am about to invade your privacy. Please say something before I embarrass us both." Her only answer was silence, so she reached in, flicked the switch to open the electric light, and poked her head around the corner. The tiny space was empty. Jerry was not at home, and the glowing numbers on the electric heating box in the kitchen said that it was nearly midnight. Ana made her way back to the sleeping area and sat on the floor, leaning back against the bed, keeping vigil.

"Jerry? Where are you?" She slid the book into the sweatshirt's pouch, wrapped her arms around herself, and remained like that, rocking back and forth, lost and unsure what to do, until she was so exhausted that she was unwillingly drawn back into the book. The sweatshirt crumpled to the floor next to the bed, with the book still tucked away in the pouch.

JERRY REGAINED CONSCIOUSNESS suddenly, as if a noise had awakened him. Alert as he was, though, he was confused. He recognized a hospital room when he saw one, but he had no memory of how he got there. He was also alone. Yes, of course he was alone. His family was back east and Ana was either a figment of his imagination or a ghost attached to some old book of poetry. The only light in his room came from the tall, narrow window flanking the half-closed door. No, he was wrong. There was a glow above and behind him, probably from some piece of health-monitoring equipment. As his eyes adjusted he saw, too, that there was light from a glow of dusk or dawn outside his window. His mind was fuzzy around the edges and his confusion wouldn't go away.

"Ana? Shvibzik? What happened?"

At the sound of Jerry's voice on the near silent ward, a nurse poked her head into the room. "Mr. Powell? Good morning. I'm Stephanie. How are you feeling?"

"Lost. Where am I?"

Stephanie came into the room and began checking the monitoring equipment and Jerry's pulse. "Royal Jubilee Hospital. You collapsed at work and gave your co-workers quite a scare." She laid the back of her hand against his forehead and seemed satisfied that he wasn't burning up. "You're looking much better now. Your colour has improved."

"I collapsed? During my headache?"

"Well, that's one of things we don't know, and now that you're awake, I'll page the doctor. As soon as he arrives at the hospital he'll come up and ask some questions. Hopefully he'll even answer a few."

"Gee, that'd be nice. What time is it?"

"Almost eight in the morning. Why don't you lie back and relax and I'll page Dr. Kelly? I'm sure you're hungry, but we'll wait to see what the doctor says before we bring in breakfast. He may need you to fast for some tests. Relax. If you need anything, the call button is here on your left." She held up the call button strapped to the bed frame.

"Sure. Thanks." He was suddenly exhausted, like someone

had cut his strings. "Maybe I'll just close my eyes for a bit, until the Doc gets in."

"Good idea." Before Stephanie had finished opening the curtains and shifting the two chairs back from the bed, Jerry was snoring.

EVENTUALLY JERRY DREAMED, and in his dream Ana pulled on his foot, trying to coax him off of the couch to go for another walk. But even as his dream gave way to reality, the gentle shaking of his foot continued. Crawling up from the dream, Jerry struggled to open his eyes only to find a short, round man somewhere over forty, standing beside the foot of the bed, shaking his foot.

"Hunh?"

"Jerry. Hello. I'm Doctor Izzy Kelly, the neuro-oncologist looking into your problem. I'm sorry to wake you, but Stephanie said you've already been awake and alert, and although I'm sure you'd like a bit more sleep, I didn't want to put this chat off any longer."

"Hi."

"How do you feel?"

"'Stupid' is the first word that comes to mind."

"No need to think like that, Jerry. What happened is quite common. What we need to know is how long have you been getting these headaches, how long do they last, is there any numbness associated with the pain, and how bad do they usually get?"

"That's a lot of questions for first thing in the A.M., Doc. Um, how *bad* do they get?"

"Yes. Do you often lose consciousness, vomit, or experience temporary blindness?"

"And what if I answer 'yes' to any or all of these questions?" The line of questioning was starting to worry him. A neurologist wouldn't be here if the headaches were caused by nitrates in his smoked meat or caffeine in his morning brew.

"Then it gives me an idea of which direction to take with your tests."

"You have a hunch, don't you?"

"There's a shadow on your x-rays that I want a closer look at, so the next thing is an MRI."

"A shadow? There's something in my head?"

"That's what the MRI will help determine. There are a variety of different possibilities and not all are as serious as you're thinking, so let's relax, and take it all one step at a time. Now, have you had any memory problems, such as trouble with names of people or places you should absolutely know?"

"I don't mean to be a smartass, but not that I can remember."

"Okay. How about confusion, unexplained exhaustion, loss of sense of smell?"

"Well, I'm new to town so I'm often lost or confused; it's a new job and I just drove three thousand miles to get here, so that probably explains my exhaustion; and when my allergies act up I couldn't smell a dirty diaper if it was on my dinner plate."

The neurologist laughed. "I've never heard it put quite that way before, but I understand what you're saying. How are your allergies now?"

"Since I arrived on the coast, they've been great. Still no problems with my sniffer, though. Are these all things I should be thinking about, aware of?"

"Simply put, yes. If you or anyone close to you notices changes in any of these areas, they are certainly indicators of a possibly more serious health issue. Also, facial paralysis, double vision, and unusual mood swings. These are all things I want you to be aware of, Jerry."

"How long am I stuck here, Doc?"

"Noon, at the latest. I've got a prescription for you to try, and it should keep any future pain from becoming so debilitating."

"Thank God. Puking and passing out were fine hobbies in college but I'd like something a bit more constructive to do in my spare time now."

"Excellent, because I'm a firm believer that a patient's attitude can affect the speed of their healing."

"Then call Billy Graham, cuz I'm ready to heal, Brother Izzy."

The doctor laughed warmly. "Yes, Jerry, I do believe you are."

TRUE TO HIS word, Dr. Kelly had Jerry discharged by noon, with the MRI scheduled for the following Wednesday. Strapped into the passenger seat of Manny's Land Cruiser, Jerry watched the orderly push the wheelchair he'd just vacated back through the hospital's main doors. Although it was midday, cloud-cover darkened the day, and as Manny moved the vehicle out of the pick-up zone, a light drizzle started. His headache was gone, but Jerry was still exhausted, and he suspected part of it was the fear of what the neurologist might find.

"Don't take it personally if I doze off, Manny. I really do appreciate all you're doing. Tell Mika I'm sorry I scared her. Just a bad headache."

"No worries, Jerr. We're not far from the loft but you go ahead and get some shut eye. I'll wake you when we get there."

"Thanks." He closed his eyes and between the soft intermittent flap of the windshield wipers and the gentle rocking of the Land Cruiser, Jerry was soon asleep, again.

JERRY WOKE UP just as Manny turned down Broad Street, approaching the loft. He shook the drowsiness off slowly, and was ready to face the world by the time Manny parked the SUV. The rain was pounding down now and Manny made him wait while he came around to the passenger side with a black umbrella huge enough to shelter both of them and a small Fiat as well.

"Carmella would have my hide if I let you get wet and catch pneumonia, lad."

Jerry laughed, but stayed next to Manny as they strode through the rain. "I'm sure she would. Thanks."

Manny let Jerry lead the way up the stairs to the loft, and Jerry was hard-pressed not to run up them two at a time. He wanted to make sure he opened the door to warn Ana they had company before the company could actually catch sight of her. He fumbled with the keys to stall their entrance, but Manny was standing back a yard, leaning the closed, wet umbrella up against the balustrade of the stairway. Jerry spoke loudly enough so that Ana might hear him and clue-in that he wasn't alone.

"So, the staff must think I'm a real girly-boy, fainting on my real first day on the new job."

"Not at all, Jerr. We all know about headaches, especially over the holidays. The tones I heard were all concern, not mockery—even the ones they didn't know I could hear." He smiled mischievously.

They entered the loft and Jerry was relieved to not be greeted by a flying royal ghost. He glanced up and around, trying to search for Ana without letting Manny know he was looking for anything. He checked the ceiling while taking off his coat and hanging it up, but no Ana.

"Thanks for the lift, Manny. Can I offer you a coffee?"

"Glass o' water'd be just fine, Jerr. Get a bit dry in winter." Manny hung up his own coat and took a couple steps into the loft.

"This is hardly winter—no snow up to your ass." Jerry gestured to the sink and then the fridge. "You want tap or filtered?"

"Tap is fine, lad, and I can get it myself."

"I can get water, Man—" Jerry started around the end of the island but Manny waved him off.

"I'm sure you can, but you aren't bloody going to. Relax. Doctor's orders."

"Everyone keeps telling me to 'relax'. Really, the headache is gone. I feel great."

"That's nice. Now sit down before I knock you down, mate."

Jerry chuckled, giving up the fight. "Yessir, Boss. I'll sit my ass down. Is here okay, Boss?" He planted himself on the couch.

"Bloody kids. Do you want one, too?"

"Sure. I'm good with anything caffeine-free, or so says the doc. No ice, though, thanks."

Manny fetched two glasses from the cupboard, let the cold tap water run for a minute and then filled the two glasses. He brought them over to the sitting area and handed Jerry one of them before lowering himself into a chair.

"Thanks." Jerry took a distracted sip then put the glass down on a coaster. The book wasn't where he'd left it on the coffee table. He peeked under the magazines on the table top and then checked under the table itself. When he still had no luck, he slipped off the couch and looked underneath.

"Whatcha looking for, Jerr?"

"A book I was reading this morning." Not finding it under the couch, he sat back up, looking around, trying to think where it might be.

"I didn't see any books in the kitchen, Jerr, but I'll go take another look." Manny slowly levered his lanky frame up from the chair and looked.

Jerry shook his head, confused. "I was sure it was sitting right here on the table when I left for work yesterday."

"Not in the kitchen, either. Guess you'll have to read one of those magazines instead." He returned to the chair. "At least you don't live with someone like my Carmella, who puts my crap away before it even hits the coffee table. Your book'll show up, lad. It's probably sitting next to the loo."

"Yeah, maybe." But not possible, Jerry thought. The one thing he was sure of was that he didn't take Ana into the bathroom with him, but he got up to check anyway, just in case.

Manny looked under the magazines, too. "Get back—what are you doing?! It's only a bloody book, mate."

Jerry came out of the bathroom, shaking his head. "It's not really my book. Sort of a loaner."

"Was it in there?"

"No."

"Maybe you took it to work . . . and don't even think about going there to look, cuz I'm on my way there and I'll check your office for you myself. Like I said—it'll pop up."

Jerry tried to appear relaxed but was starting to worry. "Yeah, you're right. Look, I appreciate you picking me up and bringing me home, Manny. I think I should relax. Maybe even have a nap."

"I'll leave you to it, then. Nap, sleep, kick back and watch porn—whatever you do to wind down. I'll see you after your days off." He got back out of the chair and retrieved his coat.

"Definitely, Manny. Does porn help you relax?"

"I'm married to an amazing woman, Jerr—I have no need for the likes of pornography." His expression was neutral but Jerry saw a twinkle in his eyes. He opened the door and stepped into the hall, picking up the still dripping umbrella. "Now rest. I'll update everyone at work so they don't keep calling to see how you're doing."

"Thanks. Çiao, Manny." He stood in the doorway and watched as the tall Aussie descended the stairs and exited out into the downpour, popping the umbrella up before stepping onto the sidewalk. As soon as his boss was out of sight, Jerry ducked back into the apartment and locked the door. "Shit, shit, shit!"

CHAPTER ELEVEN

@TheTaoOfJerr: "Music produces a kind of pleasure which human nature cannot do without."

~Confucius

JERRY RAMPED HIS search up a couple of notches. He moved furniture, yanked off the seat cushions, stripped the bed, and emptied half-filled book shelves in a fruitless effort to find Ana. After an hour, exhausted, he grabbed his jacket and headed out into the rain. He had no idea how she could have left the loft, but he would search until he found her. For all he knew, Ana went for a walk and couldn't find her way back. He headed straight for the one area he knew Ana knew—the Inner Harbour.

SITTING AT THE base of the statue of Queen Victoria, Jerry ignored the cold, sporadic drizzle as he numbly stared out at the monstrous private yacht moored in the Inner Harbour. Periodically he took out his iPhone to make sure the ringer volume was turned up. This numbness and phone-checking pattern went on for almost an hour before he decided, in some deep recess of his brain, to keep walking.

So he walked. He walked the path that he and Ana had walked two days ago. Then he walked streets and lanes he had never seen before. After an hour he was still walking, sullen and listless. The rain stopped and a fog rolled in, but Jerry didn't notice. Even as the fog thickened and the dark, clinging sensation in the air around him was one that would have suited Jack the Ripper, Jerry wandered on autopilot, led by some inner compass. Had anyone stopped and asked him where he was going he would have had no answer. In that mental and physical fog, he didn't even know where he was or where he'd been, until he was standing on the street in front of The Ipatiev House Antiques.

Recognition dawned slowly and he shuffled forward until his forehead leaned against the glass door of the shop. His breath was long and slow and a little ragged with the cold and damp, and after a minute of leaning, he stumbled away in silence, making for the loft.

Once he left the antique store he found the loft easily enough. There was still no sign of Ana when he dropped his wet coat on the floor, peeled off his damp clothes, and flopped into bed, naked, pulling the covers up tight around him. Somehow he managed to keep the phone with him and it lay on the comforter next to him, a silent sentinel.

HUNGER FINALLY DRAGGED Jerry awake and after pulling on his pyjamas and robe, and nibbling on some cold leftovers, he lit a fire in the fireplace to chase off the damp chill. He soon dozed off on the couch. Wrapped in his monstrous robe, he almost looked comfortable, but the bags under his eyes and the pallor of his skin spoke the truth. He was a mess.

ANA EMERGED FROM her darkness into the flat and discovered that not only was the morning light shining in the window, but someone had tossed the bedding around and pulled everything off the shelves. Then she heard the familiar snoring and charged into the living room to find Jerry asleep on the couch.

JERRY WOKE, SLOWLY, sensing that he wasn't alone. Sitting on the floor but leaning against the couch by his knees, Ana turned and smiled up at him.

"Ana? My God! Where have you—"

She reached up and put a finger on his lips to hush him. "Look what I can do." Holding the book up, she pirouetted and then skipped around the loft. When she got back around to the front door, she opened it with a flourish, and Jerry could hear her footsteps as she ran down the stairs and then back up again. He sat up as she returned and closed the door behind her.

"I can go anywhere! *I just have to take the book.*"

"Amazing."

She sat down next to him and hugged him. "Oh, Jerry, I missed you. Where were you? I never thought I would see you again, see you to tell you *YA lyublyu tebya*!—I love you."

Jerry's funk flooded back in. He flashed a wan smile and hugged her back, hard. "Thanks, but I might not be the best choice for your heart."

"You're perfect for me. What is wrong?"

"While you were off 'exploring'—"

"Jerry, I would never wander off without telling you. *Nikogda ne*—Never. I was here, the whole time." She took his hand, laced her fingers with his. "But where were you? I was worried."

"Yeah. About that. My headaches may be more than just diet or stress. They ran some tests while I was in the hospital."

"*Hospital*?"

"Yeah, I sort of fell down and went boom at work."

"Oh, Jerry . . . " She held his hands to her chest as if to draw the illness out and into herself.

"Then I got home and I couldn't find the book or you. I didn't know what to do. I looked for you everywhere."

"I am so very sorry." She kissed him softly on the cheek. "What can the doctors do for you?"

"They've scheduled me for a test—an MRI—next week, and I guess we'll take it from there."

"After this testing, then what?"

"You really want to know about this, don't you?"

"Of course. My brother, Alexei, was sick from the day he was born, and we saw a great many physicians and surgeons come and go, to no avail. It was not until Grigori came to us that we really saw a change in Alexei."

"The mad monk cured your brother's hemophilia?"

"He was hardly mad, although he was a very eccentric *starets*—a holy man—but he could not cure Alexei. No one could. He just helped him to build what strength he could, made him more comfortable, and helped my mother deal with the stress and pain." She stopped and sighed. Jerry gave her a gentle hug but his cheek passed through hers.

"Oops. Sorry, Jerry." She solidified and he kissed her on the forehead, smiling.

"It's okay. I need a reminder every so often that you're not like any other woman."

"Does this bother you?"

"That you're a ghost? I can see you, hear your voice, and most of the time I can touch you. That's a lot more than I can say about the women I've met through the Net."

"The 'net'? You meet women while fishing?"

"Fishing? I guess on PlentyOfFish.com I was, but not in the way you mean. The Internet is a way of communicating with the world without leaving the comfort of your home."

"Will you show me?"

"Of course."

"*Khorosho*—good . Now, what I was telling you about Grigori and Alexei is that even though Alexei could be very sick at times, he lived like other boys."

"You mean like other tsars-in-training."

"No, like any other *boy*. He ran, played, and enjoyed life. He would not allow his illness to keep him down, even though he was often too weak to even walk on his own. When he could not walk, my father carried him, or someone else if Father was away."

"Sounds like he was quite a kid."

"Kid? A goat?"

Jerry chuckled. It wasn't just a language barrier they dealt with; it was a generation gap like none other. "No, it's slang. It means 'child'."

"Oh. Yes, he is . . . *was* quite a kid. But that is not my point, Jerry."

"Somehow I didn't think so, Ana."

"You are sick. Is there a cure?"

"It depends on what's wrong. If it's cancer, then I suppose surgery or chemotherapy. I'm not sure about radiation cuz it's in my head, but I guess I'll hear all about it once all the tests are done."

Ana nodded firmly. "So there is a cure."

"I suppose so. Nothing definite. No guarantees."

"For Alexei there was no cure, but he enjoyed life to the fullest. You at least have hope, so—"

"So stop whining and live it up?"

"Precisely. Now, is there no treatment they can do until after this MIR test?"

"MRI and no, nothing but take the pain pills they gave me."

"Then if you are not in pain now, let us get 'out and about', as you say."

"You don't want me moping and hiding up here in the loft. Is that what you're saying?"

"Exactly!"

His mood improving, Jerry laughed. "And you're just the dead Grand Duchess to teach this commoner how to live?"

"If you will permit me to." Her smile faded. "I have intruded upon your life and not even asked for your permission."

"My *permission*?" He stood and pulled her close so that he could look in her eyes. "Yes, I'm sick, and yes, I'll be an asshole every so often when the pain comes back, but when you're around, I feel more alive than I have in years."

"Me, too." She winked at him. "I love you."

"You've only known me a few days, Shvibzik. Give it some time."

"Yes sir." She released his left hand and threw him a sloppy salute.

Jerry laughed loud and strong, feeling life flow back into him. "So now what, Little Imp?"

"Now? Now we explore, sir! This is *novyy gorod*—a new city—for both of us. Let us make it ours!"

"Then I guess it's time I showed you how to use your inter-net, because I have no idea what there is to see in this city."

CHAPTER TWELVE

@TheTaoOfJerr: "A painter paints pictures on canvas. But musicians paint their pictures on silence."

~Leopold Stokowski

AFTER AN HOUR of surf-the-net lessons and compiling a list of sights to see in and around Victoria, Jerry pushed the laptop away and leaned back in his chair.

"Kiddo, I'm exhausted. We have a list of almost twenty sights to see within walking distance of home, so how about I have a short nap before we go traipsing off?"

"Yes, you rest. I think I want to do some more surfing with the nets." She turned the laptop to face her and started typing and scrolling and mousing, looking very much like the curious, bright teenager she was when she died. "This is really no different from a typewriter."

"Then have at it, while I recharge my batteries." Jerry took a few sips of his herbal tea and lay back down on the couch while Ana claimed his chair and explored the new world of knowledge at her fingertips. Jerry was so wiped out that not even the Tsarevna's giggles and gasps of discovery could keep him from drifting off.

SOMETHING TUGGED ON Jerry's socked foot, dragging him from a deep, dark dream that slithered away before he could remember it.

"Jerry. You need to eat."

He looked up to see a concerned Ana gently wiggling his big toe. "Hmm? What?"

She released his toe then moved around and sat next to him on the couch. "You need to eat, my Sweet. Even if we just remain inside this evening, you need food." Ana's voice was soft, subdued.

"I agree with the food thing," he took her hand and kissed her palm, "but we definitely need to get out and see the city. It's Christmas and I won't let being a little worn out keep me in. What's on the plate, so to speak?"

"I most certainly want to get out and find something fabulously interesting—I am rather weary of the Internet. May we go see the China Town? I have never seen one and the web site makes it look so beautiful, and bright, and alive. It is also nice and close, so we will not be too far from home, should you begin to feel unwell."

"Don't you worry about me and my headaches, Honey Cakes. Chinatown sounds nice. Actually, Chinese *food* sounds good. I wonder if Carmella left the number for Chinese delivery."

Having anticipated the request, Ana held the delivery menu out to Jerry, but when he reached for it, she pulled it out of his reach.

"Ana, what are you . . . ?"

"'Honey Cakes'?"

Jerry laughed. "Cutie Pie?" He reached for the menu but she hopped up off the arm of the couch and kept it out of his reach. He followed her, slowly, still waking up.

"Keeping trying, Mr. Powell."

"Little Chickiletto?"

Ana stopped behind the kitchen island and looked at him, quizzically. "'Little Chickiwhato'?"

"Chickiletto. I just made it up."

"Your imagination needs to see a doctor, good sir."

"Borscht Babe, then."

"*Borscht Babe*?" She abruptly handed him the menu.

"Yeah, sure. Borscht Babe. Borscht is Russian, isn't it?"

"Some is. My favourite recipe is actually hot Ukrainian Borscht, although I also am rather fond of a Prussian variation with garlic and bacon—smoky and spicy."

"Smoky and spicy, eh?" Jerry leered at her.

"Mr. Powell, what on Earth are you implying?" Her hands went to her hips in mock outrage. "I am a proper young lady, sir."

"I never thought otherwise . . . Shvibzik."

"Mmm . . . yes, I think I like 'Shvibzik' best." She stepped up and kissed him on the end of his nose. "You have Our permission to address Us as Shvibzik. Not 'Honey Cakes', nor 'Chickiletto', and definitely not 'Borscht Babe'. I have spoken."

Jerry dropped to one knee in mock obeisance, his head bowed low. "Yes, Your Imperial Highness. This humble servant shall honour and obey thy Royal Command."

"Quite so? Then get up off your knee and order yourself some dinner. We must not have Our servant fading away from hunger." She giggled.

Jerry stood up too quickly and the blood rushed to his head, making him a bit wobbly. Ana grabbed his elbow to steady him.

"Jerry?"

He accepted her help and leaned on the kitchen island. "Nothing to worry about, Shvibzik—just stood up too fast. Maybe I should order some dinner."

Ana helped him onto the stool but his dizziness quickly passed. "What a terrific idea, Mr. Powell. I should have thought of that myself."

Jerry laughed. "Yeah, yeah, yeah. No one appreciates a smart-assed imp. If you really want to make yourself useful, you could find my phone for me, please."

"Of course. It is on the table." She fetched it for him. "Now, please call for your dinner, and while you are doing that and then eating, I do believe I shall have a nap."

"A nap? You don't want to keep surfing the Internet to see what's been happening for the last century?"

"No, I have seen more than enough for now, thank you. I think it best to discover the changes in person, one or two at a time. Now, if we are to discover this lovely city's Chinatown, I need to return to the book for an hour or so."

Jerry kissed the top of her head. "You *have* been out a long time, Shvibzik. Go, nap, or whatever you need to do. I promise I'll order dinner, eat, and 'wake' you when I'm ready to go out."

"Thank you. See you soon, my Sweetness." She stepped over to the coffee table and faded out quickly, blowing him a kiss as she went. The sweatshirt and jeans crumpled softly to the floor. Jerry took his iPhone over to his desk and plugged it into the charger cord before making the call. He glanced down at the computer screen and nearly dropped the phone.

"Oh, no. Dammit!" He scrolled the screen down. "I should have known. It's one of the first things a person does when they get access to the Net for the first time. Shit shit shit." He sat down heavily in the chair and started reading what was on the screen. It was the Wikipedia page for "The Shooting of the Romanov Family".

JERRY EVENTUALLY ORDERED dinner and then ate it with little enthusiasm as he finally clicked on the links he'd emailed himself and read more and more about Ana and her family; the facts and rumours surrounding their lives and deaths. When he'd had enough of both dinner and the sadness of Ana's story, he put the leftovers in the fridge, hung the sweatshirt and jeans over the divider screen, and stepped into the shower.

Twenty minutes later, freshly shaved, scrubbed, and dressed, Jerry sat on the couch with the Blake book in his lap. He stroked it gently with his fingertips, as he would Ana's own hand. After a heartbeat or two it began to glow blue, so he placed it beside him on the couch. Ana appeared, a soft smile on her face.

"Did you eat?"

He smiled back. "Yes, Your Imperial Highness, I ate."

"And you still wish to visit the China Town?"

"I think that would be the perfect diversion for both of us."

"Excellent. Then please allow me to get dressed and we can depart. What weather should we expect?"

"It's stopped snowing, but we'll take the umbrella because apparently it rains more often than it snows during Christmas here in Victoria." He noticed Ana looking where she'd last seen the clothes and he pointed at the dressing screen. "Your wardrobe awaits, m'lady." Ana giggled and walked through the screen, blowing him another kiss over her shoulder just before she was out of sight. She dressed quickly and stepped around the screen for his inspection.

"How do I look, good sir?" She did a little twirl for him, her nearly waist-length hair free-floating around her as though she were under water.

"You'd be beautiful in anything, Ana, but tomorrow we'll see about getting you some clothes of your own. You usually keep your hair tied up so I hadn't noticed how long it is. Was it that long . . . *before*?"

"Oh yes. It was only the last year when it was short. We had our heads shaved because we had measles and were losing our hair. Even though it was falling out, we cried softly when they cut our hair and shaved our heads. Such a silly thing—hair grows back, over time. If we had only known what our lives would hold in that next year, we would have seen how trivial our hair really was." She gathered her tresses and with the quick, deft motions most men never understand, she braided it loosely and tied a knot in the end to contain it. "This is a few inches longer than I ever had it, but since I loved growing it, I assumed if I was twenty-two, it would have grown like this. Do you like it?"

Jerry smiled. "I think it's perfect. I've always been a big fan of long hair, and your deep gold just shines." He retrieved the coats and the umbrella and helped Ana on with his duffel coat while he shrugged into the red parka. Noticing his camera bag at the foot of the coat tree for the first time in days, Jerry picked it up by the strap and carried it over to the couch. "I have no idea if this'll work, but I don't know why I didn't think of it before . . . " He unzipped the bag, pulled out his digital Canon SLR, popped off the lens cap, switched the camera on, and pointed it at Ana. "Smile."

She smiled reflexively but had no idea what he was doing until the on-camera flash popped up and went off. "What . . . ? Jerry, is that a *kameru*—a camera?"

"It's my pride and joy. But I'm not sure if it'll work with you. I've never tried to take pictures of a ghost. Let's take a look." He turned so they could both see the three-inch screen on the back of the camera, then he switched the camera over to "view" mode. Ana's gently smiling face filled the frame.

"Oh my! That's astonishing! The picture is immediate? Where is the film? That is me! Oh, can I try? Show me, please, Jerry! I miss my camera *ever* so much!"

"You like to take pictures?" He handed her the Canon, and she turned it over in her hands, examining each and every little angle and part.

"I had a Kodak Brownie that was always pointed at someone

or something interesting, but it was so long between taking the photograph and seeing the results that I became extremely frustrated. My tutor would have to take the camera and put it out of reach while I was supposed to be doing my studies. Ooo! This is lighter than it looks, but it is much heavier than my little box camera." She discovered the viewfinder and looked through it at Jerry. She was nearly hopping up and down with the uncontainable joy of discovering her dream toy. "Oh Jerry, please please please teach me! I do not need to know everything at once, I just want to be able to take photographs again. I am certain that film is *dorogoy*—expensive—so I will be economical with my efforts."

"It's digital, so there's no need for film. That's a fresh sixteen-gig card in there so you've probably got two-thousand high-rez shots available before we need a new card."

"Two *thousand*?" She turned the camera over in her hands, trying to grasp the concept.

"Two thousand. I can explain the digital world later, but in the meantime, shoot to your heart's content. You know where to look through, so here . . ." he touched the shutter button ". . . is the shutter release, and . . ." he turned the wide zoom ring on the lens ". . . this is how you zoom it in and out." He turned the dial on top so that the green square matched up with the shooting mode indicator. "You turn it on *here*, and I've just put it on PhD mode so you're good to go."

"PhD?"

"It stands for 'Push Here, Dummy'. Just point, hold steady, and shoot. Press the shutter release down halfway, and the camera will focus and calculate all the settings for you. Press it the rest of the way to capture the image. There's only one condition, though."

Ana lowered the camera and looked quite serious. "Of course, Jerry. Whatever conditions you apply I will abide by."

"It's not too tough—just don't get carried away with pictures of me. Capture the world around us and every once in a while let me snap one or two of you."

"That is *two* conditions, Mr. Powell, and not particularly easy ones to abide by . . . but your wish is my command." She immediately raised the camera to her eye and, giggling, snapped a picture of him.

"The word 'incorrigible' comes to mind when I think of you, young lady."

"Pierre, my tutor, often said the same thing. *Neispravimyy, incorrigible, unverbesserlich.* In Russian, French, or German, he said it was all the same. I am afraid that after almost a hundred years, this leopard is not going to change her *pyatna*—spots. Now . . . Chinatown?"

"Chinatown it is. Do we know where it is?"

"We do. A five-minute walk."

"Then let's go get some green tea or something. Maybe I can find a store that sells antelope toes or some-such as a cure for this shadow in my head."

"That would be perfect, although I would feel sorry for the antelope, having to run from lions without toes."

"Then maybe a mandrake root, or sage, rosemary, and thyme."

"Much better." She snapped a picture of Sushi, spun quickly and took another one of Jerry as he turned from the open door.

"Ana . . ."

"Sorry, but you are so handsome."

He held the door open for her. "Just step out onto the landing so I can lock up, please, Your Imperial Shvibzikness."

Ana scooped up the Blake book and dropped it into her coat pocket before dancing past Jerry and out of the loft.

THEY STROLLED ALONG Broad Street to Pandora Avenue, walking slowly while Ana marvelled at everything through the eye of the camera. Like a six-year-old, she would capture an image, then look at it on the screen and giggle when it appeared before her in seconds. Jerry got a kick out of seeing things new again through her eyes. Between the cool, crisp air, the chow mein in his belly, and Ana's enthusiasm, Jerry was feeling almost human by the time they turned north on Government Street.

Ana darted in and kissed his cheek then flitted off again down the sidewalk. "Not far now, Jerry. Fisgard Street is that next intersection." A moment later she was distracted by the Christmas lights on the trees, the blue-capped parking meters, and the Christmas banners hanging off of the red lamp posts, so Jerry was easily able to keep up.

As they neared Fisgard Street, Ana stopped, ran a few yards

ahead, and then zipped back to Jerry. "That gold and red arch up there must be the Gates of Harmonious Interest, the entrance to Chinatown."

"Since none of the other streets have a gate, I'm going to go along with you on that one." But Ana was gone again, up to the lamp post on the corner against which she propped the camera, and took a picture of the gate flanked by a pair of guardian Chinese lions, with Quonley's Grocery on one side, and Ocean Garden Restaurant on the other.

The flash went off, and Ana lowered the camera in frustration. "How do I turn off the flash-light and simply use the natural light?"

The Christmas lights all around made the whole scene sparkle, and Jerry knew exactly what Ana wanted to capture with the camera. "Let me show you." He held his hand out for the camera, and when Ana handed it back to him, he pointed out the flash button on the front. "Push this to pop the flash up." He pushed it and the little built-in flash snapped up. "Gently push the flash back down until it clicks, to turn it off." He clicked the flash back down, then turned the shooting mode dial one position. "The camera will now let *you* control when the flash is used, but it will still take care of all of the shutter and aperture settings."

"Marvellous! Thank you." She kissed him on the tip of his nose and leaned against the post to try the shot again. The flash didn't go off this time, and Jerry could see her huge grin as she took two more.

"I'm sorry I didn't bring the tripod."

"Next time, my Sweet." She changed her position slightly, snapped three more quick shots, then lowered the camera, took Jerry's hand, and stepped up to the curb, waiting for the light to change. She looked up at him, worried. "How are you feeling Jerry? I know we have not come far, but I do not want to *utomit vas*—exhaust you."

"I'm good, thanks. Just waiting for the egg rolls to kick in and give me the MSG-boost I need. It's sweet of you to ask."

"Of course. Why would I not?" She squeezed his hand.

"Some people never do." Like Haley, or his mother, he thought. This was such a nice change. The traffic light went green and Ana led Jerry across the street, to the Gates of Harmonious Interest. She maneuvered him so that he stood with his back to the Gates, facing her.

"Stand right here and smile, or make a silly face, please."

Jerry leaned back against the Gates spanning Fisgard Street, folded his arms and stuck out his tongue. Ana quickly raised the camera and pressed the shutter button, then she lowered the camera and looked at the image on the screen. She cursed in Russian then switched back to English. "It is too blurry." She popped the flash up and raised the camera again. "One more time, please." Jerry obliged and the staccato red-eye-reduction flash strobe blinded him briefly.

"Youch! Okay, your turn, missy." Ana handed him the camera and traded places with him.

"Serious or silly?"

"One of each." Ana struck a goofy pose and Jerry snapped the shot, then she lifted her chin a bit, turned her head slightly, and gave him a regal half-smile. Jerry marvelled at her transformation from silly tourist into Grand Duchess, then snapped the picture. "You're amazing. Such grace."

"And you are silly, Mister Powell. I am a clumsy lump with no more grace than a sack of cabbages."

Jerry shook his head. "I beg to differ. You shine in a way that has nothing to do with your present 'state of being'." She took the camera back from him, and he was sure she blushed, if that was possible.

"I am just a girl, out with her man." She skipped through the gate and into Chinatown.

Jerry followed her, as fascinated by her infectious exuberance as by the curiosities on display in the various storefronts. He supposed she had spent most of her short life surrounded by opulence and exquisite craftsmanship, yet here she was giggling and pointing and sharing her joy at seeing little mock-ivory Buddhas, paw-waving golden plastic cats, and pale-green jade pendants of all shapes and sizes. He put his hand on the small of her back as she leaned against a shop window. She was real, she was here with him, and when she laughed, he felt invincible in her presence. There was something about her that wrapped itself around his heart and made him think that if he let himself love her everything would be all right. And that was the thing—he was pretty sure he was falling in love. He smiled. Who was .

to tell his heart what to do?

"Look at the workmanship on this carving! It is amazing!"

Jerry looked over her shoulder at the tiny mountain village carved out of bamboo and set in a glass and lacquer case no more than eight inches tall and two inches thick. "Wow. What discipline that would take. I wouldn't have the patience to even make the frame."

"Oh nonsense, Jerry! Artistry like this does not require discipline so much as it requires *lyubit*—love. You do not do fine work like this without loving what you do. Our family had a magnificent collection of eggs created by master jewellers and they were clearly done by men and women truly in love with their craft."

"You mean the Fabergé eggs?"

She turned to him, one eyebrow arched in surprise. "You have seen them?"

"Only photos. Incredible works."

"Truly. My favourite is the Winter Egg. It is made of platinum, diamonds, moonstone, and rock crystal. The tiny, perfect basket of spring flowers inside is made of platinum, gold, white quartz, and green garnets. I would sit and stare at it for hours, shining an electric torch at it from every conceivable angle simply to watch the play of light off its perfect magnificence. It was Alma Pihl's greatest design by far. Over one thousand three hundred and fifty rose-diamonds on the basket alone."

Stunned, Jerry shook his head. "Did you say thirteen hundred and fifty diamonds?"

"On the basket of flowers. Thirteen hundred on the body of the egg, and almost four hundred on the borders."

"That makes bamboo sculpture sound pretty lame."

"Lame?"

"Unimpressive. Boring."

"Not at all! Look at the detail and workmanship that went into making the pagodas and bridges. Look at the tiny cranes. Four of them and no two alike in posture and detail. The materials and cost don't make art beautiful, but rather the skill and love poured into it."

Lifting Ana's chin, Jerry kissed her on the tip of her nose. "True enough." Yup, love.

Ana giggled and skipped back and away from him, teasing him at arm's length while searching for her next photographic subject.

CHAPTER THIRTEEN

@TheTaoOfJerr: "Those who dance are considered insane by those who don't hear the music."

~Friedrich Nietzsche

MANNY ARGUED AGAINST Jerry coming to work at all, but Jerry knew that there were some things he couldn't do from his computer at home. "Besides, I need to feel useful, and if the staff see me, maybe they'll stop worrying about me and just enjoy the Christmas season. I've had thirty-seven emails in the last day-and-a-half, asking me how I'm doing and do I need anything." Manny finally acquiesced after Jerry promised not to push himself too hard and to call if he felt even a little dizzy.

JERRY HUNG HIS coat up and closed his office door until it was only a bit ajar. Plain White T's catchy "Hey There Delilah" played over the speaker. He reached for the book poking out of his pocket, but decided to leave it where it was.

"I'm losing my damned mind. I'm falling for a ghost and carrying around a book of old poetry so I can be close to her. What is it with me and impossible women?" He slipped in behind his desk and pulled the wire mesh in-basket to the middle. He started in on the pile and after a moment the familiar blue glow radiated from his coat. He didn't look up, just kept sorting the papers into two piles.

Ana coalesced slowly. "This is your office?"

"I think so. I haven't spent much time in it since I arrived in town."

"Then I shall simply sit here, quietly. Or I can return to the book if you would prefer that."

Jerry looked up. Ana waited for his decision. He knew she only wanted to spend time with him, but she was willing to go back to whatever dark limbo waited for her in the book, just so *he* could do work he really didn't have the energy for in the first place. He smiled as big as he could. "Please, sit. Relax. Read a magazine or something." He gestured at a stack of radio industry glossies on top of the short file cabinet.

"Thank you. Just forget I am here. I used to sit and watch Father work for hours on end, and he would forget I was even in the room. I shall be quiet as a church mouse, I promise."

Jerry laughed softly. "It's okay. But if anyone comes in you have to disappear because we really didn't think this through. I should have had you come in the front door with me so that Security knows you're here." He stood up. "As a matter of fact, let's do that. If you'll go back into the book for a couple minutes, I'll take it outside and then you can come out and walk in the front door with me. Then I can get you a Visitor's Pass and maybe find someone to give you a tour. How does that sound?"

Ana leaned toward him and whispered, "It sounds absolutely marvellous, Mister Powell." Then she was gone and back into the book. Jerry shrugged back into his coat and made his way to the Reception desk, book in hand.

"Samhail, I'm just going to step out and meet a friend on her way over. I'll be back shortly. Is there a sheet I have to sign her in on or a pass to issue?"

"Yes sir, there is. You go meet her and I will have it all ready for you. What is her name, please?"

"Her name? Um, Ana."

"Ana. Guest of Mr. Powell. I'll take care of it, sir. You're welcome to wait here in the lobby where it's warm."

"Thanks, but I couldn't remember the exact address so I just told her to walk east once she turned the corner. I'll go make sure she doesn't miss the place."

"Very well."

Jerry ducked out to the street and went around the corner of the building to the alley between the old buildings. He tugged the book out, gave it a quick rub, and shielded the resultant glow from the street with his body. A moment later Ana stood before him and reached up on tiptoes to kiss his cheek.

"Quick, Jerry, you will freeze, and I am taking you away from your work like I promised I would *not*."

"This is hardly cold, but you're right, and I should get back to work so I can get enough done that we can take you shopping for clothes. You can't keep wearing my sweatshirts and jeans."

"That would be splendid. But, let us get inside, *now*. I so command you."

"Yes, your Imperial Shvibzikness." He bowed and led her out to the street and into the station. Five minutes later he was once again ensconced at his desk, while Mika gave Ana the grand tour of the station.

A LIGHT TAP on the closed office door snapped Jerry out of his daze. He'd been staring at the same Advertiser Summary Sheet for the past five minutes, and the knock seemed to be his cue to quit for the day.

"Enter at your own risk."

Mika peeked in, a cautious smile lighting her face. "How are you feeling, Boss? It's been pretty quiet in here."

"Good, thanks. I finally feel like I'm earning at least part of my salary. I'm still not sure I've earned the title of 'Boss', though." He tried to look around Mika. "Um . . . "

"Since Manny is really protective of the library, Ana's in my office listening to my iTunes. She's a real sweetie, but a little odd. I asked if she had any requests I could cue up for her and she asked for 'the one about Grigori Rasputin'. She was snickering along to Boney M when I left her. That song's older than all three of us."

"Not quite, but close. I grew up listening to jazz and Big Band because that's all my mother could tolerate. If it wasn't for MTV, I never would have known about disco and Rock and Roll."

"And you run a radio station?"

"Let's just say I did a lot of catching up once I left the nest. I had four thousand CDs and almost half of that in vinyl before I finally went digital, because the industry had me moving around so much." He logged off his computer and straightened the piles of files and reports that seemed to have doubled since he'd sat down.

"That sounds like a righteous collection."

"It took two years of spare time to digitalize it all, and even though I used the best software available, none of it compares with the original vinyl. Scratch, hiss, and pop are the only way to go."

"No doubt. My fiancé has started tracking down obscure, collectable vinyl. I sort of got him hooked on it. Oh, speaking of Danveer, you'll get a chance to meet him New Year's Eve."

Jerry raised an eyebrow. "Is that an invitation?"

"Sort of. Ana and I decided that you two should use a couple of the extra comp tickets the station was given for the First Night Gala at the Fairmont Empress Hotel. I texted Manny to clear it and he loves the idea. Most of the staff will be there so you just *have* to come. Great food, live music, and you don't *have* to dance if you're not up for it. You don't have to, but I got the impression that Ana will be seriously disappointed if you don't."

"Not as disappointed as she'll be when she sees me dance and realizes that I'm beyond bad."

"Well, whether you're dancing or not, she needs an outfit to die for."

Jerry smiled at the unintended pun. "If she really wants to go, then she'll have it. Neither one of us has been to a gala since sometime last century. Do me a favour, please, and email me the details. Are we talking 'killer' cocktail dress or fancy schmancy ball gown?"

"Last year there were prom dresses, bridesmaid dresses, and one or two fancy gowns. Floor-length was the trend. It's tux-or-stay-home for the men. I'll include a few pics from last year's event. It was absolutely amazing."

"Better send me the links to the most likely shops to carry this stuff." An idea occurred to him. "Actually, Mika, do you know of any good costume shops? Places that rent quality costumes?"

"Only one place to go for fancy—Island Costumes. We use them all the time for our Steampunk events throughout the year. They've got everything. I'll include their contact info."

"Perfect. Thank you." Jerry stood, stretched the kinks out of his back and neck. "Now we'd better fetch Ana—she and I have some shopping to do."

EVEN WITH HER gold-lacquered nails, red-and-black-dyed hair, and dangly pearl earrings, the sales girl at Island Costumes looked to be about twenty-two and was about as giddy as a sixteen-year-old when Ana told her what she was looking for in a dress. She rooted under the counter while nodding her head and saying, "Yes . . . yes . . . yes . . ." to everything Ana said. Her nametag said "Ginnius" and she seemed as mentally flighty as any genius Jerry had ever met.

"A ball gown, please," Ana described. "Strapless. Natural waist. Hemline just above the floor so I can dance."

"With whom, Ana?" Jerry didn't see the need to be specific about her dress style just so she could sway back and forth on the dance floor to "Stairway to Heaven" with him at the end of the night.

"Shush, silly man. I am picturing something in my mind."

"Then you'd better picture a clumsy oaf stepping over your feet while you're at it."

Both women frowned at him simultaneously. Ana went on imagining out loud, while Ginnius returned to searching. "Sleeveless, appliques, beading."

"Taffeta?" asked the voice from beneath the counter.

"Please."

"Embroidery? Crystals or just beads?"

"Crystals? Oh, yes. Crystals and beads both would be marvellous. And embroidery." She bounced on her toes, excited.

"Cool. Lace-up back?"

"Of course!"

"Fully lined? Built-in bra?"

"Um, yes?"

Jerry could have sworn Ana blushed. She truly was an old-fashioned girl. He'd better keep her away from a Victoria's Secret store or she'd be completely scandalized. He smiled. Her sweetness was enchanting.

"Okay. Fully lined, with a built-in bra. Boning okay? Well, *metal* boning. Plastic tends to break and can cut you or worse, and we prefer to leave real whalebone for the museums and collectors. Since you're just renting, it's about the look, not the value. So, boning?"

"Of course. Please."

"Got it!" Ginnius came up from below holding a photo album and slapped it on the wooden countertop. "We have three left. One just came back and still needs to be dry-cleaned so you've got a choice of off-white or emerald green . . . I think." She flipped through a couple more pages and finally found what she was looking for. "Sorry it took so long. Computer crashed this morning, and we're strictly old-school, low-tech until the boss gets back next week." She spun the album around and tapped a photo of a model in an emerald green ball gown. "Green or white. Not many choices at the last minute. Wouldn't even have these if all the themed New Year's parties this year hadn't gone for the Jackie O retro sixties look."

Jerry interrupted. "Even the one at the Empress is sixties?"

"Good God, no. That one is always très trad. If you're going to the Empress Ballroom, then forget the white and go with the green. It's the only green one we've got, and two whites and a pale blue have already been rented for the same party."

"The same style? I'd like Ana to feel special, not like one of a dozen women dressed the same."

"Not a problem. The others went to old women who haven't rocked an hourglass shape in *decades*. Two of them had us add trains and Queen of England crowns, and one even has a sceptre. Think more Queen Mum than Kate, Duchess of York."

Ana hadn't said a word since the photograph was placed in front of her. Her fingertips gently traced the outlines of the dress in the image, and Jerry thought she was going to cry. "You okay, Shvibzik? Are you sure you want to do this?"

When she finally looked up, Ana was grinning widely, her eyes sparkling like gems. "Oh, we are most certainly going to do this. But only if we can find you something to match."

Ginnius flipped the page over and pointed at a set of formal tails. "The real deal. Most men in this town either own tuxes and tails or wouldn't be caught dead wearing them. This suit, that dress, a faux-fur-trimmed, velvet cape, a couple simple accessories, and you two will *own* First Night, babes."

"We can get them ready in two days?"

"If we get the fitting done now, I'll do the work myself, and have them for you by ten in the morning on the 31st. Good enough?"

"It will be perfect!" Ana answered, then her shoulders slumped just a little and she turned to Jerry. "I am so sorry, Jerry. It is your decision. I should not be so inconsiderate, so loose with your money. It was a lesson Papa tried over and over to instil in us. I will be perfectly happy in a simple frock, so long as I am with my darling."

"Ten on the 31st, Ginnius?" Jerry could already picture Ana in the dress, shaming even the professional model in the photo.

"Noon, at the absolute latest."

"Sold . . . or at least rented. I sure hope you take plastic."

"Of course. Now, give me a couple minutes to find these in the back and we'll get started." She trotted off with a purpose, leaving them alone.

Ana did a quick twirl and hugged Jerry. "Are you absolutely, most definitely, without any cause for doubt or concern certain, my Sweet? There are any number of beautiful choices in the catalogue. Please do not do this for me, because I will be perfectly ecstatic just being with you."

He kissed her quickly on the tip of her nose. "Shut up, Ana. Just enjoy. Besides, maybe I'm doing this for *me*. Maybe, just maybe, I want to be at the biggest party, with the best music, and the most beautiful Shvibzik in the world."

"Now I know you're being silly! I'm the *only* Shvibzik in the world."

"Yes you are. The one and only original."

A door slammed at the back of the store and Ginnius' muffled voice interrupted them. "Okay, kiddies . . . let's get this party started!"

THE SONG ENDED, and Ana reached up and kissed Jerry's cheek before releasing his left hand. Jerry gently stepped out of her arms and reached for the tumbler of ginger ale on the kitchen counter. "So that's a waltz, eh?"

"It is."

"And you simplified it for me, didn't you?"

"Just a mite. You have excellent rhythm, though you are a bit . . . *rusty*? Is that the correct word?"

"Rusty is the *polite* word. In order to be rusty, I would have to have some skills to begin with. I don't dance. I love music, and I can sway with the best of them, but I've never danced. But I've already told you that." He moved over to the couch and sat heavily.

"Yes, you have. And that is why we are keeping it uncomplicated." She unplugged the laptop and carried it over to the couch, where she joined him. "Let me show you what a Viennese waltz can be like. This one on YouTube is the best I have seen. According to the accompanying text, they are World Champions—a husband and wife team from Austria, which is quite appropriate, as Strauss was Austrian." She started the video and the loft was once again filled with Strauss the Younger's "Blue Danube". Jerry could only stare, awed and numb, as the world's best tripped the light fantastic on the screen before them. When it was all done, he sighed.

"And you want *me* to learn to do that, in two days?"

"Of course not, silly. I simply wanted to show you what a waltz can be. Let us watch it again, but this time, forget about yourself and simply watch how Karl moves. Watch for the simple things like his posture and arm position. Watch how he bends at the waist and turns his head a certain way. Those are the simple things that anyone can master quickly but will add shine and polish to even the simplest of steps. Of course their choreography is elaborate and complicated, and far beyond us both, but his straight back and light touch on her waist are always the same.

"You cannot tell by observing this film, but what little guidance he gives her is done through small points of contact only. They have danced together for so many years that he simply has to tilt his wrist or apply two fingers of pressure on the small of her back to guide her and steer her around the dance floor. A simple dip in his shoulder communicates a world of meaning to her, his true partner. At least, that is how I was trained."

She started the video again; then paused it. "If you can manage the posture and some sure-footedness, then I will lead you with simply a touch. My sisters could dance circles around everyone at court, including myself. Tatiana was an angel in slippers, and I was just a lump, but poor Alexei could never keep up with *any* of us so we created a simplified waltz, which would not strain him and yet make him appear masterful. He was the heir, the Tsarevich, and he at least had to be able to show a modicum of grace and control in all things. I will teach you *that*."

"The dumbed-down version. Gotcha. Start that thing up

again, and let's take a closer look." He squeezed her arm and turned his attention to Karl and Agnetha doing the impossible.

THE HEADACHE WOKE Jerry so abruptly that he thought Ana was calling to him, but when his eyes finally focused in the dark, he could clearly see that he was alone. They'd danced for hours, until Ana was so exhausted that his hand passed through her waist halfway down the Danube. She blew him a kiss and faded into her book. He wolfed down a tuna-on-toasted-bagel, chugged some Gatorade, and had a quick shower before dousing the fire and climbing under the duvet. He was asleep in seconds, until the headache.

The alarm clock's red digital numbers finally came into focus, and he groaned. "Three in the morning? Damn." He popped a couple painkillers from the bottle on the nightstand and rinsed them down with warm water before sinking back onto the pillow. He listened to his body, feeling the headache growing slowly, but it levelled off at a dull roar, so he closed his eyes and listened instead to the creaks and groans of the old building, the light hum of the nearly non-existent traffic, and rehearsed the dance steps in his head. He finally fell back to sleep at 5am, with the alarm set to wake him for work in two-and-a-half hours.

CHAPTER FOURTEEN

@TheTaoOfJerr: "If music be the food of love, play on."
~William Shakespeare

IT TOOK LEE-Anne all of two minutes to convince Jerry that she knew her job.

"Manny, with all the respect and love I can muster for him, Jerry's predecessor, Dwight, was way too old school." She looked at Manny, then went on when he nodded. "He ran the station like the Internet never happened. He wasn't in touch with social media, and after that fiasco with his internal email joke getting sent to all of our suppliers, he wouldn't even *use* email. Jerry doesn't just know what a blog is, he has a considerable online presence."

"You've read my blog, The *Tao of Jerr*?"

"Your blog, Twitter feed, Facebook fan page . . . Manny sent us all the links when you made it into the top three for consideration for the job. He wanted to know what we all thought. You absolutely *killed* the competition."

"Cool. Thanks."

"My point is, bosses, we need to kick it in these areas, too. The rest of the country calls Victoria the 'City of the Newly Wed and the Nearly Dead'. Our no-repeat, oldies-to-hits pop playlist appeals to everyone, but we sponsor events like whale watching when we should be hanging out at music festivals with live Twitter feeds, and having Facebook contests. Our website is five pages of who we are and what we play. Boring! We need to invest time and money into online trivia contests and cooler giveaways. A spa weekend at an oh-so-chic resort is lovely and all, but we need to attract spenders who will attract advertisers. Trips to Seattle for Seahawks' and Mariners' games. Free passes to Van's Nicely Naughty trade show, which I, myself, will be speaking at, and can offer VIP passes for. Also, Whistler passes and transpo for the Snowboarding World Cup.

"Of course, I can and will keep signing the funeral homes, hearing aid suppliers, and carpet cleaners to mix in and fill space, but we need a transfusion of fresh advertising blood. We don't just want the Chevy dealership; we want the Subaru Customizer who makes those Fast and Furious machines the guys love, here and on the mainland. And speaking of the mainland, we need to reach beyond this colonial little island and start playing hardball against the teams in Van and beyond. Dwight hated Vancouver and kept us out of that loop, but we need *in* the loop, soon, or we'll be one of Victoria's nearly dead." Lee-Anne took a deep breath and sat back, flushed.

Jerry was silent. He'd come to all of the same conclusions when he was reviewing the numbers for the station, but the fact that his Sales Manager was on the same page, was great. He wanted to hear what Manny thought, though. He was the one who'd hired this Dwight person, so it wasn't Jerry's place to trash-talk someone he'd never met.

Manny scratched his head and looked Lee-Anne straight in the eye. "Girl, if I'd known you had these great ideas, you mighta been sitting in Jerry's seat instead of him. Two things I need from you starting right now, Missy. I need to you put all of this on paper, so to speak, and get copies to Jerry and me, both. Email is just fine. Dwight kept me out of the loop for far too long and that's my fault as much as his, but that changes, as of now."

"And the second thing?" She leaned in, pleased with herself, and Jerry did his best not to stare at her breasts, straining at her sweater's few buttons.

"Start dressing like a trained professional, please. I'll try to find you a copy of the company dress code. Lee-Anne, I don't want clients who come on board just because they like looking down your blouse or up your skirt every time you drop by their offices. Young as he is, I hired Jerry because of the respect he has in the industry. You're already the best looking one at all the sales awards banquets; so let's make sure you're the most respected, because even though this is a business built on voices, you're dead-on right about getting the faces out there. Facebook, Twitter, the works."

Lee-Anne looked like she was going to cry. She looked straight at Jerry. "Jerr, do you agree with Manny?"

"Lee-Anne, you're not stupid, so why would you think I'd disagree with my new boss, even if I thought he was off-base on this? Which, by the way, he's *not*. Your ideas are just what this station needs, and clothes one size bigger are what your career needs. I will say this once and only once, and if it's ever repeated outside this room I will deny it to the day I die, vehemently. Lee-Anne, you are absolutely one of the most beautiful women I have ever met. But, until you respect yourself, no one else will. Your awards and sales numbers are terrific, but I'll be frank and tell you that my New Year's Wish List for the station was a new Sales Manager, because you're too high risk. If no one respects our Sales Manager, no one respects us. I'm not saying I want you in baggy pantsuits and sensible shoes, just more Glenn Close in *Damages*, and less Demi Moore in *Disclosure*. Does that make sense?"

"Yes. I guess so."

"Whatever life you and Tom have at home, happy or sad, frisky or bland, I don't care. I mean, I do, but I don't. I care that all the team have lives they're happy with, but I don't care to see the fallout at work. Show us pictures of the kids, talk about your anniversary dinner with Tom, but . . . "

"I understand. Thank you. I love Tom with all my heart, and I'm sorry my behaviour has made you think otherwise. Our marriage isn't perfect, but whatever issues we have at home stay at home. I get it." She picked up the folder on the table in front of her and hugged it to her chest. "Since I hit puberty at eleven, my curves have got me more attention than my straight As or scholarships or awards. Thank you for shooting straight and giving me another chance."

Manny spoke first. "Of course. And I'm sorry we didn't have this chat sooner. We're all family, and we all want to see each of us succeed."

"Like Manny said." Jerry nodded. "Now, can I talk to you about some changes to Rolf's segment with an eye for syndication and SiriusXM Satellite Radio? His show is teetering on brilliant and if we can get him before a wider audience we'll definitely see the impact on our numbers and his career."

"My kids say he's the funniest bloke on the airwaves, so tell me what you're thinking, Jerr."

But it was Lee-Anne who answered Manny. "Podcasting. Tom loves listening to those things."

"Exactly. Manny, let's get a podcast up and use it to take Rolf and the other on-air personalities to a whole new level. Ideally, I would love to be live streaming the station over the Net, but podcasting is a less expensive foot in the Internet door."

"Podcasting? Now you've lost me. What the hell is podcasting?"

"Think of it as radio, but for subscribers only. Narrowcasting instead of broadcasting. Look, I've got a copy of *Podcasting for Dummies* I'll bring in for you. Tee and Evo—the authors—explain the whole thing better than I can. It's going to take some work, so maybe we should get back to Lee-Anne's plan and see what we can do in the immediate future to shake things up. When is this 'Nicely Naughty' show, Lee-Anne?"

"Six weeks. Valentine's Day weekend. I'll talk to the organizers and set up a VIP package for about twenty people. We can give away four passes on air every Friday leading right up to the event."

"Excellent. Perfect. I'm the new face around here, so tell me how I can help. I'll take in any event you want, and I'll bring at least one of the on-airs with me."

"And your girlfriend, Ana."

"Ana? How do you know about Ana?"

"Mika. She thinks Ana is adorable and perfect. She also said she talked you into bringing her to the First Night Ball at the Empress."

"She did. Ana's pretty excited."

Manny leaned in. "Girlfriend? I thought you left her behind."

"No, that was Haley. Ana's someone I just met here in Victoria. Is it a problem, Manny? I just gave her a tour of the station. I wouldn't exactly call her my girlfriend."

"The only problem, mate, is going to be with Carmella when she finds out she hasn't met her, yet."

"Is New Year's Eve soon enough?"

"It'll be fine. Better not make plans for dinner the next day, though. Carmella will bloody insist that you two come have New Year's Day dinner with our family."

"Ana's a bit shy." And not much for eating or drinking, he thought.

Lee-Anne laughed. "That's not what I heard, Jerry. Mika thinks we should put her on air, she's so full of life and has that cute accent."

"Ah, okay. Let's table this discussion for a much later date. *Please.* We've only just started seeing each other and mixing work and home is—as we were just discussing—a risky business."

"Whatever you say, Jerr-bear. Oops. *Jerry.* Sorry." She blushed. "Anyway, if you've just started dating, you need to wow her. Remind me after we're done here that I've got some comp tickets you two can use. Admission to Herman's Jazz Club, and a free carriage ride around Beacon Hill Park. If jazz and a carriage ride don't win her heart, she's dead inside. Just saying."

"Jazz and a carriage ride would be perfect. Thank you." Dead inside? He nearly laughed aloud. Ana was more alive than most of the living people he knew, which was probably why she made him feel so energized, even when he was exhausted.

"Right then, you two. Mr. I-Haven't-Got-A-Girlfriend and Mrs. Let-Me-Help-You-Win-Her-Heart, how are we going to promote this Nicely Naughty thing without losing our older listeners and landing ourselves in jail?"

TWO HOURS LATER they had their plan, Manny had hope for the station, Lee-Anne had solidified their respect for her and had a new confidence in herself, and Jerry had the passes in hand and a carriage ride booked for an hour after dusk that evening. He also had trouble focusing on anything for any length of time. He was thankful he'd left the Jeep at home and walked to the station.

About a block from the loft he ran into a wall of exhaustion, like someone had cut his strings, again. He found a bench and sat. "A two minute time out. That's all I need. Then I can nap at home, rest my eyes."

It was closer to ten minutes when Jerry finally admitted that his bed was calling his name louder than the bench was. He started off again and made it home quickly. Ana was nowhere to be seen, but her book was on the coffee table so he figured she was probably just saving her energy for when he got home. He hung up his coat, placed the passes for that evening's entertainment next to the Blake book, and crashed, fully dressed, on the bed. He drifted toward wakefulness when he felt a blanket draped over him and Ana climb under and snuggle up against him, but exhaustion won the battle and he tumbled back into sleep.

AT FIRST JERRY thought the Belgian draft horse was going to spook and bolt down the street with the carriage in tow when Ana approached her. The chestnut mare's eyes went wide and she pulled her head up, away from Ana's reaching hand, but as soon as the Grand Duchess placed her slender palm on the big girl's cheek, calm was restored. Ana stroked the mare's neck and spoke softly to their sixtyish carriage driver, Bryce.

"She is beautiful, sir. *Cheval de trait belge*?"

Bryce grinned widely, his big handlebar moustache wiggling. "You, young lady, know your breeds. Marie here is all Belgian and a fifth generation mare in our stable. I helped deliver her, and she's my go-to girl when the temperatures drop but folks still want to see Victoria the most romantic way there is. Are you a breeder or just a fan?"

"My family had a rather large stable, many years ago. I grew up with carriages and sleighs and these beautiful beasts everywhere I went."

"Well, then, let's get you two up where it's warm and allow me to take you back to a time when horse and carriage ruled this fair town of ours." Bryce helped Ana up and then Jerry.

Ana got the two of them settled under the blankets, Jerry helping as he could. He looked around at all of the Christmas lights and light dusting of snow. It was beautiful, almost as beautiful as the young woman beside him. He snuggled in close, allowing her to rest her head on his shoulder. She did so, then leaned away and looked up at him, one eyebrow up.

"You are very quiet, my Sweet. Are you feeling well? You are not battling another headache are you?"

"No. I'm good, thanks. Tired, I suppose. Just happy to be here, with you . . ." With who? Oh, yes, Ana. "With you, Ana." That was odd. For a split second he couldn't remember who he was with. He must be really wiped out. Maybe they'd better skip the jazz club later and just get a good night's sleep. As soon as Maury—no, *Manny*—had found out about Ana, he gave Jerry tomorrow off to rest up for the ball that night. Ana would probably have him working on the samba all day, but a day of rest would be good. Jerry drifted off, lulled by the under-blanket warmth, the rhythm of the carriage, and the bright conversation between Ana and Bryce as they passed places named "Mayor's Grove" and "Chestnut Grove" in Beacon Hill Park. He didn't even hear the clicking of the camera's shutter as Ana did her best to capture Beacon Hill Park's Christmas lights from the moving carriage.

THE CARRIAGE JINGLED to a halt and somewhere in the distance Jerry could hear Ana and Bryce having an animated conversation that seemed to be coming to a conclusion with Ana gushing her thanks.

"Oh, Mr. Smith, you are completely wonderful. Are you most certain about it? It will be on your night off."

"Miss Ana, it would be my pleasure. Besides, I don't think Maria would forgive me if I let you arrive at the biggest, fanciest ball of the year in the city's most beautiful gown without a proper mode of transportation. I only wish we had a giant pumpkin for you to arrive in with your sleepy Prince Charming here."

Ana kissed Jerry's cheek, bringing him fully awake. "He certainly is that, Mr. Smith. He certainly is that."

"Will you two be okay to get home?"

Jerry looked around. They were back where they started and not too far from the loft. "Um, thank you, but we should be good. I'm sorry I dozed off there. It's been a long couple of days."

"Not a problem at all, Jerry. Young Ana here was telling me all about it, although I suspect she didn't quite tell me everything." Ana giggled. "Now, I've given your young princess my card. She's going to have you give me a call just after noon tomorrow so we can finalize the details. What you missed while you dozed, was that somehow I believe that the beautiful gown Ana showed me a picture of needs to be delivered to the ball in true style. Maria and I were supposed to be off, being senior members of the crew, but a yellow cab is just not going to cut it for you youngsters, so we will be suited up and ready to wow the elite of Victoria with you." He climbed down from his high perch behind Belgian Maria.

"Wow. Um . . . I slept through quite a bit." Jerry looked at Ana, who busied herself with folding up the blankets and stacking them neatly on the carriage's rear-facing bench. "I guess I'll get any and all details when we get home."

"I suppose you will. She does love to talk, this one does. Made me look like a mime." He helped Jerry down from the carriage; who in turn helped Ana down. As soon as her boots were on the path, she curtsied to Bryce. "A more graceful young lady, I have never met," he returned. "Your parents raised you well, young lady."

"Thank you, Mr. Smith. They would be very pleased to hear that you think so."

"You two youngsters enjoy the rest of the evening. Jerry, good luck with the dance lessons, and I'll talk to you shortly after noon to swap details." He climbed back up behind Maria, and with a click of his tongue and a symbolic snap of the reins, they were off, back to their stables.

Ana slipped her hand into Jerry's and squeezed. "You are the most wonderful man in the whole wide world."

"This from the Grand Duchess who has charmed the top hat off of a carriage driver?"

"I am innocent of all charges."

"You are a little imp. Now, I hate to rain on the parade of fun, but do you mind if we postpone the jazz club until next week? That little nap in the carriage helped, but I'm still a bit fuzzy around the edges and an evening on the couch is probably all I can manage. I can still give you an introduction to jazz, but it won't be live, not yet."

"Returning to the loft is most satisfactory to me, Mr. Powell. Where thou goest, so wilt I."

"Then goest me home, please. I can walk just fine; I just can't read street signs too well right now. My eyes are exhausted."

"Home it is, sir." She took him by the hand and led him back to the loft, where he paused to rest on the bottom step before making the climb up. Once inside, Ana took Jerry's coat and hung it up. Gently, she escorted him to the couch and pushed him down onto it. A quick kiss on his forehead and she danced out of reach.

"I shall endeavour to cook you something mostly palatable to keep your strength up and then I hope to have you show me how to put my photographs on to the computer. To set the mood, I have put together what you in the wireless industry call a 'playlist'." With three quick keystrokes on the laptop, Ana had Ace of Base's bouncy, infectious "The Sign" filling the space. She smiled at Jerry. "Not too loud?"

He laughed. "Not at all." He leaned back against the cushions and watched Ana spin and twirl her way around the desk and into the kitchen. Some of her dance moves looked distinctly modern. "Don't tell me you learned that from Pierre in 1917, young lady."

"Ha! Not at all! Pierre would have appreciated modern music, but this is all YouTube!"

"I'm glad to see you've been putting the Internet to good use. Just don't watch Honey Boo Boo or I'll have to sell your book." He winked at her when she stopped dancing at the threat. "Never." She continued dancing, taking items out of the refrigerator, placing pots on the stove, swinging it all through the air in rhythmic arches and poses. When Ace of Base was done she froze in place, a domestic tableau. There was a beat of silence and then Ana put the bag of pasta on the counter as Roxette's "The Big L." started up. It was obvious she'd listened to the song a few times because when the band sang "Hey now, touch the sky" she was right on cue with a leap that took her straight up at the ceiling, leaving Jerry's sweatshirt behind.

"Careful!" What was he saying?! She was a ghost! Her need to be careful was long past. With a quick flip, Ana landed her feet on the ceiling and proceeded to dance across it, lip-synching to the chorus while her hair and skirt floated around her in complete defiance of gravity. Jerry got to his feet and took Ana's hands as she passed over the couch. Together the two of them danced around the loft, she, graceful on the ceiling, and he, plodding but uncaring on the floor, and their laughter nearly drowning out the music.

Roxette ended and Ana spun Jerry back to the couch and dropped into the kitchen just in time for ABBA to fill the loft, begging Jerry to "Take a Chance on Me". By the time the song was done she had pasta in the pot of boiling water, sauce simmering on the stove, and was placing sliced French bread in the toaster oven.

"Ace of Base, Roxette, and ABBA?"

"I had a needish for Swedish."

"Nice one, Shvibzik. What's next? Candy Dulfer's smooth saxophone?"

"Candy is from Holland, Mr. Smarty."

"Oh."

"But that is close enough for me." Candy Dulfer and Dave Stewart's sensuous "Lily Was Here" started up, the simple guitar and saxophone duet a perfect balance. Ana stepped through the kitchen island, solidified again, and pulled Jerry gently to his feet and into her arms. With slow, measured steps, she led him around the loft a second time, fitting their waltz steps to the slow rhythm of the guitar-sax duet.

The song ended and Ana kissed Jerry full on the mouth. He kissed her back, feeling that in that one single moment, life could not get any better. The toaster oven dinged and Ana broke away to finish preparing the meal. Pulling the golden-brown bread out of the toaster, she looked up and smiled. "Just in case you have seen fit to forget, Mr. Powell, I love you. Heart, soul, and ectoplasm."

"And I lo—*ectoplasm*?"

"I watched *Ghostbusters*. Who you gonna call?" The music changed, a high male voice with Chinese flute backing him up suddenly filled the air, and it was time for "Kung Fu Fighting". Jerry laughed, shook his head, and leaned back again while Ana did a bad imitation of Asian martial arts while continuing with the dinner prep.

Eventually the feast was served and Jerry climbed up on a stool and ate at the island while Ana cleaned up. Every so often she would blow him a kiss and he would grab it out of the air and stuff it in his shirt pocket. The entire time Al Green, Ben E. King, Amanda Marshall, and Moxy Fruvous serenaded them from the laptop. By the time Moxy Fruvous' Dave Matheson was telling the tale about when he was the King of Spain, Jerry's hunger was sated, and Ana had loaded and started the dishwasher, and was trying to open Photoshop on the laptop.

"I found this program. I do not want to shop for photographs, but am hoping it will allow me to look at them on a device larger than the camera. Is this correct?"

"Sure." Jerry picked up the SLR and popped the SD card out.

"But that program is best for manipulating—changing—your images. If you just want to see how they look, nice and big, follow me." He took the card over to the big LCD screen, slipped it into a slot on the side and then took Ana by the hand back to the couch where the remote control was. Making sure she could see which buttons he pushed, Jerry cued up the disk and started the slide show. Ana giggled and clapped her hands when the images first popped up, but she quickly became critical of her own work, condemning blurry images or ones not properly lit. Jerry got a kick out of listening to her express frustration in the same way he did with his own photos, but eventually he had to call it quits and get some sleep.

CHAPTER FIFTEEN

@o@TheTaoOfJerr: "Music expresses that which cannot be put into words and that which cannot remain silent."

~Victor Hugo

A GENTLE TOUCH brought Jerry out of an oddly dreamless sleep. He'd only closed his eyes to ward off the headache he felt creeping up, but exhaustion had snuck up behind him and dragged him down.

"Wha—"

"Just me, my Sweet."

Jerry blinked the mental blanket away and sat up, slowly. "What's up, Shvibzik?"

"I would like to go to church, please."

"Really?"

"I remember something about the Russian calendar changing the year I died, but it is still Christmas time and I would very much like to say a prayer for my family. I—" Tears welled up in her eyes. Jerry opened his arms and she slipped into his embrace, her face snuggled into his neck. Her body shook gently as she wept. Jerry held her close, not knowing what else to do. If there were such a thing as a relationship handbook, he was pretty damned sure comforting a royal ghost wasn't covered by it. He kissed the top of her head and let her emotions run.

After a short time, Ana lifted her head, wiped her eyes, and pulled out of Jerry's arms. "Thank you, sweet Jerry. I am quite ready, now."

"For church?"

"Yes, please."

He glanced over at the laptop and could clearly see a Google map on the screen. "I'm guessing you know which one."

"Of course. I did my research before I disturbed your slumber. St. Sophia would have been perfect, as I am Russian Orthodox, but they are not open today. Instead, I would like to visit Christ Church Cathedral, even though it is Anglican. It is quite close and in the photographs it appears grand and beautiful."

"Sounds good. Christ Church it is, then. I'll put on something nicer than a sweatshirt and jeans."

"I'm most certain God doesn't give a whit about your attire, only about your intention."

Jerry chuckled. "Oh, you are *not* going to get along with my mother at all. *What* we wore to church was far more important than what was in our hearts. It wasn't about faith or religion; it was about social appearances. You should have heard the muttering in the congregation when the new priest arrived with his family. The two boys had *long* hair, and his wife was a *dyed* blonde. It was scandalous in the eyes of my mother and her church ladies." He switched out his sweatshirt for a dressier sweater.

"Whether or not your mother and I are in accord on matters of church and fashion, I most certainly hope to one day meet her."

"Some day, maybe." Yeah, that's what he wanted: his humourless mother meeting the girl who resided in a book of poetry. God help him if the two of them were ever in the same room together.

"Jerry?"

"Hmm?"

"Are you certain you are feeling able to come with me? It is only six or seven blocks—I can easily walk there and back again." She slipped into her coat and placed the book in the inside pocket.

"Don't be silly. I should say a few prayers myself. Oddly enough, I find churches very comforting."

"That is not at all odd. God's house *should* be comforting."

"What's odd is that I'm not a real fan of the services or the

Hallelujah-choir-thing, I just enjoy sitting in peace, feeling the slow pulse of the place, thinking that in that single instant of time, God and I actually understand each other. Of course, just when I think I'm about to have my epiphany—life, the universe, and everything—someone interrupts and asks me if I'm joining them in the Parish Hall for coffee."

"*Coffee*? Oh, I would dearly love to taste coffee once again. My kingdom for a coffee—*and a cigarette*."

"You *smoke*?"

"Smoked. Once upon a time, and it got me into no end of trouble."

"You little imp."

"*Exactly*."

Jerry held the door open for Ana and flicked off the light switch, leaving the Christmas tree and the laptop to give the loft a warm glow. "How about we drive? Do you think you could navigate?"

She held up a folded piece of paper and smiled. "I printed a map, silly goose."

JERRY'S RESEARCH HAD revealed that Ana had been raised amongst some of the most beautiful structures in the world, like the massive, columned, white, green, and gold Winter Palace, and the five-storey, heavily gilded Mariinsky Theatre, so he really didn't expect a 20th century Anglican church to impress her; but she stood in the nave, looking down the length of the cathedral, her tears running down her cheeks and vanishing once they fell free of her face. He felt so humbled by the immenseness that he was near tears himself.

"Jerry, it is so *beautiful*," she whispered. "In Russia everything is gilded this, and solid-gold that, to make it shine and sparkle, but what has been done here with grey stone and dark wood and arches and vaults is . . . the raw, primitive power of God the Father."

"Yeah. Wow." Soft, elaborate pipe organ filled the air while they stared at the dozens of pillars arranged in four rows down the length of the cathedral, the dozen or so astounding stained glass windows filtering the crisp afternoon light, and sharp-peaked archway after vault after archway, all the way up to the roof, far above them. Alternating with the pillars were tall, white-lit Christmas trees, magnificent in their simplicity. Jerry was stunned. The nave had to be almost a hundred feet across and a hundred and fifty long, he estimated. It was the biggest non-sports arena space he'd ever been in, and yet, even with no more than twenty or thirty people scattered throughout the pews, it seemed as comfortable and intimate as his Aunt Mavis's sitting room.

Ana stepped forward, lowered herself to her knees, and stretched out, prostrate. Her forehead touched the stone floor with a soft thump, but no one seemed to notice. Jerry bowed his head, crossed himself, and waited until Ana stood beside him again and took his hand. In silence, she led him forward, to the rear-most row of pews. She nudged Jerry to the long wooden bench on the right, while she took a place on the opposite pew to the left of the wide aisle. He started to follow her, but she already had her head bowed in prayer, so he went to his "assigned" pew on the right, swung down the padded kneeling bench, and lowered himself onto it. A quick glance over at Ana showed that she was glowing ever so slightly, almost in a holy light. And then it hit him.

He wasn't just in a church on New Year's Eve, he was there with the Grand Duchess Anastasia Nicholaevna Romanova, of blessed royal blood. Not only hadn't she been struck down or banished from his world when she entered this holy cathedral, but she seemed to be *enhanced* somehow. Tears escaped his own eyes and he lowered his head and whispered a prayer. "Dear God. Um, Holy Father . . . I ask for nothing for myself because You've already given me so much, so I ask You to please give guidance to that beautiful, lost soul over there. Help her find her way. I don't want her to leave, but sure would love it if You could give her a hint of why she's here with me and not with her family, wherever they are.

"Speaking of family, Father, say hi to Dad for me, and hold him close. Tell him it's all good down here, for the most part. Also, could You send some love my mother's way, please. Some days I think she's as lost as Ana is. And please bless my new friends and family here in Victoria, and send a huge divine hug to Isis and her family. Please send that beautiful little girl someone who will appreciate her amazingness, never pity her, and take joy in everything she's capable of.

"Oh, and before I forget . . . thank You. Except for the occasional headache, you've given me a pretty cool path to tread so far. Thanks. Love Ya."

A shuffle of cloth on cloth and leather on stone told Jerry that Ana was done. He kept his head bowed and eyes closed and looked up only when he felt Ana's weight make the bench creak beside him. She smiled, but fortunately the glow was gone. No, he corrected himself; there was a little extra shine in her eyes. She lifted his hand to her lips and kissed his palm, then closed his fingers over it to hold the kiss tight. He smiled and stood, letting her take him by the hand and wander off to explore the cathedral. They drifted along, unhurried, warmed a little by the winter sunlight filtering through each story-telling piece of stained glass, feeling the solid, cold stone of the pillars, and marvelling at the Christmas tree decorations obviously done lovingly by the children of the congregation. Pipe cleaner mangers and cut-out-and-crayoned angels hung side by side with gingerbread snowmen and more tinfoil stars than they could count.

"It is marvellous, Jerry!" Ana whispered. "May I please make something for your tree?" She reached out and gently nudged a hanging tinfoil star, making it spin a little left and then back right.

"*Our* tree. Of course. I'm sure there's tinfoil in our kitchen. Pipe cleaners may be scarce, but where there's a dollar store, there's hope. We may have to wait a few days. The stores are all probably closed tomorrow, New Year's Day. But we'll see what we have at home to get you started."

"Wonderful!" And then she went back to her self-guided tour, leading them to every nook and cranny open to the public.

JERRY FINISHED UP his call to Bryce the carriage driver, confirming all of the details for the evening, and disconnected the call. He could hear Ginnius and Ana behind the changing curtain in the costume shop, giggling and whispering, and so he closed his eyes, just to rest them. He didn't hear the scuff of shoes on the worn hardwood floor, or the soft cough, but he felt the tap on his shoulder when Ginnius woke him.

She whispered softly, just between the two of them. "If you haven't already fallen in love with this chick, Jerry, you will now." She raised her voice for Ana to hear. "And now, for one night only, Anastasia, Queen of the First Night Ball!"

What sleep he didn't blink away in the instant before the curtain swung open, vanished in wisps blown on a wind of pure beauty when Ana stepped out, made a tiny curtsy, then spun slowly to show off Ginnius' work. The emerald green taffeta caught the light in such a way that Jerry was certain the dress shimmied and shivered around Ana like a living thing. He'd never seen anyone so beautiful in all his life.

Ana stopped her spin and faced him, waiting. He was silent, so she prompted him. "Jerry? Is it acceptable? What do you think?" Then another thought occurred to her. "Are you well? Are you having a spell?"

She took a step toward him, forgetting about herself, but Jerry raised a hand to stop her. He took a deep breath. "If being completely overwhelmed by the exquisite grace and refined beauty before me is a spell, then I am fatally wounded and you are my slayer. Wow, wow, and . . . *wow*."

Ginnius and Ana both laughed, then Ginnius ushered Ana back behind the curtain. "Let's get this in the box. Jerry, your tails are hanging in the men's change area, if you want to duck in and try them on, now that we've done the big reveal."

"Sure thing, though I hardly think anyone will even notice me when Ana walks in. I could be in Bermuda shorts and a tank top and I'd be lost in the blaze of her sun."

"There will be two questions on people's lips tonight, Jerry. Who is that beautiful princess, and who is the man lucky enough to be her prince? You won't be noticed first, dude, but you *will* be noticed, and talked about."

"Then I suppose it behooves me to dress my best. Give me a minute and we'll see if I measure up." He found his costume where Ginnius said it would be, pulled the curtain shut, stripped down, and climbed into the finely crafted suit one piece at a time. It took almost five minutes for him to figure out all of the various and sundry parts. Most of that time was spent struggling over the studs in place of buttons. Eventually he was ready, and took a quick, squinting look to check himself out in the narrow mirror, straightening the white bow tie and shrugging the jacket to adjust how the small shoulder pads sat. "Not bad, if I do say so, myself."

"What was that, Jerry?"

He grabbed the curtain and pulled it back. "I said, I clean up okay."

Back in her sweatshirt and jeans, Ana laughed, and threw herself into Jerry's arms. "You are the most beautiful man in the world! Yes, I think you clean up *very* well."

Ginnius stepped up to him and Ana gave her room to work. The costumer opened Jerry's jacket and adjusted the suspenders on both sides. "That should feel better. You had them a bit high. It'll take some getting used to, not having a belt and heavy fabric crowding your crotch, but the suspenders will allow you a lot more freedom of movement, both on and off the dance floor. I'm sorry about the pre-tied bowtie, but we don't have time to teach you to tie a proper one, so this will have to do." She gave it a tug and a twist and seemed satisfied.

"I am quite familiar with tying ties, Ginnius. I can help Jerry with this." Ana smiled and shrugged. Jerry wasn't surprised that tying bow ties was in her skill set.

"Cool, Ana. I'll give you one of each, just in case you change your mind." She looked at her watch. "Okay, let's get you packaged up and gone. Go home and get some food in you and relax. I've been to a few balls at the Empress and you won't eat until late and will be exhausted sucking in tummies and keeping a straight back for hours. Rest up and fuel up while you can. Jerry, why don't you get changed while Ana and I grab a couple of accessories from the back, and I'll ring it up."

"You got it, Wardrobe Mistress Ginnius."

"Ooh, I like the sound of that. Can't be a Mistress without my whip, though, and that's a whole different kind of party. Ana, come with me, and we'll find that thing you were asking about. Jerry, just hang the suit up when you're done, and I'll find a suit bag for it."

"Yes ma'am."

WHEN THEY GOT back to the loft, Ana still hadn't told Jerry what was in the hat box she and Ginnius had been so secretive about. She simply tucked it under one arm while carrying Jerry's suit bag and the bag containing her cape over her other shoulder. Jerry was assigned the task of getting the huge dress box up the stairs. They made it without calamity, and once Ana hung up the bags and put the smaller box down, she took the dress box from Jerry and indicated the couch with a nod of her head.

"You need a nap, my Sweet. You are exhausted. You are

forgetting things, your vision is still . . . what did you call it? 'Wonky'? Yes, wonky." She took the dress box to the bedroom, removed the gown and laid it out on the comforter, straightening it to prevent wrinkles. She returned to the couch and sat down next to him. "I would love nothing more than to lie here with you, to sleep in your arms, but if I am not mistaken, this evening will require a great deal of concentration so I, too, will 'recharge my battery'." She handed him the book. "Hold this to your heart and know that I will feel you close. I will set the alarm on your phone for three hours from now. Wake me and I will fix you a repast fit for a Station Manager."

A kiss on the end of his nose silenced any objection he might have had, but the truth was, he had nothing to say, he was so damned tired. Clutching the book, he lay back and let Ana cover him with the blanket. He was asleep before she'd even set the alarm and returned to the book.

THE *MISSION IMPOSSIBLE* theme called to him from the kitchen island and Jerry made a final adjustment to his tie and answered the phone. "First Night Frolics, how can I help you?"

"Jerry? It's Bryce. Maria and I are out front, whenever you're ready."

"Two minutes, Bryce. Five at the most."

"Take your time. Maria's enjoying her carrot and in no hurry to go back to the stables."

"Five, tops."

IN HIS DECADES as a carriage driver, Bryce had seen it all—girls-from-next-door all glammed up, super models in shimmering gowns, brides beautiful enough to be in catalogues, even a real prince and princess as parade marshals—but never had he seen a transformation like the one he was staring at right now. Stepping out of the old brownstone was a regal sight beyond his imagination. The dark green of the gown, the white fur of the cape's collar, the elbow-length gloves, and the simple, gleaming necklace with matching tiara reminded him once and for all why he loved the business he was in. And it reminded him why a white, one-horse-power carriage beat a thirty-foot-long diesel-guzzling, converted SUV any day. He could clearly see that Jerry was as overwhelmed by Ana as he was. It must have been a trick of the streetlight and his aging eyes, but he was sure that young Ana was even glowing, just a little bit.

His clients were at the carriage before he recovered, and he had to scramble to get the door open and the steps lowered.

"GOOD EVENING, MR. Smith. You look very elegant in your livery this evening."

"Um, thank you, miss. Special duds for a special occasion. I must admit that you are the picture of royal loveliness yourself. You *both* are. Shall we off to the ball?"

Jerry stepped aside and held a hand up for Ana to take. "A brilliant idea. This has the making of a new fairytale, don't you think? 'The Princess and the Lump'." He climbed up after Ana, who was scowling at him when he got seated. "What?"

"Tonight we are not lumps. Tonight we are grand, magnificent rulers of a perfect fairy world, and this is our First Night Celebration with friends and family. *I* am not a lump, and *you* are not a lump. You are a handsome prince—*my* handsome prince. So chin up, stomach in, and kiss me."

"Is that an Imperial Decree?"

"It is a command, for now. If necessary, I will make it a decree and it shall become law. It is your choice: kiss me because you want to, or because it is the law, within our little kingdom of two."

"Well, since you put it that way, save your lawmaking, Shvibzik, because I'll kiss you because I *want* to." And he did. It was long and tender and full of gentle emotion.

Maria snorted in her harness, and with a snap of the reins, Bryce guided the carriage away from the curb and off to the castle-like Empress Hotel, a few blocks away. Jerry and Ana broke off the kiss and snuggled under the blankets. As they rounded a corner, Bryce leaned to one side, flicked a switch, and the entire white carriage lit up with tiny, pure white lights, as if they were being escorted by a legion of fairies. Ana gasped.

"That is so wonderful! Thank you!"

"Maria's idea. We usually save them for weddings, but she reminded me that this was a night Victoria was going to remember, so, fairy lights it is."

A little girl waved frantically at them as they passed and they returned the wave. Ana even blew a kiss the girl's way, and they could hear the youngster's giggles over the soft clopping of

Maria's rubber shoes. There were Christmas lights everywhere and music drifting from doorways and windows and passing cars. Lovers strolled the sidewalks arm-in-arm, and partygoers scuttled from taxis to doorways and vice versa. It was a city alive with celebration and Jerry and Ana were at the heart of it, lulled by the creak of Maria's harness, the squeak of the carriage's springs, and Bryce's soft baritone singing Christmas carols to himself as he drove along.

CHAPTER SIXTEEN

@TheTaoOfJerr: "Music washes away from the soul the dust of everyday life."

~ Berthold Auerbach

IT DIDN'T TAKE long to reach the Empress Hotel. Bryce steered Maria onto Government Street and joined the queue of a dozen taxis and three other carriages waiting to drop off revellers for the evening.

"It'll just be a minute, folks. No need to rush it now. They're already noticing us, so by the time we get there, we might even see a few tourists with cameras, following you up the main walk."

Jerry looked across the street at the Inner Harbour. The ships in port were decorated top to bottom with festive lights. A hundred-foot-long yacht was teeming with people but his eyes wouldn't focus. "Is that a live band on the stern of that ship?"

Ana squinted. "It *is*! How lovely! New Year's on a ship! That would be my second choice, after New Year's in a castle's ballroom." She kissed Jerry quickly and turned away to look at the lights. "As long as I'm with you, my Love, I will celebrate New Year's Eve in any style you wish."

"Ditto, Shivin—um, Ana." What was her nickname, again? It escaped him, and then, just as quickly, it was back. Shvibzik. Maria pulled the carriage up a spot in line and stopped.

"Oh, Jerry, they have added more electric lights on the ivy covering the façade of the hotel! It is beautiful! I do believe my great-grandmother would have adored this!" She squeezed Jerry's arm and kissed his cheek.

"Almost there, folks. Make sure you've got everything. Gloves, tiaras, glass slippers, tickets to the ball . . ."

Jerry and Ana both checked the seats and floor of the carriage, but nothing was amiss. "Check. All accounted for, Bryce. Thanks for the reminder."

"Not a problem, Jerry. You'd be amazed at some of the things I've found back there after a trip. Once found a Stradivarius violin, left behind by a tipsy, but very much in love, virtuosa. She made it as far as the front desk of the hotel before she came fleeing back down the walkway, in a panic. I handed over her pride and joy and she hugged me for two full minutes. Got tears and make-up all over my jacket. The dry cleaning bill was worth it, just to know that they'd been reunited. She came through town last year and sent me tickets for the concert. Sweet lady. And she plays a mean fiddle, too." He clicked at Maria and they moved up even with the end of the walkway, where he set the brake and dismounted.

Bryce had been right. The slow progress to the drop-off point worked in their favour. There was now a small crowd of watchers waiting to see who got out of the carriage. Jerry could see cameras large and small, and phones with cameras, all pointed in their direction. Bryce opened the tiny half-door in the side of the open carriage and swung the steps down. He gently, but firmly took Jerry's elbow to guide him to the sidewalk, then stepped back to give Jerry room.

Ana gracefully pulled back the blanket, placed it on the bench beside her, and stood up. Hints of emerald green taffeta peeked through the long cape, but she kept the front held close. The street lights caught and refracted through the cut glass of the tiara and there were gasps among the watchers. Jerry held up his hand for Ana and she slowly, gracefully, and carefully disembarked from the carriage. She ignored Jerry's waiting arm but winked on her way past him, over to Maria. She placed a gloved palm on the Belgian's neck. "Thank you, ever so much, Maria. Happy New Year." The draft horse whinnied softly as if she understood every word. Ana stepped up to Bryce, gave him a kiss on the cheek, and whispered in his ear, “Thank you, Mr. Smith. I hope you brought business cards, because I think you are suddenly going to be *very* much in demand.”

He tapped his jacket pocket. “Right here, Miss. Now, you two go have a ball. Give me a call next week and let me know how it went.” A camera flash went off. “I think you’d best go. Your fans await.”

On the way back from the cathedral, Jerry had stopped at a bank machine and withdrawn two hundred dollars. He now handed that in an envelope to Bryce. “Thank you, sir. You will never know just how insanely happy you have made Ana. Happy New Year.”

The envelope vanished into another pocket. “That’s absolutely unnecessary, young fella, but I appreciate it. I’m glad to have played a small part in this special evening. You two go and have the time of your lives.”

A second flash went off and, smiling from ear to ear, Ana finally slipped her arm through Jerry’s. They were suddenly blinded by the flashes as everyone realized that they were leaving. A young man asked who they were taking pictures of and a woman quipped, “Who cares, Kyle? *She’s* gorgeous, *he’s* handsome, and I want *this* for our wedding!”

Jerry and Ana started up the pathway to the hotel. “Are we ready for this?” he asked.

“Of course. I believe so. *Maybe*.” She unlinked her arm and took his hand instead. She squeezed it and he squeezed back, reassuring her.

“Feeling strong, Shvibzik?”

“Very. I shall be good for hours. Is everyone from your radio station here?”

“Not everyone, but a few of them.”

“Lee-Anne, as well?”

“And her husband, Tom. I told you that Manny and I have already had a chat with Lee-Anne. It’s all good, now.”

“I believe you, but let me have just a little fun, please.”

“You will at least *try* to behave, won’t you?”

“Absolutely. For a few hours, anyway.”

“I guess I can’t ask for much more than that, now, can I?”

“Not from this ghost, you cannot.”

At the bottom of the steps up to the veranda, Jerry leaned in and Ana met his kiss halfway. He handed her the book, and she slipped it into her thin handbag before they mounted the steps.

"Let's Rock and Roll, Your Imperial Highness."

"As you wish, my Love." They approached the double doors and their little, impromptu entourage followed along, probably hoping for an inkling of who these beautiful people were. A liveried doorman held the door open for them. "Welcome to the Fairmont Empress Hotel. Are you joining us for the First Night Gala?" He couldn't keep his eyes off of Ana and her tiara. Jerry suspected that the staff didn't like being surprised by unannounced VIP visitors, and the man was trying to figure out whether the couple before him were VIPs, or simply looked the part.

"Yes, we are." Jerry broke the spell and the man shook off his wonder, back to being a professional.

"Straight ahead, and through those doors, please. Halfway there you will see the sign for the coat check on your left. Enjoy your evening."

"Thank you." They started off in the direction the doorman indicated and a handful of people from the group outside followed along, a few paces behind them. Jerry whispered to Ana, "You wouldn't by any chance be playing up the 'mysterious woman' thing would you?"

"Who? *Me*? I am just a Shvibzik, out with her gentleman, going to meet some friends for dinner and celebration."

"Yeah, nice try. I believe the Shvibzik and friends parts, but you're loving this. And so you should be. This is *your* night. If I could give you any gift within my power, it would be another night as a Grand Duchess."

"That is very sweet of you, Jerry, but for me, the greatest gift you could give me is a night of celebrating life with you. I love all of this," she swept her arm to indicate the grand hotel and festive decorations, "but if you were not here with me, it would mean *absolyutno nichego*—absolutely nothing. I am a Grand Duchess because I see it in your eyes, not because I was born with a title. I love you."

"I—" They arrived at the coat check and the clerk interrupted Jerry.

"Can I check your coat and cape, Sir and Madame?"

"That'd be great. Thanks." Jerry shrugged out of his coat and handed it over, but Ana kept her cape closed, waiting. They had discussed this moment when they were getting ready for the evening and Jerry wasn't going to diminish one iota the effect Ana's gown was going to have on watching eyes. He stepped up behind her, got a firm grip of the shoulders and held the cape in place while Ana released the clasp and stepped forward, out of the velvet and into the limelight. Of the dozen people waiting, men and women alike gasped. Jerry handed the cape to the clerk and accepted two claim tickets.

"Thank you, everyone. Is it not beautiful?"

A middle-aged woman stepped forward, timid in her own evening finery. "You're beautiful. Can I take a picture, please? Who *are* you?"

"You are so sweet. Of course you can. My name is Ana." She extended her gloved hand to the woman. "And what is your name?"

"I'm just Cathy." She shook Ana's hand.

"It is a pleasure to meet you, Cathy. Unless the 'just' is truly part of your name, I would leave it out. You are beautiful, and sparkle in a way that makes you more than 'just' anything."

Cathy blushed and released Ana's hand. "Thank you, Ana." Jerry stepped up and offered his arm to Ana once again. She took it, lifted her chin a bit, and smiled so widely that everyone else couldn't help but be infected by the smile and return it. "We have friends waiting, but if you'd like to take some photographs of these lovely costumes from Island Costumes, you are more than welcome."

"Island Costumes? Really?" Cameras flashed and photos were taken.

"Ask for Ginnius. Tell her Ana and Jerry sent you."

"Jerry?"

"JERRY!"

Everyone turned at the deep-voiced beckoning from just inside the Crystal Ballroom. Jerry could see Manny waving from the grand hall, so he guided Ana that way. "Sorry folks, my boss beckons."

They strolled off to the party, leaving Cathy and the other party guests to check their own coats and join the celebration. Two tuxedoed staff flanked the entrance of the ballroom, checking tickets, and Jerry presented theirs when asked. The numbers on the bottom of the tickets were checked against a list on an iPad and they were in.

"Welcome to the First Night Gala, folks. I would offer to have someone show you to your table, but I suspect that very tall gentleman waving at you has it all taken care of. Enjoy your evening, and Happy New Year."

"Thank you. We will. Happy New Year."

There was a bright circle of light on the floor, placed to visually highlight and announce new arrivals in a community where the higher echelons of Victoria's society all knew each other by name and pedigree, Jerry was sure. He smiled at Ana. "Shall we start the room buzzing, My Dear?"

"Oh, please!" Arm still linked with Jerry's, Ana led him into the floodlight and stopped. Jerry counted three heartbeats before the only sound in ballroom was the band, playing softly at the far end. It seemed like every single conversation came to a complete stop. Even Manny had stopped mid-stride on his way to greet them. Jerry let a half-smile creep onto his face but Ana was all teeth and dimples and nodded to him ever so slightly.

In that instant, Jerry saw the Grand Duchess, the Tsarevna, who knew the difference between walking into a room and making a truly imperial entrance. She waited two more beats, and then casually led Jerry out of the bright light, toward Manny. Conversation returned to the room, but so many eyes were directed at them that it was obvious that for the next few minutes, at least, Ana was going to be the hot topic.

"Jesus, Mary, and Joseph, Jerr! You two certainly know how to make an entrance. Carmella is going to be royally pissed that she missed it."

"Who says I missed it, Manny? Just because I wasn't at your side doesn't mean that I was completely unaware of what was happening in the room." Carmella, in a lovely, chocolate brown gown that matched her eyes, held her hand out to Ana. "You, my dear, must teach me how to make an entrance like that. I haven't seen the old codgers in this room shut up so fast since Prince Charles passed wind during a speech. I'm Carmella. Manny's warden." Ana shook Carmella's hand but Jerry interrupted.

"Manny and Carmella, may I introduce you to Anastasia, the young lady who has stolen my heart in such a short time. Ana, this is my boss, Manny, and his wife, Carmella. It was Carmella who did such a great job on decorating the loft, especially the Christmas tree."

"It is a pleasure to meet you both. Jerry speaks so very highly of you, like you are family."

"Your accent is beautiful, my dear. British with a hint of something European, isn't it?"

"Yes. English from my mother's family and Russian from my father's."

"Russian? How lovely. Not like my Manny's raw-bones, straight-to-the-gut Aussie drawl."

"Hey, don't slag Australia, lovey—after all, it's where we met."

"Of course not, dear. Now, let's get these two youngsters to the table. We don't want to wear Jerry out while the night is still young." Without waiting for agreement, Carmella hooked her arms through Ana and Jerry's and led them off, across the dance floor and to a corner table decorated like all the others with black and white helium-filled balloons, streamers, roses, and New Year's party hats and noise makers.

"Manny likes to sit with his back to the wall, so we're here in the corner."

"It's not that I like the wall, it's just that I don't want anyone having to sit behind this gargantuan head, unable to see a damned thing. Just bein' considerate, Lovey."

"I know. And it's one more reason why I love you so."

The rest of the group was seated, but with a nudge from Mika, her expensively tuxedoed, pristinely-groomed, East Indian fiancé, Danveer, stood as well. Lee-Anne's husband, Tom, joined him, getting a raised eyebrow from his wife. Her expression was more one of pleasure than of jealousy. Jerry could tell that Tom was in a rented tuxedo because he kept tugging at the collar and pulling at the sleeves, like he himself had been doing since he'd put on his own monkey-suit earlier. The two women, on the other hand, were stunning in their individuality. Lee-Anne wore a sleeveless, short-skirted, sparkly, bright red cocktail dress that would have been a dress-code violation in half-a-dozen nations if it weren't for the silky Chinese shawl-thing she had draped over her shoulders and across her chest. It didn't disguise her figure at all, but it hid a bit more skin than Jerry suspected she was accustomed to at these functions. He was impressed that she seemed to have heard what he and Manny had said to her.

Mika was all smiles as she introduced Danveer to Jerry and Ana, and Jerry could see that she was being true to her West Coast roots in what looked like something a Steampunk gypsy might wear, right down to the shiny gold, dangling earrings made of tiny clock gears. She wore a loose but conservative peasant-girl top, an embroidered corset, a pleated, crinkled skirt of rich rusts and browns, and what looked like a cashmere cape with tiny fringe. He wasn't sure of the materials it was all made of, but even he could see that the overall look was well thought-out and eye-catching. Only Ana was more striking, and the women all acknowledged it. They flocked to her for introductions and to get a closer look at her "fancy frock", as she called it. She threw him a wink just before she was surrounded and ushered off to one side by Mika, Lee-Anne, and Carmella.

Manny held up one of the two open bottles of wine on the table. "Now, can I pour you a glass? Red or white?"

Jerry shook his head. "Thank you, but the meds they've got me on don't mix well with alcohol."

"Smart lad." Manny freshened his and Carmella's glasses. "This'll last me right through dinner, which this year is being served earlier, according to the Missus."

SHORTLY AFTER ANA and the other ladies returned to the table, the buffet was opened and the band leader began announcing the table numbers. As luck would have it, Manny's corner table was in the first group and he and Carmella led the way to the food. Ana came along to keep Jerry company, but explained that she was fasting over the holidays, for health reasons. Doctor's orders. They were halfway down the buffet when Jerry noticed that sadness had crept onto Ana's usually smiling face.

"This is hard for you, isn't it?" he whispered. She nodded, not daring to speak for fear that she'd cry. "Let me jump ahead to the carving station, Shvibzik, and we'll get back to the table. I'm sorry. I should have thought this through better."

Ana gave his arm a squeeze and lifted up on her tiptoes to kiss his cheek and whisper in his ear. "I suddenly miss my family so very, very much. I am certain that when the dancing starts, I will be fine. Carmella is on her way back to the table, so I will join her. You fill your plate with delicious bits of everything and you can describe it all to me, especially the roasted carrot and mandarin salad, steamed mussels, and Yorkshire pudding. Now go. You are holding up the line." She slapped his butt with her gloved hand to urge him forward, and she started back toward the table.

Jerry caught up to the person ahead of him and glanced over his own shoulder to watch Ana glide across the dance floor, proving that even walking could be full of grace and art.

DESSERT WAS DONE and they were on their second coffee when the small orchestra shifted from "In the Mood" to "The Blue Danube" waltz. Jerry scowled at Ana. "Did you have anything to do with this, missy?"

"What are you accusing me of, Mr. Powell? Collusion with the bandleader? Plotting against your desire to sit all evening, and deny me the opportunity to show these fine people what an excellent student you are?"

"Yup. Pretty much."

"Then I shall not disappoint you." She stood and nodded politely to their tablemates. "Excuse us, please, but Mr. Powell has promised me a dance, and I would so hate to have this beautiful gown go to waste and not get a chance to show off. Taffeta is such a naughty fabric, do you not agree? It simply cannot sit still and must be up and about and dancing the night away." She grabbed Jerry's hand and pulled until he got up, dropped his linen napkin on his place. "May I steal him away, please?"

Manny laughed. "He's all yours, Ana. If he can dance to this old stuff, I'll be damned impressed."

"I may be playing my own trumpet by saying this, but I believe I am an excellent teacher. My sisters and I learned from the best. Come, Jeremy. Tonight we dance." She tugged but he didn't budge.

"Do I have any say in this at all?" He knew he didn't, but he had to at least put up a little resistance. He hadn't told Ana, but he was actually looking forward to dancing with her all dolled up in that incredible gown.

"None whatsoever." And she pulled him onto the hardwood dance floor, which had emptied out quite a bit with the change of tempo. Within a few beats, Jerry and Ana were turning and stepping and dipping. The steps were simple, but Jerry managed to stay poised and confident. Ana was absolutely radiant, leading him around with simple pressure and weight shifts. She led, he followed, and he felt like they were dancing on air. He even impressed himself with how well he remembered the steps and kept up with her.

Lesser dancers moved off the floor to watch the half dozen pairs who remained with Jerry and Ana, and as word spread that the marvellous young woman in green was dancing, people got up from their tables and moved to the edge of the dance floor to watch. Except for the band's impressive rendition of the "Blue Danube", the Crystal Ballroom was silent. As the end of the song neared, five more couples dropped out to admire Ana and Jerry and the other couple who kept pace with the fairy princess and her partner. The music came to an end and the two couples glided gracefully to a final, brief, statuesque pose. The entire ballroom—staff and guests alike—erupted in enthusiastic applause.

Jerry took Ana's hand and looked down into her eyes. "Wow. What was that?"

"It was *marvellous*, my Love." She kissed him quickly.

"Did you . . . what did . . . I felt like you guided me from inside."

"It was something like that. I simply . . . hush. We have company."

An accented, male voice spoke from behind Jerry. "In all my many years, I have never seen such a beautifully elegant and natural presence on a dance floor. That was truly exhilarating."

Jerry turned to find a distinguished man somewhere over fifty with thick, black hair, sunken dark eyes, and a black goatee peppered with grey. On the man's arm was the second most beautiful woman in the ballroom—tall, tanned, and sparkling in a long, satin, canary yellow gown. The man extended his hand. "Professor Jakob Gervaise and Danielle Madeiros."

Jerry accepted the offered hand. "Jerry Powell, and Ana . . . " He stumbled over "Romanova", and decided on a compromise. "Ana Romanski." He kicked himself, mentally. If he was trying to protect Ana, then Romanski was a pretty stupid choice.

The band slipped into "Pinetop's Boogie Woogie" and the dance floor was once again populated. Ana gently pulled Jerry away and led him off the dance floor, Gervaise and his date close behind. Once they were clear of the dancers, Ana turned to Danielle, all smiles. "You were magnificent!"

Danielle beamed at the praise from the young woman who was

obviously the centre of speculation and attention at the ball. "You flatter me, Ana. *You* were simply divine. You are a natural." She extended her own hand to Ana, which was accepted gently, and the two women exchanged a two-cheek European kiss.

Gervaise cocked his head slightly and squinted in the low light. "Jerry Powell? The new man at CKVB, 'The Best Folk 'n' Oldies on the West Coast'?"

"How the h—" He caught himself. There was no need to be rude. "How did you know that? I've only been here a week."

"I'm an avid reader of the *Victoria Times Colonist* and your station posted an announcement in the business section, welcoming you to town. We live in Vancouver now, but I taught at the university here for a few years and still have a few investments on the island. Congratulations on the new position, and welcome to the West Coast."

"Thanks, Professor." Something wasn't right about this guy, Jerry thought. His reason for knowing whom Jerry was seemed too pat, too slick. And he barely looked Jerry in the eyes when he spoke. "Now, if you'll please excuse us, my new boss at CKVB is waiting for us."

Gervaise made a small bow. "It was a pleasure meeting you. Enjoy the remainder of the evening, and Happy New Year. Perhaps we shall meet again on the dance floor." He smoothly guided Danielle away and to a table on the other side of the ballroom.

"That was strange." Jerry shook his head and held his arm out for Ana. She linked her arm through his.

"It most certainly was. I do believe I have met him before, Jerry."

"Here in town?" They strolled to their table in the corner.

"No, I do not believe so. Before."

He looked down at her and she was as confused as he was. "How is that possible?"

"I am certain that I have no idea. As you said, it is very strange."

Manny pulled a chair out for Jerry. "Sit, lad. Those were some bloody serious dance moves up there. Didn't know you could do that."

"I wasn't sure I could do it myself, to be honest. Like Ana said, she's a great teacher."

Tom shrugged. “Lee-Anne keeps trying to get me to learn that stuff, but I’m a klutz. The look I saw on her face when Ana went spinning past, though, makes me think I should at least give it a try. For her.” He sipped his beer and glanced adoringly over at Lee-Anne. “She’s a handful, but believe it or not, that shawl was *her* idea, not mine. She even went shopping for a new dress this morning, saying that she had ‘nothing with class’ for tonight, but she came home empty-handed, which is a first. I guess the pickings were slim this close to the party.”

Manny nodded subtly at Jerry. “She looks lovely as always, Tom, and I’m sure Carmella would be happy to introduce her to her dressmaker over in Port Angeles. The girls could make a weekend of it. I give Lee-Anne a clothing allowance for work, so it probably won’t be nearly as painful a weekend for you as it will for me. But, they’re our women, so what else can we do?”

Tom tried to adjust his pre-tied bow tie that seemed to be choking him. He finally unclipped it and started adjusting the slider in back. “Sure. I’d do anything to make Lee-Anne happy. Anything except wear a stupid tie every day.”

Jerry laughed. “A regular tie isn’t so bad because we can loosen them a bit when they start to choke us, but these bowties look like crap when they’re loose and turn us blue when they’re too tight.”

“Lee-Anne says a tie makes my head look big and like I have more hair than I do, whatever that means. I think the damned things are just an excuse for women to put a leash on us.”

“Hear, hear!”

“Amen to that!”

“You got that right.”

“Quiet, lads, they’re coming back. Don’t want Carmella thinking that I talk about *her* when she’s gone like she talks about *me* when I’m not in the bloody room.” He stood as the ladies arrived and pulled out Carmella’s chair for her. The other three men scrambled to follow his lead.

The women all slipped into their seats and sipped their drinks while making small talk around the table. Ana picked up the glass in front of her and although she raised it to her lips, Jerry could see that she wasn’t actually drinking. She smiled at him and he smiled back, with all his heart. She positively glowed in all the ways a living girl should. There was a sparkle in her eyes, a slight flush on her cheeks, and when she placed her hand on his own, he could feel the warmth of her touch, even through her thin gloves. He couldn't remember having been happier in his life. If this was love, he was pretty sure he could get used to it.

A delicate touch landed on his free hand and Carmella gave him a maternal pat. "Ana tells me you two haven't taken the tour, yet."

"The tour?"

"Of the Empress. The Grand Old Dame of Victoria. There's no actual tour at this hour, but I'm sure they'll let us go for a wander." She pulled her hand back as Ana squeezed the one she held.

"Yes, please, Jerry. We can all go. I am certain that they would not mind."

Carmella looked around the table. "Or we could all get up on the dance floor. Shuck, jive, shimmy . . ." The men were up and out of their chairs in a flash, including Jerry.

"A tour sounds great."

"Terrific."

"Yup, a perfect break."

"Fresh air. Need some fresh air."

The women laughed and stood up, and the men shut up. Carmella and Manny led the way toward the main doors of the Crystal Ballroom, with Jerry and Ana taking up the rear. Jerry took a few long seconds to catch his breath.

"Are you well, my Sweet?"

"Of course, Shvibzik. Just stood up too fast, I guess. Come on, let's catch up. I'm sure Manny and Carmella have a library's-worth of trivia about this place."

"You are certain? We can relax here. I am sure they would not mind."

"Nonsense. My vision's a little fuzzy, but I'm sure I'll be fine. You can be my beautiful guide dog." They started off after their friends.

"Your dog?"

"*Guide* dog. Like a blind man."

"Oh, of course. *Sobaka-povodyr*. Our cook's uncle made use of such a dog. We were not allowed to play with Ivan—the dog—but he was brilliant to watch at work, guiding his master around. In that way, I will gladly be your guide dog. On one condition."

"A condition? I'll bet Ivan didn't insist on conditions."

"Only that he be loved. All I am asking is that you agree to tell the doctor about your eyesight. I am worried."

"It's no big deal. Just stress, I'm sure."

"It *is* most certainly a big deal, Mister Jeremy Powell, because I love you and I worry."

"Thank you, my Sweet Shvibzik. And I—"

Jerry didn't finish the declaration. He didn't see who turned out the lights, nor did he see the floor rushing up at him. He most certainly didn't hear Ana's scream for Manny, and he had no idea that half-a-dozen phones were dialling 9-1-1 while someone put a folded jacket under his head to make him comfortable.

CHAPTER SEVENTEEN

@TheTaoOfJerr: "Music is moonlight in the gloomy night of life."

~Jean Paul

JERRY FELT SLENDER warm fingers loosely laced in his own, the first sensation he was aware of. He'd been at a party somewhere, recently. There'd been music, and a beautiful woman in green beside him. She looked like a princess, but obviously wasn't. Or at least he didn't think so. He heard a soft, slow beeping of machinery, with a metronome's beat. His eyes registered pale light and he opened them cautiously. He was in a hospital bed, again, surrounded by a curtain, looking up at a ceiling of hole-filled acoustic tiles. The person holding his hand stood and leaned over him, strange, smoky tears rolling off her cheeks and vanishing.

She was here. The princess was here, with him. She wasn't a dream after all. "Hi there. How*you*doin'?" She kissed him firmly on the mouth—hard enough to express her feelings, but not so hard that he felt smothered, trapped and crushed down on the hospital bed. He kissed her back, because he was sure he was supposed to. When his mental fog cleared, he was sure he'd even remember her name.

"You are awake, my Sweet." Without letting go of his hand,

she reached across him with her free one and pushed a button. "Someone should be here, soon."

"Thanks." He looked around for the bed controls and found them. The intravenous feed in his arm restricted his movement, but the controls were close at hand so he picked them up and squinted at them. He couldn't read any of the symbols. He thought they were arrows but he wasn't sure. He took a chance and pressed the up-arrow-looking button on the top right. With a whine and whirr, the top of the bed tilted and lifted him into a sitting position, just as a smiling Filipina nurse stepped through the curtain.

"You're awake, Mr. Powell? I'll page Dr. Kelly. Ana, will you be here for a few more minutes? I know you said you had to get home soon." She looked at the beauty holding Jerry's hand. Ana was her name. That's right, he thought. Ana the ghost. Ghost? Was he on drugs? He reflected on it, memories drifting and sliding in and around his awareness. No, he finally concluded, she really was a ghost.

"Of course. I still have some time before I have to leave."

"Thank you. I'll be back shortly, Jerry." She slipped back through the curtain and the squeak of her rubber-soled hospital shoes on the polished floor followed her out.

"You have to leave, Ana?"

"Not exactly. I have to get back to the book to rest. I have been here for . . . a long time. I keep fading in and out and afraid that someone will catch me."

"Where are we? *When* are we?"

"Royal Jubilee Hospital. It is the evening of January 3rd. Visiting hours were finished an hour ago, but they let me stay a little longer."

"What happened?"

"You collapsed."

"In a ballroom?" It sounded familiar.

"At the Empress Hotel. Three evenings ago."

"I've been out for three *days*?"

"The doctors had to do something about the swelling. They kept you unconscious a little longer, until they could do the surgery."

"Surgery?" He looked down at his body, counting his limbs. They were all present and accounted for.

"A craniotomy, Jerry." The answer came not from Ana, but from the tubby doctor who stepped through the curtain, medical file in hand. He placed the file in the holder on the foot of the bed and took his stethoscope from around his neck. "Hello, Ana. Jerry, we ran those tests we discussed last week—the CT scan and the MRI—and found a large mass. We need to do more tests but the pressure was building and we had to make a little hole and relieve some of the pressure. We also took a biopsy while we were in there and should have the results by tomorrow morning. I put a rush on them and the lab is going as fast as they can." He pulled up a chair and consulted his clipboard.

"Are there any changes to those things we discussed last visit, Jerry? Memory, vision, confusion, sense of smell, tremors, fatigue . . . ?"

"I was afraid you were going to ask that. Yeah, pretty much a little of everything except tremors." The doctor started taking notes. "I've forgotten names I shouldn't, I get tired really easily, and my eyes are giving me trouble, especially the right eye."

The neurologist took a shiny metallic blue penlight from his jacket pocket and got up out of the chair. "Can you focus off in the distance, please. Maybe at the fire sprinkler in the ceiling over there."

Jerry did what he was asked, and the doctor clicked the penlight on then swung it back and forth across each of Jerry's eyes twice.

"Thank you."

"So how did I do? Did you find that contact I'm missing?"

"You wear contacts, Jerry?" He consulted the clipboard, concerned.

"No. Sorry. Bad joke. You looked a little worried so I tried to make funny."

"Sorry. Yes, I'm worried. Your right pupil is dilated." He checked the second page of the report. "Yes, here it is. It was noted by the EMS team. It doesn't really surprise me, unfortunately. Having already performed the CT and MRI, I have a very good idea what we're looking at here, Jerry."

Jerry squeezed Ana's hand tighter. He was scared like he'd never been in his life, yet he felt selfish, too, what with Ana actually being dead already. Whatever the doctor was about to tell him, there was probably some slim hope for him, but there was none for Ana. The woman he had come to love was beyond help.

THEY GAVE JERRY a little something for the pain and a big something to fend off infection from the surgery, so he spent the next three days sleeping a lot, texting back and forth with Manny about ideas he had for the station, and listening to Ana read poetry from her book. He couldn't bring himself to tell Manny through text or even in person while lying on his back in the hospital bed how severe the situation was, so he asked the big Aussie to call an emergency staff meeting on Saturday afternoon. He was released from the hospital on schedule Saturday morning with more meds and a handful of hospital shower caps to protect the stitches from the closed-up craniotomy until they healed. After he got cleaned up and into fresh clothes, Jerry arrived at the station an hour early to brief Manny before speaking to the entire staff.

It had been an emotional meeting with tears on both sides, but the two men pulled themselves together in time. Manny now stood quietly against one wall of the station's modest conference room, his long arms folded across his chest and his damp, red-rimmed eyes only partially hidden behind his glasses. His staff were arranged around the room, sitting where there were chairs, standing where they had to. The engineer on duty had put on a pre-recorded thirty-minute mix of music and seasonal humour to allow the station to run on auto-pilot while everyone attended the meeting. Rolf reached up and turned off the speaker on the wall. The faces around the table were a mix of glum and confused. Stories of Jerry's collapse at the Empress had spread quickly, but few were sure what it might mean.

Jerry stood at the head of the long, oval conference table, the book clutched in his hands and a NIKE baseball cap covering his partially shaved skull and the bandage. "So. Manny and I have just had a long chat and I wanted to tell you all in person that he'll be posting my job on Monday." Gasps and whispered one-word exclamations from around the room made him pause. He took a deep breath, knowing what was coming had to be said, but not finding it any easier than it had been when he'd told Manny in private.

"It's not because I don't love the job, the station, and all of you.

It's not because Manny had a change of heart and decided I wasn't what he was looking for in a Station Manager. I am being replaced simply because Manny and you all need someone you can rely on to be here for the long run, and that's not me." He thought he'd better address some of the rumours bouncing around. "No other station has made me a better offer, and I'm not running back to Ontario to some abandoned mystery family with a dog and three-point-two kids. It's called a neoplasm. Anaplastic astrocytoma. Specifically, glioblastoma multiforme or GBM, to all the specialists and textbook publishers. Brain cancer. Advanced and aggressive. Grade 4, for those of you who understand this stuff. Probably inoperable, but brains smarter than mine are currently debating that. Radiation, yes; chemo is something called Temodar to start with, but because it's in my head and there's this blood-brain barrier thing that often prevents the drugs from reaching the cancer, they may have to go with implanted wafers of some sort. I'll be seeing the oncologist on Monday.

"Apparently they found it way too late. It wasn't nitrates in my luncheon meats, or stress, or poor posture, or any of the dozens of ideas we batted around. Unlike Ahnold, it *is* a toomah." He forced a smile, took a long slow breath, and washed it down with a sip from the glass of water on the table in front of him. Tears were already flowing around the room and he was barely holding on, himself.

"How long? Untreated, if I get six more months, I'll be the luckiest man on earth. Three, tops; more likely six to eight weeks, untreated. But I'm not giving up, because there have been great advances in treatment and they're trying to fast-track me into this clinical study they're doing here in Victoria; but the reality is that even if I beat the odds, Manny needs someone he can rely on and I'm going to be a mess for a while. We've made a compromise. He's going to offer my replacement only a one-year contract, with a healthy dose of prayer and support for my recovery in that time."

He took another sip and in that short break, Lee-Anne bolted from the room. Jerry looked up at Mika and nearly cracked when he saw the tears pouring silently down her cheeks as she stared at the table in front of her. Small sobs shook her slender frame. She looked up and he nodded at her. She nodded back and smiled weakly, then stood and quietly left. Manny snorted into a handful of damp tissues but said nothing. Jerry looked around the room, at the faces feeling his pain with him.

"That's all for now, I guess. We'll talk more, once the shock has worn off both you and me. I'm going to head back to my office for a bit, so if you could give me a half-hour or so before you swing by, I'd appreciate it. Who knew a tumour could be so exhausting?" He tried to smile and only managed to deflect a tear rolling down toward his chin.

The remaining staff stood and filed out in silence. Most looked his way, lost for words. He understood, and smiled with hope he didn't really feel. Eventually he was alone in the room. As if drinking from his glass could give others his cancer, he picked up the tumbler and wandered to his office. He could hear sniffles and tears and at least one person sobbing loudly behind a closed office door. It sounded like it came from the direction of Lee-Anne's office, but he didn't have the energy right then and there to confirm it. He'd find a time when they could sit down, after the first round of tears dried up.

Once in his office he closed the door with a firm, quiet click, and lowered himself into the desk chair slowly, like the old man he'd now never be. He placed the Blake book on the desk and rubbed his fingertips along the spine. A moment later Ana stood facing him.

"How did you fare? I would have stood there beside you, had you but asked, my Sweet."

"I know, Shvibzik, I know. But I'm not sure I could have done it with you standing there, too. It's killing me that I'm leaving them all; but knowing that I'll be gone so soon after finding *you* is tearing my heart out."

"You are not gone, yet. I heard what the doctor said. You have a chance. We are going to give this the battle it deserves. *Sushchestvuyet nadezhda*—there is hope."

"I guess. It's a really, really, long shot, Honey, and a lot depends on the decisions made in the next few days. I may not even qualify for this clinical study."

"I refuse to give up, Love. I will be your rock for as long as you need me to be, as you were for me when I awoke lost and confused in this strange world."

He laughed lightly. "I wouldn't want anyone else by my side,

Ana. Whatever I have to go through, you can be my rock, my whole damned mountain. I can pretty much guarantee that I'll be leaning on you so much you'll feel like a crutch."

"Then I will be your crutch, Mr. Powell."

"Thank you. Even when you're in the book I feel you close by, and it makes a huge difference." He closed his eyes as the room wavered slightly. When he opened them again, he felt like his heart was double its weight. "That said, you'd better get back there so I can open my door and let them all come by. You and I can be alone at home, but for now I need to let them all lend me their strength in their own way."

IT WAS MIKA who came to him first and broke the ice. She'd wiped away her tears, though fresh ones threatened to burst past the dam. She hugged Jerry close, then, with a kiss on the cheek, she let him go and sat in the spare chair.

"Lee-Anne has gone home for the day. She may be the Queen of Flirt, but I think she really likes and respects you. This seems to have affected her more than most. Most, but not all." She looked down at her hands, spinning her engagement ring in place. When she looked back at Jerry, her eyes were drier. "Do everything the doctors offer you. Agree to try it all, please, even if it sounds crazy. And in the next couple days Danveer and I will swing by the loft and we're going to chat."

"Mika, I appreciate the offer, but—"

"Not for idle chat, Boss. I want to discuss some alternate therapies for you to try. There's a healer near Tofino who's had marvellous success and he's arriving tomorrow for a family visit. He's Danveer's uncle, and he's a true swami. I've been studying with him for two years and while there's no scientific explanation for the things I've seen, there's certainly a spiritual one. I'm a Reiki Master, myself, and all I ask is that in addition to whatever traditional treatments you undergo, that you allow us an opportunity to help. If nothing else is achieved, at least maybe we can help you find peace during this time of pain."

"I'm not exactly a drum-circle-banging, incense-burning kinda guy, Mika. I don't even read my horoscope because it's all so much 'hooey and hokum' as my grandfather James used to say." Next thing she'd do would be to ask him to wear a tinfoil hat to ward off harmful rays. He knew he had to nip this line of thinking early. "I really appreciate the thought, though. Thank you."

Mika smiled. "Fair enough. But let me show you something, first. After that, just give it some thought for a day or two. I'm a full-on, West Coast, New Age Earth Cookie, as my sister says, but it's not really New Age when it's been around for millennia."

"Okay. Take your best shot at convincing me."

"Really?"

"Really." What did he have to lose?

"Cool." She closed the office door. "Stand up and face me, about a yard away." She stood, too, and moved away from the desk to give them room. "If you're more comfortable sitting, that's cool, too."

"No, I'm good with standing." And he was. He found that he was steady on his feet, at least for a few minutes. He wondered how much of his weakness in the last few days had been psychosomatic. He stood opposite Mika, with the fingertips of his right hand resting on his desk, just for the illusion of balance.

"Do you know what an aura is, Jerry?"

"Energy around the body. Some say they can see them, some say they can photograph them."

"Energy. Exactly. It surrounds our bodies and interacts with the environment around us. Many people can see them and some don't even realize it. To the Chinese it's *qi* or *chi*. The photography you're thinking of is Kirlian photography, which is thought to show the energy field around a living object, reflecting the emotional and physical states of that object. I don't take pictures, but I can see auras quite clearly. Yours is a deep gold, most of the time, though the colour shifts around your head chakra a lot, but no surprise there, now."

"And you're going to show me your aura?"

"Not today. It takes some practice, so maybe another time. All I need right now is for you to understand the concept of an energy field around your body. It surrounds and radiates off of you."

"Like the energy radiating off a hot stove burner? I can feel the heat without actually touching the metal coil."

"A perfect analogy! Can I use that with my students?"

"Be my guest." He smiled. He was really going to miss getting to know Mika.

"Wow. I don't know what you were thinking just now, but a

dark purple wave just rippled across your Heart Chakra. You okay?" She shook her head. "Sorry. Stupid question. Let me finish this up and I'll get out of your hair."

"Take your time, Mika. This is important to you."

"Thanks. Relax. Try to let the tension drain down your body and out your fingertips and toes. Take slow, deep breaths. In through your nose, and out through your mouth. With every exhalation, try to relax just a little bit more. You probably won't see anything but me moving, but it's important that you watch and see that I'm not making any physical contact with you."

Jerry followed the simple directions, curious but enjoying the relaxation. Mika lifted her arms to chest level and faced her palms to him. She closed her eyes for a second and when she opened them again there was something different about her posture that he couldn't quite pinpoint. It was almost as if she'd tensed up just as he'd relaxed. She concentrated on a spot between her hands as she extended them out, reaching for something between them. She must have found it, because her hands stopped a foot from his chest. She rocked forward, gently, and Jerry felt her push on him, rocking him back as she rocked forward. Then she rolled back and he followed.

He could feel something, but saw nothing but Mika rocking. "It feels like I'm surrounded by invisible foam and you're pushing on it."

"I am. I'm using my aura to gently push yours. Energy-to-energy."

"Holy—" This was too strange.

"That's what I thought the first time Uncle Palak showed me." In addition to the gentle forward and back of her rocking, Mika now swayed slightly from side to side, describing an oval around the anchor of her feet on the floor.

Jerry moved along with her, but just in case he was simply hypnotized by her movement and following along automatically, he willed his body to stop and he tried to stand still. He succeeded for a split second, but then a gentle tug pulled him and he was moving again. This was unlike anything he'd ever experienced, on *any* level. He held his hand up and Mika stopped. Jerry grinned, lopsidedly, a lot freaked out but getting used to surprises of both the dark and light variety. "These are not the droids we're looking for."

"He can go about his business."

"Obi Wan. Exactly." He leaned heavily on the desk. "Okay. You have my attention. Whatever the traditionalists have in mind for me, I'll give you a fair shot, too."

"Thank you. Just so you know, though, what I just showed you wasn't much more than a parlour trick. My aura simply pushed your aura. I can't reach into your head and do psychic surgery to remove your tumour."

"What about Uncle . . . ?"

"Uncle Palak is way beyond me in terms of what he can achieve with chakras and energy, but he's no Jedi master, either. All I'm suggesting is using your own energy to facilitate healing. I'll give him a call tonight and explain your situation. He'll know where best to go from here. You have to keep an open mind, though. Your attitude is the key to everything."

"The doctor said something like that, too. Ten minutes ago my attitude was becoming a problem; after this little demonstration, my attitude is *not* going to get in the way."

"Good, because there may be incense and crystals and mantras and a few other things we use."

"Bring it on. If I'm going to let them cut a bigger hole into my skull and try to remove this beast, and expose me to deadly radiation and possibly poisonous chemicals just to kill something that originated in my own body, then maybe it's time I opened my mind to the mysteries of the Far East, too. On second thought, can you Feng Shui the loft, too?"

She laughed. "And maybe an exorcism while we're at it?"

Oh crap! He hadn't thought about how this would all affect Ana. "Hell no. Let's just keep it simple. Thanks for the offer, though." He returned to his chair.

"I was kidding, Boss. Don't look so worried. It's all positive energy work. No demons, no holy water, or crosses, or other symbols of misguided faith-based politics." There was a light knock by large knuckles on the door. "I'd better get back to my office. I'm so sorry you have to go through any of this, Jerry. Just so long as you know you're not alone."

"Thanks, Mika. Auric-shoving or not, I appreciate having you in my corner more than you know. Now go get some work done. I'm still your boss and will need that report on my desk by noon."

"What report?" She looked worried, like she'd forgotten to do a task.

"I'm kidding. Go home. It's the weekend and Monday is soon enough to strap yourself to the desk and do whatever it is you do so brilliantly. Please talk to Danveer's uncle, and we'll set this all up after my planning scan on Monday."

"You got it." She smiled at him and he managed to muster one of his own. A second knock came just before she opened the door. Mika stepped back and Manny filled the doorframe, wringing big his hands and looking worn out.

"Good, you're still here, Jerr. Carmella is on her way over after making a few quick stops, and I've been commanded to keep you in the building until she arrives. Twenty minutes, tops." He stepped aside to let Mika slip out, and Jerry could see a cluster of people behind him, waiting.

"Of course. I'm feeling pretty strong, so I'll be happy to stick around until she gets here. You okay, Manny?"

"It's all still sinking in, mate. Still sinking in."

"Yeah. Me, too." He had a thought, a moment of clarity. "Would you mind doing me a favour, Manny? Something best done by you?"

Manny perked up a bit. "Just ask. I need something to distract me for a few minutes."

"Could you please give Lee-Anne's husband, Tom, a call and make sure she's okay? Mika says she left in a bit of a hurry after I dropped the bomb on all of them."

"Bloody hell. Consider it done. I should have given you a heads-up that she lost a sister to cancer last year, so your news hit her like a brick."

"Oh, shit! Maybe I'd better call her myself."

"No. It's my fault. I'll give Tom a call right now. You and Lee-Anne can have a sit down sometime early next week. Pick the restaurant and it'll be on me. Expense it. She showed a lot of strength when her sister died, so maybe she'll lend you some, once she gets over the initial shock."

"How old was her sister?"

"Six minutes older than Lee-Anne. Identical twins."

"Damn. If you'll make that call, then I'll make time for her, guaranteed."

"Thanks." He looked back over his shoulder. "I'll swing by when Carmella arrives. In the meantime, the Hug Brigade is here."

"I'll see you then." He looked out past Manny at Rolf, who seemed to be first in the makeshift line. "Come on in, buddy." He moved back around to the single chair Mika had vacated. He figured that hugs and words of support would be easier without the desk in the way. When he thought about it, he was probably just better off standing. He got up and opened his arms as Rolf entered. No words needed to be exchanged. Rolf gave Jerry a long hug, then drifted off to let the next in line come in. It was the same with each of the ten staff who came by—two-pat man hugs followed by knowing exchanges of head nods, or long girl hugs with kisses on the cheek. By the time Carmella arrived, Jerry was so infused with love and hope that he just held his arms open and welcomed her into the fold. She, too, kissed his cheek.

"So how's Ana taking all this? I'll bet she wanted to be here, didn't she? *I* would, if it were Manny."

"She's holding up pretty well. She's my rock right now, and you're right, she would have been here if I'd asked her. I just thought that people would have enough questions about what was happening with my health that having them pity the girlfriend I'm leaving behind would be a bit much for everyone."

Carmella tugged Jerry's chin down so she could glare into his eyes. "Two things, young man. One: no talk about leaving until you're gone. That's negative talk, and it isn't allowed here. Two: you let that young lady help in any way she wants. She's going to feel totally helpless as she watches you get sicker and go through the treatments, so where she can have the illusion of usefulness, you will give it to her. Is that understood?"

"Yes, ma'am."

"Okay, make it *three* things. Never call me 'ma'am' again. Anything but." She kissed him on the end of his nose and released his chin. "Now come along to Manny's office. I put together a basket of stuff to get you through the next few days. Healthy foods as well as the kind you indulge in when you're feeling blue, which is perfectly natural about now. Once you've got that in your hands, Manny and I are driving you straight home. No long-distance working, no traipsing around town, no dance lessons . . . just relax with that wonderful girl of yours. I'll explain everything in the basket to her and put her in charge."

"I'm good with that. Give me a couple minutes to grab a few

things and I'll meet you both in the lobby. Please."

"No heavy lifting, young man. That's why we have Manny."

"No lifting, I promise."

"Good. Come find us when you're ready, hon." She squeezed his arm and went off in search of her husband.

Jerry quietly closed the door, planted a gentle kiss on the Blake book and placed it on the desk. The blue glow lasted only a second before Ana was standing in front of him. She first saw his red-rimmed eyes and without a word stepped in and gave him a strong hug.

"Thanks, Shvibzik. We've only got a moment here, though. Manny and Carmella are driving me home where Carmella wants to have a chat with you about some stuff she's bringing along in a care basket. Since they won't be more than a few feet away from me the whole time, maybe I should just tell them that you've gone out."

"Nonsense. I would love to speak with them. Just tell them I am having a nap and when you step behind the screen to wake me, place the book on the pillow and return to them. I will follow you out after I put on some of the new clothes."

Jerry smiled. "You're smarter than the average Shvibzik, that's for sure. Now, let's get home." He picked up the book and with a slow pulse of blue that lingered when it ran across his hand, Ana was back between the covers in short order. Jerry grabbed his jacket, took a quick look around the office to make sure he hadn't forgotten anything, and went out to find his benefactors.

CHAPTER EIGHTEEN

@TheTaoOfJerr: "Who hears music feels his solitude peopled at once."

~Robert Browning

ANA'S PLAN WENT off without a hitch, though Jerry had forgotten that the loft had only one bed and if Ana was sleeping in it, it might imply something that wasn't true. But he needn't have worried because if Manny or Carmella thought anything was off, they gave no hint of it in their hugs and kisses for Ana when she stepped out from behind the screen.

Once the "hellos" were over, Carmella hustled Ana into the kitchen where they went over the contents of the massive basket one item at a time. On the drive back to the loft Carmella had explained to Jerry that the basket had everything from herbal teas for nausea to Callebaut Chocolate dark chocolate-covered almonds for when everything else failed and he just needed to spoil himself. There were bath oils, body oils, herbs, and even potpourri, though she admitted that the more "girly" items were for Ana because he had to take care of his caregiver. While the ladies explored the basket's contents, Jerry sat on the couch while Manny got a fire going in the hearth.

Manny looked back over his shoulder. "Whatever you need, you ask, Jerr. Our health plan had you covered from the day you walked in the front door, so with luck, that'll take a lot of the damned pressure off. It's pretty comprehensive, but Mika knows more about the details than I do cuz she built the package from the ground up with our provider. She's more into crystals than syringes these days, but she's actually got a degree in nursing, so don't turn down any advice she may send your way."

"You've got quite the strong women on your team, Manny, what with Mika and Lee-Anne blowing my expectations out the window."

"*Our* team, Jerr. Besides, in case you haven't noticed with that whirling dervish of a wife of mine, I prefer my women strong, funny, and able to stand beside me, not lean on me. My daughter is the same way, though sometimes she's more like her koala bear of an old man than the dervish of her mother." He got the fire going in the hearth and sat down next to Jerry on the couch.

"Now, a few things you're not going to argue with me about." He took a business card out of his wallet and handed it to Jerry, who read it, front and back. It belonged to a local cab company and had an eight-digit number hand-written on the back. "I have an account with these fellas. We use 'em for post-party rides and out-of-town clients, but now you're gonna use 'em if you don't feel up to driving to your appointments, or wherever. You said before that Ana doesn't drive, and as much as I'd love to be there for you, I can't always, so use the corporate account and no bloody arguing."

Jerry turned the card over and over in his hand, unsure how to respond. He had no desire to argue with his boss over such a generous offer. "Deal. You don't have to do this, but as solid on my feet as I feel today, I'm smart enough to know that's not always going to be the case. Thank you, Manny. I promise not to abuse it."

"To hell with that. Use it, abuse it, I don't care. It's deductible, so no playing 'Captain Strong' or 'the hero', or whoever." He lowered his voice to a whisper. "Use it, Jerr, or I'll sic Carmella on you." They both glanced quickly toward the kitchen but laughed when they saw that the women were too caught up in their own conversation to hear the fireside chat. "You've got that appointment with the oncologist tomorrow right?"

"Yeah. Ten o'clock. And then a scan on Monday at one. That's the long one, I think."

"I assume Ana is going with you, but do you need anyone else? I can skip church tomorrow and take time off on Monday."

"Thanks, but you really can't, Manny. Don't skip church—I probably need a few prayers said for me, and as for Monday, we're meeting with the accountant at twelve-thirty. It's important, but you'll have to handle that one without me, I'm afraid. Tax season is coming up and he wants to get us organized *before* the last minute. Mika has a good idea of what I wanted to bring up with him about some ideas to reduce the payable tax, so I suggest taking her along. I'll have Ana with me, and I promise to take a cab there and back. As soon as I'm out of the meeting and have any news at all, I'll send you a text to tell you to call when you can."

"Your word?"

"Of course."

"Done." He stuck his hand out and Jerry shook it.

Carmella spotted them out of the corner of her eye. "Manuel James Werinick, you had better not be talking business with this young man."

"Not at all, Lovey. Strictly personal."

"Good, because it's time we leave these two alone. Jerry needs to rest and Ana wants to get going in the kitchen."

"Carmella has given me a wonderful recipe that will fill you—*us*—up and give you strength, too. I had no idea that food was divided into groups and it was important to eat from each of them."

Jerry stood and looked from Manny to Carmella. "Thank you, both. I'm sorry I've been so sluggish. I'm pretty sure it's more mental than physical, but knowing that you're only a phone call away is going to make all of this so much easier to handle. You have your own lives to keep up with, too, though, so get the hell out of here and go do whatever it is you would be doing on a Saturday evening. Dine, dance, toss dwarves . . . whatever. I'm in the best hands with Ana, here, so git."

Plucking their jackets from the coat tree, Manny held Carmella's out for her and she slipped into it. "That's the Jerry I know. We've got all the confidence in the world that you're going to beat this thing."

Jerry managed a weak laugh. "I appreciate your optimism, Manny. Over the next few weeks I may have to borrow some of it."

"As much as you need, boyo. As much as you need."

With final hugs, and cheek-kisses with the ladies, Manny and Carmella were out the door and gone. Gently, quietly, Jerry pushed the door shut and leaned on it until the latch clicked. Ana kissed him on the cheek and flitted into the kitchen where she started working on dinner like a chemist preparing a formula.

JERRY PLACED THE signed consent form on the doctor's desk and laid the pen gently on top. "'Anaplastic Astrocytoma and the Brain Blood Barrier'. It sounds like the name of a Rob Zombie-Yoko Ono tribute band." Jerry tried to laugh at his own joke, but Dr. Kelly simply smiled patiently. "Sorry, Doc. I imagine you get a lot of patients who try to crack wise right about now." Jerry wanted to jump up and dance and joke and be the smartass he was in every other situation, but he couldn't even bring himself to let go of Ana's hand.

"It's a very common response to the situation, Jerry. That was quite an obscure reference, but I got it. Nicely done. I personally prefer jokes like yours to the anger some patients respond with. It doesn't happen often, but when the reaction is uncontrolled rage, my concern shifts from the patient to their loved ones. Someone that angry with me for simply being the bearer of the news is usually someone who will take that anger home and act it out. We offer counselling for all reactions, even denial." Dr. Kelly gestured at the computer screen the three of them faced. He had moved his chair to Jerry's side of the desk and spun the monitor around.

"As you can see by the blue lines and clumps, your tumour is extremely widespread." A 3D digital representation of Jerry's brain rotated slowly on the screen. "It's working its way through most sections of your brain, although it's largest near your brain stem. The technology that allows us to detect even the smaller gliomas may also allow us to treat it."

"You make it sound like there's a hope in hell that this alien-looking tumour can be beaten." Jerry waved in frustration at the screen.

"The hope is thin, I admit. I'm waiting to hear from a firm in Calgary. I've sent them a copy of your images to get their opinion."

"And in the meantime, what? Surgery?"

"No. It's too late for that. If we removed the entire tumour there wouldn't be enough of your brain left for you to function, and we still wouldn't know if we got it all. There are a few things we'll start with, but most importantly, as we discussed on Friday, we'll get you in on Monday—tomorrow—for a planning CT scan and then begin a course of radiation as soon as possible. The planning scan itself takes at least thirty minutes and it literally maps out your tumour for the radiotherapy. After the planning scan, it might be a week or two before we're ready to actually start the radiation. The computer plans the course of your therapy and when it's as complicated as yours, it can take a few weeks. This is unavoidable."

"Lovely." Except he didn't think it was. "I guess it will give me time to write a will and tie up loose ends. Doc?"

"The truth, Jerry? Yes. This is an aggressive form of cancer. The prognosis is rarely positive. The survival rate is measured in decimals below zero. If you're a stats person, I can get them for you. Many people need to hear the numbers to drive home the reality."

"Nah, I'm good, thanks. Let me summarize how I see it, and you tell me if I get anything wrong." He took a deep breath and squeezed Ana's hand. She remained silent but squeezed back. "I'm dying. Sooner rather than later. Since you can't amputate my head, a crani-ectomy isn't possible, so you'll be trying to find something that is. You'll be looking at everything anyone has ever tried with any degree of success, but this late on, the odds are so slim they've never really been measured. I'm game for anything you want to try, just so long as it doesn't make me worse or kill me faster. I guess that without a real, God-given miracle, I need to say goodbye to people, forever."

"It sounds like you understand perfectly. Any questions?"

"With or without treatment, what can I expect in terms of possible symptoms rearing their ugly heads?"

"This is your brain we're talking about, so predictions are tough, but you can probably expect more of everything you've already experienced, including memory loss, pain, nausea, seizures, even personality changes both permanent and temporary. I have an information sheet for you with links to every resource I use. The Internet is a great source of information but a massive source of *mis*information. I've vetted these resources myself and even contribute data and articles to two of them, so my recommendation is both personal and professional." He slid a sheet of crisp paper out of Jerry's file and placed it on the desk in front of Jerry. "Seizures are my biggest concern right now because you haven't really had any. You've had some blackouts and that one minor episode at your work, but nothing in comparison to what I've seen in other patients. With the extent of your tumour's growth it's only a matter of time."

"So avoid long road trips as the driver."

"Avoid driving. Period. Let Ana drive you where you need to go."

"Unfortunately she hasn't got a license."

"Not a problem. There's a network of volunteers who will gladly drive you to and from your appointments. Even without the potential of seizures, sometimes the treatments can hit you pretty hard and you need assistance. The phone number for that is on the sheet. There's also public transit and taxi. Some people don't like bothering strangers with what they see as silliness, but please know that some of these volunteers are cancer survivors themselves, or people who've lost someone to the disease, and they just want to give back or help out. It is a great service run through the Canadian Cancer Society. I know you're new to town, but cancer is part of your life now, and it levels the field and makes friends of complete strangers. There is support here. Make use of it."

"Thanks."

"I'm not just saying that to make it easy on *you*. The more you make use of the resources we have available, the easier it is on your family and friends. *Some* of them might be willing to trade places with you in an instant, but they *all* wish they could wave a magic wand over your head and make the cancer go away forever. You get to fight this disease through willpower and anger and desire to not let it win, but your loved ones can do nothing but learn about the disease, try to keep your spirits up, and help you when you need them. That's a lot of pressure for them. They'll spend more time in tears than you will because they feel so helpless."

The oncologist leaned in, to emphasize the importance of his point. "*You* don't have to look in a mirror if you don't want to,

Jerry, so you can form a thin barrier of self-denial mixed with hope. *They* can't look away from what both the disease and the treatments will do to you. Some days, inside, you'll feel just fine, but hair loss and weight loss and other changes will be right out where they see them and tear them up and make them feel like the weight of the world is on their shoulders. Terrific staff and volunteers will help, if you let them. Be strong, but don't let pride get in the way." He leaned back, again.

"Now, speaking of staff to help you, your Palliative Care Specialist should be here in a couple minutes. She would have been here from the beginning but, well, last minute calls are part of her duties."

"Palliative Care?"

"'Palliative' means 'relieving without curing'. Elizabeth can explain more succinctly what she does, but in short, while my team and I are trying to cure you, Elizabeth and her staff will be concerned with a more holistic view of your situation. In addition to your physical well-being, she'll offer professional advice, help you to understand options, offer a support system to help with the stress, and, should the disease win, help you to face it in comfort and dignity. Heck, she can even find you a lawyer to help you settle your affairs.

"You may be shocked to hear me admit that you might well lose this fight, Jerry, but you've seen for yourself how widespread it is. I plan on winning this fight with you because that's the only approach I know. I will give it everything I've got, because, frankly, I've seen miracles happen. I've seen a dying woman given six months to live only to get pregnant and have the cancer lose the battle as her baby grew inside her and their combined systems fought back. I've seen congregations pray and priests give last rights only to have a patient sit up and ask for a beer and a steak."

"That sounds like a great idea, right about now."

The doctor laughed. "Then as soon as Ms. Puleo is done with you, go have a steak and a beer. You're in for the fight of your life, literally, so you'd best start it with a full belly. In the meantime, though, I'll go confirm that Elizabeth is on her way. Would either of you like something to drink? Water, tea, coffee? We have one of those one-cup machines so my assistant has built up quite a selection. Chocolate-raspberry medium roast? Caramel decaf?

I'm going to make myself a green and white tea."

Ana looked at Jerry and raised an eyebrow. "Anything, my Sweet?"

He thought about it for a second and caved to temptation. "One of those chocolate-raspberry ones sounds great. Black. Please."

"You got it. Ana?"

"Thank you, no, doctor."

"Back in a minute or two, then."

ELIZABETH PULEO—THE Palliative Care Specialist—pretty much reiterated everything Dr. Kelly told them, so Jerry was ready for a ten-hour nap by the time the cab dropped them off at the loft. Ana helped him up the stairs, and once he was settled on the couch she made him a banana smoothie, like Carmella had taught her.

Jerry stretched and yawned. "Who knew a one hour meeting could be so draining. I feel like I've been run over by a train."

"You had best text Manny before you fall asleep." She ran the blender briefly. "Why not suggest he telephone after six o'clock this evening. That will give you time to have a nap."

"Good thinking. You must need to recharge, too. You've been up as long as I have."

"Do not fret about me, Mr. Powell. I am quite capable of looking after myself. As Miss Puleo said, I am your caregiver."

"She also said you weren't to wear yourself out."

"I will rest. I promise." She brought a tumbler of smoothie over to him. "Now drink this and I will go turn down your bed."

"Yes, boss lady," he said to her back as she stepped behind the screen. He drank the smoothie down.

"Exactly. Miss Puleo is a very wise lady and she put me in charge. You shall do exactly what I say or—"

"Or *what*, Shvibzik? You'll report me?"

"Not at all, sir." She peeked around the screen. "I will *spank* you."

"Then I'll have to report you, for physical abuse of someone under your care. I could sue you for damages. Bring you up on charges." His wink belied his words.

"You may try, sir, but the only thing I have of value is my love for you, and you already have all of it." She came to him on the couch, took the now-empty tumbler and placed it on the coffee table, then helped him up with the other. He started to protest but she silenced him with a quick kiss on the lips. In silence, Ana led Jerry to the bed. Slowly, gently, she lifted his sweatshirt up over his head and placed it on the chair. Then she undid the buttons of his flannel shirt, exposing his Property of Barenaked Ladies t-shirt. She suppressed a giggle when she read the words on the shirt, then gave him another quick kiss, handed him his pyjamas, and turned her back out of politeness.

"While you change, I will tidy up and send that text to Manny for you, if that is acceptable, my Sweet."

Jerry brushed her long braid aside and kissed the nape of her neck, his lips lingering, tickling. "That'd be perfect. Thank you, Shvibzik of my heart." She wiggled under the touch of his lips and then skipped away, to find the phone, he assumed. Exhausted, he finished changing and crawled into the big bed.

As he drifted off to sleep, he wondered how the hell he was going to have the strength to fight a battle he was probably going to lose in the end; and then he felt the sheets lift and fully-clothed Ana slipped into the bed behind him. He fell asleep with her arms around him and a silly, lopsided grin on his face.

"MANNY, I MIGHT as well come in for an hour or so tomorrow. I can double-check Mika's prep notes for the meeting with the accountant."

"Jerry, lad, you're both needed and *not* needed. I need you or I wouldn't have hired you, but I don't need you so badly that I'm going to put the station before your health."

"My CT planning scan thing isn't until just after one. We can make sure you're ready for the meeting, and then maybe I'll take Lee-Anne out for lunch."

"I don't think—"

"If I have to sit at home and do nothing, I'll drive Ana crazy. Worse still, if I have to sit on my ass and stress over everything, *I'll* snap."

"Right, then. Nine o'clock, for two hours, max."

"Two hours. Then lunch with Lee-Anne."

"I'll have to confirm that with her, make sure she's not over on the mainland tomorrow. To make it easy, though, assume the lunch is a go unless I send you a text otherwise."

"Done. See you then."

"Only because you insist, mate—*and* because your smiling face seems to have a positive effect around here. Make sure you take a cab, too."

"Yes, *Dad*."

"Smartass brat. I'd ground you, but you'd ignore me anyway. See you tomorrow."

"Will do."

Ana took the iPhone out of Jerry's hand almost as soon as he ended the conversation, and plugged it into the charger. "Now, if you please, send an email to your friend Isis. Maybe you will have time to use the Spike-thing to speak with her."

"Skype. S-K-Y-P-E." He smiled. She was right about needing to call Isis, and Skype was the only way to do it. Casual conversations were once okay for TDD telephone for the Hearing Impaired, but with the advancements of Skype and FaceTime and camera phones, there was little need for a touch-typing translator to be an intermediary in a long distance conversation with the deaf. Even when they lived twenty-feet apart, Isis Skyped Jerry whenever she couldn't drop by in person.

"'Skype'? What is the meaning?"

"I have no idea. It's not a word in English, yet."

"I will have to Google it, later." She handed him the laptop and he sank back into the cushions to send the email to Isis. The phone buzzed with an incoming text, and Ana took a quick look at the iPhone's screen. "It is from Mika. She says that Danveer's Uncle Palak is in town briefly and could she and Danveer bring him by to meet you tomorrow evening, at seven."

"Sure." He looked up from the keyboard. "I'll see her tomorrow at the office, but I suppose they want an answer tonight. Could you text her that seven tomorrow is cool, Shvibzik? Please?"

"Certainly, Jerr-Bear." She giggled, he laughed, and they both got down to sending their respective messages.

THE RAIN STARTED up just as Jerry finished cleaning the last of the spaghetti sauce off his plate with the heel of garlic loaf. The window rattled for his attention and the raindrops held that attention for a moment longer. "Looks like we'll have to postpone that walk. How about a movie, instead?"

"Something with Tom Hanks and Meg Ryan?"

"Sure. How about *You've Got Mail*?"

"A romantic story about the postal service? That could be quite interesting."

He walked his plate over to the sink where Ana was pouring the extra sauce into a jar. "It refers to email, not snail mail, though I think the original Hungarian play was about snail mail pen pals." He kissed the top of her head.

"'*Snail* mail'?"

"What we call regular postal service because, compared to email and text messages, it's as slow as a snail. Anyway, the movie is more about how true love can be hiding right under your nose the whole time."

"*That* sounds delightful."

HALF AN HOUR later they were curled up on the couch together, Ana giggling along with the staff of the Shop Around the Corner while Jerry drifted in and out of sleep.

"DARLING, WHAT IS a 'bucket list'?" Ana looked over the laptop to where Jerry was changing for bed behind the screen.

"It's a list of things a person wants to do before they die. Some people write one when they're young to give them something to aim for, and some write it when the end is getting closer, to make sure they get done the things that are important to them. Why? Where did you hear that expression?"

"On a blog titled 'Alice's Bucket List'. She was seventeen when she died of cancer but she made a 'bucket list' before she left."

"Ah." He wasn't sure where she was going with the conversation, whether she wanted to talk about cancer or dying or the young girl, Alice.

"Do you have a bucket list, my Sweet?"

He came out from behind the screen, tying the terry robe as he did. "Not really. I started one after I saw the movie, but I got distracted and never finished it."

"There was a movie about Alice?" She started typing on the laptop, searching for an answer.

"I have no idea. The movie I'm thinking of was *The Bucket List* with Jack Nicholson and Morgan Freeman. It's about two old men and their lists."

Ana looked up. "What was on your bucket list?"

"Just four or five things, I think. Go skydiving, which I did for my twenty-first birthday; swim with dolphins; manage a radio station . . . that's about it."

"That was all? That is *three* things."

He levered himself up off the couch and shuffled toward the bathroom to brush his teeth. He owed her the truth, but to actually say the words just might kill him. Remembering the last thing he wrote on that long-lost piece of paper suddenly brought home the fact that he was dying, that his bucket list was over and done. But Ana had asked, and if he owed anyone an answer, it was the ghost who finally made him think about life. "I wanted to . . . to hold my newborn son or daughter in my arms and see the future in their eyes." The weight of it all slammed into him and he stumbled. His hand reached for the kitchen counter, but Ana was there instead, catching him, holding him up. His knees gave out and he folded to the floor, her strength slowing his descent. She cradled him, and they wept together.

THE TAXI DROPPED Jerry off at the studio just before nine o'clock, after a not-so-quick detour to the downtown Tim Hortons coffee shop for two-dozen donuts and muffins. He was two steps into the lobby when Lee-Anne came out of nowhere, scooped the treats out of his hands, plunked them on the receptionist's counter, and wrapped Jerry in a huge, green, angora hug. He was surprised, but not so much that he didn't return the embrace, and then realize that his Sales Manager felt *really* good to hug. He gently broke free of her fuzzy, sweater-wrapped arms, accepting a kiss on his cheek before stepping back.

"Wow." His hand went to Ana's book in his jacket pocket, hoping that wherever she was, she couldn't sense his increased heart rate nor see him blush. If he wasn't sure about how much life was left in him, there was little doubt now, at least below the belt.

"Lunch. *My* treat, Jerry. I've got us a reservation at Puccini's. Now, you go do what you have to with Manny for two hours and I will come get you at precisely eleven." She finger-waved at him and practically skipped down the hall to her office.

"She's sure in a great mood. I hope it's catching."

"Lunch with her favourite boss has her excited." Mika stepped out of the mailroom and smiled.

"If she maintains that energy level through the whole meal she'll exhaust me." He accepted a quick but sincere hug from Mika and they started down the hall toward his office, the donuts and muffins forgotten.

"Lee-Anne feels terrible about how she reacted to your news on Saturday."

"She doesn't have to. If I could have run out of the room myself I would have. I've never dealt well with other people's illnesses, so I'm more than willing to look the other way if anyone else has trouble with mine. I sure won't take it personally."

"Please tell her that at lunch. She's been mumbling 'I hope Jerry doesn't hate me' every ten minutes. I finally just shut her office door so I could get some work done." They reached Jerry's office and Mika took her leave. "My prep notes for the meeting with the accountant are on your desk."

"Thanks, M. I appreciate it."

"Any time, Boss."

Jerry stepped into his office and Mika returned across the hall to her own office. He hadn't even hung his coat up when Manny appeared in the doorway.

"How're you feelin', Jerr? If I don't ask right off, then Carmella will have my head. She was livid when she heard you were coming in, then I told her you were driving Ana bonkers so she relented that maybe we could find you a few light duties for two hours until lunch with Lee-Anne."

"Thanks, but I can handle a little more than light duties. I'd like to talk about the meeting with the accountant but also to go over some ideas I had about our late-night format."

"Excellent. Get settled, check your emails or whatever and come by when you're ready."

CHAPTER NINETEEN

@TheTaoOfJerr: "Hell is full of musical amateurs."
~George Bernard Shaw

ALMOST ON CUE, Jerry's rumbling stomach called a halt to the work session at 10:55. "Lunch time, Jerr." The two men stood up from their notes spread on the conference room table where Jerry had moved them after he realized the printouts wouldn't fit on either his own or Manny's desks. He twisted slowly, working the kinks out of his back while Manny rubbed the back of his own neck, towering over the table. "Do you need any suggestions for lunch?"

"Thanks, but she's picked some Italian place that starts with 'P', I think." Not only couldn't he remember the name of the restaurant, but the name of his Sales Manager had slipped away from him, too!

"Puccini's?"

"That's the place, I think." He sat back down, suddenly confused. "A restaurant?"

"You bet. You all right, Jerr?"

"I'm not sure. Why am I going to a restaurant?"

"Lunch. With Lee-Anne. Damn. You've got me worried, mate. You can postpone this, you know, 'til you're feeling up to it."

"Lee-Anne? Oh, right." He shook the mental dust from his

thoughts. “No, I should be okay. It’s just lunch.”

“You sure?”

“Yeah. No problem, Manny. Just a little brain fart. I’m good.” He said the words, but he wasn’t all that certain. There were holes in his memory, like how he’d got to the office, and what he was supposed to be doing after lunch. It both scared and angered him, but he couldn’t let Manny know, or he’d tell his wife and she’d hire a nurse to look after him. He supposed he’d have to start using his phone’s Calendar and Contacts apps more, to keep track of the details of everyday life. Or maybe just lean on Ana a bit more, like Carmella said.

Manny patted him on the back and ushered him out into the corridor. “Go get your coat and I’ll go tell Lee-Anne we’re done,” then he strode silently off down the carpeted corridor and around the corner. Jerry wandered into his office and grabbed his coat. Rather than put it on, though, he slumped in the guest chair and laid the coat on his lap. For some reason he just ran out of steam. He could feel the book in the coat’s inside pocket and found some strength in that. Wondering if Mika would be willing to accept the book and its resident when he died, he finally shrugged into the coat and stepped out into the corridor, just as Lee-Anne bounced out of her office behind Manny.

“Lunch with my favourite boss! Woohoo!” She linked her arm through Jerry’s but Manny stopped her with a light touch of his long fingers on her shoulder.

“Remember what we talked about, Lee-Anne. A nice, relaxed lunch, and then make sure he gets to his appointment after.”

Her smile slipped away, but only because she wanted Manny to know that she was taking him seriously. “Of course, Manny. You really can count on me.”

“I know. Now, go. Chat. Eat. Try the Cajun Beef Lasagna. Expense it, but please spend at least two minutes talking about business.”

Jerry smiled. “A whole two minutes? You’re such a slave driver.” And he let Lee-Anne lead him out to the street where she flagged a taxi faster than he’d ever seen before. As they climbed in, he muttered, “That was impressive. It would have taken me five minutes, at least.”

Lee-Anne giggled and hugged his arm. “It’s one of the advantages of these curves. In summer they practically fight over who gets the fare. I used to be proud of it, but after what you said the other day, I'm not so sure anymore. I'm a person, not a pair of . . . well, *you* know."

"Not first hand, but I understand what you're saying."

THE TRIP WAS a short one by cab and their table was waiting in a corner, surrounded by old black and white photos depicting streets, people, and the jazz scene. As the hostess seated them, Lee-Anne turned to Jerry. "Do you mind a corner seat, Jerry? The window tables are lovely, but it's hard to talk when the world is watching us like fish in a tank."

"This is fine, Lee-Anne." And it was. The place wasn't big, but the high ceiling and quiet jazz music in the background swallowed the lunchtime chatter before it reached the other tables. If Ana ate, this would be a terrific place to bring her. He saw a drum kit in the corner. "They have music here?"

"Jazz, blues, mostly the mellow stuff."

"That's cool. I'll have to bring Ana. She's developing a taste for jazz."

Lee-Anne reached over and took his hand. "How's she doing with all of this?"

"She's holding up really well. She's my rock, along with everyone at the station, of course."

A waiter swung by, took their drink orders, and slipped away so quickly it was surreal.

"If she needs to talk to anyone about it, please have her call me. If she's half as scared as I was when my sister got sick, she's probably feeling pretty helpless. How about your family? Aren't they back in Ontario? They must be going crazy with you this far away right now."

"I'm not surprised your sister's illness scared you. Manny said you're twins."

"Identical, except she was the pretty one."

Jerry choked on his water. "The . . . ?"

"A joke, Jerry. I know *I'm* beautiful because I look just like her and I always thought she was the most beautiful girl in the world. That's not ego talking. Mary-Anne's beauty was soul-deep. She never got into half the trouble I did. The boys all noticed her, too, but she didn't care a bit. I wasn't so lucky. I probably cared too much." A glass of white wine and a tumbler of ginger ale arrived.

"Did you want to try Manny's suggestion? I love their lasagna."

"Sure. I might as well enjoy solid food while I can."

Lee-Anne smiled up at the waiter. "Two of the Cajun Beef Lasagna, please, Karl. With house salads . . ." She raised an eyebrow at Jerry and he nodded. "And the Italian dressing, please." Karl smiled back and left. "So, your family. What did they say?"

"Nothing. I haven't called, yet. It's a hard thing to do long distance. I have a young friend I'm going to Skype tonight and break the news to, so that'll probably be the rehearsal for telling my mother. We haven't always seen eye-to-eye, so it'll be an interesting conversation."

"But it's still one you have to have. Mary-Anne was a very private person, so she told just her girlfriend and me in the beginning. The first words out of her mouth to me were 'Go get a mammogram, tomorrow.' She didn't tell my parents for another month, until she was well into the treatments. They were still having trouble with her being gay, so she didn't speak to them very often." She sipped her wine. Jerry could tell it was painful for her, but he couldn't think of anything to say or do. "My parents are great people, although a bit too conservative for my taste. But as soon as Mary-Anne told them, their arms and hearts were wide open for both Mary-Anne and Charise. Tell your family. Soon."

"I will. I promise. After the planning scan today, I might know a bit more. My mother tends to be a little judgmental, with the emphasis on mental, so the more facts I have when I call, the less criticism I'll have to listen to about whether or not it's psychosomatic or something else entirely, like drugs."

She laughed. "I don't envy you. I'm glad you'll have Ana there with you. What is it about parents judging their children as inadequate or unable to make their own decisions? I never see my parents without Tom with me. That's *Tom's* idea, because he knows I'd rip into them and take out all my anger at Mary-Anne's death on them."

"Do you get tested regularly?"

She lit up and lowered her voice. "Jerr-bear, my breasts get squished so often I'm thinking of leaving Tom for the screening machine."

Their laughter was interrupted by the arrival of lunch. Karl offered fresh-grated Parmesan cheese and fresh ground pepper, and they both accepted generous sprinklings of each. He then left with a smile and a promise to come back with refills for their drinks. Jerry waited politely for Lee-Anne to take her first forkful, and then he dug in, suddenly famished. They ate for a few minutes in silence, save for mumbled approvals of taste and texture, but Jerry finally had to ask a question that kept nagging at him.

"Did she ever give up? Mary-Anne, that is. Did she ever get so tired of the whole cancer thing and just want to flop on the couch and just stay there until her time was up? I mean, I haven't even started radiation and have only known about this shit growing in my head for a little while, but I'm just so exhausted, emotionally."

"Not in the beginning, no." Lee-Anne put her fork down on her plate, gently. "Mary-Anne laughed and smiled and fought and raised awareness and funds for breast cancer research, but after her second radical mastectomy, it was like someone punched her in the gut, every day. In the beginning there was a lot of hope and promise and everyone had their fingers crossed, but when the treatments started losing ground to the disease, yeah, the couch became her best friend."

"I love my couch these days. I wish I didn't."

"And I wish I knew a secret to give you hope or cheer you up or get you off that couch. Charise was able to get Mary-Anne up for a while, but even love and affection run out of steam, as my dad said. If I let my imagination loose, and we were both single and you weren't my boss, I could come up with more than a few things to give you energy and a reason to live, but I can't. That's Ana's job and I would never insult either her or Tom by suggesting it beyond this table. Besides, that's just my mischievous sex drive talking, trying to make you smile. Charise and I have had long, long talks about this, and in the end, it was more about Mary-Anne dying with peace and dignity. We made sure she got to say everything she wanted to everyone she had to." Lee-Anne's voice softened to a barely audible whisper and Jerry had to lean in a bit to hear her. "She said her last goodbyes to Charise and me at the same time, while we held her hands to our hearts. Peace, and dignity, Jerry."

"I guess that's all anyone can ask for. She was lucky to have you."

"It's what sisters are for." She picked up her fork and continued to eat, her eyes glistening with sadness.

"Yeah, I suppose. I'm sure my sister would be glad to do that for me, but we'd probably have to gag my mother if she was in the room, too."

They finished their meals over less-important small talk about life in Victoria, Lee-Anne's children, and Jerry's newly acquired skill on the dance floor. Lee-Anne switched to green tea after her second glass of wine and they kept up the conversation right through dessert. Jerry suspected that they would have kept up the banter right up to dinner, but the alarm on his phone went off. He pulled it out and read the message on the screen.

"I've got forty minutes until my appointment."

"Lots of time. What is it they're doing today?"

"The planning scan, I think it's called. This is the long one where they scan the tumour in depth and then use the data to plan the course of treatment."

"Is Ana meeting you there? Because I can hang out with you if she isn't." Jerry believed she really would, too.

"She's meeting me at the hospital. She had to take care of a few things and wanted to let us have our lunch together."

"She's a real cutie, Jerry. She's funny and smart and there's a retro-old-Europe-kinda-thing about her that makes me feel like I'm talking to someone who's seen the whole world. She's a keeper."

"I suppose. As much as either of us can be 'keepers', I guess." He let it drop at that.

The bill arrived, Lee-Anne used her company credit card, and lunch was on Manny. They got another taxi almost as fast as the first one and pulled up at the hospital a few minutes later. Lee-Anne moved to get out of the cab with Jerry, but he put a hand on her thigh, stopping her.

"Thanks, Lee-Anne, but I've got it from here. Ana will be here in a couple minutes and Manny just said for you to make sure I got here. You've been a real boost to my spirits, but you should get back to the office to do what you do so well and keep that place solvent. Just remember that you're bright, talented, and beautiful, *in that order*. I'm sure that wherever Mary-Anne is, she's damned proud of you." Lee-Anne was speechless. Tears trickled down her cheeks so Jerry reached up and wiped one away. "Thanks for lunch. I'll see you at the office tomorrow." He got out of the taxi and walked into the hospital, looking around for a good place to free Ana from the book.

He found the Food Court and the Info Desk, but no place that he could have thirty seconds unaccosted. The ding of an elevator arriving decided it for him. "I guess we ride up and down until we're alone." There were two people on the elevator when the doors opened and although both exited, an older woman joined him. She pressed the 3 and looked up at him.

"You going to 3, too?"

"Um, no." He looked at the panel, pressed the top button, then leaned back against the comfort of the mirrored wall. He closed his eyes for a moment but the elevator arrived at the third floor. The woman left, but no one got on, so Jerry whipped the book out of his pocket, rubbed his thumb along the spine, and hoped that Ana had enough time.

The elevator started up, the book glowed blue, and Ana slowly took shape beside him. She was still too transparent for comfort when they passed the fourth floor, but Jerry sensed the elevator slow for the fifth and held his breath. As she coalesced, Ana assessed the situation and the risk and floated behind Jerry and into the corner nearest the buttons. The elevator drifted to a stop on the fifth floor and just as the door slid slowly open, Jerry felt a hand touch his shoulder and lips kiss his ear. Two doctors entered the box, too wrapped up in their own conversation about a patient with some kind of arrhythmia to pay much attention to the couple who stepped into the back corner. One of the men pressed the button for the next floor.

"How was lunch with Miss Giggles-and-Wiggles?" Ana whispered in Jerry's ear. He turned to face her.

"It was good. It was a cute little restaurant not far from the loft and they have jazz there on weekends, so all I could think of the whole time was when I'm going to take you there."

"You thought of *me*, while you were out to lunch with a beautiful woman? Silly man." The elevator stopped, the doctors exited, still oblivious. No one else got on. Jerry checked his watch. They still had twenty minutes to get over to the BC Cancer Wing. The elevator clunked upward.

"Of course. I think about you all the time. We even talked a bit about you. Lee-Anne thinks you're charming and a keeper."

"A 'keeper'?"

"It means that I'm never supposed to let you go." He pulled her in and kissed her firmly.

The elevator dinged and stopped. They reluctantly stepped back from the kiss as the doors opened. They were one stop from the top. An elderly man in hospital gown and robe rolled his IV-equipped wheelchair in and winked at them. "Don't tell them, but I'm running away." He looked at the illuminated button for the top floor. "They got a nice view from up there. I sneak out every chance I get. I figure I've got a half hour of peace and quiet before they miss me. A half hour of Heaven, away from prodding, poking, and pills."

Ana laughed, "I sympathize completely, good sir. My younger brother was always looking for places to hide from the doctors and nurses." She winked back at him. "We promise not to tell anyone you are here."

The man smiled broadly, his huge dentures dominating his tiny face. "You're a sweetie!" The doors opened and he wheeled himself out as fast as he could, rolling around the corner and out of sight. They laughed, and Jerry pushed the button for the Main floor.

"I guess we should get to that appointment, Shvibzik. You know that this scan is going to take as long as an hour. I hope you brought something to read."

Ana gently tugged the Blake book out of Jerry's hand. "Always." She snuggled into him and he put his arms around her, drawing strength from her presence.

ANA DIDN'T READ very much while Jerry was having the planning scan done. She was fascinated by the whole process and watched intently as the staff shaved a small patch of hair on Jerry's head and then drew three small marks in the area with a black pen. They explained that it was to help take measurements and aim the device, and they would do tiny permanent tattoos after this scan. They then positioned Jerry on the flat, padded table they called a couch, cradling Jerry's head in a mould made specifically for him, to keep his head perfectly still. The radiographer, Gemma, gladly explained everything as they went along, to reassure both Ana and Jerry.

"The couch will move in and out and in and out of the 'polo

hole' here as the scan is performed. It's perfectly safe. Nothing will touch you or hurt you. If you need us for an emergency, just raise your hand and we'll be right in."

Jerry tried to look up without moving his head. "You're not in here with me? That doesn't exactly fill me with confidence."

"The scan is perfectly safe for any single patient through the course of their treatments, Jerry, but we do so many of these that over our careers, the effects would accumulate. Don't your dentist and his staff step behind a shielded wall, too?"

"I suppose."

"Same thing here. Ana's welcome to come back with us. She'll be able to watch everything on the monitors. See? You're on camera, there . . . there . . . and there." Gemma pointed to three cameras positioned to keep an eye on Jerry at all times.

IT TOOK THIRTY-six minutes, according to the clock on the wall that Ana could see, and every time the mechanical couch moved Jerry back in through the hole, she clenched her fists. Everything *looked* safe, but she didn't understand most of what was happening and so she worried. When it was all over, she followed Gemma and the staff back into the scanning room where they helped Jerry to sit up and handed him a glass of water.

Gemma wheeled over an elevated metal tray like a dentist's.

"The marks I made earlier will wash off, so I'm going to tattoo three tiny, permanent marks. They'll be no bigger than small freckles." She picked a tool off the tray and quickly did her work. She helped him off the couch and back onto the floor. His steps were a bit unsteady, so Ana guided him to a chair and put his shoes on for him.

"How are you feeling, Love?"

He twisted his neck slightly, to loosen a kink. "Stiff, but okay. A strange experience, that's for sure. How did it look on the monitors?"

"I was worried. I am not one hundred percent certain what this 'radiation' is and it frightens me."

"Yeah, well, if you knew what it was it would probably still scare the crap out of you." He took a couple steps, with Gemma close at hand and Ana holding his elbow. "I'm fine, thanks. Ready to go home and relax, maybe watch a movie."

Gemma smiled and handed him a small appointment card.

"That's terrific, Jerry. I've booked you in for your first treatment on January 30th, that's three weeks from tomorrow. With a scan this complicated, it will take that long for the computer to plan your treatments; but if you have any questions between now and then, please call or email me. The information is on the back of the card. Or you can contact your Palliative Care Specialist, Elizabeth. That goes for you, too, Ana. Don't be afraid to ask us any questions at all. We want you to fully understand this process. Jerry's illness is serious, but there's nothing about the radiation treatments that you need to be afraid of."

"Thank you, Miss Gemma."

"Yeah, thanks, Gemma. I guess we'll see you in three weeks."

Ana led him out and with every step he became steadier.

"That whole thing was so painless and simple that just maybe radiation will do the trick."

"That is what I pray for."

"Prayers are always welcome."

"Home, my prince?"

"Home sounds perfect, my Imperial Shvibzik."

Three taxis waited in a queue in the front driveway, so they were back in the loft in less than fifteen minutes. Jerry swung his feet up on the couch while Ana went in search of a second blanket.

"Jerry, something is amiss."

"You mean other than you, *Miss* Romanova?"

"Yes, smarty."

"How so?"

She returned with the blanket that was usually draped over the chair next to the bed. "Before we departed the flat this morning, I made up the bed, emptied the washer of dishes, and closed the kitchen up."

"I know. Thank you." He accepted the blanket from her and spread it over himself and the spot he was saving for her next to him. Ana went into the kitchen.

"You misunderstand me, Love. I tell you this not to boast nor to receive accolades, but to point out that the bed is now unmade, three of the kitchen cupboards are open, and most of your dry goods are arrayed on the counter top."

"I'm guessing that's not how you left it."

She put boxes away and closed the cupboard doors.

"Not at all. Were you by any chance searching for something

before we departed?"

"Honestly? I have no idea. Like you once said, I can't remember what I don't remember. I have no memory of it, but obviously I was. Sorry about that. Just leave the mess and I'll clean it up later."

Ana returned to the couch. "Do not be silly. It is all done, except the bed, which can wait." She wiggled her way under the blanket and cuddled up to him. "Now, if this fair residence is run as a democracy, I wish to put forth a motion that we watch a movie."

"Seconded. All in favour?"

"Aye." She giggled.

"Aye. Motion passed. Do you have a preference?" Jerry handed Ana the remote. "Just flip through and find something that looks interesting." He closed his eyes and leaned back.

ANA FOUND A movie she was both horrified and fascinated by. Jerry must have dozed off because he was startled by her gasp. He turned his head and opened one eye to see the opening titles rolling for *Anastasia*, starring Ingrid Bergman. "Oh, shit." He struggled to sit up. "Are you sure you want to watch this?"

"Mr. Powell, that must be the silliest question you have *ever* asked me." She frowned at him. "It was one thing to listen to that offensive disco song about Grigori, but now I have found a movie about me, or someone pretending to me."

"Of course. Silly me. I've never actually seen it, myself."

"Then let me light a fire in the hearth, dim the lights, pour you a smoothie, and we will enjoy this little fiction together."

Jerry paused the film. "Sold. Since I can't see the screen too well, if I drift off again, just make sure I'm awake in time to Skype Isis." He settled under the afghan, but was unfortunately sound asleep before Ana returned to the couch with the smoothie.

Ana put the smoothie back in the refrigerator and once again slipped under the afghan and blanket with her love.

"ISIS, I'D LIKE you to meet Ana." Jerry spoke as he signed, so that Ana knew what he was saying to Isis.

"Hi, Ana!" Isis signed and waved. She spoke aloud, too, out of politeness.

Ana waved back. "Hello, Isis. It is indeed a pleasure to meet you." Although Isis could read lips, Jerry wasn't sure that she'd be able to read Ana's, due to the less-than-perfect resolution of the Skype link through the internet. He signed Ana's words for her.

"Jerry and Ana, this is Chad . . ." A slender, freckle-faced teen with bangs nearly over his eyes and a faint, blond, starter-moustache, slid into sight and waved. Isis let them all wave at each other before she dropped what she thought was a bombshell. "Chad is . . . my boyfriend." She leaned over and kissed his cheek. He blushed and Jerry did his best not to laugh out loud. Chad was just like he was at that age—wary of public displays of affection, especially in front of strangers.

Ana leaned in. "Congratulations, Isis and Chad! I am Jerry's girlfriend. I think." She winked at them.

"Yes, of course you are, Shvibzik."

Isis held her arm up for them to see. "Jerry, I'm wearing your sweater."

"I noticed that. It looks better on you than it ever did on me."

"You're silly. Do you want it back, now that we've both moved on?" Her frown told him everything he needed to know.

"Now who's being silly? That was a gift between two dear friends. Just because we have a new boyfriend or girlfriend doesn't mean that we stop being important to each other. It's yours forever. It's not like I need it, anyway."

"What do you mean? I thought you had snow out there."

"We did. It was unexpected and beautiful." Kind of like Ana, he thought.

"Then why don't you need a sweater?"

Shit. This was the entire reason for the call, but it didn't mean he was happy about it. "Isis, sweetie, I have some news. Are your Mom and Dad there, like I asked?"

"Of course. I'll get them." She turned in her chair and shouted over her shoulder. "MOM! DAD! Jerry wants to say hi! He has some news!"

Isis' parents, Teresa and Scott, slipped into the frame. "Hey, Jerr."

"Hi, Jerry."

"Hey, Teri, Scott. Good to see you."

Teresa looked closer at the screen. "Jerry, have you lost weight? Too much salmon and not enough good Ontario beef?"

"Not exactly, although Pacific salmon is incredible."

Isis waved to get his attention. "Hello! *News!* You can talk about the menu later! Holy crap, people. Priorities!"

A weak laugh escaped from Jerry, in spite of the bombshell on the tip of his own tongue. "Isis is right. If I don't tell you now, I might chicken out." He took a deep breath and Ana squeezed his arm. He rushed ahead. "Those headaches I was having . . . it turns out I have brain cancer. It's really far along, it's inoperable, it's terminal, and I start radiation in a few weeks. We have our fingers crossed and our hopes up, but, the truth of the matter is, I'm dying."

Isis sobbed, jabbed her finger at her keyboard and the connection was broken before anyone could say a thing. The last thing Jerry saw before Skype told him what he already knew about the connection was Isis' face looking like he'd stabbed her in the heart.

"Um, that didn't go so well. I guess I'd better work on my delivery before I tell my family." He sagged into the couch, cheeks wet with tears. Ana simply hugged him, having no words of her own to add.

They sat like that for a while before Ana kissed away his tears, extricated herself from his arms, and stood up. "You, my Love, must eat. Mika and Danveer will be over after dinner, but first you must eat."

"I really don't have the energy."

"You are giving up? Letting this disease defeat you already?"

"That's not fair. The whole thing is finally starting to sink in. I just told people I love that I'm dying."

"Yes, you did, and my heart breaks with yours, Love; but although I saw the damage that stubbornness can wreak when Father stood by some of his less popular and ineffective decisions, stubbornness is *exactly* what you need to face this cancer disease." She moved around the kitchen, retrieving what she needed to make dinner. "You face overwhelming odds, you are not expected to live a long life, and the doctors cannot do very much for you. Does this sound familiar? Like anyone I have spoken to you about, many times?"

"Your little brother."

"*Da*, precisely. Alexei. You two have much in common, but do not forget the one thing that is greater than all of the darkness you are facing now, and he faced back then. You both have love. *My* love. I may be a silly ghost with nothing but the dress and boots I died in and the book I am trapped in, but I love you. I will not let you face this foe alone, but I cannot fight this battle *for* you."

"I'm sorry."

"Do not be sorry, be *stubborn*. And go wash your hands before dinner. You are starting with a fruit salad and then those potato puffs you love so much, with asparagus and chicken pot pie, although the pie is in a tin foil plate and not a pot."

He pushed himself up and started toward the bathroom. "Just in case I haven't told you in a while, you are my favourite Shvibzik."

"I am your *only* Shvibzik, Mister Powell, now, less talking and more washing. Let Mademoiselle le Chef do her job." She blew him a kiss and turned away to fetch down a clean plate.

"Women . . ." He let the thought trail off, knowing that she was perfectly correct.

"I ASSURE YOU, the book was not in the apartment." Petrov couldn't stop his hands from shaking and nearly dropped the phone. "I searched high and low, Doctor Professor." It wasn't the first time he'd broken into a place to acquire an object for a buyer, but it was the first time he'd failed, and the mainland academic's voice was an animalistic growl in his ear.

"You're an idiot. *Blya razocharovaniye*. If, as you insist, he has no idea of its value, he's not going to be carrying the damned thing around with him. It was there, you just couldn't see it, old man."

"*Dah*. It must be my old eyes. I am sorry, Doctor Professor."

"I don't give a shit. This *kid* has one of the most incredible pieces of Romanov history and I will have it in my collection."

He hated what he was going to say, but Petrov knew he had to make the offer. "I will try again."

"No. You'll stay the hell away from them. I didn't get the impression that neither the radio DJ nor his dance partner are stupid. The last thing I need is them twigging to what they have and then sticking it out of reach in a safe deposit box. *I* will take care of it, and once I have this little gem in my hands, you and I will discuss your future." The call was disconnected abruptly.

The elderly antique dealer was so relieved at not having to make a second attempt that he nearly missed the threat. Petrov had never personally been the target of Gervaise's wrath, but there were more than enough rumours to frighten him. He knew that the Doctor Professor taught anthropology at Vancouver University, and he wore a delicate French surname, but there was a Bolshevik hiding behind those dark, soulless eyes. His hands started to shake in earnest and lowered himself into his chair. *I'm too old for this crap.*

CHAPTER TWENTY

@TheTaoOfJerr: "After silence, that which comes nearest to expressing the inexpressible is music."

~Aldous Huxley

DANVEER'S DIMINUTIVE, SIXTYISH Uncle Palak couldn't take his eyes off of Ana. Although he was speaking with Jerry, his eyes kept darting to Ana's shy smile. "Jerry, young sir, Mika has explained to you about auras and energy, yes?"

"Somewhat. She showed me that she could push me without touching me, which was kinda freaky, but pretty cool. I also did some surfing on the Net to learn a bit more."

"Excellent. What I would like to do—" He closed his eyes and shook his head, then looked straight at Ana. "You should not be here, young lady."

Ana stood, her smile slipping away. "I apologize. I will go for a walk if you wish." She picked up the book and started for the coat tree.

Palak waved his hands dismissively and shook his head again, his voice softer than his words. "No, no, no. Not here, in this room or apartment, but not in this *world*. You should have moved on. What is it that you desire so strongly that you have kept rebirth at bay?"

Danveer chuckled nervously. "Uncle, what are you yabbering

about? What did I say on the way over about not insulting our hosts?"

"Miss Ana, have I insulted you in any way?" He placed his palms together in front of his face and made a small bow. "If so, please forgive me. I'm only speaking of what I see."

Ana looked to Jerry for guidance but he could only shrug. He had no idea what they should say, what to admit to. He patted the couch next to him and Ana joined him, placing the book in the pouch of the hoodie she was wearing. "No insult, Mr. Palak, sir. What is it that you see, exactly?"

"Would you take my hand, please? And call me *Uncle*." He reached out to Ana, his hand open and palm up. Ana placed her hand on his and the old man gasped. He released Ana's hand slowly. "Thank you. I would love to hear your story while I work with Jeremy. Would you mind?"

Ana shrugged, unsure. "If Jerry does not mind."

"It's your story, Shvibzik. I just ask one thing of everyone, though." He glanced at each of them in turn. "Whether you believe Ana or not when she's done, none of this is spoken of outside this loft, to *anyone*. Please. Mika? Danveer? Uncle Palak?"

"Of course, Boss."

"No problem, Jerr."

"Certainly not. I mean, I agree. I will certainly not discuss it."

It was Jerry's turn to shrug. "Okay, Shvibzik, go for it."

"*Every*thing, Jerry?"

"You might as well. In for a penny . . . "

". . . in for a pound, my Sweet." She settled in beside Jerry, bringing her feet up under her and taking his hand in both of hers. "My full name is Anastasia Nicholaevna Romanova. My proper title is Grand Duchess. I was born on June 18, 1901. I died on July 17, 1918."

Danveer laughed. "Yeah. Nice try. Do we look stupid?" His uncle cuffed him on his thigh with the back of his hand and Mika flashed him a disappointed look.

"Shvibzik, you might as well show them, right off the start. It'll get rid of the doubt so that the rest will all make sense. Go slowly, though, so they can be sure." He flashed a sad half-smile and nodded at Ana. A moment later she began to fade. The sweatshirt and pants collapsed onto the couch. Mika and Danveer gasped in shock, Uncle Palak in delight. Eventually Ana returned to the book, which Jerry carefully picked up and placed on his lap. "She'll tell you all about it, but this book belonged to Ana. My great-grandfather picked it up in Russia, in July, 1918." He caressed the cover and Ana faded back in to join them. Their guests were silent.

"I died when I was seventeen," Ana continued. "This is how I appeared." She morphed to her younger self. "This is me if I was twenty-two." She returned to the age they knew her at, getting a bit taller, her curves filling out, and her hair returning to her preferred length, thick braid included.

Danveer whispered to Jerry, "Holy shit! Do you have anything stronger to drink than tea, Jerr? This is totally messed up."

"You bet. The cabinet above the sink. Help yourself to whatever you like. Anyone else? Mika? Uncle Palak?"

"No, thank you." Mika's sad eyes followed Danveer into the kitchen but she said nothing.

"Thank you, no, Jerry. And if you will lean back into the cushions, I would like to explore your illness, if I may."

"Okay." He relaxed while the swami got up and moved around behind him on the couch. Danveer went to the kitchen, poured himself a couple ounces of rye, and returned to his seat. Jerry nodded to Ana. "Sorry to interrupt, Shvibzik. Please go on."

WHILE ANA RECOUNTED her adventures in Victoria and tried vainly to answer Mika's questions about where she went and what it felt like when she was in the book, Uncle Palak's hands moved slowly around Jerry's head, never quite touching him, but never straying too far. Jerry closed his eyes and let both the gentle touch on his energy fields and the sound of Ana's voice soothe him.

As the swami worked his "magic", Jerry felt a fog clear from his head. Or maybe it was like washing a day's worth of cycling road dust off in a shower. But it also felt like a lawn might, when freshly raked of fallen leaves and once again able to reach up and feel the sunshine on the individual blades of grass. The leadenness of his limbs was brushed away and every now and then he felt a little push to one side or the other as pressure was applied to his aura or energy field or whatever was being manipulated during the strange process.

It went on and on and Jerry let himself drift, not hearing the actual words spoken, nor seeing the expressions on their guests' faces as Ana's fantastic tale enthralled them. He remembered the limestone buildings lining the steep hill of St. Marys' main street, Isis' smile when he gave her the sweater she wanted so badly, the tangy smell of the Pacific Ocean when he stood on the upper deck of the ferry, and the radiant look on Ana's face when she was dancing at the Empress Hotel. There were no headaches, no seizures, and no mental confusion. His world was all clarity and sunlight. Just when he didn't think his world could get any brighter, or clearer, he simply opened his eyes at some subtle signal from Uncle Palak.

"How do you feel, Jeremy?"

"Um, *wow*?" He couldn't stop himself from smiling and once he started smiling he couldn't do anything *but* smile. He looked to each of them in turn, Uncle Palak last, as the swami came around and once again sat opposite Jerry in the chair. Ana settled herself gently on the couch and took Jerry's hand again. He squeezed back, lovingly. "I haven't felt this clear-headed in what seems like years. Have you just cured me?"

"Sadly, Jeremy, no. What ails you, *I* cannot heal. It has spread far and wide throughout your brain. I was able to improve your blood flow, clear up much clutter, get rid of some very old clumps of emotional mud, and realign your energy fields so that you are receptive to the healing energy of the nearby ocean, but healing your tumour is beyond me, I am afraid. I certainly hope that isn't what you expected from my visit. Is that what Mika led you to believe?" He looked at Mika with confusion.

Jerry shook his head. "Not at all. She just said not to expect anything spectacular, but that you might be able to bring me a little peace. At least I *think* that's what she said. Sometimes I can't even remember Ana's name, let alone where I work or who with."

"I understand. Maybe what I have done will help with that somewhat. Maybe. I think what is most important is that you keep positive, which will understandably be very difficult in the coming weeks and months. I cannot give you the entire Hindu philosophy lecture in the short time I am here, but I will have Mika email you some links and give you some books and audio discs which will be a start."

"I'm not exactly the religious type, Uncle."

"That is, as they say, 'okay', Jeremy. You are very ill, and although the medical doctors will do all they can to extend your life, I just want to help you prepare a little for what comes next. Whether it comes in months, or years, it is a beautiful thing and thinking about it should bring you peace and joy, not stress and heartache." He smiled at Ana. "Of course, this is what I believed until I met this absolutely charming young lady. Maybe the materials will help you *both* to find peace so that when the time comes, it will be serene and blissful. In truth, that is all any of us can really ask for in this life." Checking his watch, he stood abruptly. "Please excuse my rudeness, but I have to be in court first thing tomorrow and am meeting my client at his home in Oak Bay in an hour."

Everyone else stood, Danveer and Mika going for their coats. Jerry extended his hand to Uncle Palak. "Thank you very much for your time, sir. I do feel better, and whether it's psychological or whatever, I appreciate it."

"It is my pleasure. I would be pleased to come again in a week or two, if you wish." Danveer helped his uncle into his wool trench coat.

"Of course. I'd like that a lot. Maybe on an evening when we can relax and talk more about, well, about what I have to look forward to."

"Yes, yes. I was going to suggest the same thing. Also, if time permits, I would love to hear all about this truly unique young lady's experiences in the Imperial Court. Only the joyous times, of course." He winked at Ana and she giggled.

"We would love to welcome you back, Uncle Palak, and it would bring me great joy to answer any questions you may have." She hugged the swami, much to his delight.

FAREWELLS WERE DISTRIBUTED evenly and soon Ana and Jerry were once again alone in the loft, the crackling of the fire in the hearth and the bubbling air pump in Sushi's tank the only sounds. Ana kissed Jerry on the cheek and went to the laptop where she logged onto iTunes. "I do so hope that I can find that musician Uncle Palak recommended." She was still amazed by how much information was simply at her fingertips.

"Ravi Shankar? Shouldn't be a problem. He was pretty popular, especially with George Harrison." She looked over and saw him pick up his phone, look at the screen, and then toss it on the coffee table. His other hand went to his temple.

She spun the chair around to face him. “What is wrong?”

“I wanted to call my sister but it’s too late.” He stomped into the kitchen and started rifling through the refrigerator.

“It is only half-past-eight.”

“Here, it’s eight-thirty, but she’s three hours ahead of us, in Toronto.”

“Three hours? Then it is certainly too late. Tomorrow, perhaps.”

“Dammit! I want to talk to her before I call my—*our*—mother. Shit.” He grabbed a bag of chewy chocolate chip cookies from the bottom shelf of the fridge and took them back to the couch.

“What if you sent her a text and asked her to go to your mother’s home tomorrow evening in order to speak with them both at the same time? I believe that your news will be best heard if they can share it.” She turned back to the computer.

“Like it was with Isis? Yeah, that went so well that I want to do it all over again.”

Not certain how to handle Jerry’s sudden anger, she let him munch his cookies, while she searched for Ravi Shankar. With a few clicks she found what she was looking for and Shankar’s distinct “Mishra Gara” filled the near silence of the loft. She closed her eyes and concentrated on the peaceful sitar music. “I have heard this before. A visiting British diplomat had an Indian musician with him, I believe. Or maybe it was one of my mother’s cousins. My memory of the event is foggy, at best. A beautiful sound, nonetheless. Uncle Palak was so right. Do you not think so?” She turned back to Jerry but he wasn’t listening, he was finishing a text.

“There. Sent. Tomorrow at five, our time. Remind me.” He pushed the heel of his hand against his temple. “*Please*, Ana.”

“Of course.” She took the cookies from him and kissed his forehead. She was worried. “If you are still hungry, then might I suggest something healthier than baked goods? Some fruit salad, perhaps?”

Jerry grumbled. “Fine, but make it quick, please. I’m hungry now.” He jammed his hands into his temples, but after a moment he relaxed, as if the pain suddenly vanished. “Oh, thank *God*.” He swung his feet around and up onto the couch. Before Ana could even ask him if he wanted fruit juice or green tea, he was snoring.

JERRY WOKE UP frustrated. "Let's go for a walk. I'm feeling cooped up in this one room prison." There was no answer. He was alone, which suited him fine. He grabbed his keys and coat and started for the door. At the last second he had a minor crisis of conscience, scribbled a note that he was walking down to the Inner Harbour, and left it on the coffee table next to the book.

HE STILL DIDN'T know a lot of the landmarks in downtown Victoria, but he knew how to get from the loft to the Inner Harbour and did so without much awareness of the world around him. He stopped at traffic lights, walked around fellow pedestrians, avoided the larger of the puddles, and eventually found himself sitting on a bench with his back to the Empress Hotel, staring at the private sailboats and cruisers strung with bright, twinkling Christmas lights, from "stem to stern" as his sailor father used to say.

A few people were out strolling the boardwalk, but they kept to themselves and he was okay with that. The visual slow bobbing of the craft in their moorings and the subtle sloshing of the harbour waters lulled him into a state of separateness. He knew he wasn't asleep, but he was also not really aware of the individual details of the world around him. He heard only the water, saw only the swaying of the strings of lights.

How long he sat like that, Jerry had no idea. It had been dark when he claimed his space on the bench, and it was still dark when Ana finally sat down beside him and placed her slender hand on his own. He stirred slowly up from wherever he had been drifting and discovered that he was cold and damp with fresh rain. Lost within the waves and lights, he hadn't noticed either the temperature or the wet.

"Jerry, you need to get up, get moving. I will wave down a cab for us."

"No cab. The walk will do me good, warm me up, I guess."

"But you are wet and shivering. You will catch—"

"What? My death from a cold?" He *was* shivering, too; and somewhere along the line his fingers had acquired a pale blue tint. "It's not far. We'll be home soon and I'll go straight to bed."

"First you will take a warm bath, then to bed."

She was right. Even his currently primitive mind could see that. He let her lead him up from the boardwalk to street level, away from the anesthetizing bobbing lights and sloshing harbour. With the fingers of his left hand tightly laced with those of her right, she guided him along the drizzle-dampened streets, and eventually up to the loft. At some point he sensed her undressing him, but she left him alone to remove his boxers and climb into the tub.

Jerry drifted off again, but it couldn't have been for long because when he awoke, the water in the tub was still hot, a hint of steam drifting up. At some point Ana had taken his damp clothes away and left his folded pyjamas, fluffy robe, and a clean baseball cap on top of the toilet seat cover. He twisted the kinks out of his neck and felt pretty good—much better than he had when Ana found him on the bench. Slowly, he dipped the washcloth in the hot water and washed away the last of the rain dampness. After a vigorous finger-tip-scrubbing of most of his scalp, careful to avoid the small bandage on his head, he rose up from the steam and climbed carefully from the tub. Even the process of drying himself off with the big towel seemed to give him a boost. By the time he was dressed in his goofy fleece pyjamas and cocooned in the robe, he was ready to face the world.

A subtle, sweet scent greeted Jerry when he stepped out of the bathroom. "Chocolate?"

"Hot cocoa." Ana rose from the couch, a mug in her hand and a worried half-smile on her face.

"Perfection. Just what Dr. Romanova ordered." He accepted the mug from her and kissed her gently on the lips. "You are a life saver. Thank you."

"And you are my heart and soul."

"So, what's the plan?"

"Drink your cocoa and then bed."

"Doctor's orders?"

"Shvibzik's command, which is much more serious."

A gentle wave of vertigo bumped into Jerry and he stumbled a half step on the way to the couch. "Change of plans. I'd better take the cocoa straight to bed." He stumbled in that direction.

"Jerry?" She took his elbow.

"I'll be okay, once I lie down."

They reached the bed; he placed the mug on the bedside table, and fell face-first on top of the comforter. Ana was about to call 9-1-1 for help, afraid that he had collapsed, when his snoring cancelled the alarm. She hoisted him up and the rest of the way onto the bed, struggled to maneuver the covers from under him to over him, and once again, climbed in with him, wishing she could pray him to good health.

HALEY HAD ONCE asked Jerry, back when they lived together in the small apartment in St. Marys, what would be his favourite way to wake up, other than with sex. Jerry's unhesitating answer was "bacon". His favourite way to wake up was to the smell of perfectly cooked bacon. When he was a child it was to the smell of toast being made but when someone told him that smelling phantom toast was a sign of having a stroke, he adapted quickly and decided that cooking bacon meant the same thing—that breakfast would be ready soon, and someone else was making it.

On Tuesday morning, when Jerry finally found his way up from a foggy, dream-filled sleep of which he remembered no details whatsoever, it was because a slender tentacle of airborne bacon drew him up and into the word of reality. He heard Ana puttering in the kitchen and Ravi Shankar's sitar in the background. "That smells great, Shvibzik!" At least, that's what he tried to call out. Instead, what came out was a soft, slurred moan. Then his face started twitching and both his hands curled into tight fists. His toes clenched, his back arched, and suddenly all he could see was the fluttering of his eyelids.

He shook and twisted and kicked, and he was sure he was going to swallow his tongue or shit himself, but although the seizure went on for another endless four or five seconds, his tongue stayed where it was and his pyjamas remained clean. When he once again got control of his own body, he desperately needed to throw up. With one hand clamped over his mouth, he stumbled for the bathroom, knocking over one of the bar stools and startling Ana into dropping the frying pan she was scrubbing. He heard the clang of steel on steel and her shout of alarm, but he staggered on, his legs protesting that they were still too weak.

With what his father had called the Powell Luck of the Irish, Jerry somehow made it in time, and as the toilet seat lid flew up, what little there was in his stomach spewed out. He retched a second time, but that seemed more to make sure that his body was done expelling than because he was still nauseated.

A slender hand gently squeezed his shoulder, then released it. He heard the tap running next to the toilet and the plastic tumbler being filled. When he finally sat back and opened his eyes, Ana handed him the tumbler. Without a word between them, he took a mouthful of cool water, rinsed, spit the bile aftertaste into the toilet, and then drank the rest of the water in the tumbler, grateful. He handed it back to her and she wrapped him in her arms.

He squeezed her back. "I'm okay. Thank you for not getting all freaky on me."

"'All freaky'?" She released him and they got to their feet. He put the lid down on the toilet, flushed, and followed her out of the bathroom and into the living room.

"All weird. Strange. Melodramatic. You reacted, but you didn't *over*react. Thank you."

"You needed me. I had no idea of what was happening to you, but you needed me. If you wish, I can get 'all freaky' on you after you've had breakfast." She winked at him and moved into the kitchen while he set the stool back on its feet and sat at the kitchen's island.

"No, I think we can let that lapse go. Do I smell bacon?"

"Yes . . . and no. What you smell is tofu bacon, compliments of Carmella. She said something about 'nitrates' in real bacon so you get this delicious 'facon'. With real eggs and hash browns, which are really potato puffs chopped up and fried." She placed a glass of grapefruit juice in front of him.

"'Facon'? Did you just make that up?"

"No sir. I am not that imaginative. When I Googled cooking instructions, the website used that terminology."

"Ah. It smells lovely, my Sweet, but will it keep for a little bit? After my recent cookie-tossing, I think the juice is about all I can manage, at least for a few minutes." He took the juice to the couch and settled into it. "I hope you're not offended. It really does smell wonderful."

"I promise not to be offended if you tell me why you vomited."

"I felt nauseated." Part of him was still trying to process what *had* happened. "I think I had a seizure. One second I smelled facon and the next I was all clenching and writhing on the bed, trying not to swallow my tongue. I don't know if I threw up because that's what happens after a seizure or because it scared the crap out of me."

Ana planted herself next to him, her legs folded up under her, facing him directly. She took his hand in both of hers, lifted it to her face and kissed his palm, tears streaming down her cheeks, fading away once they went into free-fall. He pulled her in and they held each other close until Jerry leaned back.

"You know, that facon smells too good to resist. I'm pretty sure I can handle breakfast now." He tried to get up off the couch but Ana shoved him back down.

"Sit. Stay. Obey. I will bring breakfast to you." She strode off to retrieve the prepared plate.

"Now you're treating me like a dog?"

"You vomited like a cat, so maybe *that* would be most appropriate."

"Have you ever seen a cat sit, stay, and obey?"

"We only had dogs. Jimmy would sit, stay, roll over, fetch, sneak along the floor like a spy, and dance on his back legs."

"He was a beagle, right?"

"Yes. He was just a puppy, but he was a very smart puppy." She placed Jerry's breakfast on the coffee table in front of him and set the knife, fork, and napkin next to it. "He loved Alexei almost as much as he loved me, but Alexei—Lyoshka—was too weak to hold him, which is why Jimmy was in my arms when we were taken into that basement." She sat back down, this time giving Jerry a bit of room to eat. "I tried to protect him with my body, but those Bolshevik bastards were determined to not let anything living leave that room that was not part of their damned revolution."

"I'm sorry."

"As am I. *Spasibo*. Thank you."

Jerry ate while Ana leafed through the Popular Science magazine that had arrived in the mail on Monday. The sitar music played on from the laptop, adding an eerie atmosphere to the dark topic still hanging in the air.

Eventually Jerry cleaned the last crumb from the plate and returned it to the kitchen, despite Ana following him and trying to take the plate from his hand while he switched it from hand to hand and around his back, keeping it just out of her reach. She gave up when he kissed her quickly and deposited everything into the sink.

"This is not what I meant about being stubborn, Mr. Powell."

"Stubborn is as stubborn does, I suppose."

"Fine. What is your plan of operation for today? What exciting things will we be doing?"

"Today? I promised Manny I'd stay away from the office, but there are some forecasts and plans I have to work on. I emailed the files to myself so I can do that work here, at home. I have to call Mom and Carole at five, and the Palliative Care lady, Elizabeth, wants me to complete that Will Kit she sent home with us. I'm not sure how much fun is in all of that, between telling my family I'm dying to writing down who I want to get what after I do die. This isn't crap I expected to be doing in my twenties."

She kissed him on the cheek again and his concern slipped away.

"Was there something you wanted to do, Shvibzik?"

"Since you have asked, I thought it would be absolutely marvellous if you called Dr. Kelly and told him about your seizure."

"Really? It's come and gone, over and done."

"And what if you have another one? Maybe there is a medication that you can take to prevent them."

"Fine. I'll add that to the list, somewhere between 'Work' and 'Will'."

"Thank you."

"WHAT DID THE doctor say?" Ana stood with her arms crossed in anger, but her facial expression was all worry and concern.

"He said that working from home today was probably a good decision. He said that it sounds like I had just a minor seizure. If I have another one today and it lasts any longer, that I should come in and we'll talk about some anti-seizure meds. But if there are no more seizures for a few days, we'll hold off on the medication because he doesn't want to start pumping me full of chemicals that aren't intended to fight the cancer. He also said that throwing up isn't uncommon and he wanted me to tell you that if I don't come back out of a seizure within a minute or two, you're to call 9-1-1."

"So he was not concerned?"

"Oh no, he was very concerned. But he also knew that sooner

or later I was going to start having seizures. He's going to call Gemma and see if there's absolutely anything they can do to speed up the planning process. I got the feeling that he already knows the answer is 'no', because of the technical limitations, but he was trying to reassure me that he takes this all very seriously."

"Well, I should certainly hope so."

"He does." Jerry hugged her. "We can't go second-guessing the professionals. I realize that wasn't always the case back when, um, when . . . when they were treating your brother, but medicine has come light years since then. At least most of it has." He looked down into her eyes, and was amazed at how much life there was in their sparkle. He kissed the end of her nose and opened his arms. "Now, shall we look at this Will Kit and decide who gets what should all of medical science not be able to put me together again?" Grabbing the kit off the desk, he took it over to the couch.

"It is such a grim thing. Is it *absolyutno neobkhodimo*—absolutely necessary?"

"If I die without a will, there'll be a huge mess and the government will get involved. I've been thinking that maybe I should leave my few investments to Manny in lieu of continuing to rent this place for you."

"No! I do not want to be here if you are not here!"

"Where will you go, Ana? Your destiny is your own, now that you can carry the book and go wherever you want. If you had a Social Insurance Number, you could get a part-time job and even stay here. Maybe I can arrange something with Manny."

Ana grabbed his chin and forced him to face her. "Jeremy What-ever-your-middle-name-is Powell, if you are not in this world then I do not want to be, either. I would rather return to the book for all eternity."

"I wish I knew how you got in there in the first place, because then I could join you, if there's room. I could donate the book to a good library with a rare book collection and we could live out eternity haunting a library and reading our way to the end of time."

"*That* sounds absolutely wonderful. While you decide what goes to whom, I will look for an appropriate library." She went to the desk and opened up the laptop. "Of course it will all be moot because I have faith in you. In my heart of hearts, Darling, I know that this cancer will not kill you."

"If I were betting my money, I'd go with the prognosis on this one, but if I'm putting my hopes and dreams on the line, I like your thinking, Shvibzik."

"Excellent. Now write out that ghastly Last Will and Testament and I will do the *ghostly* Googling and find us the perfect library. Any particular city?"

"I've always wanted to see Paris, or even London, and they're both a lot closer to Moscow than Victoria is. I'd love to see where you grew up."

"And I would love to show it to you. Once you have beaten this nasty cancer into submission or remission, maybe we should plan a trip."

Jerry's hand holding the pen trembled violently and his tongue felt heavy, but it passed as quickly as it came. "Okay. A trip." He struggled to make the words sound normal, so as to not alarm Ana. "When I'm better." He turned his attention back to the will, knowing full well that as sweet as Ana's wishes, plans, and predictions were, the facts were pretty damning. He wouldn't be visiting Russia in this lifetime.

ANA NARROWED IT DOWN to two academic libraries in France and three in the British Isles, all of which had special collections of Tsarist Russian documents. She printed out the list and went about making Jerry a late lunch while Ofra Harnoy's cello softly reimagined the music of the Beatles in the background.

His own task hadn't gone as well, and he was still torn between leaving everything to Ana outright or leaving it to Manny and Carmella to administer for Ana. If he did that, though, he would have to bring them in on Ana's not-so-little secret so that they understood the whys and wherefores of his unusual bequest. A headache rolled in just before he finished his list of possessions but he pushed through, lastly leaving his digital music collection to Mika. He'd have to make a copy to another external hard-drive for Ana, but he wanted the original files to go to Mika and Danveer. He dropped a couple painkillers into his palm from the bottle he now carried everywhere as religiously as Ana carried her book. Summoning a bit of saliva, he tossed the capsules back and read over his notes.

The sound of rain pounding on the windows finally drew his attention away from the paper in front of him so he wandered over to the window. It was a cold, ugly rain, matching his mood exactly. No lightning flashed nor thunder rolled. It was simply wet and relentless. He sat on the window bench and stared out at the greyness as the heavy raindrops pounded the streets empty of civilization. So far as he'd seen in his few weeks here, it was a quiet street most days, but today it looked abandoned, like the zombie apocalypse had rolled through and left only two survivors—a ghost beyond their appetites, and a guy soon to join their ranks.

He let the steady, thumping, hum of the rain lull him and soon Ana joined him, silently placing the plated sandwich in front of him. She seemed to understand his melancholy and gave him the quiet he needed. He blew her a quick kiss, started in on the sandwich, and the two of them turned their attention back to the rain.

"I should probably have a nap before I call Mom and Carole," Jerry eventually suggested.

"Would you care for some company?"

"Always." He led her to the couch and they stretched out, he with his back to the cushions and she with her back to him and his arms encircling her, symbolically protecting her from a world that could no longer hurt her. She wiggled in close to him and giggled when he kissed the back of her neck.

"Sleep tight, my shining knight."

"You, too, my glowing Shvibzik."

CHAPTER TWENTY-ONE

@TheTaoOfJerr: "A gentleman is someone who knows how to play the banjo and doesn't."

~Mark Twain

"MOM, BEFORE WE go any further, you have to promise me that you won't hang up or disconnect, no matter how much you might want to."

"Now, Jeremy, why would I do that? You're just being insulting."

"That's not my intention. I had a similar conversation yesterday with friends back in St. Marys and they hung up on me."

"I'm not your so-called friends back in that dinky little town you never should have moved to in the first place, I'm your mother. Now, what's so important that this conversation couldn't be between just you and me on a real telephone on the weekend, not this ridiculous video thing when I should be playing bridge?"

Jerry's younger sister, Carole, huffed at their mother. "Mom, give it a rest. Skype is better than that tinny speakerphone feature on your old handset. This way we can actually see Jerry's face and he can see us."

"This new technology is just a waste. I don't know why you even have to live all the way out there, anyway. If you moved back to Toronto we could be having this conversation face to face. I don't even have any idea how this Skype-thing works."

"You don't have to, Mom. I'm handling the technical end of it. You just have to look at the camera and talk." Carole's hand reached up and blocked her laptop's camera for a moment while she showed her mother where it was. "And I *know* you can talk."

"Don't get smart with me, young lady. You know what I mean."

Jerry took a deep breath and cut them off. "Are you two finished? Mom, if there were any other way to have this conversation, we would do it, but there isn't. Carole, thanks for setting this up. Jean-Marc, I see you back there. If you want to run screaming from the room, I completely understand."

Jean-Marc waved and smiled. "Thanks, Jerr. I'm good. What's up, *mon ami*?"

It was time. He felt Ana squeeze his hand from off-camera. They felt it best to wait until after he dropped the bombshell before doing any introductions. "I've been to see a doctor. It turns out that my headaches aren't the result of a lumpy mattress or changes in the weather or—"

"It's those damned luncheon meats you eat. I told you they would make you sick. Maybe someday one of my children will listen—"

He'd had enough. It was time for tough love and damn the torpedoes. "Mom, shut up. As usual, you have no idea what you're talking about. You see two articles on the Internet or have a conversation with the ladies during a 3-Spades hand and suddenly you're an expert. This time you're dead wrong." Deep breath.

"Jeremy Powell, I will not take this abuse, especially via some stupid computer thingy. This call is over." She reached for the computer mouse but Carole slapped her hand away, hard.

"Touch that mouse and Jerry and I will suddenly be orphans. You will sit down, shut up, and listen to what Jerry has to say. Jerry, go ahead, before I choke the living shit out of Mom."

Not only did their mother look shocked, but Jean-Marc in the background looked like he was going to cheer out loud. Much to his credit, he didn't.

"Um, thanks, Carole. Mom, I have cancer. Brain cancer."

Carole sobbed. Jean-Marc went white and covered his mouth

with his hand. Jerry's mother paled a little, but lifted her chin. He could see her clench her teeth briefly.

"That is *not* funny. I know you want my attention, but trying to shock me into silence with one of your cruel practical jokes is unacceptable."

"Glioblastoma multiforme or GBM. A brain tumour. It usually kills in nine to fifteen months, max. They're pretty sure I haven't got that long. We caught it pretty late."

Carole got up out of her chair and turned away from the camera, her face in her hands. Jean-Marc took her place. His eyes were damp, too, but he was holding it together. Next to him, Jane held one hand to her mouth. Her eyes were wide, and Jerry could see her hand trembling. Jean-Marc leaned in.

"Tell us what they've got planned for treatment, Jerr. Surgery? Radiation? Chemo? Clinical study?"

Thank God at least one of them was being strong. Jerry nodded. "No surgery, because it's too wide spread, even to the brain stem. There a few technical tricks they can try to get the chemo around the blood-brain barrier, and I start radiation therapy in three weeks."

His mother found her voice. "Three weeks?! Start tomorrow! Don't put this off like everything else you've procrastinated in your life. The sooner you start, the better."

"Thanks, Mom, for finding a way to blame *me*. Actually, it's going to take three weeks for the scan they did yesterday to plot out the extent of the tumour and the specifics of the treatment. They can't just blast away at my head with a laser cannon and hope they get more tumour than brain. My oncologist is going to try and speed up the process, but this is one aspect of the treatment that isn't too flexible. They're also looking into available clinical trials. With the disease so far along, the odds of me becoming a lab rat are actually pretty good."

His sister traded places with Jean-Marc again, having recovered from the initial shock. "What can we do? Can you come home for a visit before they start the treatments? Can you get the time off?"

"No travelling. My boss is great, fantastic even, so that's not the problem. But I've started having seizures, which was expected, so I don't dare risk flying. If I had a major seizure mid-flight . . . I wouldn't wish that on the flight crew or the other passengers. Besides, I want to stay close to the medical team I've already started working with. What I'd like to do is fly the three of you out for a visit. Can you spare the weekend?"

"Of course!"

"*Mais oui*!"

"Which weekend?"

"Mom! Jerry's sick! It doesn't matter which weekend!" Carole hung her head. "I swear we were both adopted."

Her mother turned slowly to look steadily at her. For the first time since the conversation started, she truly looked sad. "That's not funny, Carole. I'm asking simply because we have to book the flights."

Jerry held a hand up to stop the bickering, as he'd done for years when they still had regular family dinners. "I'd like to fly you out this weekend. Friday." He sensed movement beside him and turned to see Ana staring at him, tears welling up in her own eyes. He simply nodded to her and her floodgates opened. He squeezed her hand and looked back at the camera.

Carole finished some mental calculations and nodded. "Definitely. Jean-Marc and I will find a way. Mom?"

"This Friday?"

"Yes, please."

"It's that serious?"

"I wouldn't ask if it wasn't."

"I know. You joke around a lot, but . . . *of course*. Friday is fine, Jerry. I can even stay with you for as long as you need me to, to make sure you eat properly, and drive you to your appointments. You don't need to worry about anything but getting well."

Jerry chuckled. "Thanks for the offer, Mom, but I should be okay." He squeezed Ana's hand, again. "I've got a great support team here in Victoria. My new boss and co-workers have become an instant family. Of course they'll never replace you three, but, well, you'll see when you meet them. I'll book it at this end and email Carole everything you need to check in and get your boarding passes. I'll take care of your hotel, too."

"Jeremy, that's too expensive. We can just stay with you. I'm sure you have a couch, and can find sleeping bags."

"Mom, this is a bachelor apartment and definitely not big enough for f—" He almost said "five". "Not big enough for four, even if some of them are camped out in sleeping bags on air mattresses. I'll take care of it. End of discussion."

"Okay. Thank you."

He had to lighten the mood before they disconnected. "One last thing. Jean-Marc, can you check and see if you need a passport to get here, please. Being from Quebec and all, I'm not sure how well you'll be received in the West."

"Me? They love us in the West! I'd be more concerned about your mother and Carole. They're not just from Ontario, they're from *Toronto*, the Centre-of-All-That-is-Wrong-With-Canada."

"Nah, I'm pretty sure they're okay, just so long as they don't have to stop over in Alberta. Victoria is so British that Torontonians are relatively safe."

"Then I think we're all good to go, *mon ami*." He smiled, and it was just what Jerry needed to see.

"Excellent. I'll make the bookings and email the information to each of you, as back-up. If I don't talk to you before then, rest assured that I'll meet you at the airport. All you have to do is pack your bags and make the flight."

"Okay, Jerr."

"You got it, big brother."

"We'll see you Friday, Jerry. I love you. *We* love you."

"I love you guys, too. Bye." He disconnected the call, placed the laptop on the coffee table, and tilted over sideways on the couch, into Ana's lap. "Holy crap. I'm exhausted, and it has nothing to do with being sick. I'm sorry I didn't introduce you, Shvibzik. It'll be easier in person, when you can work your charms on Mom and tame her with your smile."

"I look forward to it. She may anger you and make you want to scream, but remember that you live a long way from home and she is most likely frustrated that she cannot help you in your time of need. I remember more than one night when Mother cried herself to sleep because Alexei's health was declining and the doctors were less than useless."

"Maybe so, but Mom has been like that all my life, even when I was a kid at home. She's the main reason I haven't lived in Toronto since I graduated from high school. I love her, I just can't be around her for any longer than a few minutes. I don't know how Carole does it."

"Daughters are different. I cannot explain how, but although Mother loved us all immensely, she had a special bond with

Alexei which had nothing to do with either his health or his being the Tsarevich."

"Yeah, I guess."

"You will see, when she arrives."

"If you say so. Are you sure you want to meet her? Haven't you had enough trauma in your life?"

Ana flicked his ear with her finger.

"Ouch!"

"Mr. Powell, I certainly hope you are not comparing your lovely mother to the Bolshevik bastards who butchered my family. I do not care how cruel you think your mother has been over the years, there is no comparison."

"No, I suppose not."

"Good. Now relax while I massage the lumps on your head."

"Yes, ma'am."

"That's 'Yes, your Highness', Mister Powell." She kissed his brow and then massaged his skull with such delicate skill that he soon drifted off. When he finally awoke, Ana was watching *The Hobbit: An Unexpected Journey*. From his sideways position, it looked like the adventurers were just leaving Rivendell. Jerry sat up slowly.

"Jerry, I want to be an elf." She paused the movie.

"An elf?"

"Galadriel is so full of grace and beauty. A true royal who would be perfectly at home in any royal court I have *ever* visited."

"She's a good choice, but I think you're more like Arwen, an elf from *The Lord of the Rings*. In those movies, she's a brave, fearless warrior who would do anything for her true love. I always felt that Galadriel had a dark side that gave me the creeps, made me uncomfortable." He picked up the laptop, checked the charge on the battery, then took it to the desk where he plugged it in and turned it on.

"Then I must watch *The Lord of the Rings* next."

Jerry laughed, kindly. "There are two more movies within *The Hobbit* trilogy, which adds up to about six more hours of viewing because I'm a fool for owning only the extended director's cuts. *The Lord of the Rings* trilogy runs a little over nine hours, too, so you may need to take a break in there somewhere. Even *I* couldn't watch them all straight through, from beginning to end, in one sitting. I've tried a couple times."

"Eighteen hours, for *two* stories? Oh my."

"Two stories that are really just one story, split into two, with a fifty or sixty year gap in the middle, and a different hero for each part."

She sighed. "This could take quite some time."

"True enough, but it would take you longer to read the books."

"There are *books* for these films? They must be as long as *War and Peace*. It is a good thing they never made a film of *War and Peace*—it would go on for *days*."

"They did, quite a few times. There was a mini-series that ran something like fifteen or twenty hours that we had to watch in History class. I slept through most of it." He logged onto one of the discount-travel-booking websites, quickly realized that he would need his credit card.

"That is *quite* understandable. It was required reading for us as well, and I remember falling asleep numerous times, struggling with Tolstoy's lumbering prose." She watched Jerry sit, then get up for his wallet, and then sit back down again at the computer. "What are you doing, Love?"

"Booking the flights and hotel for Mom, Carole, and Jean-Marc. I know my mother is old-fashioned, but I hope she can deal with Carole and Jean-Marc sharing a room."

"I am certain she will be fine with it, but if she is not, from what I observed of your sister, Carole will convince your mother otherwise." She turned back to the fifty-inch screen. "Will it distract you if I continue to watch the movie?"

"No. Go ahead. This will only take a few minutes but I just need to pay attention to what I'm doing."

"Thank you." She restarted the movie and Jerry returned to the task at hand. He cringed when the final total for the tickets came up, but it was important, and it wasn't like he had anything else to do with his money. Then Ana giggled at something on the screen and he remembered that he still needed to provide for her in some way. At least he assumed he'd have to. He had no idea if her being "awake" was linked to him or whether she was independent now and whether he lived or died made no difference to what happened to her. The idea that the two of them could both be bound to the book and spend eternity exploring the world had a certain bizarre appeal.

Once the airline tickets and hotel rooms were booked, he

forwarded the email confirmations to all three of Jean-Marc, Carole, and his mother, then printed off a copy for backup. The streets of Victoria were still being pounded by the rain, so he abandoned the hope of a walk and returned to the couch.

THEY MANAGED TO make it to the end of *An Unexpected Journey*, but Jerry could see that Ana was starting to flicker and fade, and he was doing his own living version of the same, so before she could even suggest watching the second movie he shut off the Blu-Ray player and the screen. "We're both done in, Sweetie, so let's call it a night. We can pick this up tomorrow after we've both recharged our batteries."

She flopped her head on his shoulder. "You are a very smart man, Jeremy Powell. I think that is the most excellent suggestion I have heard all day. As a matter of fact—" She faded so quickly that they were both caught off-guard. Her clothes collapsed into a pile on the couch. Jerry picked her things up, confirmed that the book was in the hoodie's pouch, then took everything and placed it on the bed. After a moment he changed his mind and draped them over the divider screen before shuffling off to the bathroom.

THERE WAS A window open somewhere. Jerry could smell the ozone and dampness, and feel the chill. There was smoke, too. At this rate he'd freeze to death before the cancer killed him.

"For crying out loud, can't a man get some goddamned sleep without some moron setting the place on fire and trying to freeze him out?!" He dragged his ass out of bed, grabbed his robe, and charged straight to the window on the far side of the loft, overlooking the street. He slammed it shut and spun around to confront Ana. His head throbbed and the sudden motion made him want to puke. Though everything was a blur, he could make out someone sitting on the couch, watching him. He wanted to tell them to stop being an idiot, but suddenly he was more interested in keeping his belly still and stopping the pounding in his head. He flopped in the nearest chair.

"Enough of the pain already. Just let me die in goddamned peace."

"Gladly, but not until you give me Anastasia's book." It was a man's voice. One Jerry thought he recognized. "Once you do that,

I'll even help you along to whatever afterlife you wish. Heaven, Valhalla, Fields of Auru . . . whatever."

Jerry squinted but could only make out thick dark hair and a goatee. "Who the hell are you and what are you doing in my home?"

"Give me Anastasia's book, and you won't need to worry about who I am." There was a metal-on-metal sound like gears, or like *the hammer of a revolver being cocked.*

"I have no idea what you're talking about. If you want a book, go to the damned library, but leave your gun at home."

"You're being a smart ass, facing down the barrel of a .38 Special? I mistook you for a much smarter man, Jerry."

"Nervous reaction. Sorry." Was he dreaming? Where was Ana and why was this killer sitting on his couch wanting her book? "What's so important about this book that you break into my house and point a gun at me?" His eyes were starting to focus, but his headache was tearing him a new lobe, so there was no way he was going to put up any kind of fight. His only hope was to play dumb, which wasn't much of a stretch right now.

"Where is goddamned the book, Powell? And where is your little dance partner?"

Oh shit. "She's out. Getting groceries."

"Good. But if I'm not out of here with that book in my hand before she comes back, the first bullet is for her."

"Is this what you want, Bolshevik pig?"

Both men turned at the sound of Ana's voice. She was calmly holding the book in front of her, sidestepping towards Jerry.

"Give it to me and you both live." He pointed the revolver at Ana's chest.

Whatever reply he was expecting to his threat, he probably wasn't expecting both Jerry and Ana to break out laughing.

"Get lost, asshole. You can go ahead and shoot, but you're not getting the book, *Professor*." He now recognized the university prof from New Year's Eve. "It's not mine to give and it sure as hell isn't yours to take."

"I know why he wants it, Jerry. And I know who he is." Ana stood next to Jerry's chair, tall and angry.

"He's that professor from the Empress—the fancy ballroom dancer."

"No, he's a Bolshevik bastard." Ana took a step toward

Gervaise, ignoring the threat of the gun.

The gun lifted to point at her head. "What makes you think I'm a Bolshevik, little girl?"

"Because I know that face. When we first met, I thought you looked familiar and I told Jerry so, but now that I see your eyes in better light and hear your voice without the music playing, I know you, Yakov Yurovsky."

"How—?! My name is Jakob Gervaise. *Professor* Jakob Gervaise."

"Maybe so, but you are also the direct descendant of Bolshevik assassin, Yakov Yurovsky."

Jerry was confused as hell, but he kept quiet. He was nowhere near his phone to call 9-1-1 and there was no way he could reach the fireplace tools to use as a weapon before he got shot. He didn't care if he died, he just didn't want this asshole to get Ana's book, and therefore, Ana.

The gun in Gervaise's hand shook. "How could you know that, *shlyukha*?"

"You call me a whore? *Vy ne chto inoye, kak sobaki , kotoryye ne mogut lizat' svoi yaichki.*" Gervaise's eyes went wide and Ana smiled. "Yes, a dog who cannot lick his own testicles. I know you, son of Yurovsky, as I knew that Bolshevik dog himself."

"Impossible."

"Possible. Very possible. After his men shot me and stabbed me with their bayonets, I still would not die. The jewels sewn within my garments had protected me, kept me alive long enough to watch my entire family butchered by your kin. I looked him straight in the eye and he shot me in the head." She tapped her forehead with a fingertip and the bullet hole appeared.

Gervaise scrambled to his feet. He still had the weapon, but Jerry was pretty sure he was no longer in control of the situation. "You are insane! *Sumasshedshiy*!"

"Perhaps I *am* crazy, but I am still Anastasia Nikolaevna Romanova!" Suddenly Ana was her old self, the young girl Jerry first met, complete with all of the bullet holes, bayonet piercings, and blood.

Six gunshots and a pair of empty-chamber clicks shattered the relative quiet of the loft. Acrid gun smoke filled the air and Jerry gagged. He pulled himself up out the chair, needlessly worried for Ana's safety, but she still stood tall and unharmed. Of course, he thought. What could bullets do to her that they hadn't already done?

Gervaise threw the gun and Jerry ducked just in time. The weapon slammed into the wall behind him with a thud and fell to the floor. Jerry didn't think he could take the older man in a fight, but it suddenly became very apparent that he wasn't going to have to. Without moving from where she stood, Ana stretched her arm out, grabbed the man by the throat, and picked him up. She looked over her shoulder at Jerry.

"I now know why I am here, Love. It is to avenge the murders of my family. God has given me the opportunity to slay he who slayed us."

The professor gagged and kicked and grabbed at Ana's impossibly long arm, his beady eyes looking like they were going to pop out of his head from both fear and constriction of his airway. But he was no longer armed, or even a threat.

"Ana, put him down."

"It is my sacred duty, Jerry. For the honour of my family."

"There's no honour in murder." His headache was fading.

"It is an execution, not murder."

"That's what this guy's great-grandfather thought, too, I bet."

"Yakov Yurovsky murdered innocent children. He murdered *me*!" Gervaise stopped struggling, although he was still conscious, barely.

"'Vengeance is mine, saith The Lord', or something like that. Would God want you to avenge your family? Isn't that something only He can do?"

"But—" She lowered Gervaise to the couch and loosened her grip enough to let him breathe.

"What would God want, Shvibzik? What would Alexei want? Or Tatiana, Olga, or Mashka?" He stepped up beside her and put his hand on her arm. "Would they want you to become a murderer, like the Bolsheviks who executed them? *This* man didn't kill your family. *This* man didn't put a gun against your head and pull the trigger." Suddenly Jerry understood it all. Understood not just how to get through to Ana, but why. "What would Grigori want you to do?"

"Forgive him?"

"Exactly. But not just *him*. Forgive his great-grandfather. There was too much bloodshed and horror in 1918. End it here.

Be the better person. Be the Grand Duchess that Queen Victoria would have been proud of. Right here and now, the Last of the Romanovs holds in her hand the power of life and death. Reverse all of the mistakes your well-meaning father made before you. Do what your Papa is not here to do. Forgive."

"But . . ."

Sirens approached. Someone must have heard the shots and called 9-1-1. Jerry had no idea how he was going to explain all of this. He scooted over to the fireplace and grabbed the poker. He wasn't at his strongest, but he was pretty sure that the fight was out of Gervaise. "Ana, my Love, forgive him."

"He killed Mashka."

The sirens were nearly there. "Ana . . ."

"And Jimmy. What could my puppy ever do to your precious revolution?" She tightened her grip once again.

"Ana! Shvibzik!"

She released Yurovsky's heir, and the man slumped, barely conscious. She looked at Jerry and nodded, then dropped to her knees in front of Gervaise. She took his hands in hers and lifted them to her lips. She kissed the dark, curly-haired back of each, straightened her back, and lifted her chin. Three or four car doors thumped shut out on the street, but Ana paid them no heed. "Jakob Gervaise, descendant of Yakov Yurovsky, I forgive you, and your forefathers; not in the name of the Russian Imperialist Romanov family, but merely in the name of my Papa, Nicholas, my Mama, Alexandra, my sisters Olga, Tatiana, and Maria, my little brother, Alexei, and myself, Anastasia. I forgive you."

Jerry could hear glass smash down the stairs at the street level and indistinct shouts. The cavalry had arrived.

ANA COULD SENSE that something was seriously wrong. She looked up at Jerry, thinking that maybe he was having a seizure, but her vision started to mist over. Panic set in and she shook her head violently, trying to shake her head clear, but the flat she had called home ever so briefly wavered and faded. She tried desperately to solidify, but something fought against her.

She stood quickly, rushing into Jerry's arms, confused, but she ran right through him! She spun around and reached for him again, and he dropped the fireplace tool and reached for her, but she was undone. The new half-life she had come to love so much was being ripped from her and she had no idea what came next. The flames in the fireplace seemed to grow, to seek her attention, like a hungry beast, and within the flames something stirred. A darkness moved like a flame, but it was completely without light or warmth. It writhed weakly and reached for her, finally making its move, after nearly a century.

Then the tension deep within her snapped like a rubber band stretched too far and all of her fear, all of her worry, all of the terror for her future vanished. She was *free.*

"*Vremya prishlo,* Shvibzik." It's time.

Ana spun at the voice. Standing tall and straight, Alexei stood beside the Christmas tree, some of the needle-filled branches appearing to grow right out of his arm and a glass ornament sort of hung from his elbow.

She looked at Jerry to see if he could see what she was seeing, but her darling only stared at her, stunned. She looked back to Alexei. "Lyoshka?"

He saluted her and smiled. "That is Lance Corporal Lyoshka, to you." His smile saddened just a bit. "It is time to come home, Shvibzik. We have been waiting."

"'We'?"

"The family. Everyone."

"In *Nebo*? Heaven?"

"*Da*, I believe so. Even Jimmy."

"They have *dogs* in heaven?"

"Silly Shvibzik, it would not be Heaven without dogs."

Tears coursed down Ana's face. She was ready to explode from the magnitude of the emotions bouncing around in her heart and head.

Alexei held his hand out. "Come, big sister. You have done what the rest of us could not. Father is so proud of you."

Ana took a final look at Jerry, his tears matching her own. She had felt so at home with him. Like she had never belonged anywhere until she was with him. And now she had to leave. Alexei tugged her sleeve. The flat was fading quickly. Before it was too late, she signed "I love you" to Jerry and blew him a kiss.

JERRY COULDN'T BELIEVE his eyes. Ana was leaving. She walked through the couch, toward the Christmas tree. Fading fast, Ana turned and her fingers flashed the signs he had taught her. He flashed back "I love you, too!", but she was gone. Did she hear him? Did she see his signs? Did she know that he loved truly her? That he always had? He felt like his heart was being torn out of his chest, then the door to the stairs flew open and police in SWAT gear charged in with their weapons drawn.

JERRY SAT, STARING out at the rain again, empty. Why hadn't he told Ana sooner how he felt about her? The police came and went, taking Gervaise, the revolver, the six mysteriously flattened slugs, and his statement. They could tell that he wasn't well, so the lead officer gave him his card and asked him to come by tomorrow and answer a few more questions. He refused their offer of medical assistance, so they left him alone.

He got up and looked around. He wanted to smash his fist into the brick wall surrounding the fireplace, but restrained himself and simply started a fire to chase away the damp chill that seemed to permeate Victoria since he'd arrived and only subsided when Ana was beside him. Once he was sure the kindling had caught and the flames wouldn't sputter out, he shuffled around the loft in his pyjamas, restless. The headache wasn't any better, but it wasn't any worse, either. He dropped a few flakes of food into Sushi's bowl, but ignored the Betta when it looked at him from just below the surface of the bowl while picking at breakfast.

"Maybe I just need a little caffeine to ease the pain," he said to no one in particular. There was a dull pain in his chest and a lump in his stomach that didn't seem to be connected to the agony in his head.

Switching on the single-cup coffee maker, he knew he'd find his salvation in coffee. It was another minute before the "Ready to Brew" light came on and with a push of the button, Jerry had sweet flavoured elixir dispensing into his mug with gurgles and splashes and a wafting scent of delicate caramel teasing him. With mug in hand, he went in search of his painkillers. He knew they were obviously right where he'd left them, but it took him a few minutes of hunting to remember that he'd left them in his pants pocket. The caramel washed down the pair of capsules as he made his way to the desk, turned on the laptop, and started ruthlessly deleting emails from people he'd never see again. Part of him just wanted to curl up on the couch and cry, but he could almost hear Ana's voice telling him to stop wallowing in self-pity.

Halfway down the page, he saw an email from Haley, back in St. Marys. "What does she want?" He opened the email and read it aloud. "'Dearest Jerry, I hope your new life in Victoria is all you'd dreamed it would be.' Yeah, I dreamed of cancer and death and losing the woman I loved just when I found her. 'I miss you, Jerry. Things are not the same here at home since I came back.' Of course not! You walked out on your husband and girls because you were bored and then wandered back into their lives because you were curious if it could be better, not because you wanted to actually work on it and fix it. 'I wish I was out there with you, feeling sand between our toes, watching the whales swim past, and making love in some little inn overlooking the ocean.' There's more to love than sex, Haley. Sorry. Dee-lete." He clicked on the trashcan icon and the email was gone.

He scanned his email inbox, saw nothing more that caught his attention, and pushed the laptop away. "Enough of that junk. I don't need to enhance my performance, collect my Ethiopian inheritance, or lose weight like Jennifer Biels; I need a cure for Stage Four, terminal, brain-sucking cancer. I need . . . *whatever*." He stomped over to his couch cocoon, turned the big screen on, and went through the tedious process of booting up Netflix. Once he was in, he searched for Ingrid Bergman's *Anastasia*.

He didn't even make it through the opening credits before he was up off the couch, suddenly restless. He knew he was hungry but had no idea what to eat or why he should even bother. It was all so senseless. Why was he even going through the motions of life when it was going to be over soon? Now that the seizures had started, Jerry knew the stark, lonely reality was that he *maybe* had weeks left. Weeks. Weeks of what? Seizing, puking, sleeping? And he had his ever-positive, always-loving mother coming out for a weekend. Yippee.

The world expected him to put on a brave face and fight this stupid disease right up to the end, his chin held high as he lost weight, lost his hair, and died from the inside out. But that's not how he wanted to die. It's not how *anyone* wanted to die. What was it the Palliative Care woman had said? "With dignity and peace", or something like that? Surrounded by people watching him fade away, tears of pity in their eyes, but secret thanks in their hearts that it's not them whose light is being snuffed out in slow, agonizing increments. Someone would hold his hand, someone would say some crap like they loved him, and then everything would go dark.

Jerry knew he wasn't going to get to come back like Ana. When he was done, he'd be *done*. No mystical, Hindu reincarnation. No waiting virgins, no welcoming arms seated to one side of God. No blaring trumpets, no wings, no reunion with his father while they ate cream cheese and drifted in the clouds. One second he'd be alive, and then he wouldn't. Game over. So why didn't he just get it over with right now? Why didn't he tell the pain and the disease to just piss off? It's too bad he hadn't let Gervaise finish him off. Instead, he'd have to hang himself, or cut his wrists in a tub of warm water. Yeah, the tub would be best. The mess would be contained and he'd already be naked so they could just tag and bag him and shove him in an oven so they could cremate him down to fit in a pickle jar and be shipped back home where his mother could dig a hole on his father's grave and drop him in. That way she could visit and natter at the two of them at the same time. She'd *love* it, and *he* wouldn't care.

He pulled a clean plate out of the dishwasher, trying to decide what he should eat, but all he could think of was an untouched bucket list and the ruins of his wasted life. Jeremy George Powell. Twenty-four. Never married. Never had kids. Never wrote that novel. Never learned to fly a plane or ride a motorcycle. Never swam with dolphins, or tried stand-up comedy, or rocked the house in a band. Never made love in an inn overlooking the ocean. Never spent a month in Paris soaking up French jazz. Never traced his family roots back to Ireland. Never really, truly, fell head-over-heels-spend-the-rest-of-eternity-together in love . . . until now, at the end.

He cocked his arm back and threw the plate. It smashed against the tile backwash over the sink and shattered, shards flying everywhere while the biggest pieces crashed down into the sink. Next, the coffee mug hit the faucet, broke into two, and bounced away.

"All right. End of the pity party, people. I need air and I need it *now*." He snatched his baseball cap and coat off the tree and that's when he noticed Ana's book. His breath caught in his throat. He'd managed to keep the book because he told the officers that he had no idea what Gervaise was doing in the loft, and Gervaise was oddly silent as they led him away.

He tucked the book in the jacket's inside pocket and clomped out of the loft. He made it three steps down off the building's stoop before he realized that not only was he still in his pyjamas, but he was also barefoot and it was still pouring rain. He stopped, felt stupid for a second, and then continued on. "Screw it. At least I'm wearing a hat and my skull won't fill with rainwater."

CHAPTER TWENTY-TWO

@TheTaoOfJerr: "The only truth is music."

~Jack Kerouac

BY THE END of the block, Jerry was soaked and shivering. "This is getting to be a habit, buddy." He looked ahead, left and right, down streets he was only vaguely familiar with. He glanced over his shoulder. He was alone. No fellow pedestrians, no taxis, no horse-drawn carriages, no Ana chasing after him. The frigid rain pounded down on his cap, ran down his back, soaked him from top to bottom, bottom to top, inside and out . . . and it washed away his hurt, his frustration, and most importantly, it scrubbed him clean of the fear that had been threatening to overwhelm him.

He turned around, slipped a bit on the cold, wet cobblestones. It was time to face the world, and he would start back in the warmth of the loft. He went home. At the front door to the building he jammed his hands into the coat's pockets and found his keys buried at the bottom of the right one, under a layer of fast-food napkins and plastic-wrapped restaurant mints. He looked Heavenward. "Thank you."

The freezing cold caught up to him and he stumbled up the stairs, fumbled with the keys and lock, and would have broken in the door if he'd had the strength. Eventually the key fit the lock and turned. He shuffled into the loft, placed Ana's book carefully on the mantelpiece, then shed his rain-soaked coat and shuffled into the bathroom where he peeled off his soaked pyjamas and the hat, dropped them on the floor, stepped into the tub, pulled the plastic curtain around himself, and turned on the shower. He didn't wait for it to warm up and really didn't need to since he was much colder than even the cool spray that preceded the hot. He sat there, curled up under the spray, numb.

WHEN THE SHOWER began to cool after he'd used up all of the hot water, Jerry shut it off and climbed out, ready for nothing more complicated than sleep. Sleep, and more painkillers. The frigid rain and the hot shower had washed away the headache, but his soul ached and throbbed and was numb, all at once. He went through the motions of drying off with the big bath sheet. Eventually he tossed it over the shower rod and wandered out into the heat of the loft proper.

Standing naked by the bed, he couldn't find his pyjamas at first. Then he remembered the wet lump on the bathroom floor, and instead grabbed sweatpants and a hoodie from the ever-present pile of clothes on the chair next to the dresser. He swallowed two more capsules and curled up in a fetal position with the pillow hugged close. Once again, sleep found Jerry, and he welcomed it.

A CHIME SOUNDED in Jerry's dream and he reached for the old, black dial phone on the desk next to his dream self. He picked up the receiver. "Hello?" No one answered. "Helloooo? Is there anybody out there?" The chime sounded again and he concluded that it wasn't the phone. He looked around the vintage office of his dream but it slipped away, revealing the walls and framed photographs and dim light of the loft. "What?"

The chime sounded a third time, and he finally clued in. "Skype?" Who the hell would be calling him? Not his mother, that's for sure. Maybe Carole. By the time he got to his desk and the laptop, the chime was silent. The caller ID was still on the screen, and although he had to squint, he could see that it was Isis' number. With a couple quick taps of the laptop's touchpad, he called her back. While it rang, he dropped his butt into the desk chair. Isis couldn't have gone far from her computer because she answered quickly.

"Jerry! You're there!" She signed rapidly. "I love you I'm sorry I hung up on you Mom is mad as shit at me for doing it!"

He waved at her to stop, and signed with strong gestures to get her attention. "Isis! Slow down! You'll melt your nail polish you're talking so fast. It's okay. My mom almost hung up on me, too, when I told her last night."

"So it's true? You have cancer?"

"Yes, it is. It's not something I would joke about." He found himself comforted by talking with Isis. His anger at being awakened thinned and dissipated.

"You're dying?"

"Yes."

"When?"

"Probably within the next month or so. The doctors think I have longer but I'm not so sure."

"Am I going to get to see you again, before you go?"

"I'm not sure. I'm flying my family out to see me this weekend, while I'm still healthy enough, but I hadn't planned on doing any travelling, because of the seizures I've started having."

"Oh. Can I come visit you?"

"I don't think your parents would be too impressed with their fifteen-year-old daughter flying out to see an old man."

"They're cool with it. It was Dad's idea. He cried as hard as me when you told us you were sick. That big tough cop is just a softy inside. If he can come, he will, but he says Mom and I can come out if you let us."

He thought about Ana and how much she would have loved meeting Isis in person. "I'd love to see you, but let's see how the next week or so go. I may need some recovery time after my mother's visit."

"Is it okay with Ana if we visit? I'll ask her myself, if you think that would be better, more polite."

Shit. "Um, Ana isn't here anymore, Isis. She's gone."

"*What did you do?!*" Her signs were sharp and angry. "I could tell by the look on both your faces that she is the best thing to ever happen to you! I don't care what you do, you get her back!" He tried to say again that he had no idea where she went, but Isis didn't let him get a sign in edgewise. "Call her number every ten minutes, go pound on her door, email her, text her . . . I don't care what you have to do. You need to have someone there who loves you and, most important, you deserve to have love in your life. Haley is a bitch and I'm glad you got away from her, and I'm too young for you, so find Ana and be in love." Her hands slowed down so that he could make no mistake in the translation. "Or I will fly out there and kick your ass myself. Is that understood?" She folded her arms over her breasts and waited for his answer.

Ana was never coming back but he didn't need to argue with Isis over it. "Yes. Clear as glass, Miss Bossypants."

"You can call me all the names you want, Jerry, but at the end of the day I will *still* kick your ass. Now, tell me about your cancer. Brain cancer?"

"Brain cancer. Glioblastoma multiforme." He spelled it out for her because he didn't know the signs for the proper medical name, if there even were any.

"It's growing in your head?"

"Yes. It's the cause of my headaches and lately it's making me want to throw up, my eyesight sucks, I've started having seizures, my memory is like Swiss cheese, and my moods are swinging like crazy."

"Can they operate on it? Chemo? Radiation?"

"They haven't decided, yet. I just told them to cut my head off because I don't use it that often anyway."

She smiled for the first time since they'd started chatting, but it didn't last long. "Is there anything else you can do? Acupuncture, psychic surgery, leeches?"

"Leeches? You've been watching too much History Channel. I do have a Hindu swami who has aligned my chakras and is going to do more energy work to make me more at peace, but even he reluctantly agrees that I need a real miracle to get through this alive."

"Even more reason to find Ana and make up. If you have to die, at least don't be a lonely idiot when you do."

"Yes, boss."

"Good. Mom and Dad are out at a Lincs game, but I'll tell them that we talked and everything is cool. I mean, except for you dying soon. *That's* not cool." She wiped away sudden tears with the sleeve of her sweater.

"I know what you mean, Kiddo. I'll call next week after my family has left, but in the meantime, tell your folks I love them, and tell your dad to be safe."

"Always. You, too. I love you."

"Right back at you."

"Now go find Ana."

"Yes, boss."

"Later, 'gator."

"On the flipside."

"Isis out."

"Jerry . . . out." They disconnected simultaneously. He sat, staring at the screen, but was interrupted from forming any great, world-changing thoughts when his stomach rumbled. He squinted at his watch. "Six o'clock? I'm sleeping what life I have left away." Getting up, he whipped up a simple microwave omelette, made toast, and chased it all down with a couple of painkillers and a glass of thick-pulp orange juice, before returning to the desk. He stared at Sushi, who probably wondered where the strange floating lady who fed him had gone.

"I'm sorry, buddy. She completed her mission and moved on. We're back to just you and me."

JERRY WAS HALFWAY through his second attempt to watch the fake Anastasia deal with the doubters of high society when his phone buzzed with an incoming message. It was from Mika, wondering how he was doing.

Not sure he wanted to talk to her, he replied with a text. "Not at all good. Ana is gone, forever, this tumour is kicking my ass, and I'm losing. Good news is my mom and sister are arriving Friday." Once the text was sent, he turned on the laptop, started the music, then shuffled into the kitchen and started cleaning up the mess, careful not to cut himself on the shards of the plate and mug. She'd only been in his life for two weeks, but he kept expecting Ana to pop up and do something silly, to make him laugh and distract him from, well, from *dying*.

The sixties playlist he'd selected buoyed his mood, brushed off some of his funk, and gave him a little more energy. When the kitchen was relatively clean, he moved on to the bathroom, where he wrung the rain-soaked pyjamas out over the tub, then hung them up to dry. A passing glance in the mirror startled him and he realized that he hadn't shaved in a day or so, his hair was sticking up at odd angles, the bandage over his stitches needed changing, and he had dark bags under his eyes. "I can't do much about the baggy eyes, but I can manage an electric razor and a comb without hurting myself. The bandage may be a bit tricky."

He managed to shave, comb, and awkwardly re-bandage, then made his way out to the couch when he was done. On his way past the computer he shut off the music. By the time he was settled into the couch, he was ready to stay there for the evening. He called up Netflix on the big screens again and scrolled through until he found BBCTV's *Sherlock*. "Not too dark, not too cheesy, just what Doctor Watson ordered." The intercom buzzed, indicating that someone was down at the street door. "Ana?" He rushed to the speaker mounted on the wall and pressed the "Talk" button.

"Hello! Ana!"

"No, Jerry, it's me, Mika."

That's when it truly hit Jerry. No matter how many times he answered the door or picked up the phone or opened a book, it would never be Ana. He buzzed Mika in and slid to the floor, so great was the weight on his soul. Even if he weren't dying, he would have wanted to after losing Ana.

MIKA FOUND HIM sobbing, just inside the door, and helped him up and onto the couch. She tried to get him to talk, but he just couldn't get the words out past the sobs, so she held him close. She hoped that when his tears ended she'd be able to get him to explain what had happened, but instead he fell asleep. She shifted their positions on the couch a bit, lay Jerry down, nestled in behind him, and pulled the afghan off the back of the couch and over them both. She didn't know what else to do.

"SHE FORGAVE HIM and then faded away? There's no sign of her anywhere?" Mika handed Jerry a cup of tea and sat down beside him with her own cup. The afghan wrapped Jerry like a cocoon with two pale hands poking out to hold the cup and saucer.

"Nothing. There's the bullet hole, the bloodstains, and the inscription from her mother . . . but no Ana." He sipped the brew slowly, careful of the heat.

"She didn't go into something else? Another book, a photograph? Your fish?" She nodded her head toward Sushi's tank.

He almost smiled. "No. She just faded away. I can feel her absence. I can't explain it, but it feels like there's something missing, like I'm standing in front of a crowd of people and my zipper is undone. There's something wrong, but I just can't pinpoint it until someone glances down at my crotch and *then* I can feel the breeze. Except that there's no breeze here. She's gone." He stared at the floor.

"Like Uncle said, she shouldn't have been here in the first place. That book wasn't a place of safety for her; it was chains and a prison. She's free now. She should have moved on a long time ago. Maybe your last words to her were brief, but you gave her the greatest gift you ever could—your heart. She's gone where she's supposed to be, and you helped with that. You can spend the rest of your life—"

"My *short* life."

She slapped his leg reproachfully, but left her hand there. "The rest of your life beating yourself up, but in the end you woke her up and loved her. You gave her the chance to have happy memories close off her existence here before moving on. You gave her a chance to fulfil her destiny and put old sins to rest."

Jerry put the cup on the saucer and placed his free hand on top of Mika's. "Thank you." He squeezed her hand gently and smiled at her. For the first time, he noticed bright green flecks in the light brown of her eyes. Then she leaned in and kissed him on the forehead, before standing up and letting him have his hand back. "You're leaving?"

"Are you going to be okay?"

"Yeah. I hurt, but she did what she needed to do and has moved on."

"If you're sure you'll be okay, I'd better go."

"Really?"

"Jerry, you're hurting from your loss of Ana, and I'm a little sad from my breakup with Danveer so—"

Jerry levered himself up off the couch and dropped the afghan. "Danveer dumped you?"

"No, *I* broke up with *him*. When we were here with Uncle Palak on Monday, I finally saw how dissimilar we are. I think I was more attracted to the idea of having Uncle Palak as a mentor than I was of having Danveer as a husband. He really doesn't have a spiritual bone in his body. I spoke with Uncle Palak about it and he agreed completely. Actually, he wondered why it took me so long to figure it out."

"I'm sorry to hear that. Or I'm not, I guess. If you're not rushing home to him, stay awhile and watch a movie, chat, help me with my chakras." He just wasn't ready to be completely alone in the loft.

Mika shook her head and moved toward the door, where her coat hung. "I'll be honest, Jerry. From the few days we've spent working together at the station, I'm more attracted to you than I *ever* was to Danveer. You and I are on the same wavelength on so many things. You may not think you're a spiritual person, but the way you talk about music and life and how you find a way to tickle the laughter out of every situation, is straight from the spirit, the soul. And it's damned sexy . . . If I don't leave now, I'm going to take advantage of your heartbreak and mourning for Ana, and take you to bed. Or at least try to."

"Um . . . " He didn't know what to say, but mostly because he knew that under different circumstances she would have been his dream woman—if his dream woman weren't already a dead Russian Grand Duchess.

"Jerry, I'm going. The roads are a little slippery, so I'll text you when I get home safely. I'll talk to you tomorrow. If you feel up to coming into the office, I'll gladly come by and pick you up." She shrugged into her coat, not giving him a chance to help her, and perhaps get too close to her.

"You're sure?"

"I'm sure. I shouldn't have said anything in the first place. You probably think I'm no better than Lee-Anne, flirting with the new boss like he's fresh meat and I'm starved for attention." Her smile faltered.

"Not at all." He put the cup and saucer on the kitchen counter and closed the distance to Mika, where he took her hands. "You're not like that and really, neither is Lee-Anne. You're an amazing woman, and I *can* feel some kind of energy between us, but my heart really and truly belongs to a silly little Russian ghost. You're right that Danveer is wrong for you. Even this thick-as-brick man could see that. He's a nice enough guy, but you walk different paths. You have to promise me, though, that you'll keep walking your own path, confident that the right someone will someday step right up beside you and let their path overlap with yours."

Mika laughed between tears. "Now you sound like Uncle Palak! That's practically what he said to me."

"He's a wise man. In my case, though, my wisdom comes from listening to too many deep, soulful lyrics, and from a Deepak Chopra book I read last year."

She moved a half-step closer and her voice softened. "Jerry, I . . ."

It was Jerry's turn to kiss Mika gently on the forehead. "I know. Go. I'll be fine." He turned her gently around, opened the door for her, and patted her on the butt to scoot her out. "Text me when you get home, and I promise to let you know if I need a ride in tomorrow. Good night, Mika."

"G'night, Jerry. Namaste."

"Namaste right back atcha."

Mika snickered and made her way down the stairs. Jerry closed the door gently behind her and clicked the deadbolt over as quietly as he could.

"It never rains but when it pours." He looked over at Sushi. "If I'd known this whole I'm-dying-soon shtick worked so well on women, I'd have tried it years ago." The fish looked at him and tilted his head as if he understood him. Jerry shook his own head. "Yeah, you're right. That's unfair. Mika's better than that, and so was Ana." He sighed and dropped back onto the couch. "Ana . . . where the hell did she go? Did that darkness she was so worried about suck up her soul?" The idea made him shiver, and he grabbed the afghan off the floor, wrapped it around himself, brought the television out of nap mode, and let the modern-day Holmes and Watson distract him. Fifteen minutes later Mika's text came in saying that she was home safe and sound and thinking about him. She also urged him to call any time if he needed to talk. He texted back a quick note that he was glad she was safely home and he would call if he needed anything. He'd have written more, but he could barely read what he typed and the strain on his eyes threatened to bring on another headache. He did close off with a colon-bracket smiley-face, just so she didn't misinterpret his brusqueness. Holmes himself was sending a text on the screen so Jerry put his phone and dark thoughts aside, and got lost again in the twisting, turning plot.

CHAPTER TWENTY-THREE

@TheTaoOfJerr: "Jazz isn't dead. It just smells funny."
~Frank Zappa

AT EIGHT O'CLOCK, his small travel alarm beeped only twice before Jerry silenced it. He'd been up for ten minutes already, staring fuzzily at the ceiling and listening to the sounds of the street outside. There was a single honk and a short-lived distant siren, but generally speaking Victoria just didn't seem to have the traffic and energy of even the suburbs of Toronto where he grew up. Only St. Marys was quieter than Victoria, though not after a hockey game, when the car and truck horns of either celebration or frustration punctured the night.

Last night had been a quick one. He'd fallen asleep immediately, had no dreams that he could remember, and woke up before the alarm sounded. He felt emotionally pummelled, but surprisingly well-rested. He was also fed up with what he'd called the "pity party" yesterday and was determined to get stuff done today. He still had the most recent quarterly reports to review for Manny, and his overly cautious nature told him he'd better call and confirm his family's flight and hotel reservations. Online booking from the comfort of his pyjamas allowed him to bypass a travel agent and maybe save a few bucks, but it also meant that he had to do all the calling around himself, to confirm that the ducks were in a row for his mother's visit.

There was something else he was supposed to do, but that part of his to-do list had fallen through his Swiss-cheese memory and might never reappear. He remembered that he planned to drop by the station later on, but since Mika would already be at work, he would cab it or walk, depending on what shape he was in when the time came. He nuked a couple of eggs, tossed them on toast, and washed them down with black coffee while scrolling through the reports he'd emailed himself. He had to enlarge the spreadsheet immensely so that his failing eyes could make out the numbers, but he quickly saw a couple areas of possible overspending he'd bring to Manny's attention and highlighted them, just to jog his memory later on. He thought about it for a moment and decided that the highlighting wouldn't be enough. A few taps of the laptop's touchpad opened a blank document and he typed a quick note to himself with the dates and entries in question. His new motto was "Leave nothing to chance." What he remembered today could be gone tomorrow, or even by lunchtime. He squinted at his note, rereading it to make sure he'd got everything down he wanted to remember. He did this with five more points before he finished going through the report. "It's really not too bad at all. There's nothing here Manny can't fix quickly and almost painlessly.

"Speaking of painless, I suppose I should post a few tweets just to say I'm still alive . . . while I am." He pulled up his list of quotable music quotes, logged on to his @TheTaoOfJerr Twitter account, and posted a couple quips he hadn't used before, including his favourite one from Frank Zappa. He considered working on his blog, but it could wait until he dropped by the station. With Ana gone, he really needed to see some friendly faces, especially Mika's. "You know, Sushi, it's probably time I do that Last Will & Testament thing. If I leave everything to you, will you just blow it all on one of those bubbling scuba divers for your tank?" He really *did* need to do a will, though there was something troubling him about the idea. Something needed doing or . . . *had already been done*! He opened up the desk drawer and there was the will kit, all filled out and ready to be notarized or whatever the lawyer had to do. "Shit. Two wills would have been as bad as none. Easily fixed." With a quick phone call he set up a five-minute appointment with Manny's lawyer, and with a second call, ordered a cab to pick him up in an hour. "Time to shit, shower, and shave."

MANNY FRESHENED JERRY'S decaf and leaned back in his chair. "I hate the idea of a young feller like yourself even having to fill out a will, but I'll honour whatever requests you've made, provided you do your best to hang around as long as possible and make it all unnecessary."

"Deal. I'm not really asking you to do much, really. Just take a little of my ashes and sprinkle them in the Pacific and send the rest to my mother. There's a list of my possessions that my sister and mother get first dibs on and then the rest goes to Mika."

"Mika? Not Ana?" Manny raised his considerable eyebrows.

"Ana's gone. She never really expected to be here that long anyway."

"Why Mika?"

"She's been great to me. She's probably the smartest one you've got on staff, and that's saying something with this staff. I want her to have a copy of my digital music collection and anything else she wants after my family has picked over it. If there's any meat left on the bones after that, maybe open it up to the staff or donate it to a women's shelter."

"I like how you think, mate. Since that's not going to happen for some time, what have you got on that cost analysis you were so keen to talk to me about?"

"I found three immediate ways you can trim your overhead without anyone losing their jobs, and a couple that might require some reconfiguring of job descriptions as well as letting one of the part-timers go, or convincing one of the full-timers to shift gears to part-time."

"Close the door, Jerr, and show me." Manny reached for the printouts Jerry had brought into the office with him. Jerry nudged the door shut with his foot and leaned over the reports his boss was spreading across the desk.

THE TWO MEN went through the figures and then Jerry's proposals line-by-line, and only quit because Jerry could feel his frustration and anger building quickly, and knew that he was going to snap at any moment. Part of it was probably the tumour's interference, but he also knew his blood sugar was low and he needed to eat. Mika nearly jumped out of her chair when he suggested the two of them go for Vietnamese subs.

"I was afraid you weren't going to talk to me, Jerr. I sort of crossed a line last night."

Jerry shook his head. "Not at all. We both stepped *to* the line, but nothing was crossed. I didn't do more than wave at you when I came in because I didn't want to get distracted from the task at hand, and with my shot-to-hell attention span, your smile would have been too much of a distraction." He held the lobby door open for her and followed her out onto the chilly street. "Let's just relax and get a bite to eat and not worry about all that other stuff for now. Deal?"

She squeezed his hand quickly and released it. "Deal, Boss."

FOR TWO PEOPLE in the radio industry, they were both unusually quiet while enjoying their sate beef or vegetarian subs. They split an order of fresh salad rolls and washed it all down with a pot of green tea. Jerry smiled across the table as he folded up his empty sub wrapper.

"I'd forgotten how nice it is to eat *with* someone."

"What about Ana?" Mika wiped a bit of sauce from the corner of her mouth.

"She loved to cook and was terrific at it, but she didn't eat."

"I suppose she wouldn't have to, really." She took a moment to gather her thoughts. "That must have the most surreal experience, having a ghost in your life. I mean, I was both freaked out and intrigued for the short time we were over at your apartment, but that was just for a few hours."

"I gotta admit that it was the strangest experience I've ever had happen to me, but after a few days it just seemed normal."

"You're a lot more open-minded than Danveer, that's for sure. All he wanted to do when we got home was run back over and get Ana to do it all again so he could film it and put it on YouTube or Instagram. The true miracle of it all completely escaped him. That was the breaking point for me." She finished her tea and moved the cup and saucer to one side so she could lean her elbows on the table and move closer to Jerry. "You should write a story about it. Use only the facts, but tell the whole thing as fiction so people don't try to lock you up."

"Maybe I should. I could do it on the blog."

"Or an ebook. That's what Uncle Palak does. He's written ten books so far and made a few thousand dollars for the spiritual institute he founded. He's even recorded the first two as audiobooks."

"I'd love to read his stuff but would have to go with the audiobooks, since my eyes are so bad now. I have to magnify Manny's spreadsheets by 400%, just to squint at them. I don't think that would work so well for books. Besides, Uncle's voice is so soothing and calming that it would be like having another session with him."

"Speaking of which . . . he emailed me his court date schedule and would love to come by and see you next week sometime, after your family has left. I think he was hoping to speak with Ana again, but when I explained that she'd finally moved on, he was excited for her. He really will help you see the big picture with all of what's happening to you, Jerry."

"Will he help me to understand where you fit into all of it?"

Mika laughed lightly. "I'm your friend, your assistant, and your shoulder to lean on. Anything else can evolve as it's meant to be."

She was rewarded with a big smile. "Then I am the luckiest man in Victoria." Mika blushed, but at that moment their waitress arrived to top up their teapot and so they were both rescued from saying anything awkward. They took turns refilling their cups, and sipping the brew.

"When does your mother arrive tomorrow, and where have you got her staying? Not the sofa in your apartment, I hope."

"They land about noon, and I'm putting them up at the Empress, smart ass." A cell phone rang three tables away with the retro real-bell ring so popular with tech users, and when the woman answered it her voice was so loud that it felt like she was sitting right at their table. Jerry's temper surged and he was about to turn and say something snarky, but Mika grabbed his hand and distracted him.

"the Empress is a great choice." She nodded toward the loud woman. "Let's get out of here." She tugged him firmly up out of his seat and he let her. The fury was followed by a growing headache and he knew the cool winter air was a better choice than the loud, humid air of the tiny restaurant filled with the sound of the woman's whine.

"Hmmm?" What had Mika just said?

"How old is your sister?" She released his hand, now that they were outside.

"Um . . ." He couldn't remember. She was younger, but he had trouble concentrating. "Three years younger than me, I think. Maybe four." The sidewalk was wobbling and Jerry had trouble standing still. "I think I'd better call a cab." He abruptly sat down on a bus stop bench.

"Jerry? What's wrong?!" Mika crouched in front of him, holding her hands in his and trying to look at his eyes, as if she could see what ailed him that way.

"A headache, triggered by that bitch on the phone." He lowered his voice and took a long, steady breath, filling his lungs with the chill air. "A taxi . . . now. *Please.*"

"Yes. Um, of course." She stood and turned to face the road, looking up and down the hill for any sign of a cab. It was midday, on a busy downtown street, and so it took only a few moments for a cab to come around the corner. Mika waved frantically and the cabby pulled up right in front of them.

Jerry pulled himself ungracefully to his feet. Mika took his elbow and guided him to the cab. "Broad Street." He pulled the door open and climbed in. Mika made to follow him but he stopped her. "No, thanks. It's just a headache. I'll go get some sleep. You go back to work." She tried to follow him again. "I'll be fine, Mika, but Bruce Banner has left the building and I don't want you to see me if I get all green and mean."

"You need help, Jerry."

"No, I need to go home and sleep." His anger was growing without any real justification and it was tearing him apart that it was aimed at Mika. "Please. I'll text you when I get home." He leaned over and pulled the car door shut before she could make another attempt. "Let's go," he directed the driver.

JERRY ENDED UP sending Mika a brief apology email from his laptop when he got home because he couldn't read the tiny texting screen on his phone. He took a double dose of meds and passed out face down on the bed, with no music, no television, and no Ana to keep him company.

THE ONLY LIGHT on in the loft when Jerry finally woke up was the tiny one on Sushi's fish tank. He rolled himself off the bed and shuffled to the bathroom. When he was done, he worked his way to the desk, still in relative darkness. As he rolled his chair out, he kicked something soft at his feet. He clicked on the desk lamp and found the camera bag when he bent down to investigate. He knew he'd been out taking pictures recently, but he couldn't quite grasp the memory of when and where. He popped the SD card out of the big Canon, slipped it into the card slot on his MacBook, and brought the computer up out of Sleep Mode.

It took a few moments for Photoshop to open up but he was soon scrolling through the image previews, starting from the beginning of the disk. He swiped the touchpad and the blurry images moved past, right to left. He squinted hard, seeing Sushi in his travel bowl sitting on top of the Jeep back in St. Marys in a set-up shot implying that he'd forgotten his sidekick. "Yup. Fun times. You did pretty well on the trip, buddy, though your navigating sucked." He scrolled onward, seeing the various "Welcome to . . . " signs at each state line, a few sunrises, some mountains, an eagle here, a hawk there. He finally got to the photos of the ferry landing in Victoria and his first view of the city. The next shot popped up and caught him completely by surprise. It was the first photo of Ana, taken right there in the loft.

"Oh, shit." He pushed the chair back from the chair, not sure whether he was ready to see these pictures. But the Apple OS gave him a hint of the photos both before and after the preview he was seeing, so it was already too late. He could see what came next. "Then I guess I'd better get myself a drink." He got up, started the coffee maker, loaded a K-cup of House Decaf, then sprinkled some flakes into Sushi's tank, and waited. After a moment he realized he was hungry and so fetched a plastic tub of crunchy coleslaw from the refrigerator and a spoon from the cutlery drawer. The coffee was ready within a minute and Jerry took both his steaming cup and the slaw back to the desk.

He sipped his coffee or munched his salad as he scrolled through the photos, squinting, thinking he'd have to invest in a cheap pair of reading glasses tomorrow. Even with the photos as unclear as they were, he could see that Ana had a terrific sense of composition. Some of the angles she shot from gave her subjects an air of whimsy, especially the parking meters. A tear trickled down his cheek. "Dammit." He wiped it away and continued. There were the shots where she'd clearly wanted to get the Chinatown lights but was stymied by the flash, then the flash-less shots followed. He stopped when he got to the photo he'd taken of her in front of Chinatown's Gates of Harmonious Interest in her chin-raised regal pose.

"That's the one right there." He clicked on the Eject Disk icon, then removed the little SD card and took it over to the big screen. He fumbled getting it into the slot on the side of the plasma screen, turned the card around and finally got it to fit. He booted the screen up, then moved to the couch, grabbing the remote control as he shuffled past the coffee table. The buttons were tiny and his eyesight sucked, but he'd gone through the process of putting his images up on the screen so often that he really didn't need to clearly see what he was doing. After a minute or two of slow scrolling through the screen's menu and then the files on the card, he had the same regal photo of Ana up bigger than life. From this distance the image still wasn't perfect, but he could now make out many of the details, including some of the sparkle in her eyes. He carefully placed the remote on the couch beside him, leaned back, and wept.

He wept for losing Ana, and for what the cancer was doing to him. He wept that he'd never see Isis again, or her parents. He wept for his new family at the station, and he especially wept for Mika. Then he wept for his mother, for Carole, and for Jean-Marc. Finally, he wept for his father. Of all the people he needed with him most right now, when the odds weren't particularly good, it was his dad. A former Navy pilot and lumberjack, his dad had once been described by his future in-laws as a big teddy bear, and at this moment, in a city at the far end of the country his family had helped found and build, Jerry really, really needed to be held by that big teddy bear, and told that it was all going to be okay.

MIKA CALLED A little after eight in the morning. "I hope I didn't wake you."

"It is damned early, but we're radio folk, so I'm used to the early hour." He'd slept on the couch with the afghan pulled over him, and it had been one of the most restful sleeps he'd had in years.

"Manny has given me the day off to make sure that you get to the airport on time to pick up your family. He's even ordered a limo."

"What? Mom will go nuts. She's not one for flashy. I should make him come with us so he can explain it to her in person."

"He was going to, but he has a meeting with a member of the local CRTC staff. He wants to make sure your cool proposals are kosher with the Radio and Television Commission before we start implementing them."

"Smart man."

"He says it was *your* idea."

Jerry laughed. "At least *one* of us remembers our conversations."

"So, what's your Mom's flight number and exact arrival time, please? I'll drive over to your place and have the limo meet us there an hour before they land."

He knew the flight info, but at the same time, he didn't. "Noonish. Westjet, I think. How about I forward you the email I sent to Carole with everything from flights to hotel?"

"Perfect. In the next ten minutes would be great, if you can, please. I want to give it to the limo company."

Jerry walked the phone over to the laptop and woke it up. "I'm at the computer now. Give me just a second to find that email."

"Sure." She went silent on the other end of the line, letting him work. Eventually he found what he was looking for and forwarded it to her. "Done, I think. Hard to tell when I squint like Gilbert Gottfried. If it's the wrong one, give me a call right back. Otherwise I'll let you figure out the timing and I'll see you whenever you get here."

"It's a plan."

"Good." Damn! He still needed to shower and clean up a bit. The alarm sounded on his phone and when he strained to read it, he was pretty sure that the alarm's reminder note told him to call and confirm the hotel and ask for early check-in. He'd even added the phone number for the Empress so a quick tap of the link and in three minutes he confirmed the reservations, secured 1pm check-ins, and even pre-paid the entire stay and guaranteed incidentals to his credit card, just to eliminate any argument from his mother that he couldn't afford to look after the charges. Now it was done and locked in. She was probably going to be pissed off and the thought made him snicker. He opened his iTunes Barenaked Ladies playlist, set it to play randomly, and shuffled off to the bathroom. Steve and Ed's voices followed him, telling him what they'd do if they had a million dollars.

JERRY SHOWERED AND shaved, mostly by feel because he couldn't exactly see his whiskers. On his way back through the kitchen, with the now dry pyjamas draped over his shoulder, he hid the dirty dishes in the dishwasher, tossed two slices of bread in the toaster, and started the coffee maker. He was pretty sure he was low on decaf, so that would have to go on the list he hadn't started yet.

The bed was easy to straighten up, even with his wonky vision. He stuffed his dirty clothes into the big orange laundry bag in the closet, and then gave the entire loft a quick squint to see if he'd forgotten anything. The place was a bit chilly, but he was going out, so starting a fire would be risky.

By the time Mika arrived, he'd started the draft of a blog post about his diagnosis and the direction things were going. He left out any mention of Ana, preferring to save that story for a fiction, like Mika suggested. He buzzed her into the building and opened the door to the stairwell a crack so she could get into the loft. He'd left his coffee somewhere and he wanted to find it before it got cold. Seeing his mother again had him needing fuel, even if it was decaf. He probably should have had something more than toast, but he planned to take them to lunch at the Empress once they were checked in to their rooms, so his belly's rumblings could wait.

"Jerry?" The door swung open and Mika came in. Jerry looked up from the kitchen island, mid-sip of his coffee. He waved and Mika finger-waved back at him. "Hey, mister."

"Hey, lady. You're looking good, I think."

"That's a compliment?"

"From a guy with crappy eyesight, yeah. I can see dark boots—probably leather—an almost floor-length dark coat that doesn't shine, so it's probably wool and not leather, and a jaunty bright yellow beret. So, yeah, you're looking good."

"Thanks."

He couldn't see if she blushed, but her voice was soft and a bit huskier than usual, so she probably had. "Coffee? Tea?"

She hung up her coat. “The limo won’t be here for half an hour, so a tea would be nice. I can get it, though. You relax.”

“Done.” Jerry remained on the stool and Mika found the mugs, the tea for the one-cup maker, and set about fixing herself a cuppa.

“Are you ready to see your Mom and sister?”

“I suppose.”

“Are you really saying goodbye?”

“Even if I see them both—and Jean-Marc—again, I’ll say goodbye this weekend. When my other grandmother was sick a few years ago, every time we saw each other we knew it might be the last time, so we made sure we always said our goodbyes. When she did eventually die, I’d made sure I said everything I wanted to. The last time I saw my dad I turned around as I was leaving his hospital room, wanting to go back and tell him I loved him, but I figured I’d just tell him the next time I saw him. He died three days later, before I could get back into town to see him. I’ll never forgive myself for that. Even though we flashed a few finger signs at each other, Ana and I didn’t really get to say goodbye, and that hurts. Rest assured that I’ll be saying goodbye to everyone before I go.”

He stared off toward the window, not really seeing anything but the square of morning light. “The thing about cancer is that they may not be able to say exactly when I’ll be done, but based on the rate of the disease’s progress and how I’m holding up, they’ll probably be able to give me a few days’ notice to at least make a few calls, kiss a few cheeks, and return a few hugs.”

Mika turned quickly away from Jerry, her shoulders shaking as she bawled. He put his mug down and slipped off the stool. As usual, he had no idea what to say so he just turned her around and pulled her close, leaning his head against hers and letting his own tears flow. He’d already wept for himself and for Ana, so his tears quickly ran dry. Mika soon regained control, too, and finished with sniffles. Jerry kissed the side of her head and whispered in her ear, “Yeah, I know.”

They pulled apart, giving a last squeeze to acknowledge the shared moment, then each found a sink, splashed water on their faces, and were towelled off and back to smiling when the street door buzzer sounded. Mika checked her watch. “Five minutes early.”

"Better than five late." He buzzed the limo driver up.

"Are we ready?"

Jerry crossed himself like a lapsed Catholic checking his pockets. "Spectacles, testicles, wallet, and watch . . . yup. Good to go." He also surreptitiously checked his pocket for his meds.

"You're a goof." Mika slipped into her coat, and then helped Jerry with his.

"Yeah, tell that to my mother. She thinks I'm a wandering wastrel avoiding his mother at all costs."

"She's pretty astute. I'm looking forward to meeting her."

"Well, brace yourself, because we're heading into the storm of storms."

They stepped out of the loft just as the trim-moustached, retired-military-looking limo driver arrived on the landing. "Morning, folks. I'm Eldon. Any luggage?"

"Not yet, thanks, Eldon. We're picking my family at the airport so I'm sure there'll be bags then."

"Excellent. Follow me, then, please Mr. Powell," and Eldon led the way down the stairs and out to the dark blue stretch limo that looked almost black under the overcast sky.

Once they were settled in, Jerry closed his eyes to ward off a threatening headache.

"You okay, Jerr?"

"Just a little head-thumper. Nothing I'm not used to, thanks." He opened his eyes, smiled at Mika. She shifted to face him.

"So, is your mother really as bad as you say? She's probably a dear sweet lady with a heart of gold."

"She is and does." The limo was warm so he unzipped his coat. "But she has also spent the better part of my life telling me that I'm doing it all wrong."

"Everything?"

"Pretty much. I think she had seriously high hopes for me to become a doctor or lawyer like some of her friends' sons, but I chose the uncertain, low-paying world of radio. I got to be a professional goofball and she can't see that loving what I do is more important than filling my bank account. Dad died of a heart attack working a stressful sales job for a disrespectful employer, trying to give us a terrific life. He did a great job, too, but it killed him. I swore I'd never work at something I hated so much that it'd stress me to death. Even though the pay was low in the beginning, and the hours are absolutely abusive, I love radio. I'm even going to try and talk Manny into letting me sub in for the gang periodically, to keep my hand in. I love music, people, and laughter, and life is best when all three are combined."

"Have you ever told your mother that?"

"I tried, just after graduation, but I was young, Dad had just died, she had to go back to school to upgrade her computer skills now that she was back in the workforce, and I probably didn't articulate it too well. I was pretty angry back then. Mostly at Dad, for leaving, but also at her for, I don't know . . . probably for not finding a way we could save him. That sounds stupid when I say it out loud."

"It makes sense to me. I'm angry as hell that you're sick and I can't just align your chakras and heal you. Nothing I have been trained to do as a nurse or a Reiki Master is of any use right now, and I want to scream."

"Yeah. Me, too."

They slipped into silence, each looking out a window as the city slipped past and the limo left the core, driving to the airport in Sydney, north of Victoria.

ELDON PULLED UP in front of the small, fog-enshrouded terminal with twenty minutes to spare. He opened the door for Mika and Jerry, then indicated a small parking lot a short distance away, barely visible through the fog. "Folks, you both head inside where it's warm and dry, and I'll park Big Blue then follow you in. Once your family arrives I'll bring the luggage out to the curb, go get the car, and swing around to pick everyone up. It sounds convoluted, but it's a small airport, and they need this area kept clear for the shuttle buses."

Jerry nodded. "That sounds great, Eldon. We'll go find some seats. Can we get you a coffee? I desperately need one myself." He was feeling a bit light-headed.

"Thank you, sir, but I have a fresh thermos in the car with my wife's special vanilla-hazelnut brew. I appreciate the offer, though. Go on in and get settled. I'll join you shortly."

"See you inside, then." Mika linked her arm through Jerry's and led him in through the sliding glass doors.

It was almost as warm inside the airport as it was in the limo, so they shrugged out of their coats and looked for a Starbucks,

Tim Hortons, or some sort of café.

"It's about time, Jeremy." The voice came from off to their left. Jerry spun at the sound but wobbled a bit before Mika steadied him.

"Mom?"

Jane Powell approached him with her own coat over her arm, and Carole and Jean-Marc behind, with a cart loaded with their luggage. "Didn't you double check our arrival time? We caught a tailwind or something and got here ten minutes ago. All you had to do was make a simple phone call and we wouldn't have had to stand here waiting."

Carole stepped around her mother and went straight into open Jerry's arms. "I promised I wouldn't cry in public, big brother."

"You lied, little sister."

"Jerk."

"Brat." He kissed her cheek and let her go. Jean-Marc stepped up and Jerry didn't hesitate to take him into a bear hug as well. Jean-Marc and Carole had been together long enough for Jerry to consider him his brother. "*Mon* chum. *Ça va*?"

"*Ça va bien. Et toi*?"

"*Comme si, comme ça*. Cancer suck-la."

"*Oui. Beaucoup de merde*." Lots of shit.

They stepped out of the hug, managing only half smiles.

"Jeremy, are you going to introduce us to your friend?" Jane nodded at Mika.

"Hmm?" His concentration slipped and the terminal wavered for a moment. "Um. Sorry. Of course. Mom, Carole, *et* Jean-Marc, this is my assistant and dear friend, Mika. Mika, this is my fam."

"It's nice to meet you, Mrs. Powell. Jerry has—"

Jerry abruptly leaned into Mika, interrupting her. "Oops. Sorry."

His mother suddenly sobbed, her hand going to her mouth and her eyes filling with tears. "It's true. You're . . . my . . . oh, *shit*."

"MOM?!" Carole and Jerry were both stunned. Jerry almost laughed, but the sombre situation robbed the moment of its humour. "Mom, the last time I heard you swear was . . . *never*." He held out his arms for her and without another word, dirty or otherwise, tiny Jane Powell gave her son the hug of their lifetimes. Mika stood silently behind Jerry, her hand on his shoulder to steady him. "Yeah, it's true." He led his Mom over to a bench and sat down beside her. "Like I said before, I'm dying. We're not giving up, the doctors will do what they can, but it ain't lookin' good."

"Isn't."

"What?"

"It *isn't* looking good." She caught herself, wiped her eyes with a tissue that seemed to appear out of a pocket. "I'm sorry. It's an old habit."

"It's okay, Mom. I finally get it. You take your job seriously."

"My *job*?"

"Being my mother. You've always just wanted what's best for me, even when I was being a goofball. I'm sorry I've given you such a hard time for so long."

"No, *I'm* sorry. I should have encouraged you be who you wanted to be, and just let you grow up without all my poking and prodding."

"As someone recently pointed out to me, that poking and prodding was just your way of showing that you love me. I get it. Thank you."

"Well, of course I love you. I'm your mother. That's just the silliest . . ." She stopped mid-sentence and looked at Jerry over her glasses as if seeing him for the first time. "You're . . . welcome. Thank *you*."

"For what? I'm a pain in the ass. Just ask Mika. She's all ready to quit, after only a few weeks of my bullshit."

Jane looked at Mika, who was shaking her head and smiling, then looked back to Jerry. "Thank you for being my son. For making me so proud. You're silly and stubborn and have moved too far away from me, but you've always had the biggest heart of anyone I know, except your father. The two of you . . . " She trailed off, dabbing at her damp eyes again. Jerry hugged her with one arm and the other three sniffed back their own tears.

"Sorry to interrupt, Mr. Powell." Eldon stood to one side. "I'm guessing that the flight arrived early. I'll go get the limo, sir. I'll hurry, because the shuttle bus is due out front at any minute, and there's no room for both of us."

"Thank you, Eldon. That'd be great. We'll be right out." Eldon jogged off at a brisk pace.

Jane stood up quickly. "Jerry, you didn't hire a limo, did you? That was just silly." She followed after Eldon. "Excuse me, sir, we don't . . . " But the driver was already out the doors. She followed him, and the others scrambled to catch up, Jean-Marc bringing up the rear with the cartload of luggage. When the doors slid open for Jane, Jerry was right behind her, but Eldon was disappearing into the fog, on his way to Big Blue. Jane waved at him. "Sir, we don't need a limousine, we'll just take a taxi—"

Jerry heard the bus before he saw it. In slow motion, like a glass-faced behemoth, it parted the fog and appeared just as Jane reached the curb, intent on getting Eldon's attention. "MOM!" He lunged for her, got a hold of her arm and pulled her back to safety, but he couldn't reverse his own forward motion and tripped over his own feet, directly into the path of the shuttle bus. He thought he heard screams, but they were cut off by immense pain on the left side of his head, just before everything went black.

AS INTENSE AS it was, the pain only lasted for a blinding lightning-flash of a moment, which Jerry thought was more than a little odd. It vanished as quickly as it hit him, literally. He concentrated for a moment, then realized that his headache was gone, too. There wasn't even the faint buzz of threatening pressure he'd grown accustomed to over the last year or two. There was just quiet.

"Are you simply going to lie there in the road, my Love, or will you get up so that I can finally introduce you to my family?"

"*Shvibzik*?"

"That's *Grand Duchess* Shvibzik to *you*, sir." Ana giggled, and Jerry laughed.

SPECIAL THANKS TO:

Dr. Jennifer Rahn for helping me to understand brain cancer and its treatment. Any mistakes in the story are my own, not hers.

Cheryl Hingley, Katherine Salter, Jennifer Rahn, Adrienne Greenwood-Cruise, and Shannon Allen, for all of the editing, critiquing, and butt-kicking.

Tony King, for insights into the world of radio broadcasting.

Jack Whyte & the 2012 Jack Whyte Workshop participants for the in-depth critiques and encouragement when I asked "Do you think this story is worth finishing?".

ABOUT THE AUTHOR

2016 Baen Fantasy Adventure Award finalist, Timothy Reynolds, is a 'former everything', including stand-up comic, teacher, editorial cartoonist, short-order cook, game show contestant, canoe-wrangler, paparazzo, accountant, and trainer of bus drivers.

His ancestors have been at the forefront of history, including arriving on The Mayflower, being chased from Salem, Massachusetts, and fathering Canadian Confederation, so it's only natural that he has become a 'twistorian', mixing history with fiction to tell his tales.

"Canada's modern-day Aesop"* was born in London, Ontario, raised in Toronto, and has called Alberta home since 1991. "Waking Anastasia" is his second novel, based on his own original screenplay, "Ana".

Tim blogs at www.TheTaoOfTim.com, tweets at @tgmreynolds, and jams all the other stuff he does onto the Book of Face. Also check out *www.tgmreynolds.com*.

*Barbara Budd on CBC Radio's "As It Happens"

CPSIA information can be obtained at www.ICGtesting.com
Printed in the USA
LVOW11s1939161016

508873LV00002B/2/P